DAYS LIKE THIS

Jackson Falls Series Book 3

Laurie Breton

*Special thanks to Patti Korbet for acting as
proofreader/editor/idea person
and all-around cheerleader.
Without you, this book would never
have made it to the finish line.*

PREVIOUS BOOKS BY LAURIE BRETON

Coming Home: Jackson Falls Book 1
Sleeping With the Enemy: Jackson Falls Book 2
Black Widow (Ellora's Cave)
Final Exit (MIRA)
Mortal Sin (MIRA)
Lethal Lies (MIRA)
Criminal Intent (MIRA)
Point of Departure (MIRA)
Die Before I Wake (MIRA)

PRAISE FOR LAURIE BRETON'S
COMING HOME:

"Lyrical and gorgeous...just beautiful in its portrayal of the devastating changes of love over time."

-- Judith, *I Love Romantic Fiction*

"a beautifully told, beautifully written story of love and loss"

-- Jessica Van Den, *Experiment: Life*

"wonderfully written"

-- Shelly, *{Dive} Under the Cover*

Casey

August 1991
Jackson Falls, Maine

Becoming a member of the Jackson Falls Public Library Committee had, quite possibly, been the worst decision Casey Fiore MacKenzie had made in her entire thirty-five years. The six of them had spent the last two hours embroiled in a heated debate about book censorship that had ended in a stalemate. Now she had the beginnings of a headache and was seriously rethinking this whole community service gig. It was all part of the *What-is-Casey-Going-to-do-With-the-Rest-of-Her-Life* self-actualization program that she'd recently embarked on. Not that it had been her idea. As far as she was concerned, at thirty-five, she had plenty of time to figure out the next sixty years.

But Rob had been prodding her, and when he got like that, it was usually easier to just give in. The man could be relentless, and the fact that he was nearly always right didn't make it any easier to take.

She'd stopped writing after Danny died. It wasn't that the well had dried up; she'd simply turned off the spigot and hadn't bothered to turn it back on. Without him, without that golden voice to bring her music to life, there no longer seemed to be any point to it. Rob had remained uncharacteristically silent on the issue, although she knew it bothered him more than he wanted to admit. They'd worked together as partners since they were little more than kids. But aside from a couple of half-hearted attempts at persuasion that had fallen flat in the early days following Danny's death, he'd avoided bringing it up. It was probably better for both of them if he stayed away from that particular can of worms.

But he'd been working without her. He hadn't said so, but she recognized the signs. All those hours he'd been spending out in the zillion-dollar studio they'd built in the barn. She knew damn well he was out there working on new material, which meant that she needed to start pushing harder with the self-actualization thing. New material meant a new album, and a new album meant he would be going back out on the road. She'd seen the restlessness in him for a while, knew him well enough to recognize the signs.

He was a musician; performing was programmed into his DNA. He would almost certainly ask her to come with him, but they both knew she'd rather have bamboo shoots shoved under her fingernails. Been there, done that, bought the tour shirt. He would leave, and she would be left alone for three months while he was out there playing rock god with his Fender Strat. She'd better find something constructive to do with her time, because Rob MacKenzie was a strong proponent of tough love, and he was apt to plant one of his size-eleven Reeboks up her backside if he thought she was going to spend those three months sitting in her rocking chair, waiting for him to come home.

She'd fully expected that by this time, there would be some indication that they were percolating the newest little Fiore-MacKenzie collaboration. But so far, nothing. Even though thirty-five was still young, she knew that once a woman passed thirty, her chances of conceiving decreased with each passing year. She was nowhere near ready to accept defeat, but sometimes, lying awake in the wee hours, her thoughts danced all around the dark possibility that it might not ever happen. If it didn't, they would deal with it. There were always other options. She would love any child, no matter the age or race, that was placed in her arms. They both would. But she so wanted that child to be a part of both of them.

She turned the car into the driveway and parked under the giant elm tree that shaded the old Gothic revival farmhouse. When she and Danny had bought the place four years ago, she'd privately dubbed it Fiore's Folly. The house had been his baby from day one, and they'd spent months pouring money and sweat equity into it. With the clarity of hindsight, she suspected that for Danny, the home rehab had been an external symbol of the very personal rehab he'd been doing on the inside. Somehow, they'd managed to turn the place into a real home.

And then he'd died. Sometimes it was hard to believe she'd lived here with Rob longer than she had with Danny.

As soon as she stepped into the shed, she heard the music, Steely Dan's *Dirty Work* from *Can't Buy a Thrill*. He'd been playing that damned album for two decades. Something about the cool, sophisticated, jazzy flavor of Becker and Fagen's compositions had grabbed Rob MacKenzie the first time he'd heard one, and in the intervening years, it had never let go of him.

She opened the door to the kitchen and it hit her smack in the face, the mouth-watering aroma of something spicy and pungent and swimming in garlic. Her husband stood at the stove, poking at the old steel wok. Whenever Rob cooked, the kitchen ended up looking as though a series of small explosions had just been detonated, but the end result usually made up for the disaster, so she tried to turn off the compulsive housekeeper inside her and just roll with it.

He turned, saw the expression on her face, and said, "Bad one?"

"*Au contraire, mon ami*. Bad would be a vast improvement." She dropped her purse on a chair, hoisted herself up onto the wooden tabletop, and demurely crossed one leg over the other. Reaching up to sweep her dark hair back over her shoulder, she said in disbelief, "My god, Flash, those people are lunatics."

He picked up the glass of white wine he'd already poured and had waiting for her, crossed the room and handed it to her. "I figured you'd be needing this." Both palms braced against the edge of the table, he leaned into her. She reached her free hand up to cup his cheek and they kissed, his mouth soft against hers. He moved back a few inches, and those warm green eyes studied hers. "Hey," he said.

Casey brushed a wispy blond curl away from his face and said, "Hey."

She'd never been much of a drinker, but drastic times called for drastic measures, and he'd been plying her with wine since she was eighteen. She raised the glass and said, "I realize you probably think it's all that hot jungle sex, but the real truth is that this—" She twirled the wine glass by its stem. "This is why I keep you around." She took a sip of wine, rolled it around inside her mouth, and swallowed. Sighing, she stretched her shoulders to release the tension and said glumly, "The Brochu sisters. Somebody needs to point out to those two darling ladies that this isn't the nineteenth century. And Al Frechette. The man is a Neanderthal. Please remind me why I'm doing this."

"Because you're an incredible human being. And because it gives you a chance to show the world how hot you look in that red suit."

She rolled her eyes. "Easy for you to say, MacKenzie. You're not the one being tortured. And stop staring at my legs." She reached down and tugged at her skirt in an attempt to make it cover a little more thigh. The suit she wore was a screaming shade of scarlet, light years outside her comfort zone, which ran more to neutrals like navy or gray. He had, of course, picked it out. He had, of course, been right. With her olive complexion and the straight, dark hair that fell to midway down her back, the color looked stunning on her.

"Don't be such a prude, Fiore. You'll spoil all my fun. It's been so long since I saw my wife wearing anything besides jeans, I forgot she had legs."

Since the legs in question had been wrapped around his waist less than twelve hours ago, it seemed doubtful he'd really forgotten. Instead of responding, she reached down and peeled off the high-heel torture devices she wore on her feet and dropped them on the floor. And wiggled her toes. "Cook," she ordered, pointing with her wine glass.

Aided by the wine, the music, the wonderful garlicky aroma, and the sight of him working, her stress began to dissipate. She loved to watch him, six feet of long, loose, rangy man in faded, snug-fitting jeans, loved watching the way he moved as he chopped vegetables and dropped them into the sizzling wok. All of it intimately familiar and yet at the same time new and exciting. He needed a haircut; the tangled mess of golden curls that fell to his shoulders was getting out of control again. But then, when hadn't he needed one? He'd been her best friend, the one solid, stable thing in her life, since she was eighteen years old. And sometimes, even after a year of marriage, it still didn't feel real, the two of them together like this.

They'd taken a long and circuitous route to get here. She'd seen him through two failed marriages and a half-dozen years as a card-carrying member of the girl-of-the-month club. Every time Danny had broken her heart—and she'd lost count of the number of times—Rob had been the one to pick her up, dust her off, and glue the pieces back together. There was an intimacy to their bond that couldn't be easily explained. It hadn't been about sex, not back in the days when she'd been blind to every other man but Danny Fiore. Their relationship had been based on brutal honesty, blended creativity, and a willingness on each of their parts to open up a vein and bleed for the other.

Rob MacKenzie had seen her through the darkest times in her life, and some of those times had been very, very dark. She'd loved him forever, and although neither of them could pinpoint a precise moment when their feelings for each other had turned into something that went light years beyond platonic, somewhere along the way, with a fatal inevitability, they had. After Danny died—a long time after Danny died—they'd finally decided to stop running from the way they felt about each other and do something about it instead.

She clasped the stem of her wine glass in both hands and said to his back, "So, hot stuff, what did you do all afternoon while I was out battling the dragons of small-town narrow-mindedness?"

"Oh," he said, focusing his attention on his cooking, "this and that."

Evasiveness was so unlike him that Casey narrowed her eyes and took a closer look. There was something in the set of his shoulders that hadn't been there fifteen seconds ago. With the better part of two decades of history between them, she was intimately acquainted with his body language, and red flags were flying everywhere. He was getting ready to dump something on her. And she wasn't going to like it. "What's wrong?" she said.

"Nothing's wrong. But we have to talk."

She'd been about to take another sip of wine, but she stopped dead with the glass an inch from her mouth. "That sounds serious."

Rob picked up a fistful of shrimp and tossed them into the wok. "It is serious."

"Now you're scaring me."

"Don't be scared. Everything's fine. But something happened this afternoon and I've spent the last two hours trying to wrap my head around it. I'm not sure I'm there yet."

He still wasn't looking at her, and her rapidly expanding dismay sent her stomach plummeting. He moved to the sink and turned on the water, soaped and rinsed his hands to rid them of the *eau de* shrimp. Tearing a paper towel from the roll on the counter, he finally met her eyes. "I was planning to wait until after we ate," he said, drying his hands, "but you know me too well. Listen, babe, this came at me out of the blue, and I don't have any idea how you'll react. I'm still not sure how to react myself. I'm still having trouble believing it."

Casey looked at her glass of wine, closed her eyes for an instant, then tipped her head back and finished it off in a single long slug. Rob turned off the stove, filled a plate for each of them, and carried the plates to the table. She sat down across from him and picked up her fork. "All right, MacKenzie," she said. "Spill."

He rested his elbows on the table and ran the fingers of both hands through his tangled mess of curls. "I had a call this afternoon from a lawyer in Boston. Do you remember Sandy Sainsbury?"

"Of course. You had an off-and-on thing going with her back in the day."

"She died two weeks ago. From cancer."

"Oh, Rob, that's terrible! She was so young!"

"Thirty-five. And she had a fifteen-year-old daughter."

"That poor girl. It's so hard to lose your mother at such a young age. I know how it feels."

"Yeah. I thought about that. It's a lousy thing to have in common." He was looking at her oddly, and she couldn't figure out why. "The lawyer," he said. "He's in the process of settling Sandy's estate."

"I see," she said, although she really didn't.

"When she first got sick, Sandy had a will drawn up. She didn't have much, and she wanted to make sure her daughter ended up with what little she did have. But that wasn't her main concern. Both of Sandy's parents are long gone, and she never had any brothers or sisters, so the only family she had left was a couple of distant cousins. She was worried about what would happen to Paige—that's her daughter's name—if she didn't beat the cancer. So she spelled it out in her will. If anything happened to her before the kid came of age, she wanted custody of Paige to go to the girl's biological father."

"And?"

He didn't respond, just looked at her with those green eyes, and suddenly it all came together. Lawyer. Custody. Fifteen-year-old daughter. Biological father. She quickly did the math. Set down her fork. And took in a hard, sharp breath. "Oh, my God," she said.

"Um…yeah."

"You're telling me that you have a fifteen-year-old daughter?"

He raised his shoulders, looked at her helplessly, and said, "Apparently."

She saw her own shock reflected in his eyes. A million thoughts raced through her mind, but when she opened her mouth, only one came out. "Holy mother of God."

He cleared his throat. "She's staying with her downstairs neighbor right now, but the woman's already got four kids and no husband, and she can't take on another kid, not on a permanent basis. If I don't take her, the kid will go into state custody and end up in foster care." He paused. "I won't blame you if you want to bail. You didn't sign up for this."

"Oh, for the love of God, MacKenzie! After everything we've been through together, you still don't know I'd walk through fire for you? I've probably heard something more colossally idiotic coming from that mouth of yours at some point in the last two decades, but right now I can't remember what it could possibly have been."

He closed his eyes. When he opened them again, they were suspiciously damp. "I don't deserve you," he said.

"Shut up, you fool. I love you, and after everything you've done for me over the years, we have a few miles to go to even up the odds. And I so hate that this is the first question coming out of my mouth, but I have to ask it. How do you know for sure she's really yours? And don't say it's because Sandy wouldn't have any reason to lie. Considering that she couldn't manage, at some point in the last fifteen years and nine months, to call you up and say, *Hey, by the way, you have a kid.*"

"Don't feel bad, it was the first question I asked, too. He faxed me a copy of her birth certificate, Sandy's will, and a couple of Paige's school photos. Once you see the pictures, you'll stop wondering. She's mine."

He reached for a folded sheaf of papers she hadn't noticed and slid them across the table to her. Casey picked them up gingerly, glanced at him across her untouched dinner plate, and unfolded them. Skimmed the will until she reached the part where it said *Full custody of the minor child to be retained by the biological father, Robert K. MacKenzie.* She swallowed hard, then studied the birth certificate. Name of child: *Paige Morgan MacKenzie.* Mother: *Sandra Louise Sainsbury.* Father: *Robert Kevin MacKenzie.*

She glanced at him again before looking at the photos. The adolescent girl who stared back at her had a mass of thick golden curls, a strong, square jaw, a face with more angles than curves, and a light dusting of pale freckles across her nose. Although it was impossible to tell from a black-and-white photo, Casey would have bet the farm that her eyes were the trademark MacKenzie green. A tear ran unbidden down her cheek. "Oh, babe. She looks just like you."

"Poor kid got my hair."

"There's nothing wrong with your hair, MacKenzie. You just need to comb it a little more often. So of course you told him we'd take her."

"I did not. I told him I had to talk it over with my wife. This is a life-altering decision, Fiore. It was hard enough springing this on you as it is. I wasn't about to give you the news as a *fait accompli.*"

"Um, sweetie? This *fait* is about as *accompli* as it gets. Of course we're taking her. We don't have a choice."

"There's always a choice. But whether or not we bring her here, she's still my responsibility. At least until she's eighteen."

"She's not a responsibility, she's a child. Your child." She took in a sharp breath. "Oh, Flash—" Another tear trickled down her cheek. "You have a kid."

"I'm so sorry." He picked up his napkin and reached across the table to swipe away her tears. "I know it's a shock."

"That's not why I'm crying. I'm crying because I'm thinking about all those years you missed because that damn woman couldn't be bothered to tell you that you had a daughter. She stole fifteen years of a relationship with your child away from you. And of course I'm sorry she's dead. I always liked Sandy. But—damn her! How could she do this to you?"

"I don't know. But if we do this—"

"There is no if. This is your little girl we're talking about. We're doing it."

"Damn it, Casey, this will change everything! We've only been married for a year. We've barely had any time together as a couple. And it took us so long to get here. What if this screws things up for us? I'm not willing to jeopardize what we have. This isn't a matter of trying her on for size and changing our minds if she's not a good fit. This is a permanent commitment. One that's so unfair to you. How can I ask you to raise another woman's child?"

"Rob, she's *your* child. Part of you. And of course it's a permanent commitment, one that'll change our day-to-day life, but we're solid, you and I. Nothing will change the way we feel about each other. We'll work through whatever problems arise like the rational adults we are. We won't let this come between us."

"That sounds great in theory. But in practice? It might not be so easy. You're my first priority. Always. The way I feel about you is the most important thing in my life."

"Sweetie, I hate like hell to burst your bubble, but it doesn't work that way. The minute you step into that little girl's life, she becomes your number-one priority. That's the way parenthood works. Trust me when I say this. I know it from experience."

He let out a long, ragged sigh. "This isn't the way it was supposed to be." He took her hand and threaded fingers with hers. "It was supposed to be you and me and a couple of babies. Our babies. We weren't supposed to start out with a teenager I fathered with a woman I haven't even thought about in fifteen years."

She brought their joined hands to her lips and kissed his knuckles. "Life is what happens while you're making other plans," she reminded him. "And you and me and those babies? It'll still happen. This just means our kids will have a big sister to look up to. And we'll have a built-in babysitter."

Darkly, he said, "Right."

"You listen to me, MacKenzie. This is a miracle! Something wonderful like this, coming out of the tragedy of Sandy's death, like the phoenix rising from the ashes. You're going to have a relationship with this beautiful daughter you never even knew about. No matter how you look at it, my friend, that is a miracle."

"Have I told you lately what an extraordinary woman you are?"

She released his hand, got up, and walked around the table. He pushed back his chair, and she settled on his lap and wound an arm around his neck. "You," she said, resting her head on his shoulder, "are going to be an amazing father."

He buried his face in her hair, and they sat for a long time before he said, "I don't know anything about teenagers."

"Neither do I. But we have Rose and Jesse just down the road. Between the two of them, they know pretty much everything there is to know about kids. We *will* be calling them frequently."

"Oh, shit. I have to tell Rose. And my parents. I can deal with the rest of the family later."

"First, you need to call the lawyer back." She kissed his cheek and got up from his lap. "I'll clean the kitchen and put supper in the fridge. We'll reheat it and try again later."

While he took the cordless phone and went out onto the back steps to make his call, she sprinted upstairs to change out of the suit. Then she stood in the hallway outside her bedroom, contemplating all those closed doors. She had three empty rooms up here. Would Paige feel more comfortable near them, or would she prefer to maintain some independence, some distance between herself and these new parents fate had forced upon her? Casey couldn't forget the emotional roller-coaster she'd ridden after her own mother's death. There had been grief, and frustration, and resentment at being forced to grow up overnight at the tender age of fifteen.

But what stood out most in her memory was the terrible feeling of isolation. What she'd needed more than anything had been simple human contact. Closeness with the living, to ease the pain of the dead. She'd been lucky; Dad and her sister Colleen had been there, and she'd had extended family nearby. Paige, on the other hand, would be with strangers. Blood relative or not, Paige's father was a stranger to her. It wouldn't be easy for the girl.

Casey went back downstairs, and while she loaded the dishwasher and wiped down the mess he'd made cooking a meal neither of them had touched, she listened to the soft murmur of

Rob's voice as he talked to the lawyer. She couldn't hear what he was saying, and she was tempted to go outside to eavesdrop, but if he'd wanted her to hear, he would have stayed in the kitchen. This was his personal business, and she couldn't step into the middle of it unless she was invited. He would share whatever he chose to share when he was ready.

Nearly a half-hour later, just as she was rinsing the last of the soap suds from the kitchen sink, he came inside and set the phone in its cradle. He stepped up behind her, folded his arms around her and pressed his face to her hair. "We're driving down to Boston in the morning to pick her up."

Casey turned in his arms, saw the terror in his eyes, and melted. It was true, what she'd told him earlier; she would walk through fire for this man. "This will turn out fine," she said. "We'll get through this together."

"I talked to her. Paige. I got her number from the lawyer and I called her."

"That's what took you so long. I was starting to wonder. How did it go? How did she sound?"

"Like a typical teenager. Mostly monosyllabic. I told her how sorry I was about her mother, and how excited I was to find out I had a daughter. I made sure she understood that if I'd known about her before, I would've been there for her, right from day one. I told her about you, said we were good people and we'd give her a good home, and she'd have aunts and uncles and cousins and grandparents. Lots of extended family, on my side and yours. I hope I didn't overwhelm her. Family isn't something she's ever had. I didn't know what else to say, except that we'd be down tomorrow to bring her home."

"I'd say you did just fine."

"I called Rose, too. I didn't tell her what was going on, just asked if they were planning to be home because we wanted to come over and talk to them about something important. This is kind of a big thing to tell people over the phone. As a matter of fact, I think we should stop in and tell Mom and Dad in the morning, since we'll be in Boston anyway."

"I agree. This isn't the kind of news a man wants to give his mother over the phone. Listen, I've been thinking about where we should put her. The poor kid is going to feel so alone. I think we should give her the room next to ours."

"Great. There goes my sex life."

She raised an eyebrow. "Surely you knew that was inevitable once we started having kids?"

Darkly, he said, "I figured we had a few good years left before it all went to shit."

"I'm teasing you, MacKenzie. Your sex life isn't going anywhere. Trust me." She brushed a single curl away from his face. "We'll just have to be a little quieter, that's all."

He raised both eyebrows and gave her a knowing look, and she said, "Never mind. I forgot myself for a minute there. Maybe we should give her the downstairs guest room instead."

"That's a much better idea, Fiore. Unless you want to give her an advanced sexual education at the age of fifteen."

"Surely you jest. At fifteen, she probably knows more about sex than we do."

He let out a snorting laugh, then quickly sobered. "This isn't funny, is it? This is my daughter we're talking about. She's fifteen years old, and if those school photos are any indication, she's a knockout. Does this mean I have to go out and buy a shotgun to keep the hordes of teenage boys away?"

"It could come to that." She patted his cheek affectionately, gave him a quick kiss on the lips, and said, "Welcome to parenthood."

***

Rose and Jesse Lindstrom lived in a two-hundred-year-old Colonial on thirty acres with over a thousand feet of prime river frontage. Considering the going price of waterfront property, if Jesse ever decided to sell, he could make a fortune. He'd grown up in this house, and after his parents became snowbirds and started spending winters in Arizona, they'd sold him the family homestead for a ridiculously low price. The house had needed major updating, and Jesse had dropped a ton of money on renovations. The end result was a wonderful family home that would probably stand for another two hundred years.

The Lindstroms were one of those "yours, mine, and ours" blended families that had come about totally by accident. Both of them divorced parents of teenagers, Rose and Jesse had met last summer at Casey and Rob's wedding. The attraction between them had been instantaneous and intense, so intense that a few weeks later, Rose MacKenzie Kenneally had started throwing up every morning.

Casey had thought they were crazy when her sister's ex-husband and her husband's sister had announced they were getting married. They came from different worlds, their personalities were complete opposites—Rose was fire, while Jesse was ice—and they didn't even know each other. Except, apparently, in the biblical sense. But somehow, they'd made it work. Rose had moved her entire household, including two teenagers, an iguana, and a dog the size of a Frigidaire, from South Boston to rural Maine to live with Jesse and his teenage son. Four months ago, their daughter Beth had been born, and nowadays, nobody even remembered their unconventional start.

When they knocked on the door, Chauncey began barking frantically. Jesse opened the door, dog collar in hand to hold back eighty pounds of slavering mutt, and said, "Come on in." Upstairs, the stereo was booming as Axl Rose screeched an ear-splitting rendition of *Welcome to the Jungle*. With Chauncey's toenails tick-ticking elatedly on the hardwood floor, they followed Jesse to the kitchen, where Rose was just finishing up the dinner dishes.

Out here, it was a little quieter. "Hey, guys," Rose said. "Coffee, tea, beer?"

"Coffee," Rob said. "Times two. Decaf, if you have it. We have to be up early tomorrow."

"Coming right up." Rob's sister was a striking woman, with the MacKenzie green eyes, an angular face that was just this side of pretty, and wild, curly hair like her brother's, except that hers tumbled down her back in a fiery red tangle that was a perfect match for her personality.

"So," she said, taking mugs from the cupboard and setting them on the countertop. "Do you two have some kind of—" She glanced meaningfully at Casey's flat stomach. "—exciting news?"

"We have news," Rob said, "but not that kind of news. At least, not exactly."

Rose looked puzzled by his statement as she made instant decaf and carried two mugs to the kitchen table where Casey and Rob had settled side by side on wooden dining chairs.

Setting the mugs in front of them, she said, "So what's up?"

Rob said, "You might want to sit down for this."

"Whoa." Rose shared a quick glance with her husband before dropping onto a chair at one end of the long dining table. "What's going on?"

Rob took a breath. Beneath the table, Casey squeezed his hand. He said, "I just found out this afternoon that I have a fifteen-year-old daughter."

Nobody spoke. He exhaled, and Casey squeezed his hand again. "Her mother died two weeks ago, and I'm taking custody of her. Her name is Paige. Casey and I are driving down to Boston tomorrow to pick her up, and—what the hell, Rose? Why aren't you looking even remotely surprised by any of this?"

All eyes fell on Rose, who squirmed uncomfortably before getting up and making her way to the refrigerator. From behind the open door, she said brightly, "Does anybody want coffee cake? I'm sure we have one in here somewhere—"

"You knew," Rob said in a stunned voice. Casey rested a restraining hand on his arm, but it was too late. He vaulted to his feet and stalked across the room. Slammed the refrigerator door shut with so much force that his sister jumped out of the way to keep from being decapitated. "You fucking knew, and you never told me!"

"Back off, little brother, or I swear to God I'll—"

"Like hell I'll back off! How could you know something like this and not tell me? How long have you known?"

"If you can't be civil, I'm not saying a damn thing!"

"Civil, my ass! How long, Rose?" He advanced on her, inching forward until they were nearly nose to nose. "How goddamn long have you known?"

His sister held her ground, not in the least intimidated by him, probably because she was eight minutes older than he was, and they'd been squabbling like this since the womb. She squared her shoulders and her jaw and said, "Six years."

"*Six years?* SIX FUCKING YEARS you knew this, and you couldn't bother to tell me? What the hell is wrong with you? How do you even know about this?"

"Stop yelling at me, Robbie, or I'll toss you out on your ass!"

"I'll stop yelling when I'm damn good and ready. How'd you find out?"

Rose glanced at Casey, then back at her brother. She raised her chin and said, "Mom told me."

Casey winced and closed her eyes. *Worst possible answer.* Across the room, Rob said in disbelief, "*Mom* knows about this? How is that possible?"

"She ran into Sandy in the grocery store six years ago. Sandy had the kid with her. Mom took one look—"

"The kid has a name. It's Paige. I'd appreciate you remembering!"

"Mom took one look at *Paige*—" Rose over-emphasized the word, glaring at her brother. "—and almost had a heart attack. She's the spitting image of you, right down to the green eyes. But before Mom could ask any questions, Sandy beat feet. So she called Meg—"

"Meg knows, too? Jesus, Mary and Joseph!"

"—for confirmation. She knew Meg and Sandy were always tight. And Meg said that yes, the kid was yours, but Sandy had begged her not to tell you. So Mom called me to ask what I thought she should do."

"I don't believe this." He began pacing like a caged tiger before rounding on her again. "Who else knows? Does the whole family know? Does Mo Branigan down at the corner store know? Do Father McMurphy and my fourth-grade teacher know? Is there anybody from Southie who doesn't know? Besides me, of course." He paused to run trembling fingers through his hair. And said in an odd, strangled voice, "Does Dad know?"

"We decided not to tell Dad."

"*That was really big of you!*"

"Damn it," she shouted, "stop yelling at me!"

"Why?" he shouted. "Why would you keep this from me?"

"Sandy made Meg swear not to tell, and we couldn't—"

"So you did this to keep Sandy happy? Whatever happened to blood being thicker than water?"

"Your life was a mess!" she shouted. "A total flipping mess! You were on the road all the time, living out of a suitcase, traveling from gig to gig, flying to London, and Tokyo, and Sydney. There was no stability. No house, no wife, not even a serious girlfriend. Just an apartment you hardly spent any time in, and dozens of interchangeable women. You'd been divorced twice, and you weren't showing any signs you'd ever settle down and start acting like an adult. We decided it would be better for both of you if you didn't know about the ki—about Paige."

"So you just made that decision for me, arbitrarily? You and Mom and Meg, without knowing anything about my life, without even considering my feelings, just decided it would be best to keep this from me, for my own good? Well, *thank you very much!*"

"Mom almost told you a few years ago. When you and Casey were living together in Boston, and—" Rose paused, glanced at Casey, then back at her brother. "We were all so sure the two of you would end up together—but then Casey got back together with Danny, and you were a basket case, and we decided it would be better if we didn't say anything."

"Wait a minute," Casey said. "What do you mean, he was a basket case?"

"Never mind!" Rob snapped.

"When you and Danny got back together," Rose told her, "my little brother fell apart for a while. He was in pretty bad shape."

"Shut up, Rose! Stay the hell out of what's none of your business!"

"I'll shut up when I damn well please! Maybe it's time she heard this! Maybe it's time she found out just what she did to you when she dumped you for—"

"SHUT. THE. HELL. UP!"

"Oh, for the love of God," Casey said, getting up from her chair and marching across the room to stand between them like a referee at a boxing match. "To your corners, people! You're both acting like four-year-olds. Rose, just for the record, I didn't dump your brother. We were not a couple back then. He was sleeping in my guest room. As for you—" She met her husband's eyes. "Sit. Now!"

He sat. And buried his face in his trembling hands. "Jess," she said, "do you have any hard liquor in the house?"

"There's a bottle of Jim Beam in the den."

"I think my husband could use a drink. Just a shot, to calm his nerves. He's had a rough day. This was shocking news, and I believe we're experiencing a little delayed reaction."

Rob said, "I don't need to be treated like a—"

"Shut up," she said firmly but gently, kneeling on the floor in front of him. "For once in your life, let me take care of you. God knows, you've done it enough times for me."

His eyes met hers, and she watched as the fight drained out of him and he said with quiet resignation, "Fine."

Jesse returned with a shot of Jim Beam. "Thank you," she said, and put the glass in Rob's hand and wrapped his fingers around it. "Drink," she told him.

He upended the glass and took the shot in a single swallow. Closed his eyes and let her peel the glass from his fingers. She handed it back to Jesse and took Rob's hands in both of hers. "You okay?" she said.

His fingers slowly curled and tightened around hers. "I will be," he said. "Eventually. I'm just a little overwhelmed."

"And rightly so. It's been quite a day. Now, apologize to your sister."

His eyes opened and stared, a little unfocused, into hers. "What?"

"You heard me. Apologize for being a jackass."

"You're on her side now?"

"I'm on your side. In everything, always and forever. But you had no business going off on her like that. Maybe she didn't do the right thing. I'm not qualified to judge. But if she did the wrong thing, she did it for the right reason. Because she loves you, and she cares about the welfare of your daughter. And you're acting like a spoiled brat. I love you more than I can say, but I don't particularly like you when you're a brat."

He gaped at her in disbelief, glanced over at his sister, who was still scowling at him, then at Jesse, who was deeply involved in counting the floor tiles in his kitchen. "Fine," he snapped. "I'm sorry."

"Not good enough," Casey told him. "Say it like you mean it."

He glared at her and said, "Who do you think you are, my mother?"

"No, my friend, but I am the woman who can withhold all, ah—intimacy—from you if I don't get my way."

"Hah! With a teenager in the house, there won't be any more *intimacy*, anyway."

Jesse glanced up from his study of the floor tiles. "Try three teenagers and a four-month-old. Maybe once you've had your teenager for a few weeks, we can compare notes."

Rose snorted, and just like that, the tension was broken. "Ah, hell," Rob said, rubbing his eye with the heel of his hand. "I'm sorry, Rosie. I promise I won't scream at you again. At least, not until the next time we have something to fight over. I'm even sorrier now that I know you're not getting any."

Rose's eighteen-year-old daughter, Devon, walked into the room just in time to hear his last sentence. "Is no place in this house sacred?" she said in exasperation. "Not even the kitchen? Just three more weeks. Three more weeks, and then I can leave this House of Crazy for college. I cannot wait!" And she turned and stalked back out again.

"I'm sorry, too," Rose said, as though Devon had never been there. "Mom and I really did think we were doing the right thing."

"Mom. Ugh." He grimaced and rubbed both hands over his face. "You'll have to talk to her. Right now, I'm afraid of what I might say." He glanced up at his sister. "You have to understand that I'm scared to death. This morning, I was just me, living my life, and everything was normal. And tonight, I'm somebody's father, and I didn't even get the requisite nine months of prep time. Just—boom. Instant dad, without any warning."

"You guys will do fine," Rose said. "Casey's a whiz with kids of all ages, and you're still a kid yourself. Jesse and I will do anything we can to help you through this. Between the two of us, we have an encyclopedic knowledge of teenagers. If there's anything we don't know, Trish will. If Paige gets out of hand, just send her to Trish for a day or two. She'll whip the kid into shape."

Trish was Jesse's sister, married for more than two decades to Casey's oldest brother, Bill. Trish was kind-hearted and wise, and the nearest thing Casey had to a big sister. But at times, her sister-in-law could be bossy and overbearing, and a little too interested in other people's lives. Sometimes, behind her back—and Bill's—she was known as the Drill Sergeant.

Rob grinned, then sobered. "I know. It's just—hell, I don't even know what to say to her. The kid just lost her mother. She's bound to be fragile right now. No matter what I do, I can't make that go away."

"She's not expecting you to, hon. She's old enough to know her mother isn't coming back. Casey will probably be better at helping her with that, anyway. She's been there. She understands. And kids are remarkably adaptable. You'd be amazed by what they can survive. Just don't push her too hard. Let her adjust to you in her own way and her own time."

"We'll be fine," Casey said. "The three of us will get through it together."

"If you need us," Rose said, "call. Any time, day or night."

Rob stood and hugged his sister. "Thanks. And I really am sorry for losing it. None of this is your fault."

"You're an idiot," she said, "but you're still my baby brother and I still love you. Even when I want to strangle you."

"Touching," Casey said. "So touching, the two of you, when you're not trying to kill each other."

"Look," Rose said to Casey, "I didn't mean to imply that you'd done anything wrong, taking Danny back after the separation. It's just that Rob was in such bad shape afterward, and—"

"Rose," Jesse said quietly, "zip it."

"Oh, hell. Fine." And she zipped it.

Rob

The bathroom door opened, and his goddess of a wife stepped into the room, dressed in her blue silk robe and carrying an open bottle of wine. She closed the door silently, then leaned against it, while on the tinny-sounding clock radio, the Delfonics sang *La-La-La-La-La*. Green eyes met green eyes and shared a wordless conversation. She untied the belt to her robe, shrugged it off, and let it fall to the floor. Naked, she crossed the room and handed him the wine bottle. She leaned over the tub, gravity exerting its pull on those perfect breasts she always insisted were too small, and trailed slender fingers through the bath water.

Satisfied that she wasn't about to be scalded, she braced a hand on the rim of the massive claw foot tub, stepped over the edge, and lowered herself to her knees between his outstretched thighs. Eyes locked with his, she gave him one of those Mona Lisa smiles and leaned in to kiss him. Then she turned around and lowered herself to a sitting position, settling between his thighs. He wrapped an arm around her, pulled her close, her back silky-smooth against his chest. She rested her head against his shoulder and he cupped her breast and leaned back against the tub, sliding them both lower until the hot water reached her chin.

"Hi," she said.

"Hi."

"Wine, please."

He handed the bottle to her. She raised it and took a slug, then passed it back to him. He took a drink and propped the butt of the bottle against the rim of the tub. And sighed. "I'm so sorry about the meltdown. It was not my finest hour."

"Shush." She reached up, found the back of his neck, and began rubbing it, the way she knew he liked. He closed his eyes and shut up. He'd violated their unspoken agreement to leave all negativity on the other side of that door. In their bedroom, they talked about anything and everything. But the tub was sacred and inviolable. This was the place they came for comfort, for connection, for healing. For re-centering. Not for rehashing what had brought them here.

"This is nice," she said.

He nibbled her shoulder. "You're nice."

"It reminds me of Paris."

They'd spent three months in Paris, the honeymoon of all honeymoons, staying in a shabby little rental flat in the 3rd arrondissement with outdated plumbing and the deepest bathtub he'd ever seen. How many hours had they passed in that tub, drinking cheap French wine and eating baguettes smeared with country butter, while the pipes clanked and thudded and spewed water that was sometimes icy, sometimes scalding?

He raised the wine bottle, took another sip, and said, "We'll always have Paris."

"Funny boy. Unhand that bottle, son."

"Lush."

"You've made me what I am today." She took a sip of wine. "I could've just stayed there forever, you know."

"*In vino veritas?*"

"In Paris, idiot."

He nuzzled the back of her head, inhaled the scent of woman and faintly floral shampoo. "Maybe we can retire there. A couple of grizzled old ex-pats, living on faded memories of youth and glory."

"*Grizzled?* Speak for yourself, my friend. I intend to be a fabulously gorgeous and well-preserved woman of a certain age. Think Zsa Zsa Gabor or Barbara Cartland. With snow-white hair tinted pale pink." She handed the bottle back to him. "I'll be known across the Continent as the glamorous *vielle américaine*. The one with the grizzled husband."

"And my Zsa Zsa will open her own little *patisserie*, where she'll introduce all of Europe to the pleasures of genuine Maine whoopie pies."

"But of course, *dahlink*. And you'll sit cross-legged and barefoot on a street corner with your guitar, and you'll take off the little black beret you wear to cover your bald spot—"

"Hey!"

"—and you'll play beautiful tunes for the tourists, who'll toss coins into the beret so you can buy your next bottle of wine. Because, you see, by this time, we'll both be winos—"

"We're already winos."

"Stop interrupting. And when we get bored and need a change of scenery, we'll hop on a jet and fly home to visit our grandkids."

"Grandkids?"

"Lots and lots of grandkids."

"I like that part of the story."

"Me, too."

She let out a sigh of contentment. He adjusted their fit, stretched out a leg and, with his toes, turned on the hot water. "Not too much more," she said. "We're already lapping at the edges. I don't want to drown."

"I won't let you drown."

"You haven't yet, have you? Not in two decades."

"You came close a couple of times." He turned the water back off, eased them both a little higher. Slowly, so he wouldn't flood the place. "But I always pulled you back to shore."

"My hero."

"Am I your hero?"

"You are. More wine."

"I'm not too sure about me," he said, giving her the bottle, "but you're definitely a lush."

"See what you've done to me? I may need a twelve-step program."

He let out a soft snort of laughter at the idea of his straight-laced wife needing substance abuse intervention.

"There. I made you laugh. Mission accomplished."

He tightened his arms around her. "Have I told you lately that I love you?"

"Indubitably."

"Indubitably? You do like your sixty-thousand-dollar words, don't you, Fiore?"

"Are you having trouble keeping up, MacKenzie? Should I get you a dictionary?"

"Witch."

"I'm just trying to be helpful. Accommodating the handicapped."

"Woman, you are *so* going to pay for that later."

"But not right now."

"Nope. Not right now."

She turned on one hip, her movement sending a soapy wave sloshing over the rounded edge of the tub. It hit the floor with a splash. "Oops," she said.

"Watch it. We'll have water dripping all over the dining room table."

"We have plenty of money. We can buy a new table."

"You get too much water on these old floorboards and we're apt to end up in the middle of that table. Tub and all."

She pressed her cheek to his neck and wound an arm around him. "We can't be having that, can we?"

He set the wine bottle on the floor, wrapped both arms around her, closed his eyes and smiled. "Nope. We can't be having that."

Lesley Gore was singing now. "Have you ever actually listened to the words of this song?" she said. "I've always liked Lesley Gore. But who on earth wrote these dreadful, misogynistic lyrics?"

"I haven't the foggiest."

"It's okay that he's cheating, because she knows that deep down, he really loves her? And she's sure he'll come around one of these days? Good God."

"That was the Sixties, babe. It's a whole new world now."

"We must be talking the Brill Building. In that era, everything that didn't come out of Detroit came out of the Brill Building. But which of our oh-so-talented predecessors is responsible for this travesty?"

"I'll buy you the record. We'll read the fine print together. Then we'll know."

"Whoever it was, it seems they had a skewed view of love and life. Good thing you didn't share their viewpoint when we started writing together. I would've very quickly disabused you of such a ridiculous notion."

"Not to mention after we got married."

"That goes without saying."

"I'm nobody's fool. I know just how sharp you keep that filleting knife."

"It's a very effective tool, isn't it?"

"Hush now," he said. "Just cuddle."

"How lucky am I, to marry a guy who actually likes to cuddle?"

"Wait a minute. Am I missing something? Men don't like to cuddle?"

"Not in my experience. Which, admittedly, isn't vast, but to my understanding, enjoyment of cuddling is not among the top traits of most manly men."

"I guess I never got the memo. Better keep it to ourselves, then. Wouldn't want to destroy my studly reputation. The last thing I need is for anyone to think I'm not a manly man."

She shifted position again, rising to her knees and sending another gush of water over the side of the tub. Took his face in her hands and kissed him. "Trust me. There's no question in anybody's mind about your manliness."

He reached up and cupped a wet, soapy breast. "Good to know."

Casey

The dream began the way it always did.

They were in the BMW, snow falling around them so thick and fast it nearly obscured visibility. They were bickering, the way married couples do in stressful situations, and he was trying to keep the car on the road and still put some miles behind them. When she told him he was driving too fast for the conditions, he asked her if she wanted to drive. That shut her up. The car slipped, lost traction, and began to skid. Her heart slammed into her throat. He steered into the skid and brought it back under control. And she said, "I swear to God, Danny, if you kill us, I'll never speak to you again."

"I'm not going to kill us," he said. "I'm not going to crash and burn. I'm going to be right there beside you in your dotage."

Then, from out of nowhere, there it was, the tanker truck, lying on its side, blocking the highway directly in front of them. It all happened so quickly, yet at the same time she could feel it unfurling in slow motion, like a movie where the director wanted you to experience a potent, gradual build-up of terror. He pumped the brakes and they began to spin, at first slowly, then faster and faster. Just before they reached the truck, he pulled out of the spin and they tore through the snow bank instead, came out the other side, and she thought, *We made it. We're okay.*

Then they started falling, rolling, side to side and end over end, small objects catapulting like crazed pinballs around them. She screamed his name and reached out into nothingness, unable to find him in the confusion, and it really was true that your life flashed before your eyes, because she saw it all so clearly, saw everything she'd done wrong in her life, everything she'd done right, saw all the people she'd loved, even those who had already passed on: Mama, and Grandma and Grandpa Bradley, and then there was Katie, her Katydid, gazing solemnly at her with Danny's blue eyes, the color of a summer sky, and she understood she was going to die, and she didn't mind dying, because dying meant she'd be with Katie again.

They slammed hard against a boulder and came to a creaking, shuddering halt. Something hit her in the face, and the world went black. And cold. So cold that at first, she thought she really had died. Until something soft and wet and insistent kissed her cheek, and she forced her eyelids open, licked a flake of snow from her bottom lip.

The windshield was shattered, broken glass everywhere, snowflakes falling cottony and silent all around her. A thin layer of smoke hovered on the air, and she panicked until she realized it was powder from the deployed airbags. In the distance, she heard voices shouting. She turned her head and gazed impassively at the hideous Thing that had been her husband. *Blood.* So much blood, it mingled with the snowflakes drifting through the open windshield and ran in crystalline rivulets down his face. Blood trickled from his nose, from his mouth, from the massive chest wound where the steering column had impaled him. Instantly, she knew he was gone, knew the man she'd loved for her entire adult life was no longer in there, knew there was nothing left of him but this broken, bloody shell.

And then, in the way of nightmares, he opened his eyes, and they weren't Danny's eyes at all. Instead of that summer-sky blue, they were hard and evil and yellow. The hideous Thing-That-Wasn't-Danny reached out a bloody hand toward her, and it had claws where there should have been neatly manicured fingernails, and she had to get away, had to escape from this monster before she suffered the same fate.

She yanked frantically at the door handle, but it wouldn't budge. Tried to roll down the window, but it was jammed. She began kicking at the passenger-side window, kicking harder and harder as the Thing drew ever closer, until she felt its hot, rancid breath on her neck. But the window refused to break, and the Thing smiled, showing razor-sharp teeth, and it was going to tear her to shreds, and she couldn't escape, couldn't do anything but scream and scream and scream—

She awoke with a jolt, her heart hammering, her breath coming in short little gasps. *Oh, my God*, she thought. *Oh, my God.*

Trying to slow her breathing, she glanced around the bedroom to orient herself. The room was hot and sticky, and the fan they'd put in the window, its whirring blades fluttering the curtain, wasn't doing much more than redistributing the thick, humid air. Parched, she desperately needed a drink. Beside her, Rob slept hard and peacefully, the way he always did.

Still trembling from the nightmare, she eased away from him and sat on the edge of the bed. Took a long, cleansing breath and stood. Reached for the robe she kept on a nearby chair.

From the darkness behind her, a groggy voice said, "Where you going?"

She hesitated, the robe in her hands. Slipped it on, tied the belt, and turned back toward the bed. "I'm just going downstairs to get a drink. Go back to sleep."

The kitchen was cooler than her bedroom had been. Moving swiftly and surely in the darkness, she took a glass from the cupboard and filled it with water, icy-cold, refreshing and wonderful. She drank until the glass was empty, then set it in the sink and stood there running cold water over her wrists.

This December would mark four years since that terrible night when Danny died. Yet the nightmares hadn't started until a year ago, so soon after she married Rob that the connection was impossible to miss. Dr. Freud would certainly have something to say about that. Was it guilt that generated these gory horror-fests? If so, she had no reason to feel guilty. She'd done nothing wrong. They'd waited nearly two years, a respectable length of time for a widow to mourn her husband before becoming sexually active again. Rob had—for the most part—kept his distance, had allowed her to come to her own conclusions about the direction their relationship was headed.

But Danny had been her love and her life for thirteen years, the only man she'd ever slept with, and even though she knew it was ridiculous, in some small part of her, it still felt disloyal, being with another man that way—and enjoying it so damn much. She'd been so young and innocent when she met Danny, only eighteen, and she'd fallen hard and fast. Being with him had been heaven and it had been hell. She'd worked incredibly hard to keep their marriage intact. But there had been something missing in him, something broken that couldn't be fixed. Looking back from the vantage point of thirty-five years spent living on this planet, she couldn't help wondering: If she were to offer advice to that naïve eighteen-year-old version of herself, what would she say?

Step away from the Magic Man. Yes, he may be pretty and shiny and shiny and sparkly and new, and yes, he may offer untold delights. But along with those delights come heartaches. Sorrow. So much pain. In the end, you may not find him worth it. Run away now, while you still have time!

And yet. And yet. She didn't regret those thirteen years. They'd loved each other with a desperation bordering on obsession. No matter how bad things got, no matter what wedge drove them apart, she and Danny were always drawn back to each other by some force she'd never been able to explain. Even after Katie died and everything went to hell, even after she recognized that her feelings for Rob had turned into something complicated and unnerving and sexual, even then, that same sick obsession had driven her back to Danny.

And there was still the other side of the coin, the side she couldn't ignore. If she'd never met Danny, she wouldn't be here with Rob today. She would probably be married to Jesse, and living in that big house by the river, with three or four kids and a husband she cared for but didn't love. A thirty-something housewife, aging too rapidly, mourning her lost youth, trying to minimize her regrets, and yearning like some lovelorn teenager for the kind of passion she would probably never experience.

The kitchen light came on, startling her, and she blinked rapidly to adjust her eyes. She hadn't heard his footsteps. Casey turned off the faucet, dried her hands on a dish towel, and turned to face her husband.

He'd thrown on a pair of jeans. Tight ones. Long and lean and rangy, he had wide shoulders and well-developed biceps—honed by years of playing scorching rock guitar—a flat stomach and narrow hips, and a dark triangle of silky chest hair tapering to a slender vee that pointed directly toward paradise. After the better part of two decades spent trying to fatten him up, she'd finally managed to put a few pounds on him over the winter, and those pounds had landed in all the right places. Shirtless and barefoot, the man was a walking advertisement for sex.

Her mouth went dry, and everything inside her melted. He had no idea how the sight of him like this affected her, and she had no intention of ever telling him, because it seemed undignified for a woman her age to lust so heartily after her own husband.

Maybe his lack of ego was part of his charm; in spite of the long list of women who had come and gone before her, he still didn't recognize his own attractiveness. Rob MacKenzie wasn't handsome, not in any conventional sense. At first glance, he seemed quite ordinary, until you got close enough to look into those soft green eyes and see the kindness there. Even then, a woman might dismiss him as a lightweight, a nice guy who would always finish last, until he flashed one of those zillion-megawatt smiles, his secret weapon, and reduced said woman to a helpless puddle of goo.

"Another nightmare?" he said.

She should know better than to try to sneak around his built-in radar. He always knew. Always. "I'm okay."

Rob knew she kept reliving the accident in her sleep, knew the dreams were horrifying. But she'd never told him the details, and she never would. He knew better than to ask. There was only so far they could take the *no boundaries* thing. Even she and Rob had certain lines they didn't cross, places they didn't go. They never discussed his first wife. And they never talked about the accident.

He stepped closer, slipped his arms around her waist. She pressed her mouth to the center of his chest in a soft kiss. Silky chest hair tickled her nose. "Hey," she said.

"Hey."

Her hands idly sliding up and down his back, she lay her face against his chest and let herself wallow in the absolute rightness of being with him. He tucked her head under his chin and they swayed together, contentment rolling off them in waves. This was the way marriage was supposed to be. Easy and open. Not tainted by rivers of darkness that ate away at its foundations until it could no longer stand without assistance.

Eventually, he said, "Can't keep your hands off me, can you, Fiore?"

Against his warm skin, she smiled. "I'm just admiring all that delicious male pulchritude."

"Pulchritude," he said. "That's a big word."

"It is. Do I get extra points for all those syllables?"

"You get extra points, sweetheart, just for breathing. You hungry?"

She tilted her head and looked up at him. "It's always the same with you, isn't it, MacKenzie? Food and sex, sex and food. That's all you ever think about."

"Hey, a man has to survive, and there are certain basic building blocks to survival. One is food, the other one's sex. And maybe indoor plumbing, although the jury's still out on that."

"If my vote counts for anything, I'm all for indoor plumbing."

"Of course you are." He patted her fanny, let his hand rest there. "You're a girl."

"And aren't you glad I am?"

"I remain ever grateful that you're a girl. This whole relationship would be really awkward if you weren't. So what do you say? I'm starving. We never ate dinner. Let's heat it back up."

The kitchen clock read 2:37 a.m. It wasn't as though it would be the first time; they had a tradition of late-night eating going back nearly two decades. "Why not?" she said, and stepped out of his arms. "You open a bottle of wine, and I'll reheat the food."

"Babydoll," he said, and leaned to kiss the tip of her nose, "you read my mind."

Rob

He hated like hell to wake her.

She looked so relaxed, so comfortable, sleeping face down with her dark hair spilling over her bare shoulders and across the pillow, that he wished he could let her stay this way forever. Casey was typically an early riser, but they'd been up for half the night. After the wine and the reheated dinner, they'd managed to squeeze in a very satisfying round of canoodling.

This morning, he'd let her sleep as late as he dared. He'd been up for two hours already, had gotten in an eight-mile run and a long, hot shower and had sipped his first cup of coffee on the way into town to top off the Explorer's gas tank. Under normal circumstances, he might have crawled back into bed and stayed there with her, their limbs intertwined in a random tangle of post-dawn wedded bliss. But their particular brand of normal was about to undergo a sea change, and he had no idea what the end result would look like.

Atkinson, the attorney, was expecting them around noon, and it would take at least three and a half hours to get to Boston. Maybe longer, depending on traffic. So he crouched down beside the bed, coffee mug in hand, swept aside her dark cloud of hair, and pressed a kiss to her bare shoulder.

"Mmph."

He recognized that sound, knew it well. Translated, it meant, *Go away and leave me alone.* Prepared for the challenge, he ran a finger down the center of her spine. She reached for a pillow and draped it over her head, and he used the final weapon in his arsenal, tilting the coffee mug so the aroma of fresh-ground Colombian beans wafted directly up her nose.

That did the job. She flung the pillow aside and with obvious reluctance, opened her eyes.

"Morning, gorgeous," he said.

She wet her lips and said in a groggy voice, "You fight dirty."

He grinned. "I know your weaknesses."

She sat up, wrapping the sheet around her modestly, as if he hadn't already seen and explored in depth every inch of that hot little body. Prudishness was one of her quirks that he found alternately endearing and maddening. He leaned forward, gave her a lingering kiss, and handed her the mug of coffee. "Thank you," she said, and took a sip. "What time is it?"

"Almost eight. We really need to roll. You want to grab breakfast on the road, or should I just make toast?"

"Toast is fine." She took another sip and closed her eyes. "Once I get a shower and some caffeine, I'll be human again. I promise."

"You're dragging this morning. I guess I was too much for you last night. Must be a *looove* hangover."

She opened her eyes, studied him at length. "Don't flatter yourself, MacKenzie."

He grinned. "Woman, do you have any idea how much irreparable damage you just did to my poor, battered ego?"

"Tell your poor, battered ego to stop fishing for compliments. If I have any complaints, I'll let you know."

"So I at least performed adequately on what may have been our last opportunity for the next decade to have hot jungle sex?"

She reached out a hand and straightened his collar. "You got the job done, Flash. And it won't be a decade. It'll only be three years."

"Only three years without sex. I feel so much better."

Over the rim of her coffee mug, she gave him one of those heart-stopping smiles that always turned him inside out. "Hand me my robe, my incredibly oversexed man, and go make toast."

He picked up the ice-blue silk robe she'd hung neatly over the back of a chair. "Oversexed?" He handed it to her. "Hardly. No pun intended."

"Toast," she said. "Vamoose! Give me ten minutes to shower and get dressed."

Most women, when they said ten minutes, meant an hour. But his wife was a low-maintenance woman, and when she said ten minutes, she meant ten minutes. Punctuality was another of her primary character traits. Twenty minutes later, beneath clear blue skies, they were on the road, both of them nursing coffee and private thoughts. He glanced over at her, took a sip of coffee, and said, "You're quiet this morning." He suspected the enormity of this had finally hit her.

She turned to look at him, her opaque sunglasses hiding her eyes, making it impossible to gauge her mood. "It's a lot to take in."

"Are you sure you're really cool with this? It's different for me. She's my kid. I have a blood connection with her. But for you—"

"Come on, Rob. Do you really think I'm that shallow?"

Eyes on the road ahead, he said, "Of course not. I didn't mean it that way. But part of me feels like I'm forcing her on you, and you're too polite to tell me to take a long walk off a short pier."

"I believe being polite with each other for the sake of politeness went out the door around 1975. Believe me when I say that if I had any objections, you'd know about them."

"Good to know."

"I also believe it's crucial that we're open and honest about this situation. Because if we're not honest—with each other, with ourselves—that's when things will start to go sour. And that's the absolute last thing we want."

"Agreed."

"I'm not sure how I'm supposed to feel. I'm absolutely one hundred percent behind you in this. She's your daughter, and we will take her into our home and raise her. I've never for an instant considered not taking her in."

"But?"

"But. You pointed it out yourself. This will change things. Now that I've had more time to think it over, it makes me a little nervous. Fear of the unknown can do terrible things to your psyche. And—" She paused. "Even the act of admitting this makes me feel small and petty, and I hate it. But there's a part of me that's jealous."

"Jealous?" he said blankly. "Tell me you're not afraid I'll cast you aside in favor of my daughter. Because if you are, I can assure you that hell would freeze rock solid before that would happen."

"It's not that."

"Then what?"

"You have this wonderful opportunity to get to know your daughter. To watch her grow up. To have a relationship with her."

"And?"

She gazed out the passenger-side window, away from him. "And my daughter is buried up on that hill beside her father."

It struck him without warning, a hard, sharp pain, somewhere in the vicinity of his breastbone. That beautiful little girl, who'd inherited the best of both her parents, had broken so many hearts when she died. Including his. "I'm a cretin," he said, wishing there were some way he could apply his size-eleven foot to his own posterior, and kick hard and repeatedly. "I never even thought about Katie, or about how this might stir things up for you. You cannot know how sorry I am."

"You have your own daughter to think about right now. I wouldn't expect you to be thinking about mine."

"But I should've been. It just didn't occur to me."

"Don't beat yourself up over it. This has nothing to do with you. This is me being petty and small and selfish. And that's just a fraction of what I'm feeling right now. My emotions are springing around like a pinball out of control."

"Mine, too. And you are not petty, or small, or selfish. You're a bereaved mother."

"I should be over it by now. It's been five years."

He set down his coffee cup, reached out and took her hand, threaded fingers through hers. "It's not the kind of thing you get over, babe. It gets easier, but it doesn't go away."

"The only reason I survived it is because you were there."

Squeezing her hand, he said, "I know."

They were both silent for a while. Sometimes she went away, to a dark place where he couldn't follow her. And it killed him that he couldn't, but there was no changing it, no matter how much he loved her. She was a mother who'd lost her child, and nobody, except another parent who'd gone through the same thing, could ever understand.

"But let's not be maudlin," she said. "Because another part of me feels as though I've been given a second chance at motherhood. I don't expect to take the place of Paige's mom. But the opportunity to give her the guidance and the love she'll so badly need...I'm excited about that. I know we'll hit rough patches, bumps in the road. Yes, I need to be a mother, and yes, I want your babies. But Paige *is* your baby. And I get to help you raise her to adulthood. I feel so honored."

She was a truly amazing woman, his wife. He brought their joined hands to his mouth and kissed her fingers. "I love you," he said.

"I love you, too. So what are you feeling about all of this? Now that you've had some time to think it over?"

He dropped her hand, wiggled his shoulders around a little to ease some of the tension. "How do I feel? We can start with terrified, because I don't know where to even begin to be a father. Pissed off at Sandy for keeping me in the dark for fifteen years. Resentful about having my life disrupted like this, just when you and I have finally found our way to being *us*. Excited to have a kid. I've wanted kids for so long, and I'm bringing her home with me, where I can be her dad. A little giddy, because from here on in, she's ours, and you and I get to watch her grow up. Sad, because she's lost her mother, and Sandy won't have that same opportunity to see her grow up. Then I remember she deliberately denied me the opportunity to experience those first fifteen years, and I bounce right back to pissed off again."

She saluted him with her coffee cup. "That's what I call honesty, my friend. I'm so glad to know I'm not the only one who's bouncing all over the place."

"What if she hates me? What if she hates you? What if she's more than we can handle? What if she needs psychiatric help to deal with the trauma of losing her mother? What if—hell, I don't even know. All these *what ifs* are circling around in my head like vultures, and I'm the carcass they're waiting to pick."

"Don't borrow trouble. If she needs counseling, we'll get her counseling. Your sister's a social worker, she knows everybody. She'll be a great resource if we need her. And as far as resources are concerned, we certainly don't have to worry about money. We're so lucky. Whatever Paige needs, we can afford to pay for, including a decent college education when the time comes. This will all work out. You'll see."

Traffic on I-95 was heavy, and he popped in Mellencamp's *Lonesome Jubilee* and focused on his driving. Music was an obsession for him. He craved it, needed it flowing through his days the way most people needed caffeine flowing through their veins. But when Casey was with him, unless he could find an oldies station, he never played the radio, for fear the deejay would spin a Danny Fiore record and she would freak. Silently, of course. His wife never said a word, but her body language was eloquent. Almost four years after his death, she still couldn't handle hearing Danny sing.

And Rob understood. He really did. She and Danny had been an institution. She'd lost the love of her life, and that wasn't the kind of thing a woman ever got over. If he had half a brain, he'd get down on his knees and kiss the ground, because even though he couldn't begin to fill Danny's shoes, for some crazy reason she loved him anyway. She just didn't love him the way she'd loved Danny. He'd long since accepted it as truth, and did it really matter at this point? Danny sure as hell wasn't coming back. He, Rob MacKenzie, was the one who was upright and breathing, the one whose ring she wore, the one who slept in her bed every night. So he accepted second place in her life, silently thanked the gods for his good fortune, tiptoed around the elephant in the living room, and stuck to the safety of cassette tapes.

His response to hearing Danny sing was vastly different from hers. Sure, he felt nostalgia and a little sadness. Danny had, after all, been his best buddy. But beyond the sadness, there was exhilaration, for every time he heard one of those hit songs, he was blown away by the magic the three of them had created. That magic had given him a life he never could have imagined when he was a scrawny nineteen-year-old guitar player with vague, unformed dreams about making a living with his music.

Everything that was good in his life today he owed to Danny Fiore: the woman who was sitting beside him; the career that was exponentially bigger than his wildest dreams; the money sitting in the bank that allowed him to work when he felt like it and loaf when he didn't; even the house he was living in. Without Danny Fiore, he would have none of those things. Without Danny Fiore, he would probably still be playing the Boston bar scene. Or worse, he would have given up his music years ago for some dreary nine-to-five job that would have sucked the soul right out of him.

Instead, thanks to Danny, he'd led a charmed life. Oh, there had been a few bumps in the road. He'd had his heart broken a time or two, had gone hungry for a few years while they struggled to achieve success. That had been hard, but it was a cakewalk compared to Danny's death. That was the toughest thing he'd ever had to face, losing his friend, his front man, the guy whose voice gave brilliant life to the music he and Casey wrote. He'd loved Danny like a brother, and losing him had felt like the sky falling on his head.

But it hadn't always been that way. He hadn't much liked Danny Fiore at first.

As cities went, Boston wasn't a big one, and in the summer of 1973, the local music scene was small and incestuous: if you were out there playing, sooner or later, you knew everybody else who was out there playing. And if you didn't know everybody, you knew everybody's bass player, or everybody's cousin who used to play with your drummer's college roommate. That was the kind of place it was. For a couple of months, he'd been hearing about this singer named Danny Fiore, who had a voice, they said, that could peel the wallpaper off the walls. Rumor said he'd been bringing down the house everywhere he played, and at the age of twenty-two, he was already achieving local legend status.

One Saturday night when they had nothing better to do, Rob and a couple of his friends went out to Somerville to check out Fiore and his band. The bar was crowded, the audience about three-quarters female, and the instant Fiore stepped up on stage, Rob understood why. The guy was a total chick magnet. He had a face like a Greek god, and he oozed sex appeal like ketchup from a bottle. Disappointed, Rob was ready to dismiss him as just another pretty face. All flash and no substance. He figured he'd stay for a couple of songs, finish his beer, and find some better way to spend what was left of the evening.

Then Fiore opened his mouth to sing, and any thought of leaving went *cha-cha-cha* right out the door. It was strictly garage band stuff, but holy mother of God, could the guy sing. Rob instantly forgave him for the pretty face because it didn't take more than fifteen seconds to realize that Danny Fiore was going places. But not with this band. The bass player wasn't bad, but the drummer was weak, and the lead guitarist sucked. Rob nursed his beer and watched and listened and ruminated. When the set ended, acting on an impulse that came from someplace he didn't even recognize, he thrust his beer bottle into his buddy Eric's hand.

"Hold this," he said, and stalked resolutely through the crowd to the stage. "Hey, Fiore!" he shouted.

The Greek god glanced up, eyed him from stem to stern, took in the tangled mess of curly blond hair, the long, scrawny legs encased in ragged denim, the scruffy army jacket and the wrinkled Led Zeppelin tee shirt underneath it. And said, "What?"

"Your guitar player's for shit."

For five long seconds, they took each other's measure. And then Fiore said, "So, Junior, do you think you can do better?"

He snorted and said, "With one hand tied behind my back." He might be barely nineteen and still wet behind the ears, but he knew his way around a guitar. "How about I show your friend here how it's supposed to be done?"

Fiore raised a single, cynical eyebrow. "Hey, Trav," he said to the bass player, "this kid thinks he's Jimmy Page. What do you think? Should we put him to the test?"

The bass player grinned and said something that sounded like, "This should be fun."

"Come on up, kid." Into the mic, Fiore said, "Eddie, get your ass back up here, we need you on the drum set. Dave? This kid here says he wants to show you how it's supposed to be done."

Rob sprinted up onto the stage, shrugged off the army jacket and tossed it to Dave, and picked up the guy's piece-of-shit guitar. When Fiore said, "You have a name, kid?" he just shrugged.

"Okay, then," Fiore said into the mic. "Looks like we have an anonymous guest guitarist tonight. Let's see what this kid can do."

There was a smattering of applause, a few catcalls, a handful of beer bottles raised in salutation. Rob ran his fingers up and down the neck of the guitar to get the feel of it, plucked a couple of notes, tightened his B string, and launched himself into the opening riff of Clapton's *Layla*.

He didn't have the bottleneck slide Duane Allman had used to play that legendary guitar riff, but he managed to do a damn fine job without one. The look on Danny Fiore's face was priceless. Their eyes met, and something passed between them, an acknowledgment, an instantaneous understanding. Rob lifted his bony shoulders as if to say, "Told you so." Fiore nodded and, without missing a beat, jumped into the vocals. The rest of the band fell in, and Rob MacKenzie closed his eyes and just played, making that piece-of-shit guitar sing and wail and scream like a woman in the throes of ecstasy. It was a beautiful thing, and when they got to the piano solo, because there was no piano, he improvised, made the guitar weep as sweet and as tender as a mourning dove at the break of day.

When he was done, the applause was gratifying, but that was never what it was about for him. For him, it was about the music. Always, it was about the music. He hopped lightly from the stage, handed a stunned Dave the guitar in exchange for his jacket, and walked away into the crowd.

"Hey, kid!" Fiore shouted into the mic. "Who the hell are you?"

He didn't answer, just kept going, out the door and onto the sidewalk. If Fiore wanted to find him, it wouldn't be hard. This was, after all, Boston. Everybody knew somebody who knew somebody who knew somebody. What he'd done was a little over the top, not his usual style. But he'd always believed that if you wanted something, you had to go after it. And he'd never been fazed by a challenge.

Besides, something about Danny Fiore had provoked him, had brought out a perverse side of his nature he hadn't known was there. He'd liked seeing the guy sweat. Now the ball was in Fiore's court. It would be interesting to see how long it would take him to volley it back.

Thirteen-and-a-half hours later, he got his answer when his mother yelled up the stairs, "Robbie! Somebody here to see you!" He came loping down the staircase and found Danny Fiore standing in his mother's kitchen. Rob glanced at the wall clock, silently counted the hours, and nodded. Not bad. Not bad at all.

"MacKenzie," Fiore said, by way of greeting.

"Fiore," he said.

Without another word, Fiore tilted his head in the direction of the rusty and dented '64 Bel Air parked at the curb, and Rob followed him outside.

Inside the car, Danny Fiore handed him a twelve-ounce Bud from the six-pack on the floor, took one for himself, and lit a cigarette. He drew the smoke in deeply, exhaled it in a blue cloud, and flicked an ash out the window. They popped open their bottles and sat in a comfortable silence, sipping beer and scoping out each other's vibes.

"Okay, kid," Fiore finally said, "here's the deal. Because I'm the front man, my name goes on the band. I bring my bass player, and you find us a drummer that knows his ass from his elbow. We split the money four ways, except that I get an extra ten percent, because it's my name and my band."

Rob took a long, slow pull on his beer, slithered down onto his tailbone and propped his size-eleven sneakers on the dashboard of Fiore's beat-up Chevy. And said, "Your name goes on the band, because we'd be fools to do it any other way. You can bring your bass player, and I already found us a drummer. We split the money four ways, and you don't get any extra, because I'm as good at playing guitar as you are at singing, and you don't intimidate me one iota. You and I will be equal partners in everything, because it's *our* band. We play the covers the audience wants to hear, but we also play some of my original stuff, because covers won't break us out of the bar band ghetto. And if you call me kid, or junior, one more time, I'll put my foot up your ass so far you'll need dental work."

"Anybody ever tell you that you have brass balls, MacKenzie?"

"Right back atcha, Fiore."

Danny Fiore exhaled a cloud of smoke and said, "You must be some kind of wizard to play like that. I think I'll call you Wiz. How long you been playing?"

"Ten years. Five on the electric."

"Christ, how frigging old are you? You look like you're still in high school. You're a long drink of water, but you're scrawny as a wharf rat."

"Nineteen. Just finished my second year at Berklee."

"Berklee," Fiore said. "That explains a little. Tell me, can you sing?"

"Not like you, that's for sure. But, yeah, I can sing."

"Nobody sings like me, MacKenzie. But you can do harmonies?"

"A real humble guy, I see. And yes, I can do harmonies."

"If you're looking for humble, you're barking up the wrong tree. What else can you do?"

"A little piano. A little composition, a little arranging, a little transcription."

"God bless Berklee! I think this just might be the beginning of a beautiful friendship."

"What about you, Fiore? What else can you do?"

"Piano. Years and years of lessons. A little guitar. Self-taught. Nothing like what you can do—Jesus Christ, I've never met anybody who could do what you can do—but I can pinch-hit on rhythm if I have to. What are you playing?"

"A third-hand Fender Strat with an ancient Marshall amp that I picked up cheap a couple of years back. Temperamental bitch. Sometimes she works, sometimes she doesn't."

Fiore took a sip of beer and ruminated for a while before saying, "We'll have to get you some better equipment. And maybe some decent clothes. Because, my friend, we are serious musicians, and we are going to go far together."

Rob raised his beer bottle and said, "I'll drink to that." They clinked bottles together, sealing a partnership that would, indeed, take them far. It would take them to places neither of them could have ever anticipated, and it would cement their standing in the pantheon of rock-and-roll history.

"What you did last night," Fiore said, and took a drag on his cigarette, "that was really ballsy."

He crossed his ankles up there on the dash and said, "Don't take this the wrong way, Fiore, but as soon as that first note left your throat, I saw my future in your eyes."

"That's okay, MacKenzie, because I'm pretty sure I saw God when you played that first guitar riff." Fiore snickered. "You should have seen the look on Dave's face when you picked up his guitar and started wailing on it. I thought he'd cry. It was a beautiful moment." He drew on his cigarette, exhaled. "So who's this drummer?"

"Guy named Jake Edwards. Used to go to Berklee with me."

"So you called him, and he said yes, just like that?"

"I called him at six-thirty this morning and dragged him out of bed. His wife was royally pissed. He didn't say yes until I told him who I'd lined up to be the lead singer in my new band."

Fiore raised both eyebrows and said, "Pretty sure of yourself, aren't you, MacKenzie?"

"Nope. Pretty sure of you, though."

Fiore studied him at length, then said, "You really are nervy for a wharf rat."

"Thank you."

"And now, my audacious friend, we have to find a place to rehearse. I strongly suspect that Dave won't let me use his garage any more." Fiore tossed his cigarette out the window, into the street. "Especially since I fired him and Eddie five minutes after I found out your name."

"Pretty sure of yourself, aren't you, Fiore?"

Fiore grinned and said, "Nope. Pretty sure of you, though."

"We can rehearse here. My folks will be cool with it. They've been putting up with my music for years. They figure it keeps me off the streets and out of jail. We have a big family room downstairs. With a piano."

"I think this is a marriage made in heaven, MacKenzie. You suppose we should at least ask first?"

He grinned, said, "Details, details." Set down his empty beer bottle, opened the car door, swung his long legs down off the dash, and said, "Come on in. Let's get this party started."

Casey

She would have gotten hopelessly lost trying to find the address, but Rob navigated the streets of South Boston with the familiarity of a native. While he drove, she read house numbers. "Right here," she said when they reached number 36. "The blue one." He slowed, craned his neck to get a better look, then found a parking space two houses down and wheeled the Explorer into it as though he'd been parallel-parking behemoth four-wheel-drive vehicles all his life. He turned off the ignition, and they looked at each other in silence before opening doors, exiting the car, and meeting on the sidewalk. She stepped into his arms, and they held each other, warmth to warmth, giving and receiving strength to deal with whatever lay ahead.

He let out a ragged breath. "Looks like this is it."

She touched her palm to his cheek. "Are you ready?"

"I don't think that's possible. We just move straight ahead, ready or not."

"This is a good thing, MacKenzie. A moment of great significance."

He kissed her palm. "Just be there to catch me in case I pass out."

She heard a car door slam, then footsteps approached, and they stepped apart and turned to look at the man who had just crossed the street. He was about their age, dressed in a gray suit, and he carried a briefcase. "Mr. MacKenzie?" he said. "Greg Atkinson."

Rob shook his hand, then said, "My wife, Casey."

"Mrs. MacKenzie." Atkinson shook her hand. "I hope your trip was pleasant."

"It was. It's a lovely day for a drive."

"Before we go up," he said, getting right down to business, "I want to make sure you're both fully on board with this. It's not something you can undo, and you're both looking a little shell-shocked right now. She is your responsibility, Mr. MacKenzie, but nobody's forcing you to take physical custody of the girl."

"We are absolutely both on board with this," Casey said. She took Rob's hand, threaded fingers with him. His hand was damp, and overly warm. And a little shaky. "One hundred percent. Of course we're taking custody of her."

Atkinson studied her face, nodded, and turned to Rob. "She's my daughter," Rob said, and squeezed Casey's hand. "She'll be going home with us."

"Good!" Atkinson turned and they began walking toward the blue house. "Paige seems to be a pretty resilient kid. She's been through a tough time, but she appears to be weathering it as well as any kid could. This all happened very quickly. Sandy was only sick for a couple of months. In hindsight, that was probably a blessing for both of them. It could have been so much worse if she'd lingered for months, but her illness was mercifully brief. On the other hand, it happened so quickly I'm not sure Paige has had time to absorb the significance of it. You may want to handle her with kid gloves for a while." They reached the house, and he turned to Rob. "You talked to her last night?"

"I did. It was a pretty brief conversation. And a little awkward. I didn't know what to say, and neither did she."

"Just guessing, I'd say you should expect that awkwardness to continue, at least for a while. Yes, you're her father, but she doesn't know you, and you're taking her away from everything and everyone she's ever known."

They stood for a moment, staring up at the faded triple-decker, with its peeling paint and sagging porches. "Second floor," Atkinson said, and they began to climb the worn wooden stairs.

"Do you have any idea," Rob said, "what Sandy told her about me? How long she's known I'm her father?"

"I don't. But considering that she has your last name, I have to assume they addressed the issue at some point. I don't know too many kids who'd reach the age of fifteen without asking why their last name is different from her mother's. Or, for that matter, without asking who their father is. But I have no idea how forthcoming Sandy may have been."

They reached the second-floor porch and stopped at a battered wooden door. A half-dozen banana boxes were stacked next to it, beside two large suitcases. The boxes were neatly labeled in thick black marker. BOOKS/VIDEOS. STEREO

EQUIPMENT. MISCELLANEOUS. PRIVATE! RECORDS. LEROY.

Leroy? Casey exchanged glances with Rob, raised her eyebrows, and he shrugged. A purple ten-speed bicycle leaned up against the peeling paint, next to a battered guitar case. Atkinson knocked on the door, and a small dog began yapping.

The door was opened by a fortyish woman with a tired face and worried eyes. "Good morning!" the attorney said, stepping into the entryway. "Lorraine Harriman, this is Casey and Rob MacKenzie." The woman nodded but didn't offer her hand.

Rob said, "Hey," and moved past her into the house. Casey gave the woman a brief smile and followed him inside. The dog, some kind of miniature mixed breed, danced and darted and sniffed around their feet in an enthusiastic attempt to determine whether they were friend or foe.

The entryway opened directly into the living room. To her left, through an open doorway, Casey caught a glimpse of an avocado-green refrigerator. In the living room, a boy of about eight and a teenage girl were sitting together on the couch, watching MTV. The girl glanced up at them, whispered something to the boy, and stood, unfolding her body until she reached her full height. She had to be at least five-six, because she towered over Casey's five-foot frame like Gulliver in the land of the Lilliputians. Lost in the voluminous folds of a man's button-down shirt worn with slender jeans and high-top sneakers with lime green laces, the girl sported multiple earrings that dangled in a noisy cluster. She'd gone a little heavy-handed with the make-up: bright red lipstick, rosy cheeks, too much eye liner.

Casey stared at her, stunned by her resemblance to Rob. Paige was built just like her father, tall and lanky, with long arms and legs and big feet. Whippet-thin, just like he'd been at twenty. She had his eyes, his strong jaw line, his thick, curly blond hair, except that his stopped at his shoulders, and hers tumbled in a wild cascade down the center of her back.

Atkinson took the girl by the hand and drew her forward. "Paige," he said, "I'd like you to meet your father and your stepmother, Rob and Casey MacKenzie."

The girl squared her jaw. Glanced at Casey, then at Rob. "Hi," she said.

Casey returned her greeting, but Rob remained silent. She glanced over at him, concerned for an instant, until he reached out a hand toward his daughter. The girl hesitated, then shrugged and reached out her own hand. He took it in his and held it while they studied each other.

A tear rolled down his cheek. He cleared his throat. "Is there some place we can talk in private?"

"The kitchen," Lorraine Harriman said. "Right through that doorway."

He shepherded his daughter into the kitchen, leaving the rest of them standing awkwardly in the living room. Over the sound of the television, Casey could hear the soft murmur of his voice, but couldn't tell what he was saying to the girl. "Sandy and I were friends," Lorraine Harriman said. "I've watched Paige grow up. I'd figure out a way to keep her if I could. But Sandy was determined that Paige would go to her father." Lorraine's mouth thinned. "I'm still not sure it was the right decision."

Casey reached out and took the woman's hand in hers. "I want you to know that my husband is one of the good guys. I've known him since he was twenty, and I'd trust him with my life. We're not living any kind of wild rock-and-roll lifestyle. He hasn't even been out on tour in more than a year. We live a quiet, normal life in the little rural town where I grew up, in an old house just down the road from my dad's dairy farm. She'll have aunts and uncles and cousins nearby, and her grandparents are right here in South Boston, so she'll get the chance to see you when we visit them. And we have so much love to give her! We have a strong marriage, but so far, it's been just the two of us. Paige will make us a family. I won't lie and say this hasn't been a shock, because it has. But we're both thrilled about Paige. We'll do right by her, I promise you."

Rob and his daughter returned from the kitchen, both of them silent, but some of the tension seemed to have dissipated. The little dog ran to Paige and danced in circles around her feet, and she crouched down to rub its ears. Atkinson glanced at his watch and said, "If I can have just a few minutes of your time, Mr. MacKenzie, we have some business to go over."

Rob disappeared back into the kitchen with the lawyer. "Are those your things on the porch?" Casey asked the girl. Still playing with the dog, Paige nodded. "Okay, then," she said briskly. "We might as well start loading the car while your father's tied up with Mr. Atkinson."

She stuck her head into the kitchen, where her husband and the attorney were sitting at the table with a thick manila envelope between them. "Sorry to interrupt," she said. "Car keys?" Rob pulled them from his pocket and tossed them to her, and she blew him a kiss.

Outside, on the porch, she eyed the stack of boxes and said, "Is this everything?"

Paige nodded. "Everything else—all my mom's stuff—went into storage."

"Okay, then. Grab a box, and let's get started."

Together, they carried boxes, suitcases, guitar, and bicycle down the long flight of stairs and up the hill to where Rob had parked the Explorer. Casey opened the tailgate and began packing the rear cargo area tightly with boxes, while Paige squeezed the suitcases and the guitar into the back seat. They debated how to fit in the bicycle, finally managed, after a couple of failed attempts, to maneuver it in and close the tailgate.

Brushing grit from the bicycle tires off her hands, Casey said, "There. We did it!"

Paige shrugged, and for the first time, Casey saw a bit of Sandy in the girl. "You remind me a little of your mother," she said as they began walking back toward the house. "I knew her, years ago. I liked her."

"You knew my mom?"

"I did. She and Rob dated, off and on, for quite a while."

After a moment of deliberation, Paige blurted, "Were you the reason they broke up?"

The stricken look on the girl's face almost broke her heart. "Oh, no, honey. Rob and I have only been together for a short time. I was married to Danny Fiore for thirteen years. I knew your mom because we were all friends back then. I don't know why they broke up. If you want to know, you'll have to ask your father."

They reached the house, began climbing the stairs. "I'm so sorry about your mother," she said. "I can empathize with what you're going through. I lost my mom when I was fifteen, and it was a terrible thing to live through. I know this is scary for you, because we're strangers. You don't know us, and we don't know you, and this is a whole new world for all of us. But we're so glad to make you part of our family. We look at you as a gift, one that just dropped into our laps from out of nowhere. And those are the best kind of gifts. The unexpected ones."

In a flat tone, Paige said, "That's pretty much what he said to me. My father. In the kitchen."

"I'm not surprised. We're generally on the same wavelength. Your dad's a really good guy, Paige. But he's scared to death right now, because he doesn't have a clue how to be a father, and he doesn't want to screw it up and disappoint you. Or himself. Try to give him a chance, and don't expect him to always get it right. Just remember how hard he's trying."

Inside, Rob waited with the lawyer and Lorraine Harriman, the manila envelope tucked into the crook of his elbow. Atkinson shook hands all around, wished them luck, and saw himself out. "You didn't have to load it all without me," Rob said when the attorney was gone.

"We are two strong, independent women. Fully capable of doing it for ourselves. Right, Paige?"

Paige just made a soft snorting noise.

"Well, then," Rob said. "I guess we're ready to roll."

Paige said goodbye to Lorraine and the boy, then picked up her purse and a bright pink leash from the couch. "Come on, Leroy," she said. The dog ran to her, and she snapped the leash onto his harness.

Casey and Rob exchanged startled glances.

"The dog's yours?" he said.

"You didn't know?" Terror, mixed with defiance, filled her eyes. Frantically, she said, "You won't make me get rid of him? I've had him since he was a puppy, and he sleeps with me every night. He's my best friend. My only friend."

Casey and Rob exchanged glances again and held a silent conversation. This would not go over well with Igor, Rob's cantankerous Siamese cat, who was cranky under the best of circumstances, and who still, after all this time, hadn't accepted Casey as part of his family.

Without speaking a word, they reached consensus. *Oy*, she thought. *This should be interesting.*

"Of course we won't," Rob said. He crouched down to the dog's level and held out a hand. Leroy daintily lifted a paw, and Rob shot Casey a quick grin. "Hey, Leroy," he said, taking the paw and shaking it. "Welcome to the family."

They stopped at a McDonald's somewhere in the urban sprawl on Route 1 north of Boston for lunch, a bathroom break, and a dish of water for Leroy. Paige had very little to say, and once they were back on the road, Casey attempted to draw the girl out. "So you play guitar?" she asked, turning in her seat to see the girl's face.

Paige shrugged. "Some."

"Maybe you and your dad can play together. He's an amazing guitarist."

"I've heard him play."

"Really? Where?"

"MTV. And Mom had record albums. I don't live under a rock."

Casey looked to Rob for help, but he glanced at her and shrugged, his shoulders clearly conveying his message: *Don't look at me. I don't know thing one about teenagers.*

When she checked the back seat again, Paige had put on her headphones. With Leroy curled up beside her, his head on her lap, she was pointedly ignoring them. Casey looked at Rob. He glanced in the rearview mirror, picked up the manila envelope he'd tucked beside his seat, and handed it to her.

The envelope contained a notarized copy of Sandy's will and other legal paperwork detailing custody arrangements. It also held an official copy of Paige's birth certificate, her school records, her medical records, her baptismal certificate. Casey skimmed them. All the girl's immunizations were up to date. She'd had chicken pox at age four, and impetigo at age seven. Her tonsils had been removed when she was nine. She was a solid B student, had been a member of the school chorus in middle school, and would be entering tenth grade when classes resumed in September. "Wow," Casey said quietly. "Atkinson was thorough."

"If you dig deep enough," he said, "you'll even find Sandy's family medical history."

"I'm impressed."

"We'll sit down and go over it together when we have time. It doesn't have to be today. I just wanted you to get a quick look at it."

"We really did this, didn't we, Flash?"

"We really did it, babydoll."

She stuffed everything back into the envelope and closed it. After a few minutes of silence, he took one eye off the road, shuffled through the cassettes in the center console, chose the one he wanted, and handed it to her. She opened the case and popped the tape into the stereo, and Gene Pitney began singing in his unique, pained vibrato about a town without pity. She hid a smile, secretly tickled by the fact that her diehard rocker husband was a closet Gene Pitney aficionado.

Or maybe not so closeted, considering that lately, he'd been bringing Gene to the regular weekend get-togethers at her brother Bill's house. Most of the adults there, who were all old enough to remember Pitney's angst-y ballads from the dusty reaches of childhood, found his choice of music perfectly acceptable. Most of the kids, on the other hand, were reduced to eye rolling and occasional emergency trips to town so they could wash away the taste of Pitney with some speaker-blowing Guns n' Roses.

From the back seat, there was absolute silence. Casey glanced over at her husband, and he shot her a wink. She smiled, leaned back into soft leather upholstery, and they listened to oldies the rest of the way home.

Paige

Sunlight spilled through the gauzy curtain fluttering in the breeze from the open window. At first, she didn't know where she was. Confused, she blinked at the brightness, looked around the room, saw the boxes piled in the corner. And remembered. The pain hit her hard, low in the stomach. Her mom was gone, life as she'd known it was over, and she'd been shipped off to live with strangers in this old house at the end of the earth.

She reached out for Leroy. When she didn't find him, she rolled onto one hip and looked down the length of the bed. She was alone. Panic clutched her insides. Paige rolled out of bed and walked to the window. Outside, on the back lawn, her father's wife was on her knees, weeding the garden. Leroy lay nearby, basking in the sunshine, his leash hitched to a wooden stake that had been driven into the ground.

The panic receded, but her stomach still hurt. She threw on jeans and a tee shirt and padded barefoot to the kitchen. The refrigerator didn't offer anything exotic or exciting. She settled for a bowl of Cheerios, rinsed the bowl and spoon when she was done and left them in the sink. Somebody in this house, probably Casey, was a serious neat freak. Wasn't it usually the woman who kept the house in order? Not that she actually knew. The closest she'd ever come to a normal household, with a mother and a father, was all those TV sitcoms she'd grown up watching.

Paige glanced around the kitchen. Her Walkman had died yesterday. Somewhere in this house, there had to be a package of batteries. They'd most likely be found in the junk drawer, and even rich people had junk drawers. Although this didn't look like a rich person's house, she knew he—her father—was worth *beaucoup* bucks. His wife was probably even richer; Danny Fiore had been a huge star, and when he died, all that money must have gone to his widow. Why had they buried themselves in this half-assed town, when they could have lived in Paris or London or frigging Hollywood? There were cows—*cows, for Chrissake!*— just up the road. The road itself wasn't even paved. Who in their right mind would choose to live in a place like this?

She began opening drawers in search of the holy grail. After several false starts, she found what she was looking for. The drawer held an assortment of mismatched screwdrivers, a pencil with a broken lead, a random selection of screws and nails and cup hooks, a piece of sandpaper, slightly used, and beneath that, *voilà!* An unopened 4-pack of AA batteries. She popped it open, dropped a couple into her palm, and returned the pack to the drawer.

With her Walkman revived, Paige took a long, hot shower, dressed in cut-off jeans and a Metallica tee shirt, and stepped outside to see just what she'd gotten herself into. She was immediately struck by the quiet; it was a little creepy, the complete absence of car horns or sirens. Instead, there was the buzzing of insects and the annoying chirping of birds.

The grass was soft and springy against the soles of her feet. She circled the house, moving toward the only other human who seemed to exist in this rural hell. Casey was on her knees in the garden, methodically murdering weeds and tossing them aside. The resulting pile of dead soldiers reminded Paige of a photo her eighth-grade history teacher had shown the class of one of the death chambers at Auschwitz, limp bodies stacked like firewood. Her father's wife was wearing some kind of lame-ass wide-brimmed straw hat. Its pink cotton print straps, designed to tie under the chin, instead fluttered loose around her face.

The two of them—her father and his wife—had hovered over her last night like a pair of fussy old hens, pouring on the niceness and the bogus concern until Paige was ready to scream. Did they really think they were going to win her over with pizza and fake smiles? He had made a huge deal out of helping her set up her stereo (as if she didn't know how to do it herself!), even going so far as to unearth a dusty set of speakers that were twice the size of hers and could really bark.

She'd offered him a stilted thank-you. She didn't even know what to call him. *Dad?* Not in this lifetime. *Father?* Too snobby-rich-socialite. *Rob?* That seemed far too friendly. *Mr. MacKenzie?* Utterly preposterous. She'd finally settled on the generic pronoun: *Him. He. You.* It seemed the most appropriate choice. Just because they shared DNA and a last name didn't mean he could waltz into her life and take it over, as if the first fifteen years hadn't meant a thing. He was not her dad, and would never be; she'd gotten along quite nicely for fifteen years without a father. Rob MacKenzie was nothing more than some random stranger who had once known her mother, and who looked a little—okay, if she wanted to be honest, a lot—like Paige herself. A sperm donor. They did not have any kind of father/daughter relationship, and she intended to keep it that way.

Leroy wagged a greeting, and Casey looked up from her work. She rocked back on her heels and, gardening trowel in hand, adjusted her ridiculous hat. "Good morning!" she said in a tone so saccharine it make Paige's teeth ache.

"Hey."

"Did you sleep okay?"

Paige shrugged and said, "Why do you do that? The weeding? It looks like so much work. I'm not sure I get the concept."

"If I don't pull the weeds, they'll take over. They'll strangle my poor vegetable plants, and then I won't get any peas or beans."

It still didn't make sense to her. All that work, when you could just go to the grocery store and buy vegetables in a can. "So what's with the hat?"

Casey cocked her head to one side. Sounding surprised, she said, "You don't think it's the height of fashion?"

It took her a minute to realize she was being teased. Paige hardened her resolve, not intending to give an inch. "Ha," she said.

"I spend a lot of time in the garden. In the sun. I don't want to wake up one day at the age of fifty with a face like a dried-up old prune. The hat protects my skin."

Paige wasn't sure whether to be relieved or disappointed that Casey was wearing the hat for practical purposes, and not deliberately trying to look like Whoopi Goldberg in *The Color Purple*. The hat was still lame and ugly, but she supposed it served its purpose. "Where's, uh—"

"Your dad? He's in the studio. Out in the barn. You're welcome to go check it out. He won't mind. Or I could show you."

"No! No, I don't need to go there. I was just…curious."

Casey went back to weeding. "Just in case you're wondering," she said, "I've known him for seventeen years, and he hasn't bitten me yet."

Good to know. "What is there to do in this godforsaken wilderness?" she said. They'd driven through what passed for a downtown yesterday afternoon, and it hadn't looked promising. "Is there a movie theater? A McDonald's?" At this point, she'd settle for a bowling alley.

"Negative and negative. They have both in Farmington, though. It's not far. About twenty miles away. There's a video rental place here in town. The selection isn't great, but it's what we have."

Not far? *Twenty miles?* Was the woman on drugs?

With the back of her hand, Casey shoved the brim of her hat away from her face. "There's also a drive-in movie in Skowhegan. There aren't many of those left around. But that's not so close. I think it's about an hour's drive."

Shit. This was worse than she'd feared. She was going to be trapped here for the rest of her life with these two clueless old fogeys. She would be climbing the walls by the time school started. "I don't suppose," she said without much hope, "there are any kids my age around here?"

"Actually, you have a bunch of cousins. Some by blood, others by marriage. Mikey and Luke are both sixteen. The girls are a little older."

Cousins. Oh, yay. She remembered now that *he* had mentioned them, when he'd called to introduce himself. *Hello. I'm your father. I'm here to rescue you from a fate worse than death.*

She should have taken off for Fiji while she had the chance.

"We generally get together at my brother's house on Saturday nights." Casey yanked at a weed until it loosened its hold and broke free. "We barbecue, play music, talk and laugh and generally have a good time. Tonight, we'll introduce you to everyone."

Outstanding. Disgusted, Paige scooped up her dog, turned without responding, and stalked back across the grass to the house. She let the screen door slam behind her. Once inside her room, she locked the door—it wasn't even a real lock, just one of those pathetic hook-and-eye things—and popped her favorite MC Hammer cassette into her stereo. With the volume on full-blast, she sprawled on the bed, clutched Leroy in her arms, and let the music take her away.

Rob

He could hear it from the driveway as he approached the house. Loud, repetitive, obnoxious noise. When he opened the door to the kitchen, it slapped him in the face, like walking into a wall of sound. It wasn't a good sound.

Casey was at the stove, stirring something in a big stainless pot. "What in bloody hell is that horrible noise?" he shouted.

"I believe," she shouted back, "the appropriate term would be rap."

He moved closer so they could converse without yelling. Peering over her shoulder to see what was in the pot, he said, "Jesus Christ on a Popsicle stick. How long has this been going on?"

"A couple of hours."

"You have to be kidding."

She shot him a look. It wasn't a pleased look. "You're the one who gave her the massive speakers. Thank you for that, by the way."

"Does she have that poor dog in there with her? His ears are probably bleeding."

"I don't know about his, but mine certainly are. It must be terribly lonely out there in the studio. I might have to go out there with you after lunch. Just to alleviate some of your loneliness."

He swore under his breath. "The worst thing I ever offended my parents with was Zeppelin's *Immigrant Song*. And maybe a little Doors. *Light My Fire*. The long version."

"Strange, but nobody in my house ever objected to Herman's Hermits."

He let out a soft snort of laughter. "Have you said anything to her?"

"She's your kid, hot stuff. Maybe you'd like to broach the subject."

"How the hell am I supposed to do that?"

"Gee, MacKenzie, I don't know. How about something like this: Approach her door, tell her to turn down the music, and announce that lunch is ready. A novel concept, I realize, but it might actually work. You'll never know unless you try."

"As a professional musician, I feel I have to say this: That is not music."

"I know, babe, I know. It hurts, doesn't it?"

"In more ways than one." He stared at that closed door and felt a knot the size of Rhode Island tighten inside his stomach. He'd never, in his thirty-seven years, had a problem expressing his opinion. And he didn't have a shy bone in his body. Why was he so reluctant to confront his own kid?

"Just as a reminder," Casey said, "you're the one who gets to play the dad in this little scenario."

"Ha-ha. Very funny."

"I think you need to take the proverbial bull by the horns and act as if."

"As if what?"

"As if you had a freaking clue what you were doing."

"She's fifteen years old. Why am I so intimidated by her?"

"I don't know, but if you're thinking of taking away her precious music, you should probably offer her something in exchange. Psychology 101."

"Such as?"

"I don't know. Maybe a post-luncheon tour of your studio. Not the fifty-cent tour, but the full monty. Show her all the awards. Give her an in-depth explanation for each and every one. Tell her some of your more interesting road stories."

"Most of my road stories are dull enough to make your eyes glaze over. And the ones that aren't are definitely not suitable for the ears of a fifteen-year-old."

"Then let her play with some of your ridiculously expensive toys. Let her push buttons and spin dials and pretend to be a big record producer."

"Bite your tongue, woman. You just want a break from the bloody massacre."

"I freely admit that thought was foremost in my mind. You could always give her a guitar lesson. A long one. Teach her to play *Layla*. All seven minutes of it."

It would be a small sacrifice if it would bring an end to this torture. "Okay, then," he said, steeling himself. "Cover my back. I'm going in."

She flashed him that Mona Lisa smile, and he headed for his daughter's bedroom door. He rapped twice and waited. When there was no response, he knocked harder. From this proximity, the noise had him clenching his teeth. His central nervous system, despite having been subjected to continual overdoses of screaming rock music for the past two decades, was on overload and moving rapidly toward doom. The door itself was vibrating. "Paige!" he shouted. "Lunch!"

"Coward," Casey said from across the room.

"Bite me." He knocked again, hard, and raised his voice a few decibels. "PAIGE!"

The noise—he refused to think of it as music—ceased abruptly. The door stopped vibrating, and his central nervous system slowed in its headlong rush toward the death star. A second later, the door opened a crack. "What?" she said.

"Lunch is ready. Come on out and join us. Leroy still alive in there?"

"Um, yeah." She appeared puzzled by his question. "He's fine, but he peed on the floor."

"Great. Did you clean it up?"

"I didn't have anything to clean it with."

He turned helplessly to Casey, who rolled her eyes. "I'm on it," she said.

"Before we eat," he told Paige, "we should probably take him outside for a walk, so he won't do something even worse on the kitchen floor."

Paige didn't argue, just clipped the leash to Leroy's harness and moved, barefoot, to the door. He followed her, and they ambled in a meandering circle around the house, Leroy stopping at every other blade of grass to mark his territory. "So what's with the pink leash?" he said. "Aren't you worried about giving poor Leroy a complex?"

She looked at him blankly. "Why?"

"Boy dog? Hot pink leash?" At her continued stony look, he said, "Never mind." Apparently the kid lacked a sense of humor.

He kept throwing her furtive little glances, trying not to get caught at it. But he couldn't stop staring at her. She looked so much like Meg had at fifteen, it was scary. Or what the fifteen-year-old Meg would have looked like if she'd painted her face like

a two-dollar hooker. As if Mary MacKenzie would have ever
tolerated that from any one of her daughters. He had an
overwhelming urge to grab a wash cloth and scrub all that shit off
until there was nothing left but fresh-faced fifteen-year-old. But
that might be a tad over the top, and would do nothing to endear
him to the kid. He needed to exercise restraint. "Do you know my
sister Meg? She and your mother used to be best friends. That's
how your mom and I met."

He'd finally grabbed her attention. "Meg is your sister?"

"She is. You didn't know she was your aunt?"

"I just remember her as Mom's friend. She used to be around
all the time when I was a little kid, but I haven't seen her in years."

"She moved to Seattle a few years ago. You look just like
her." When the kid simply shrugged, he said, "You hit the family
jackpot with the MacKenzies, kiddo. There are nine of us, and the
extended family just goes on and on."

"Lucky me."

"Oh, we're not that bad. Except maybe Kevin. And you
won't have to meet everyone *en masse*, at least not until Christmas.
Tonight, we'll introduce you to my sister Rose and her family.
The rest of tonight's gang belongs to Casey's side. You'll like
'em. They're good people."

"Woo-hoo," she said darkly. "I can hardly wait."

If he'd ever spoken to his father that way, he would have
ended up with a mouthful of soap. But he should probably cut the
kid a little slack. This situation they'd been thrown into was
awkward for both of them. She'd just lost her mother, and he and
Casey were total strangers. At least she was responding to his
half-assed attempts to make conversation. It might not be much,
but it was a start.

Leroy paused to sniff at one of Casey's beloved rosebushes,
and Rob snagged the leash and dragged him away before he could
lift his leg and destroy it. "See that?" he said, pointing. "That's a
rosebush. Casey has a bunch of those planted around the
foundation. If you let Leroy pee on 'em, she won't be a happy
woman. And you don't want to see my wife when she's unhappy.
I'm just offering this as a little friendly advice. Keep Leroy away
from Casey's roses. *Capisce?*"

"Yeah. I *capisce.*"

Leroy finally accomplished what they'd brought him outside for, and Rob handed the kid the paper towel and baggie he'd brought along for the occasion. "What's this?" she said.

"Poor man's pooper scooper. You leave that lying around, Casey will really get riled up. And you don't want to see her riled up."

She gave him a look so frosty he could feel his testicles shriveling, but she bent over and cleaned up after her dog. Holding the bag with the tips of her fingers, as far away from her body as she could get it, she said, "Now what?"

"Now," he said, "I show you where the trash cans are."

They deposited Leroy's little gift and headed back to the house. He shot her a quick glance and said, "So you like rap?"

"Yeah."

One of these days, he'd sit her down and they'd have a real conversation about it. He'd find out exactly what it was that made the stuff appeal to her, and maybe it would give him a glimpse into her psyche. One of these days. But not today.

"Casey and I," he said, "do not like rap. As a matter of fact, that stuff you were playing earlier causes me actual physical pain."

She glanced at him out of the corner of her eye. "Is that a broad hint?"

He decided not to leave anything open to interpretation. "It is. You'll have to cut the volume. Drastically. Or my wife may pack her bags and move out. Or worse, toss you and me out into the street. Considering that the house belongs to her, she'd have a perfect right."

"If you're married, doesn't it belong to both of you?"

"I'm not sure about the legal ramifications, but she and Danny bought the house three years before we were married, so for all intents and purposes, it's hers. And you know, it could get pretty cold living in a cardboard box on a downtown street corner, come February."

"We wouldn't be living in a cardboard box. You have plenty of money."

He raised his eyebrows. "And you know this because?"

"I didn't just fall off the turnip truck. You're loaded. You're a friggin' rock star."

That term had always made him uncomfortable. Not to mention the kid had a potty mouth. "Danny was the star. Not me. I'm just the guy who stood up on stage behind him and played guitar."

"And wrote and produced all his albums. And had a successful solo career after the two of you split up."

His eyebrows went higher. "You make it sound like we were dating. And you seem to know a lot more about me than I do about you."

"You think? Considering that you apparently didn't even know I existed."

Apparently? What the hell did she mean by apparently? Before he could ask, they reached the door to the shed, and he decided to let it go. For now. "After lunch," he said, swinging it open and letting Paige and Leroy enter the house ahead of him, "I'll show you around the studio. You can bring your guitar with you. We can jam a little."

"Oh, joy," she said.

He stepped into the kitchen, met Casey's eyes. "Wash your hands," he said to Paige. She disappeared in the direction of the bathroom, and he crossed the room to his wife. Took her in his arms and buried his face in her hair. Only half-joking, he said, "Just hold me."

"Oh, come on, Flash, it can't be that bad."

"It is that bad. She accused me of being a rock star. And she hates me."

"She's a teenager. She's supposed to hate you. It's an unwritten law of adolescence."

"I am not a rock star. Danny was a rock star. I am a Berklee-trained professional musician."

"You dropped out of Berklee after two years."

"Everybody drops out of Berklee. Your point is?"

"Look, I know you have a tendency to get all hinky about stuff like this, but, well…you sort of are. A rock star, that is."

He looked at her in mock horror. *"Et tu, Brute?"*

"Semantics, MacKenzie. You're quibbling over semantics."

He sighed and said, "I'm taking her out to the studio after lunch like you suggested. That'll give you a break from the screaming meemies. I'll collect payment later." He kissed her eyelid, nudged her cheek with the tip of his nose. Cupped her chin in his hand, tilted her head, and pretended to peer into her ear canal.

"What the hell are you doing, MacKenzie?"

"Checking for bloodstains."

She rolled her eyes. He couldn't actually see them, but he knew her well enough to know exactly what she was doing. "You're a lunatic," she said.

"Yeah, but you love me anyway."

"I do. Most of the time." She wound those gorgeous arms around his neck and tilted her head back and studied him through exquisite green eyes. "Kids need structure. They respond well to it. We just have to provide it."

"Which could be problematic, as I am possibly the least structured person on the planet."

"Well, then, isn't it a good thing you have a regimented person like me around to offset all that loosey-goosey stuff?"

He pressed his mouth to the line of her jaw. "It's a damn good thing, Sarge."

"Don't worry. Give it time. It'll get better."

"I know what would make it better." He waggled his eyebrows. "You could kiss me."

"Kissing always makes everything better, but can you promise to behave? We have a fifteen-year-old chaperone now. No more groping each other in the kitchen."

He slid his mouth down the slender curve of her neck and said, "That is a tragedy of epic proportions."

"It is." She leaned into him and kissed him, sweetly, tenderly, thoroughly, with a heated, open-mouth, full-body-contact kiss that had his engines revving in high gear until behind them, the kid cleared her throat. He hadn't even heard her come into the room. He'd probably sustained hearing damage from all that noise.

His eyes popped open and looked directly into Casey's, mere inches away. "Busted," he said.

His goddess of a wife offered him a game, secretive little smile that hinted of future delights, and gave him one last kiss for good measure. And said briskly, "Paige, the soup bowls are in the right-hand cupboard, next to the fridge. Saltine crackers are on the shelf in the pantry. I'll get the spoons. Leroy's welcome to stay, as long as he exhibits good manners. But if he's going to sit and beg the whole time we're eating, you'll have to shut him in your room."

Paige

These people she'd been sent to live with were total freaks.

Earlier today, she'd gone into the bathroom to wash her hands before lunch. When she came out, there they were, her father and his wife, wrapped around each other and making out like a couple of teenagers, right in the kitchen. Did people their age actually *do* that kind of thing? Certainly not her mom. Or the parents of any of her friends. It made her ill just to think about it. And they'd acted like it was no big deal. They'd just gone ahead with lunch, as if the sight of them like that hadn't done irreparable damage to her adolescent psyche. She wanted to scream at them to get a room, but of course if they'd really wanted privacy, they could've just gone upstairs.

The freak factor continued from there. They actually had matching license plates on their cars. Hers said C-MKNZ. His said R-MKNZ. An excess of cuteness that made Paige want to hurl. He had a second car, an older-model Porsche 944. Shiny, black, classic. The plates on that one said WIZARD. Hah! Ego problem, much?

After lunch, he'd given her a guided tour of his studio. She'd pretended not to be impressed, but he had a real honest-to-God recording studio out there in his barn in the middle of Nowhere. The walls were lined with gold records. Paige had never seen one before, except on TV. And there was a shelf holding a half-dozen Grammy awards. All of them his. His and Casey's. He said they were songwriting awards. And he told her a little about himself, about how he'd gone to Berklee on a scholarship, but he'd left when he met Danny Fiore and they started a band together. Paige wasn't about to tell him that Berklee had been her dream from the time she was nine years old. The last thing she needed was for him to think she was trying to follow in his footsteps. Her music was her own private thing, totally unrelated to him. She might have inherited his musical talent, but it went no further than that.

Tonight, they were planning to parade her in front of the family like some exotic zoo animal. She could hardly wait to be forced to meet aunts and uncles and cousins and try to remember who was who. According to her stepmother, Luke and Mikey were just a year older than she was. Maybe they'd be simpatico, although she didn't hold out much hope. If they'd grown up in this heinous place, they were probably hicks who wore muddy L.L. Bean boots and had never heard of LL Cool J.

She missed her mom so much.

Her father turned the car into the driveway of a little yellow ranch house, surrounded on three sides by cow pasture. Paige had only been in this delightful little burg for twenty-four hours, but already she'd seen enough cows to last her a lifetime. The driveway was lined with pickup trucks and 4-wheel-drive vehicles. She'd seen so many of them in the brief time she'd been in Maine that she was certain they must multiply, like rabbits, while people slept at night. Her father gathered up the stack of record albums his wife had been holding in her lap, and they all piled out of the car.

They were greeted by a dark-haired man going gray at the temples. Casey's brother. The family resemblance was unmistakable. Behind gold-rimmed glasses, his blue eyes were lively. "Hey," he said, "it's the man with the music! About time you got here." He and her father exchanged some kind of complicated handshake—one of those stupid guy things—and then he turned to her. "This must be Paige. I'm Bill. Nice to meet you."

She shook his outstretched hand, then a smiling, matronly blonde rounded the corner of the house and bore down on them like a ship at full sail. "Hi, sweetie," she said, slipping an arm through Paige's. "I'm your Aunt Trish. Let me introduce you to everyone."

Before Paige had time to blink, she was swept away to the back yard, where Trish proceeded to introduce her to more than a dozen people. There was her red-headed Aunt Rose, who was her father's sister, and her husband, Jesse Lindstrom, who was Trish's brother. Their infant daughter, Beth, was adorable. Next came Casey's father and stepmother, Will and Millie Bradley, and several neighbor couples whose names escaped her. Then the cousins: Billy and his very pregnant wife, Alison; their toddler son, Willy; Ian and Jenny and Kristen Bradley who, like Billy, were Trish and Bill's kids. Devon and Luke Kenneally, who were her Aunt Rose's kids and, like infant Beth, her first cousins. And

Mikey Lindstrom, who was Jesse's son and crushingly handsome, with his father's dark eyes, and hair so blond it was almost white.

She'd never be able to keep track of everyone; not only were there more names than she could retain at one time, but the relationships were so complicated that she finally gave up on trying. Everybody seemed to be related to everybody, although if she was interpreting it correctly, there were actually four families: the Bradleys, the MacKenzies, the Lindstroms, and the Kenneallys. They were just embarrassingly intermarried, like hillbillies from Appalachia.

If she stayed here for any length of time, eventually she'd probably figure it all out. For tonight, she would focus on the boys, with whom Trish had left her after the whirlwind of introductions. Mikey, because he was possibly the best-looking guy she'd ever seen, and Luke, because he seemed so familiar.

"I know you," he said, studying her with eyes that she already recognized as the MacKenzie green. "From South Boston. We went to school together."

That explained the familiarity. "So we're cousins, and we never knew it? How'd you wind up here, at the end of the earth?"

"My mom married his dad." He elbowed Mikey, who stood silently at his side, looking gorgeous but inexplicably grim. "So we moved here."

"How do you stand it? Do you even have cable TV? We—I mean they—*he* and his wife—don't. I can't even watch MTV. All they have is the local channels."

"It's not so bad here. School's okay. I've made a lot of friends, and Uncle Rob gives me private guitar lessons. I've started a band with a couple of the guys. There's no cable TV this far out, but we have a satellite dish. You're welcome to come over and watch it any time you want."

Her interest was immediately piqued. "You have a band? A real band?"

"Well, we're not playing anywhere yet except Tobey's garage, but, yeah, we get together a couple times a week to practice."

"What do you play?"

"Rock. Blues. A little of this, a little of that. You can come to practice with me sometime if you'd like."

"I'd like. So where do people shop around here? I'm used to just hopping on the T to Downtown Crossing. How far is it to the nearest mall?"

The boys exchanged glances. "Girl stuff," Luke said, and Mikey nodded agreement.

"There's a few stores in town," Mikey said. "Bookstore, five-and-ten, drugstore, shoe store. That kind of thing. The nearest mall is in Auburn, but it's pretty small. If you're looking for a real mall, you have to go to South Portland. It's about a hundred miles."

"Oh. My. God."

Without warning, the stereo speakers on the deck started blaring some kind of bouncy pop song so ancient it might have come over on the Mayflower. Something about a girl crying at her own birthday party because her boyfriend took off with another chick. Why did she suspect it was one of the records *he* had brought with him? "What on God's green earth is this dreck?" she asked.

"Something old," Mikey said. "From when they were kids. The Sixties, I think."

"Would that be the 1860s?"

The solid wall of ice that was his face thawed just a bit, and she saw it in those dark eyes: the beginnings of a smile. So he wasn't always grim. "Are you telling me," she said, "that you put up with this crap every weekend?"

"We put in an appearance," Luke said. "Greet everyone, have a burger or a hot dog, a little potato salad, make nice with the relatives. And then—"

"We escape," Mikey said.

Casey

"So Chuck told him to take a long walk off a short pier." Paula Fournier raised her beer bottle and grinned. "It was a beautiful moment."

Paula upended the beer and chugged it, and they all laughed at her story. Casey glanced around the group of women. She'd missed this kind of female camaraderie. All those years she was married to Danny, she'd acutely felt its absence. She had been a woman living in a man's world. Even after they bought the Malibu house and Katie came along and they settled into a fractured kind of normalcy, she'd still felt isolated, her life devoted exclusively to her husband, her daughter, her songwriting. His career. There had been no girlfriends, nobody to laugh or vent with about the trials and joys of marriage and motherhood. Nothing more than a nodding acquaintance with any of her neighbors.

Her best friend, her only real friend, had been Rob. She'd been friendly with his first wife—the four of them had lived together in New York during that brief marriage—and later on with Kitty Callahan, a singer she met on Danny's first tour. But neither of those superficial relationships had ever developed into real friendship, and she hadn't realized, until now, just how much she'd missed the company of other women.

She sensed Rob's presence an instant before he slipped an arm around her from behind, took her hand in his, and fluidly danced her from side to side in time with the music playing on the stereo. "Excuse me, ladies," her husband said, "but I need to borrow my wife for a second."

At least one pair of eyes watched in appreciation as he spirited her away from the group and halted a few feet away, where they could speak privately. Over her shoulder, he glanced at the group of women. "I'm sorry to drag you away," he said. "You looked like you were having fun. Listen, I can't find Paige. Do you know where she is?"

"I'm sorry, I forgot to tell you. She's not here. She left with the boys an hour ago."

He raised both eyebrows. "You let her go off with them?"

She reached up to straighten his collar. "Stop worrying. She's perfectly fine. Mikey and Luke are both good kids, and Mikey's a careful driver. He won't let anything happen to her." At his stricken expression, she moved her hand to the back of his neck and began to rub it. "You know how bored the kids get at these gatherings. They never stick around for long."

"I know, but it was never *my* kid not sticking around before."

"She's fifteen. Yes, we have to keep her on a leash, but unless she gives us some reason not to trust her, we want to keep that leash relatively loose. With kids, you have to choose your battles. It's a trade-off. Giving in on the little things helps you to build up more ammunition for the big things. And believe me, there will be big things. You just have to follow your instincts, because it isn't always easy to tell the difference between the two. But if she wants to leave an adult party to go into town for a burger with her cousins, I don't see any reason to tell her no."

"We have burgers right here."

"When did you turn into such a curmudgeon? Have you forgotten what it was like to be a kid? Did you want to hang out with your adult relatives and their friends when you were fifteen?"

He sighed. "You're right. I know you're right. Why is it so hard to accept?"

Still rubbing his neck, she said, "It's a heavy responsibility you've taken on your shoulders, the responsibility for somebody else's life. It's scary. Just remember, you're not bearing it alone. I'm right here with you, taking half the load."

He wrapped his arms around her and she rested her cheek against the front of his shirt. "I feel eyes on us," he said. "Why are they watching us?"

She raised her face to his. "They're just jealous because I have the hottest date here."

He let out a soft, choked laugh. "You are so full of shit, Fiore."

"But I made you laugh, didn't I?"

"You did. So what's the real reason they're staring at us?"

"They're just jealous because I have the hottest date here."

He rolled his eyes. "I am not hot."

"Oh, stop it, Mister Broken Record. You know as well as I do that women find you attractive. And they're curious about us.

It's natural, isn't it? The places we've been, the things we've experienced—"

"Like starvation? And cockroaches?"

"Like winning Grammy Awards. Like playing on stage in front of fifty thousand people. Like that nasty 'R' word you so hate."

"What 'R' word?"

"Rock star. Ring a bell?"

"Damn it, woman. Now it's my ears that are bleeding."

"I hate to have to break it to you, my friend, but because of these things, by the standards that plague small towns like this one, you and I are considered exotic and fascinating."

"I don't want to be exotic and fascinating. I just want to live my life in peace. I'm just an ordinary guy."

"Now there is where we disagree, but I'm not going to argue over it."

He glanced over her shoulder again. "Maybe we should give 'em something to talk about."

"Make up your mind, Flash. You either want to be the center of attention, or you don't."

"I just think we should make it clear to all of these women that I'm taken."

She raised an eyebrow. "You're wearing a wedding ring."

"Oh, of course. I forgot. Wedding rings scare off even the most predatory of women."

"I don't think there are too many predators in our little group. Also, lest we forget, one of those women is your sister, one is your sister-in-law, and one is my nephew's very pregnant wife. That leaves just three possible predators."

"Who are all looking at me like I'm their next meal. You have to save me from a fate worse than death."

"You're so transparent. You're just looking to cop a feel."

"Every chance I get."

Inside the house, the music changed, and Lenny Welch began singing in his sweet, plaintive tenor about getting the blues most every night. Green eyes met green eyes and held a brief, wordless conversation, and there on the grass, they began swaying together in time with the music. "They're still watching," he said.

"And they won't stop until you remove your hands from my butt."

"We're married. I can legally feel you up any time I want."

"This reminds me of high school. They used to have this unbending rule at school dances. If a teacher couldn't slip a sheet of paper between a couple, they were dancing too close."

"Hunh. Too close for what?"

"Alarming social diseases. Like syphilis. And pregnancy."

"So what you're telling me, in your delightful roundabout way, is that we're in danger of getting detention."

"Exactly. And since we're already in deep trouble anyway—" She tilted her head back, took his face between her palms, and kissed him until every nerve ending in her body was on red alert and both of them were breathing heavily. She drew back, studied his eyes, gone a soft, smoky gray. And said, "Now see what you started."

He waggled his eyebrows and said, "We could go home early and finish it."

"I think not." Toying with the top button on his shirt, she said, "I'd suggest you go find something to keep yourself amused. Try not to break anything or injure yourself. When your daughter gets back, we'll think about going home. If I determine that you've behaved properly, you might get to finish what you started. If not..."

"It's off with my head."

"I'm not sure I'd go that far, but I can safely say that if you misbehave, you won't be getting any tonight."

"Guess I'd better walk the straight and narrow, then."

"If you're hoping to get lucky tonight, then yes, you'd better."

"Got it, Sarge." He clicked his heels together and saluted smartly.

"Glad we have that clarified. Now can I go back to what I was doing?"

"Only if I get to stand here and watch you walk away."

She gave him a secretive little smile. "Letch."

"And damn proud of it."

She planted another quick kiss on the corner of his mouth, stepped out of his arms, and walked away without a backward glance.

But because she knew he was watching, she added a little extra sashay to her walk.

Paige

Comfortably buzzed.

That was the only way to describe how she felt. She wasn't stupid enough to get really drunk. She knew enough to eat something first, knew she needed to pace herself, knew when it was time to stop, but she hadn't reached that point yet. She took another swig from the bottle of Jim Beam that Luke had pilfered from his stepfather's liquor cabinet, then handed it to him, lying beside her on the blanket at the edge of the old granite quarry. From this vantage point, with the massive quarry in front of her, all that wide-open treeless space, the night sky was like a wide swath of velvet, hung heavily with stars. She'd never seen so many stars in her life, dancing across the heavens, melting into a band of white that Mikey said was the Milky Way. He'd pointed out various constellations, and when she'd asked him how he knew all this, he'd said his dad had taught him, years ago, when he was just a little boy.

Luke drank from the bottle and handed it back to her. She offered it to Mikey, sitting on her other side, but he declined. Earlier, both boys had stripped down to their skivvies and taken a swim. Mikey said the quarry was a hundred feet deep, and there were any number of things at the bottom, including a car that somebody had pushed over the edge a couple of decades ago. It was rumored that there were even a couple of skeletons down there, but Paige suspected that was nothing more than a ghost story manufactured by some horny teenage boy in the hopes of scaring his pansy-ass girlfriend into letting him get a little closer than she ordinarily would.

Paige was not a pansy-ass girl, and ghost stories didn't scare her. To be truthful, not much scared her, but on the other hand, she didn't have a death wish. Since she wasn't that good a swimmer, while the boys dove and splashed, she'd stayed on the blanket, clutching the bottle and studying the stars, swatting at the occasional mosquito, enjoying the warm summer night.

She had never been a religious person. She wasn't even sure if she believed in heaven or hell. But lying here, gazing up at that vast, star-spangled sky, she couldn't help wondering if her mom was up there somewhere, looking down on her. If so, Sandy wasn't pleased to see her fifteen-year-old daughter drinking whiskey straight from the bottle. She might not be surprised, but she definitely wouldn't be pleased.

Paige took another sip. It burned all the way down, but left a comfortable warmth in her belly when it was done. She handed the bottle back to Luke. He was an okay kid, laid back and carefree and fun. Mikey, on the other hand, was an enigma. She couldn't quite figure him out. He seemed so serious, appeared to have no interest in drinking or smoking or partying. Although, now that she thought about it, he hadn't been the least bit fazed by her seeing him in his underwear, so he couldn't be quite the stick-in-the-mud that he seemed.

"I suppose we should be heading back soon," she said. "He'll be looking for me."

"He who?" Luke said. "Your dad?"

"He's not my dad. He's nothing more than a sperm donor."

"I don't get it. Uncle Rob is the coolest guy I know. Why do you hate him?"

"He deserted us. Why wouldn't I hate him?"

"He didn't desert you. He never even knew about you."

"Hah! Says him."

"I'm telling you, you're way off target. I was home the night before last when he and my mom got into it because he'd just found out about you, and Mom and Aunt Meg and Grandma all knew, and nobody bothered to tell him. It wasn't pretty."

"You were eavesdropping on their conversation?" She liked the idea of her cousin snooping around, hiding in corners, practicing clandestine surveillance on his elders.

"Trust me, when two MacKenzies get into an argument, eavesdropping is totally unnecessary. The neighbors can hear for a mile around."

"Yeah, well, he probably just wanted to make himself look good. Because there's no way my mom would have lied to me. She told me he left because he didn't want the responsibility of being a father. He didn't want *me*. And I can never forgive him for that."

"You can go on believing whatever you want, but you're dead wrong. And you're not the only one with parent problems.

My dad's a real jerk. He treated my mom like crap, then he went out and got a new wife. One who's not much older than my sister. And Mikey's mom left when he was just a kid. So don't think you're special just because you grew up without a dad."

Her head swiveled around, and she studied Mikey, who thus far hadn't uttered a word. Outraged, she said, "Your mom *left* you?"

Lying beside her on the blanket, Mikey folded his hands behind his head and closed his eyes. "It's not as bad as it sounds," he said. "Mom got pregnant at seventeen and married my dad, and I think she didn't have any idea what she really wanted. She was too young. When they split up, Dad was the stable one, so they agreed that I'd stay with him. It's not as though I never see her."

"Wow," she said. "That must have sucked, all those years without your mom." She'd gone just two weeks without hers, and the pain was almost unbearable.

"I had Aunt Trish, and Grandma Millie, and Aunt Casey. And now, I have Luke's mom. My dad's amazing. I wasn't raised by wolves, if that's what you're implying."

"Wait a minute. I'm confused. Why do you call her Aunt Casey?"

He opened his eyes and looked at her like she was an idiot. "Um...because she's my aunt?"

She scrunched up her nose and studied him while she tried to work it out in her head, but finally gave up. "How is that possible?"

"My mom is her sister."

"Holy batshit. Are you people all inbred, or what?"

"It just seems that way," Luke said. "Once you get all the relationships worked out in your head, it makes more sense."

Still trying to puzzle it out, she said to Mikey, "Let me make sure I understand this. Your father's sister is married to your mother's brother. Do I have it so far?"

Those dark eyes were indecipherable. "Correct," Mikey said.

"So that means...you and the Bradley kids are double cousins."

"Also correct."

"Jesus." She sat up and screwed the cap back on the bottle of Jim Beam. Handed it back to Luke. And said, "I think I have a headache."

Rob

When he got home from his morning run, Casey had breakfast going: sizzling bacon, fresh-sliced cantaloupe, scrambled eggs, and pancakes loaded with lush, ripe blackberries she'd picked just after sunrise. The way she cooked, it was a wonder they weren't both morbidly obese. He snagged a strip of crisp bacon from the paper towel where it was drying and went to the refrigerator to take out the milk. He was stirring it into his coffee when Paige came out of her bedroom, shuffled past him without speaking, and slammed the bathroom door behind her.

He met Casey's eyes. "Little Miss Sunshine," she said.

Grimacing, he returned the milk carton to the fridge and reached for another strip of bacon. "Hey, you!" his wife said, playfully slapping his hand away. "Leave some for breakfast."

"I'm a growing boy. And you're just scared that I'll take your share."

"Make yourself useful while I finish this. Set the table."

He popped the pilfered strip of bacon into his mouth and gathered up plates and flatware, glasses and napkins. In the bathroom, Paige was running water in the sink. He arranged the table, found the salt and pepper and a dish of softened butter and set them in a splash of honey-colored sunlight next to the vase of flowers she'd cut from the garden while she was out picking berries at the crack of dawn. He had no idea what the tiny blue and purple blossoms were, but fresh flowers on the breakfast table were classic Casey.

The bathroom door opened, and Paige came out, dressed in jeans, a white tee shirt, and red suspenders. She'd made an attempt to tame her hair, but he knew from firsthand experience that it was pretty much a hopeless task. She yawned, sniffed bacon-scented air, and said, "I usually just eat cereal and toast."

"That's because you haven't tasted my wife's pancakes."

The kid shrugged, pulled out her chair, and collapsed into it as though every bone in her body had dissolved, leaving her spineless and limp. Casey brought the food to the table, and they sat down to eat. Paige eyed the scrambled eggs with disdain, took a single slice of cantaloupe, and studied the stack of pancakes. "What are those purple things?"

"Blackberries," Casey said. "Just picked this morning. They're out of this world."

"I don't think I like blackberries."

Casey raised an eyebrow. "You don't like blackberries?"

Paige squared her jaw. "I've never had them."

Rob wondered briefly just what kind of mother Sandy had been, until he remembered the price of supermarket blackberries and realized she'd probably been a frugal one. "Well, then," he said, "you're in for a treat."

Paige didn't look convinced, but she helped herself to a single pancake and smothered it with syrup. "Butter?" Casey offered.

Paige shook her head. "That stuff will kill you before you're fifty."

He and Casey exchanged glances before he shrugged and smeared his pancakes with artery-clogging saturated fat.

Paige sliced her pancake with her fork, pulled out a blackberry, and nibbled at it warily. Eyes focused on her plate, she ate in silence. The tension around the table lay heavy and thick, in stark contrast to their usual relaxed meals. He glanced at his wife. She raised her eyebrows and gave him a brief smile. "So," she said to his daughter, "what do you think of the blackberries?"

Paige shrugged. "They're okay."

"If you want to make me a list of the foods you like, I'll be happy to stock the pantry with your favorites."

"Whatever."

Casey cleared her throat. "Where'd you go last night with the boys?"

Paige raised her head, coolly met her stepmother's eyes, then went back to eating. "Nowhere special."

"I've been thinking. School starts in just a few weeks. I thought maybe we could go school shopping at the mall. All three of us. We could make a day of it."

Paige threw down her fork and scraped back her chair. "Why don't you just back off? You're not my frigging mother! You will *never* be my frigging mother! So why don't you just stop pretending, and leave me the hell alone!" She staggered to her feet and slammed out of the house.

In the silence, the clock ticked. For an instant, his wife's face looked as though she'd been slapped. "Goddamn it," he said.

"It's all right. She's hurting."

"It's not all right, and hurting is not a valid excuse to lash out at you for no reason."

"I'm fine. Let it go."

He squared his jaw, studied her face, considered his options. "No," he said, and shoved back his chair.

She set down her napkin. "Rob, don't—"

But her protest came too late. He was already out the door and circling the old farmhouse through the lush beauty of a late-summer morning. He found his daughter on the back porch, huddled on the swing, looking as miserable as he felt. When he rounded the corner, she glanced at him briefly, then went back to staring off into space.

He climbed the steps to the porch slowly, sat down on the swing, leaving a good distance between them. Leaned back, propped his feet on the porch railing, and began lazily rocking.

"Look," he said. "This is an awkward situation we've been thrown into. I know how you must feel about losing your mother—"

"You don't know a goddamn thing about how I feel."

He hesitated, considered her words, realized she was right. "Fine," he said. "I probably don't. Both of my parents are still alive. But I've lost people I cared for. I've felt the pain of loss, so maybe I do know a little bit. And because of that, I'm trying to give you the benefit of the doubt. But there are lines we don't cross, and you just crossed one."

She glanced at him from the corner of her eye, but said nothing.

"You will not speak to my wife like that again. Ever. I don't care how much you wallow in self-pity, it's not an excuse to be rude to her. That woman has been nothing but kind and gracious to you, and you owe her an apology. I may not know what you're going through, but let me tell you, little girl, she does. She lost her mother at fifteen, her daughter at twenty-nine, and her husband at thirty-one. If there's anybody in this godforsaken place that you might ever want in your corner, it's her, because she's been there, done that. And survived it all."

He was met by a stony silence.

"Look at it from her point of view," he said. "She's trying to rebuild her life after absolute devastation. Then she finds out that the yahoo she just married sowed a few more wild oats than she'd ever guessed, and now, surprise! It's a bouncing baby girl. Only the kid's fifteen years old. Talk about shaking things up. And you know what? A lot of women would've said, 'You're on your own, buddy.' A lot of women would have booted me out on my ass. But she didn't. Even when I was questioning the wisdom of taking you in, she was already sizing up bedrooms and mentally redecorating. You know why? Because that's the way she rolls. She's a good person, the best person I've ever known, and it never even occurred to her to question taking in somebody else's kid to raise. Even this morning, after you were unforgivably snotty to her, she told me to let it go. Because she knows how bad you're hurting inside, and it's breaking her heart. That's the kind of woman she is.

"So if you have anything to say to her, you will act like a mature, civilized human being. If she offers you something you don't want, you'll just say, 'No, thank you' and leave it at that. Is that understood?"

"Fine. Are we done now?"

He leaned back on his tailbone and clasped his hands behind his head. "You know," he said, "I'm going to tell you something about me, something you could use against me if you ever wanted to. But I'm telling you anyway, because I trust that you have enough integrity to not do that."

"Don't trust me. You'll be disappointed."

"Oh, I don't know. You act tough, but I have this feeling that underneath that hard shell, there's a soft, marshmallow center."

She snorted.

"Everybody has a weakness, right? Something they can't control? Something that controls them? For some people, it's drugs, or booze, or greed. For some of us, it's something a lot simpler. You know what my weakness is?" He closed his eyes, felt the warmth of the sun on his face. "It's that woman in there.

If you want to hurt me, the quickest and easiest way is through her. You stick a knife in her, I'm the one who bleeds."

They were both silent, the only sounds the buzzing of insects and the twittering of birds. "There are three billion women on this planet, give or take," he said, "but there's only one of her. And for me, that woman is *it*. There are no others. There've been two things that defined my life. One is my music. The other is the way I feel about her. And for the most part, they've been tangled together from the beginning." He opened his eyes, crossed his ankles on the railing. "That woman is what keeps me upright and breathing. She always has been. So if you want to know who your old man really is, kiddo, I'm just a washed-up old guitar player who'd gladly lay down his life for the woman he's loved since he was twenty years old."

"I suppose there's some kind of lesson buried in there somewhere."

He smiled, leaned his head back and studied the porch ceiling. "You ever go running?"

"Running?" she echoed, as if he'd said something foul.

"Like it or not, kiddo, you're built just like me. Long and lean. That's what they call a runner's body."

"And your point is?"

He turned his head. "I go running every morning. Rain or shine. I think you'd make an outstanding running partner."

Various emotions flickered across her face: disbelief, uncertainty, disdain. And back to disbelief. "You're serious."

"You just put on loose clothes, your most comfortable pair of sneakers, and you put one foot in front of the other, and you sweat and grunt and gasp for breath until the endorphins kick in. Then it gets good."

"Endorphins."

"Way better for the psyche than happy pills. Runner's high. Makes you feel good. Legally."

"Is this supposed to be some kind of father/daughter bonding ritual?"

"Do I look like a manipulative guy? I just thought you might take to running."

She narrowed her eyes. "Why are you being nice to me?"

"Because, like it or not, you're my kid. I'm stuck with you, and you're stuck with me. That's what they call family. And I think everybody deserves a second chance. Which is why we're going back into the house, and you're going to apologize to Casey, and we're going to move on from there. If we're lucky, maybe we can still salvage breakfast. If she hasn't already tossed it in the trash."

"Fine."

They found Casey in the kitchen, scrubbing industriously at the stove top. Their uneaten breakfast still sat on the table. He cleared his throat. "I believe Paige has something to say to you."

Casey paused in her scrubbing, turned slowly, waited. Stiffly, Paige said, "I'm sorry I was rude to you. And if you still want to, I'd like to go shopping with you."

"Apology accepted," Casey said. "Now, let's eat breakfast, before it's inedible."

Paige nodded, sat, and began eating. He met his wife's eyes. One corner of her mouth turned up, ever so slightly, and she gave him an almost imperceptible nod of approval.

And over his daughter's head, he shot her a wink.

***

He hadn't expected much to come of their little chat, so when he came downstairs the next morning, he was surprised to see Paige waiting for him in the kitchen, dressed for running.

"Don't think this means we're friends or anything," his daughter said as she tightened the lace to her sneaker. "Because it's nothing like that."

"Of course not."

"Running's good for your health." She finished with the first foot, and swapped it for the other.

"Absolutely."

"And if you don't have your health," she said, tugging at her laces, "what do you have?"

He nodded gravely. "I used to smoke. A pack a day."

She looked up, surprised. "You did?"

"I did. Then, about five years ago, Casey badgered me into running with her. It was torture at first. I could barely make it to the end of the block. But she was a true friend, the best kind, the kind that doesn't accept any bullshit excuses. She applied the toe of her running shoe to the crack of my ass and bullied me into losing the cigarettes. Smartest thing I ever did."

They went out together into a glorious summer morning, pale pink tinting the eastern sky as the birds awoke for the day and began their good-morning songs. "You need to stretch first," he said. "Like this." They did a few stretching exercises together, until he decided they were both sufficiently limber. Then they started down the road, Paige deliberately positioned on the shoulder, away from traffic. He slowed his pace considerably to accommodate her. "You want to run facing traffic," he said, "so you can always see what's coming. Especially here in the sticks, where there aren't any sidewalks."

For a time, they ran together in silence. She moved with a lengthy stride, strong and even, in spite of her lack of experience. *Youth*, he thought. It made all the difference. He studied her from the corner of his eye, marveling at her lean strength, blown away by the fact that he'd fathered this amazing creature.

"Why are you staring at me?" she demanded.

"I guess I'm just wondering how a guy with an ugly mug like mine managed to create a kid as good-looking as you."

"You're not ugly. Besides, you had help."

He tried to picture Sandy's face, but it had been too many years, and his memories were vague and indistinct. Guilt gnawed at his gut. He and Sandy had dated off and on for nearly two years. Shouldn't he be able to remember her more clearly? In his own defense, it hadn't been any great love match. She'd been his sister's best friend, and their relationship had been based more on proximity than passion. For the most part, it had been—and he hated to use this word, but it was the only word that fit—casual. At least from his point of view. They'd had fun together, but the relationship had been so unremarkable that he barely remembered its final death knell. Their parting had been so low-key, he wasn't sure they'd even said good-bye. It had simply been understood that he was leaving for New York and moving on with his life, and Sandy was staying behind in Boston. Not once had he considered asking her to come with him. It hadn't been that serious a relationship.

Besides, Sandy wasn't the only girl he'd been involved with. When their off-and-on relationship had been in on mode, they were monogamous, but during their off periods, there had been other girls. He was a young guy, and he'd done what young guys do: whored around, just because he could. But he hadn't been stupid. He'd always practiced safe sex. It hadn't occurred to him that there might be consequences, until now, at the advanced age of thirty-seven. Paige might not even be his only offspring. In spite of the precautions he'd taken, there could be other kids out there carrying his DNA. After all, he and Sandy had been careful, and look how that had turned out.

The thought was terrifying. He supposed there came a time in every man's life when his past came back to bite him on the ass. His personal Day of Reckoning. If so, Rob MacKenzie had just met up with his. Nothing could slam reality home to a man more quickly than the knowledge that he'd fathered a child. Or the understanding that there could be others. All those years, he'd thought he was being so careful, but the teenage girl running beside him was living proof that at least once, he hadn't been as careful as he'd thought.

And then, there was the whole mortality issue. This wasn't the first time that knowledge of his own mortality had stared him in the eyeballs. For most of his life, time had been of little consequence. He'd simply lived from one day to the next, blissfully unaware of the passage of the years. Until Danny died, and he found himself lost, rudderless, acutely and painfully aware that he was well past thirty and his life was going nowhere.

It had been Casey who saved him. He didn't believe she even knew that he'd been hanging on by his fingernails and about to go splat on the pavement. It was her friendship, her love, her warmth and tenderness, that had pulled him back from the edge. By that time, he was in love with her, fully and desperately. But he understood that if he pushed, he might lose her. So for the first time in his life, he familiarized himself with two utter strangers: patience and celibacy. For nearly two years, he'd led a solitary and celibate existence while he waited for his best friend's widow to come to the same conclusion he'd already reached: that they were meant to be together.

"So," Paige said, dragging him back to the present, "why'd you desert us?"

He realized they'd been running for some time, had actually picked up speed, yet she hadn't lagged, didn't seem tired or winded, hadn't even broken a sweat. He was beginning to get the distinct impression that he'd been hustled. "I don't know how many ways I can say this, but I didn't desert you. I never knew you existed." He quickened his pace, lengthened his stride, watched as she effortlessly adjusted hers to match his. "I thought you weren't a runner."

"I never said I wasn't a runner. Are you calling my mom a liar?"

"You might not have said it, but you clearly implied that you weren't into running. And let's just say that your mother's interpretation of the situation differs from mine."

"My mom was a saint. And I didn't imply anything. You chose to believe what you wanted to believe."

"As did you."

"I happen to believe what she told me. Why would she have any reason to lie?"

"You tell me. You sure as hell knew her better than I did."

"I run on Carson Beach at low tide. Three times a week. And she said you left because you didn't want the responsibility of a kid."

"That's not a safe place for a young girl to run alone. And what your mother said is utter bullshit."

"I'm not stupid. I carry pepper spray. It's a moot point now anyway, since I'm a world away from Carson Beach. And you *are* calling her a liar."

"My leaving had nothing to do with you. I moved to Manhattan with Casey and Danny to further my career. Your mother never told me she was pregnant."

"And if she had, would you have stayed?"

He hesitated for just an instant too long. Paige snorted. "Right. That's about what I thought."

Casey

She was watering her flower garden when they came back from their run. Casey leaned back on her heels, set the hose to mist, and watched them approach. Father and daughter, two long, lean bodies, so alike it was scary. They separated, walked up the driveway individually, Paige a half-dozen paces ahead of her father. She passed Casey without acknowledging her, flounced up the steps and into the shed, and slammed the kitchen door. A moment later, M.C. Hammer began rapping in glorious, vibrant stereo.

Rob approached more slowly, looking tired and defeated. He glanced at her, shook his head, and kept walking.

Oh, boy.

She gave him his space, finished watering the garden, came back inside and started her morning household chores, gradually working her way from the kitchen to the upstairs bathroom. Picked up his wet towel from the bathroom floor and hung it over the shower rod, made their bed, opened the blinds to allow morning light to spill in. Then she went back downstairs and heated a pot of water. She prepared two cups of Earl Grey and, teacups in hand, went outside in search of her husband.

She found him exactly where she'd expected, on the porch swing, his favorite spot. Slumped on his tailbone, his hair damp from the shower and his long legs stretched out, bony ankles propped on the porch railing, he swung listlessly in the sweet morning air.

She sat down carefully beside him, handed him a steaming cup of Earl, kept the other for herself. "Hey," she said.

"Hey." He balanced the cup against his thigh, dangerously close to an area where no man wanted to be scalded. "Thanks."

She waited with bated breath until he raised the cup. "You okay?"

"I've been better."

"What happened?"

"She was right. That's what happened."

"About?"

"She asked me if I would've stayed in Boston if I'd known Sandy was pregnant. I couldn't tell her yes. Because it would have been a lie." Troubled green eyes sought hers. "What kind of hypocrite does that make me?"

She rested a hand on his thigh, smoothed worn denim with gentle fingertips. "There is not a hypocritical bone in your body, MacKenzie."

"That first time we talked on the phone, I told her that if I'd known about her, I would've been there from the beginning. But it's not really true. There's no way I would have stayed in Boston. You and I and Danny—we had places to go, things to do, people to see. I had a budding career as a musician, and that took precedence over everything. Every. Damn. Thing. Oh, I wouldn't have left the two of 'em high and dry, but I would have been a long-distance dad. I would've sent money whenever I could, but think about how poor we were. Pretty soon, the money would've stopped, too. Let's face it. I would've been a shitty father, no matter what."

"Come on, Rob. You were twenty-two years old. Just a kid. You weren't ready to be anybody's father. Not financially, not emotionally."

He let out a soft, cynical laugh. "Hell, I'm not sure I'm ready yet."

"And don't you think maybe Sandy knew that? And that's why she never told you? She knew you well enough to understand that you would have tried, and failed. And failing would have broken your heart, and Paige's. Because you would have loved that little baby to distraction. You just wouldn't have known how to be a father to her. Sandy probably believed her daughter would be better off with no father than she would be losing one she'd come to love. So she protected Paige, by keeping the truth from both of you. And her heart was the only one broken."

Somber green eyes studied her over the rim of his teacup. "Maybe," he said.

"I've been a mother. I understand sacrifice. And heartbreak."

He reached out, touched a strand of her hair. "Yeah," he said. "You do."

"It'll be okay. Just give her some time."

He was quiet for a while, considering. Finally said, "But how do I make it up to her? Fifteen years of not being there for her? I don't know what I should do."

"There's nothing you can do. You can't make it up to her. It's too late for that. Those fifteen years are lost. You can only move on from here."

He let out a long, poignant sigh. Said, "Ah, shit."

She leaned back, propped her bare feet on his legs, and rested her cheek against his shoulder. Studying the row of pink roses that ran along the rim of her teacup, she said, "Will this be us in fifty years? Sitting on the porch swing with our walkers and our hearing aids, drinking Earl Grey and talking about our glory days?"

"Would that be such a bad thing?"

"Are you kidding, MacKenzie? I would be honored to still be drinking Earl Grey with you fifty years down the road."

"This is why I married you. All that wisdom you're so good at dispensing. You always seem to have the answer to my problems. And it's a definite plus that I don't have to pay a shrink three hundred bucks an hour, since you dispense advice for free."

"I'm flattered. Even though you make me sound like a vending machine."

"You should be flattered. I meant it in only the most positive of ways."

"And here I thought it was my drop-dead-gorgeous legs that attracted you to me."

"That, too. But it was mostly the wisdom. Hey, I'm sorry I stood you up in favor of the kid."

"You didn't stand me up. We can run together any time. I think it's important for you to spend time with her. Even if said time is spent arguing. You're building a relationship. It may be a prickly one, but at least it's a starting point."

He lifted his arm. She scooted under it and lay her head against his chest. He wrapped the arm loosely around her shoulders. "What'd I ever do to deserve somebody like you?"

"Two-way road, my friend. Two-way road."

Paige

"Excuse the mess," Luke said, tossing his amplifier cord into the back seat to make room for her. Doing her best to avoid the empty soda cans and fast food wrappers that littered the floor of the rattletrap old car, Paige climbed into the passenger seat and shut the door.

"Nice ride," she said, settling in and fumbling with the seatbelt.

"Hey, I inherited it from my mom, okay? It was free. Free makes everything better. Even dings and dents and rusty fenders."

He had a point. She glanced into the back seat, where his guitar case lay atop a pile of wrinkled clothes. "Dude, if you want to impress chicks, you might want to consider excavating this deathtrap. Chicks dig clean, you know."

"Thanks for the advice." Her cousin adjusted his sunglasses, shifted the car into gear, and backed down the driveway.

"No offense meant. I'm just saying."

"None taken." He looked both ways, checked his mirrors, backed out into the road, and headed for town.

"So where is practice?"

"My friend Tobey's place. On the River Road, out on the other side of town. We practice in his garage."

"And your band mates know I'm coming?"

"Yeah. They're cool with it."

"So, in other news…I was right."

"About what?" Luke tapped the steering wheel in a rapid, rhythmic motion.

"About *him*," she said. "My old man. He's just as much of a dick as I always knew he was."

He glanced at her from behind mirrored sunglasses. "What happened?"

She folded her arms and said, "He as much as admitted to me that he never wanted me."

Luke thought about it for a while. "That doesn't sound like him."

"Yeah, well." She shrugged and glanced out the side window at the lovely view of trees, trees, and more trees.

"What, exactly, did he say?"

"He said that if he'd known my mom was pregnant, he would've moved to New York anyway."

"Wow. That's harsh."

Bleakly, she said, "I don't think he ever loved her."

"You can't know that. You weren't there. Life isn't black and white. There are shades of gray. An infinite number."

"You just say that because you have this twisted hero worship thing going on with him."

Luke shrugged. "Maybe. I just think you should reserve judgment until you've had time to get to know him."

"What's there to know? He's a big jerk. End of story."

"Your opinion," her cousin said. "Not mine."

"I guess we'll just have to agree to disagree, then, because you're not changing my mind." She was silent for a time. Then she said, "Where's Mikey today?"

He eyed her long enough to send a flush across her cheeks. "Is that the way the wind's blowing?"

"I have no idea what you're talking about."

"Of course you don't. I bet you never even noticed that face of his. Let me give you a word of advice. Don't even bother to go there. My stepbrother has so many girls chasing after him that his head's spinning. The last thing he needs is another one."

"Jesus, Luke, all I did was ask a question. Don't build a federal case out of it."

"Besides, he's your cousin."

"Step-cousin."

"I thought we were hanging today because we're friends, not because you have the hots for my stepbrother."

"Oh, for the love of God. We *are* friends!"

He studied her a moment longer. Then said, "He's at football practice."

She wrinkled her forehead. "Football practice? But school doesn't start until next week."

"What planet did you come from? The first game is a week from Saturday. The team has to be ready. They practice for three hours every weekday morning for the entire month of August."

"In this heat?"

"Yep."

"What a bummer."

"Mikey doesn't seem to mind. Maybe it feeds his ego. He is the star quarterback, you know."

She rolled her eyes. "Of course he is. Are you saying he's conceited? Because he doesn't seem that way to me."

"Not conceited. Just aloof. And way too serious."

"Yeah. I kind of got that. He always has this grim look on his face. Why do you suppose that is?"

"I don't know. I think it's a Lindstrom family trait. Jesse's that way, too."

"Really?" She thought about it. Luke's stepfather did seem somber. "So how do you suppose he and your mother ever got together? They seem so different."

"To tell you the truth—" Eyes still on the road, Luke reached out to adjust the radio. "I have absolutely no idea. Listen, Mikey and I are spending Saturday at Old Orchard Beach. The last hurrah before we go back to hitting the books. Want to come with us?"

"How far is Old Orchard?"

"A couple of hours. We're taking Mikey's truck. I don't dare to go that far in this thing."

"Wise decision. Sure, I'd love to go. I can't believe summer's almost over. School next week."

"Devon's already headed off to college. I'm giving it a couple of weeks, then I'm asking if I can have her room. It's bigger than mine."

"You think they'll give it to you?"

"Just testing the waters. It never hurts to ask."

Luke's friends were a motley crew of misfits, all of them appearing to be as laid back as her cousin. He carried in his guitar and amp, plugged them in, and introduced her around.

"Tobey on drums," he said. The drummer spun his sticks and saluted. "Corey on bass." Another wordless greeting. "And this dude over here, on the keyboard, is Craig."

"Hey," she said.

A chorus of mumbled *heys* came back to her. "So where's Nate?" Luke said.

"Nate," Tobey said, "is sick. Again. I hear her name is Emily."

Luke scowled. "How the hell are we supposed to get anywhere with this band if our lead singer keeps blowing us off?"

"I don't know, dude. I'm just passing on the message."

"You need a singer?" Paige said.

"It's hard to play without one," Craig said.

"Well, hell. I can sing."

The boys exchanged dubious glances. "You can sing," Luke said.

She grinned and said, "Like a little bird."

Her cousin glanced around at his band mates. They all shrugged. "Okay, then," he said. "Let's see what you can do."

It took a few minutes to figure out what songs they knew in common, what they could play well enough so it wouldn't sound like a cat in a blender. They finally settled on Janis Joplin. She'd been Sandy's favorite singer, and Paige had grown up listening to her music. While the boys did their best to keep up, she belted out her own distinctive version of *Piece of My Heart*, putting everything she had into that song.

When she was done, there was a moment of astonished silence. And then Luke, in a voice that sounded remarkably steady when you considered the look in his eyes, said, "Somebody call Nate, wish him good luck with Emily, and tell him he's fired. I think he just got replaced."

Rob

Saturday morning, he was alone in the kitchen, a cup of coffee in his hand and Igor draped over his shoulder, when his daughter bounced into the room wearing an unbuttoned man's dress shirt and, beneath it, a pink bikini so small it would have been banned in Boston. Above hot pink Converse sneakers, her long, bare legs reached almost to her neck, and between the two tiny scraps of fabric a long, slender stretch of youthful skin was on flagrant display. Giant pink hoop earrings dangled from her earlobes, and she'd glopped on the make-up so thick he barely recognized her.

His blood pressure shot high enough to put him at serious risk of suffering a coronary. "What in bloody hell is this?" he said.

The kid raised both eyebrows and widened innocent green eyes. "This what?"

He waved both hands in a gesture that encompassed the entirety of her. "This…THIS! The way you're dressed."

She seemed genuinely puzzled. "What's wrong with the way I'm dressed?"

"Jesus, Mary and Joseph. Where do I begin?"

The kid glanced down at herself and shrugged. "I'm going to the beach with Luke and Mikey. This is how I always dress for the beach."

He plunked his coffee cup on the counter so hard that hot liquid sloshed over the rim. At the sudden movement, Igor leaped to the floor and slunk off toward the living room. Grimly, he said, "Not any more, it's not."

"What are you talking about? It's just a bikini. Mom always let me wear it. Everybody—and I mean freaking everybody— dresses this way!"

"Yeah? Well, your mom isn't in charge any more. I am, and you are not leaving this house looking like a two-dollar hooker. I've known drag queens who wore less make-up."

Her eyebrows went higher. He'd snagged her interest. "You know drag queens?"

"That's not the point! You are not going anywhere dressed like that. Sure as hell not anywhere with two sixteen-year-old boys! I may be an old fogey now, but I was once a sixteen-year-old boy, and I'm not so old I've forgotten what it was like."

"You're kidding, right? They're my cousins!"

"At sixteen, hormones trump blood every time. And only one of them is your cousin. Mikey's only a pretend relative."

"Oh, my God. I can't believe you! Are you trying to ruin my life?"

"You're fifteen years old. You're not supposed to have a life."

His daughter squared her jaw. "You are seriously behind the times, and I am not dressing like something out of a Dickens novel just to please you!"

"Hold that thought." He marched to the wall phone, picked it up, and dialed his sister's number. When Jesse answered, he said, "Just the person I wanted. I need an expert opinion."

"Go for it," his brother-in-law said.

"Fifteen years old. Make-up six inches thick. A bikini that leaves nothing to the imagination, and a belligerent attitude. Thinks she's wearing this attire to go to the beach with Luke and Mikey. As I just reminded her, I was a sixteen-year-old boy once. I need your take as someone who spends a lot of time with teenagers. Is this appropriate attire? Does everybody—and I mean freaking everybody—dress this way?"

"Those are two very different questions. Yes, it's pretty much what they all wear these days. The bikinis get smaller and smaller every year. And no, it's not what I'd consider appropriate attire under the circumstances. I was a sixteen-year-old boy once, too. Not all that long ago, if you count it in dog years."

"So I'm not overreacting?"

"Trust me. If there's one thing I know, it's teenagers. Locking her in a chastity belt and a suit of armor wouldn't be overreacting."

"And you won't be offended if I read your son the riot act before I allow my daughter to get into the car with him? And threaten to kick his ass from here to Chicago if he so much as lays a finger on her?"

"In your shoes? It's what I'd do."

"Thank you." He hung up the phone, turned back to Paige. "The jury's in. Go back into your room and change into something presentable. Shorts and a tee shirt will work just fine. *Decent* shorts. The bikini can stay here. While you're at it, you can scrub that crap off your face until you look a little less like Mae West."

"I don't even know who Mae West is, and I hate you. I really, truly hate you."

"My heart bleeds."

"If Casey was here, she'd tell you how ridiculous you're being!"

"Casey's not here right now, and I'm the king of this particular castle. Of course, if you really value her opinion that much, we can always wait for her to get home. You'll probably miss your ride, but, hey, that's your funeral, not mine."

She squared her jaw. Her shoulders. Glared at him. He glared back. For a full ten seconds, they stared each other down. And then she turned, stalked across the kitchen, and slammed into her room.

He reached for his cup of coffee, abandoned on the counter, and realized his hands were shaking like a wet dog after a rainstorm. He picked up the cup, tossed its contents into the sink, and left it sitting there. Crossed the room, opened the fridge, and took out a beer instead. Popping the cap, he brought the bottle to his mouth, upended it, and took a long, slow swallow.

And said to nobody in particular, "That went well."

Casey

Her meeting had run late, so she'd swung by the bowling
alley and picked up a pizza for lunch. Clutching the box to her
chest while spicy and delicious aromas wafted directly up her nose,
she kicked off her shoes in the shed and let herself into the house.
The kitchen was silent, peaceful, the lack of rap so blessed, she
nearly fell to her knees in gratitude.

Somewhere in the distance, Junior Walker softly asked the
musical question, *What does it take (to win your love)?* Casey set
down the pizza and followed the music to the living room. Rob
was slumped on his tailbone on the couch, those endless legs
extended, bare feet resting on the coffee table, Igor purring softly
in his lap. He held a half-empty bottle of Heineken tilted against
his thigh, and with his head leaned back against the cushions and
his eyes closed, he wore a look of such supreme bliss, she was
reluctant to interrupt.

She moved silently to the couch, knelt on the cushion beside
him, and settled there, curled up with knees folded and her feet
tucked neatly beneath her. He opened his eyes, looked at her, and
struggled to focus. "It's that sax," he said. "It gets me every
time." He thumped his chest. "Right here."

She took the Heineken from his hand, raised it to her mouth,
and took a sip. "I brought pizza."

"I know. I can smell it."

She helped herself to another sip of beer. "Tomatoes,
mozzarella, pepperoni, green peppers and onions—"

"I might've done something that maybe I shouldn't have."

She glanced at Igor and said, "Do I even dare to ask?"

The cat didn't answer, just stared back at her, his huge, blue
Siamese eyes wide with mistrust.

"I was right. Damn it, I was absolutely, one hundred percent
right! It's just that...maybe I could've been a little gentler about
it."

"Oh, Flash. What did you do?"

"If only you'd seen the way she was dressed. You remember
that bikini you wore in Nassau?" His eyes sought hers. "The one
that, um...snagged my interest?"

"The one you picked out? It would be hard to forget."

"This looked just like it. Except it was on my daughter. My friggin' daughter! All that skin. All that damn bare skin. She's only fifteen! And she'd slapped on make-up so thick she could've grouted tiles with it."

"And you freaked."

"What was I supposed to do? She was headed to the beach with two sixteen-year-old boys. There's no way I could let her out of the house half-naked like that. I have to protect her against her own stupidity. It's my job. Except...I maybe went a little overboard." He paused, sighed. "I wasn't very nice to her."

"How not very?"

"I told her she wasn't leaving the house looking like a two-dollar hooker."

"I bet that went over well."

"And I made her change into shorts and a tee shirt. She wasn't impressed. She invoked your name. Told me that if you were home, you'd let me know what a flaming ass I was being. She didn't use those exact words, but that was the gist of it."

She ran a fingertip around the lip of the beer bottle. "What am I going to do with you, MacKenzie?"

"This is tougher than I thought it would be. This whole parenting thing. I didn't expect it to be easy, but this is ridiculous."

She nudged an annoyed Igor away, eased herself over and took his place on her husband's lap. Handed him the beer bottle and, combing her fingers through his hair, said philosophically, "We'll survive this. If we survived disco, we can make it through anything."

He let out a soft snort of laughter. Fiddled a little with the collar of her shirt. "I guess we are bulletproof, aren't we?"

"Able to leap tall buildings in a single bound. That disco—" She took a sip of beer. "That was some nasty stuff."

"Like a persistent rash of unknown origin." He tucked a strand of hair behind her ear. "And then, there was New Wave."

"We survived that, too. A Flock of Seagulls. I mean, what was that hair all about? And don't forget rap."

"I'm trying to forget rap, but I keep being reminded about it. Up close and personal."

She slipped a hand beneath his collar and rubbed the back of his neck. He sighed and said, "We're dinosaurs, aren't we?"

"Yes, but take comfort in knowing you're my favorite dinosaur. Don't let this get to you. It's bad for your health. Sitting here brooding, while your daughter's probably frolicking on the beach and doesn't even remember the two of you had words." With her free hand, she began kneading his shoulder. "Look at you. Your muscles are all tied up in knots. What you need is a good massage."

He made a slight adjustment to her fit on his lap, left a hand resting lightly on her thigh. "That's not the only thing I need."

"You have sex on your mind *again*, MacKenzie?"

"When do I ever not have sex on my mind?"

"Point taken. You know, I had no idea when I married you that you'd turn out to be such a hot-blooded stud."

This time, he let out a full belly laugh. "I have to keep you around, if only for the entertainment value. And don't be coy with me. You knew what you were getting yourself into. You shacked up with me for three months before we said our vows. That should've been sufficient time for you to get the picture."

"I suppose that is a valid point. Although you make it sound really tacky."

"Damn right, it's valid. And, tacky or not, you like it as much as I do. So..." He ran a fingertip down her bare arm. "The kid won't be back for hours. Are you listening, Fiore? HOURS. We're all alone. While the cat's away, I think the mice should do a little howling."

"That's one whopper of a mixed metaphor, MacKenzie."

"I have a whopper I'd be glad to share with—"

"This conversation," she said archly, "is rapidly deteriorating into twelve-year-old-boy territory."

"Sorry. I forgot you're still in lady mode until you take your clothes off. Let me rephrase that. Come upstairs with me to the Love Shack, and I'll show you a good time. A very, very good time."

"Why, in the name of all that's holy, have you built your life around snippets of song lyrics?"

"I have no idea. Maybe to annoy you?"

"Then you've certainly accomplished your mission. What about the pizza? It's already getting cold."

He leaned forward and kissed the corner of her mouth. "That, my sweet, is why God invented microwaves."

"Well," she said. "We can't argue with that logic, can we? Give me five minutes to take the dog out, and I'll meet you upstairs."

Paige

While Luke sat under a neighboring beach umbrella, doing his best to impress some little blond chickie in a yellow string bikini, Paige and Mikey left their stuff on the blanket and walked the hard-packed sand at the water's edge. "I'm sorry," she said. "Sorry that he put you through the Spanish Inquisition. He's a total jerk."

Hands tucked in the pockets of his tropical-print shorts, Mikey walked with a loose, measured stride. "Don't be so hard on him. He's just doing his job as a dad."

"I've managed to survive for fifteen years without one of those, and I don't need one now, poking his nose into my business, where it doesn't belong."

"Maybe, but you know he'd argue that that's exactly where it does belong. In your business. And if you think that's bad, try having a dad who teaches at the high school. And watches your every move."

The breeze blew a strand of hair into her face, and she brushed it away. A few yards ahead of them, a gull strutted into the surf, wings spread wide, skinny little legs braced against the rushing water. "Yeah, I guess you win that one. It's just...we had a wicked fight before you got there. He didn't approve of the way I was dressed. He made me go back to my room and change."

"Don't worry about it. You look great. Some of these girls here—" He raised his head and glanced around. "—look like they're advertising it for free. Like the kind of girl you don't bother to call the next day."

Heat flooded her cheeks. "I don't think they're advertising. It's just fashion. It's what girls wear."

"Well, it looks trashy to me. I mean—sure, I'm a guy. I'm not blind. But just because they look good on the outside doesn't mean there's anything good on the inside."

"Wow. An independent thinker. I suspect most guys don't see it that way. For instance, Luke. He doesn't seem to be having any problem with it."

The corner of his mouth twitched. "In case you hadn't noticed," he said, "Luke and I are not cut from the same cloth."

"No kidding."

"But we're friends. Don't ask me how that happened, because we don't have a thing in common. Not one thing. But I like the guy. He's solid. Somebody I'd want on my side in a fight."

"I guess you're lucky, then, since you're stuck with each other. I had a friend in Boston who absolutely hated her stepbrother. The guy was a total douche. But she was stuck with him anyway." Paige folded her arms across her chest. "So your dad teaches high school?"

"Yep. English. Pretty much every kid who's gone through Jackson High in the last ten years has had the privilege of taking English with Mr. Lindstrom."

"Did you have to take it with him?"

"I did. We pretended like we didn't know each other, even though everybody knew we did. It was brutally painful."

"But you get along, right? Out of school?"

"Sure. My dad's an okay guy. Tough, but fair. I think yours probably is, too. If you give him a chance."

"Why does everybody keep flogging that same horse?"

"I don't know. Maybe you should start paying attention to what they're saying, before the damn thing dies."

Another breeze caught her hair, and she was glad she'd worn the hooded sweatshirt. Here at the Maine coast, it was chilly for late August. Most of the girls in their tiny bikinis had goose bumps in places she didn't want to think about. "So," she said, "college in another year?"

"If Dad has anything to say about it, yes. He thinks I don't stand much of a chance of success in today's world without a college education."

"You don't agree with that?"

"I'm still undecided. He'd like to see me go to Farmington. That's where he went, and it's a good school. I wouldn't have to live on campus if I didn't want to. I could commute. That's what he did."

"You could still live at home. That would be good."

"Oh, I don't know." He kicked at a stone, slick and smooth, packed hard into the wet sand. "I kind of like the idea of being on my own. It's not bad, living here with my family. But sometimes

I get the urge to pack everything I own in a suitcase, hop in my truck, and head for the West Coast. See some of the country along the way. Figure out what I want to do with my life. That's hard to do in a little backwater town like Jackson Falls. How am I supposed to know what I want to do, where I want to be, if I've never done anything or been anywhere?"

"You don't strike me as a wanderer. I'd imagine you as more of a homebody."

He leaned down to pick up a long strand of seaweed. "Things," he said, "aren't always what they seem."

"No," she said. "They aren't."

"So, Luke tells me you're a singer."

"Not really. It's just something I fool around with."

"Not what Luke says. He says you're good. Are you planning to do something with it?"

She hunched her shoulders and tucked her hands into the pockets of her sweatshirt. "I don't know. I'm not sure I want to live that kind of life. Putting yourself out there, knowing you'll face rejection, that you might never make it, no matter how much effort, no matter how much heart and soul, you put into it. But—" She shrugged. "Music is what makes me feel good. You know? Sometimes I think I could really do something with this. And then I think of my old man, and it's like having a bucket of cold water dumped over my head."

"Why? He's had a really successful career. He could probably help you. Give you a leg up on the competition."

"That's the thing," she said. "I don't want his help. I want to prove I can make it on my own. Because if he helped me, and I was successful, I'd spend the rest of my life wondering if that success was because I was good, or because my old man was an aging rock star who called in a few favors."

"You might not want to let him hear you talking about him that way."

They exchanged glances, and then she let out a snort of laughter. He smiled, and his whole face changed. "Come on," he said. "Let's go see if we can drag Luke away from Lolita and find some onion rings or something."

Casey

He'd closed the bedroom blinds so that only soft light filtered through. At one open window, a whirring fan exchanged stale air for fresh. In the dim light, he was fiddling with the stereo. She stood there for a moment, drinking him in, head to foot. Something tightened in her throat. What was it about those damn bare feet of his that got to her every time?

He turned, studied her face. And smiled. "Dance with me," he said.

She crossed the room and stepped into his arms. He felt warm and solid, lean and lanky and wonderful. She lay her head against his chest and said, "Flash? There's no music playing."

"Well then, babydoll, we'll just have to fake it."

Beneath her cheek, his heart beat steady and strong. "But we don't need to fake it. You see, whenever you take me in your arms, I automatically hear music playing."

"Wow, that's good, Fiore. Really, really good. Slick."

She tilted her head and looked up at him. "You think? I sort of thought it was."

"You should try setting it to music." Still holding her, he leaned back and reached out a hand to flip a switch on the stereo, and Smokey Robinson's sweet falsetto filled the room. *Ooh, Baby, Baby.*

"Ah. That's so much better."

"Of course it's better, woman. The man is a god."

She tightened her arms around him as they swayed to the music. "No matter what terrible things people might say about you," she told him with exaggerated sweetness, "nobody will ever be able to accuse you of having bad taste in music."

"I think there's a backhanded compliment in there somewhere." Without warning, he dipped her so low she nearly touched the floor. She let out a little shriek and clutched a fistful of his shirt. She was giggling when he smoothly pulled her back upright. "You might want to pipe down," he said, "or we'll have Leroy up here, sniffing around to make sure there isn't an intruder in the house."

"Leroy's tucked away all safe in his crate, so there's no danger of that."

"What a relief. He'd definitely put a damper on my plans for the afternoon."

Smokey stopped warbling, and Aretha took over, saying a little prayer. He spun her away from him and then back into his arms. "You know," she said, "this whole overprotective *shtick* is pretty normal. It's a guy thing. You should have seen the fit my brother pitched when we told him we were getting married."

"I figured something like that went down. You and Travis went into a huddle in the kitchen and stayed there for quite some time. Of course, you have to cut him some slack. We came at him out of left field. He didn't even know we were together until we showed up at his door, with you wearing a rock the size of Texas on your left-hand ring finger."

"It's a family tradition. Trav always disapproves of my choices when it comes to men. It took him years to forgive me for marrying Danny. How dare I marry yet another rocker? So while you were in the living room making polite chit-chat with Leslie, Travis dragged me off to the kitchen and proceeded to express serious doubts about your suitability as husband material. He simply didn't believe you had it in you to settle down and go the long haul with just one woman. He made a point of reminding me about your dismal track record, including, but not limited to, all those years you spent as a manwhore."

"That is not a real word. You just made it up."

"*Au contraire*, my friend. And if the shoe fits, does it really matter?"

"Moving right along, I imagine you set him straight."

"Oh, I set him straight, all right. I told him that: A) You were thirty-five years old and you'd finally pulled your head out of your ass and grown up, and I wasn't even remotely concerned about you going astray."

"Nice, Fiore. Very complimentary picture you painted of me. I can't wait to hear B."

"Ah, yes. B. I furthermore told him you'd known me long enough and well enough to understand that if I ever did catch you dipping it someplace where it didn't belong, I'd amputate first and ask questions second."

"You've turned really bloodthirsty in your old age. Is this supposed to serve as some kind of warning to me?"

"Stay in line, MacKenzie, and you'll have nothing to worry about."

"I'm shaking in my shoes."

"You're not wearing shoes." .

"Smart-ass." He dipped her again, and again she let out a startled yelp. "You just don't learn, do you?" he said cheerfully. "I swear, if this keeps up, we'll have the cops knocking on the door, telling us to keep it down because the neighbors are complaining about the noise."

"We don't have any neighbors. And payback is going to be such fun."

"Bring it, baby. I have broad shoulders. So?"

"So. Since his first volley fell short of its target, he tried a different tack. He put on this somber, mournful face, and told me he was afraid that someday, I was going to regret settling."

"Settling?"

"Yes. That's the exact word he used. He said I was too young, at thirty-three, to trap myself in a loveless marriage with an old friend just because we were both alone and looking for companionship."

"He did *not* say that."

"Oh, he said it. And he was dead serious."

She could feel the laughter rumbling up inside his chest before it spilled out, starting as a choked snort and ending in a deep belly laugh. He had the most amazing laugh. "Oh, man," he said, wiping a tear from his eye, "where does he come up with this stuff?"

"I have no idea. It seems he thought I was recruiting a shuffleboard partner for my sunset years."

He snorted again, made a choked sound in the back of his throat. "What did you tell him?"

"Oh, you know," she said offhandedly, as he spun her away and then back again, "I told him you were hung like a racehorse and we were spending all our spare time having screaming sex in every room of the house, and if he didn't believe me, he was welcome to drop by and check it out for himself."

He froze for a split second before the anticipated explosion came. "Jesus H. Christ, Fiore! Don't do that to me!"

And she grinned. "Had you there for a minute, didn't I?"

"Who the hell are you, and what have you done with my baby?"

"It's all your fault. You've been a very naughty influence on me, MacKenzie. And I did warn you about payback."

"You only had me for about half a second. Damn, woman. That mouth on you is unbelievable. Now that you've taken ten years off my life, what did you really tell him?"

Etta James replaced Aretha, telling her unfaithful lover that she'd rather go blind than watch him walk away. Casey closed her eyes and pressed her cheek to his chest, and while they swayed in time to the steamy blues ballad, she said, "After I stopped laughing hysterically, I told him he was way out in left field and couldn't be more wrong. I said we'd been crazy about each other for years—"

"Emphasis on the plural?"

"Emphasis on the plural, just in case there was any possibility he might miss the point. And that we'd finally decided to stop screwing around and do something about it before we both got so old that neither one of us could remember how to insert tab A into slot B. Or why we'd even want to."

"You said that to your brother? Those exact words?"

She looked up at him and batted her lashes demurely. "I did."

"Oh, man, I can just picture his face. You're thirty-five years old and you've been married twice, and Trav's still in denial about the fact that you gave up your virginity a long time ago. I bet that shut him up."

"Let me put it this way: That was a year and a half ago, and he's never said another word to me about it."

He let out a soft, breathy laugh and rested his cheek atop her head, and for a time there was just the two of them and the music, weaving its magic spell in and around and through them. "If this song got any hotter," she said, "I think we'd both go up in flames."

"Congratulations, Fiore. You just figured out the method to my madness. I know you. I know the blues works on you the way booze does on most women. Gets you all hot and loose and slutty."

"Slutty?"

"You know what would make this whole scenario even more fun?"

"I suppose if anybody knows slutty, it would be you. And the very thought of asking makes me feel faint."

"It would be even more fun if we ditched all the clothes."

"And danced naked?"

"That would be the idea."

"Do you have a clue how quickly things would deteriorate if we did that, MacKenzie?"

"I suppose that would depend on your definition of deteriorate. Maybe we should just skip the dancing and get right down to business."

In response, she wound her ankle around his and ran the sole of her bare foot across worn denim, up the calf of his leg and back down again. "I'd like to revisit that slutty thing. I could use a little clarification."

"If you're in the mood for show-and-tell," he said, running his hands down her backside until they reached her thighs, "I'd be happy to give you a little demonstration. That might clarify things for you."

"Give me some time to think about it."

"Time's up." Without any effort, he boosted her up into his arms. She tightened her arms around his neck, locked her legs around his waist, found his mouth with hers and kissed him, slow and hot and sexy, in rhythm with the music, until they both ran out of breath and were in danger of passing out unless they took in some oxygen. Lungs afire, she pressed her face to his shoulder and listened to his attempt to regulate his own breathing. Etta was still singing and, locked together like a single unit, they were still moving in slo-mo to that hot, seductive rhythm. Casey tangled both fists in his hair, kissed his neck, and took a hard little bite of his earlobe.

And said, "I vote for show-and-tell. Dancing is so overrated."

Rob

They'd been playing together for a year when, out of the blue, Trav's kid sister, who had this idea in her head that she wanted to be a songwriter, sent her brother a cassette tape of songs she'd written. Casey Bradley was just out of high school, barely eighteen years old, living on the family farm in a one-stoplight town somewhere in the wilds of western Maine, and she was a month away from tying the knot with some guy she'd grown up with. She had a strong, clear singing voice that sounded a little like Carly Simon, and the songs were pretty good. A little too pop-ish for Rob's taste, but Danny had gone gaga over them, and being Danny, he'd badgered the living shit out of Travis to take him up there to talk to the kid about using her material.

Trav had finally caved, and the two of them had driven the Chevy to Maine to talk to his kid sister. Danny had, of course, steamrolled right over her. What eighteen-year-old girl could say no to that face? There'd been just one snag. The girl couldn't read music. She'd been doing it all by ear. Because there was only one person they knew who was any good at transcription, Travis and Danny had dragged her back to Boston with them, to Rob, with this half-assed notion that the girl could play the songs that were inside her head, and he could transcribe them onto paper.

He'd taken one look at Trav's kid sister and thought, *whoa.* She was gorgeous. A little bit of a thing, with big green eyes and long, black hair that fell all the way to her waist. But her beauty wasn't all of it; there were any number of gorgeous girls out there. This girl really had something special. She wasn't like the chippies who hung around the stage on a Friday night while he was packing away his equipment, girls with short skirts and low-cut shirts and too much lipstick, girls who made it clear they were available if he was interested. It hadn't taken him any time at all to learn that if you put a guy up on stage and stuck an electric guitar in his hands, even if he couldn't play for shit, even if he looked like Godzilla, he'd have no shortage of girls ready and willing to spread their legs for him.

Casey Bradley wasn't that kind of girl. There was a purity about her, an innocence that shone like a beacon in the night. She was cool and self-assured and smart, with just enough naïveté to sweeten the package. She was, quite simply, a nice girl. A girl who was yet another victim of the infamous Fiore charm.

Rob tried to be philosophical about it. There was no way in hell a girl like that would look twice at a guy like him, not with Danny Fiore in the picture. The very idea was laughable, and the chemistry she had with Fiore was so palpable it was scary. Three days after she arrived in Boston, Travis phoned him around nine-thirty in the morning, dragging him out of bed, and barked, "Is my sister there?"

Rob yawned and raked the fingers of one hand through his tangled mop of hair. "She's not here," he said. "She left around midnight, with Danny."

"Well, she's not here, either. Her bed hasn't been slept in."

"Maybe she went home."

"She didn't go home. Her stuff's still here."

"Well, I wouldn't worry. If she's with Danny, I'm sure she's fine."

"What the hell would she be doing with Danny?"

"Jesus Christ, Trav, what do you think they're doing? I highly doubt they're playing pinochle."

There was absolute silence at the other end of the phone. And then Travis said, "If you're implying what I think you are—"

He rolled his eyes. "Have you seen the way she looks at him?"

"My sister's not that kind of girl. She's engaged, for Christ's sake! Besides, I warned her to stay away from him. I told her what kind of guy he is." Travis went silent for a few seconds. "You don't really think—oh, man, he wouldn't dare. Would he? I swear to God, if that son of a bitch so much as lays a finger on her, I'll cut off his gonads and cram 'em down his throat!"

This probably wasn't the time to divulge to Travis what Casey had confessed to him the night before, that she'd thought she wanted to marry the fiancé back home, until she met Danny Fiore. She'd asked Rob for advice, and he'd told her to follow her heart. In Rob MacKenzie's book, that was always the best policy. Keep a cool head, and make your choices in life based on what you really wanted, not on what other people thought was best for you.

It was the way he lived his life, and he believed it would be a much happier world if everybody followed that philosophy.

So he and Trav wandered over to Avery Street and banged on the door of Danny's crappy room, but the only answer they got was from the guy across the hall, who cracked open his door, glared at them, and said, "Nobody's home. Some people work at night, you know. Get lost!"

By this time, Travis was a wreck. "Should I call the cops?" he said.

"And tell them what? That your sister, who's a grown woman, seems to have taken off with your buddy without telling you? Sure. I think that's a great idea. Let's go find a pay phone right now."

"Fuck you, MacKenzie."

He patted Trav's shoulder and said, "They'll show up, sooner or later."

And they did. Eighteen hours later, the two of them were sitting in a huddle on the front stoop of Trav's Joy Street apartment building when they saw Danny's Chevy chugging up the hill. In classic Boston driver style, Danny nosed the Bel Air to the curb in a spot that would have nicely fit a Volkswagen Beetle, leaving the ass end hanging out into the narrow street. Danny stepped out of the car, drew Casey out the driver's door behind him, and closed the door. Then he backed her up against the car and laid one on her, right there in front of her brother and anybody else who happened to be looking. She took his face between her hands and they proceeded to steam up Beacon Hill like it had never been steamed before.

Travis started to rise to his feet, and in the hopes of preventing a homicide, Rob grabbed his arm and yanked him back down onto the stoop. Then, as casually as though they'd just come back from a five-minute trip to the corner store, the two lovebirds strolled hand-in-hand to the front stoop where Rob and Travis were sitting.

This time, he couldn't hold Travis back. On his feet with both fists clenched, Trav said to Danny, "You are a dead man."

And Casey said quietly, "Trav."

"Shut up," her brother said without looking at her. "I'm not talking to you. I'll deal with you later. After I clean up the street with this motherf—"

More forcefully this time, she said, "Travis!"

Her brother's head turned in her direction, and he scowled. "What?"

And she and Danny held aloft their left hands, sporting shiny new matching gold wedding bands.

Casey

The curtain fluttered at the window, nudged by the same air that cooled the sweat from their skin. She lay on one hip, drowsy and sated, her head on his shoulder, an arm wrapped around him, their legs tangled like limp strands of spaghetti. From her vantage point, she had an up-close-and-personal view of the entire lean length of him. He had a beautiful body. Beautiful was probably a silly word to describe a man, but it was the only word that fit. Rob MacKenzie was built for speed. Slender, but nicely put together, with broad shoulders, a narrow waist, and that sexy triangle of hair, shades darker than the hair on his head, that marched from breastbone to pelvis. A hard, flat belly, and muscles in all the right places.

Farther south, he was generously endowed, those slender hips of his born to fit between a woman's thighs. His long legs were lanky but strong, knees and ankles still bony, no matter how much he'd filled out over the years. And there was something about his feet, those exquisitely sculpted feet, that always made her mouth go dry.

If anybody had told her, seventeen years ago, that one day they'd wind up here, she wouldn't have believed them. Not that she hadn't loved him right from the beginning, but she'd loved him in a sweet, best-friends kind of way. She'd certainly never thought of him as husband material. Not back then. At twenty, Rob had been gaunt, scrawny, all knees and elbows, still growing into his feet. Cute as a button, with those green eyes and that glorious mass of golden curls he hardly ever remembered to comb, but he'd possessed a fashion sense that was nothing less than abysmal. Although he was always immaculately clean—and smelled heavenly—he dressed as though he'd picked his clothes, blindfolded, from a Goodwill box.

In spite of his fashion sense, or lack thereof, he'd been smart. Scary smart. When they first started working together, she hadn't even known how to read music. She'd been pulling the notes out of her head with the help of a pitch-perfect ear, her mother's antique concert Steinway, and a portable cassette recorder. He'd been the one to teach her. Pretty much everything she knew about music, Rob MacKenzie had taught her, so long ago that the two of them had been little more than the amorphous, embryonic beginnings of the people they would eventually become.

He'd been a scrawny twenty-year-old guitar wizard, still living at home in Southie with his parents, and fresh from a two-year stint at Boston's Berklee College of Music. She'd been an eighteen-year-old bride, radiant after her elopement with a sinfully handsome blue-eyed singer with huge ambitions and a powerful, soaring tenor that sent chills racing up and down her spine. She and Rob had been drawn to each other, two creative souls who somehow instinctively understood that whatever they created as partners would be exponentially greater than the sum total of its individual parts.

Seventeen years later, he was still teaching her. Except that the things he taught her now were more likely to be X-rated.

She knew women were supposed to reach their sexual peak in their mid-thirties. But she'd never expected this kind of raging inferno. Was it her age, or was it the man himself? Generic, thirty-something female hormones, or Casey-and-Rob-specific pheromones? There was no way to determine, with any degree of certainty, the answer to that question. All she knew for sure was that sometimes she wanted to inhale him. Wanted to swallow him alive. Wanted to meld with him in a frantic, violent coupling, wanted to wrap herself around him and rock him hard and fast until they both forgot their own names.

She'd always liked sex. What was there not to like? But in spite of the thirteen years she'd spent as Danny's wife, she'd been woefully naïve about a lot of things. Rob MacKenzie had taken her to places she'd never even imagined. Despite the fact that her first husband had been an international sex symbol, Danny had been surprisingly Puritanical and vanilla in his approach to sex, and she'd been too innocent to know the difference.

There was nothing vanilla about Rob MacKenzie, in or out of bed. There wasn't a shy bone in his body, and he possessed a "damn the torpedoes, full speed ahead!" attitude towards life that sometimes left her breathless and scrambling to keep up. An inventive lover, he enjoyed experimenting, and was willing to try anything at least once. For her part, she was an enthusiastic participant in his experiments, even the ones that left them rolling in hysterical laughter. He liked to talk during sex. Sometimes, he whispered sweet nothings so touching she melted. Other times, his language was crude enough to be shocking. Embarrassing.

And extremely titillating, a heated turn-on for a woman who'd been raised to wear her skirts at a respectable length and her shirts buttoned all the way to the collar, a woman who'd barely uttered any word stronger than "hell" or "damn" until she was past thirty.

Sometimes, even after a year of marriage, the transition from friends to lovers still felt awkward. Sometimes, she was overwhelmed by the complexity of her emotions. Her feelings for him had seemed clear-cut before, but now those clear waters were muddied. Who was this gorgeous, sexually-charged man who could turn her limp and pliable and ready to rumble with nothing more than a heated glance across a crowded room? What had he done with the sweet, funny, kindhearted guy she'd married, the man who was her best friend, her mentor, her keeper of secrets? What had happened to the demure and idealistic young woman she'd once been? Surely, she could find that woman again, if only she could figure out how to meld, in her own mind, the best friend and the steamy lover into the same man.

"You okay?"

She raised her head to look at him. Swept her damp hair back from her face and said, "I'm fine."

"Then why am I suddenly getting all these weird vibes?"

"They're all in your head. There are no weird vibes."

"You can't say that. They're my vibes. You can't take 'em away from me. What's wrong?"

"Nothing's wrong. I'm just thinking, that's all."

"About?"

She closed her eyes, burrowed back against his shoulder, and ran a finger down the center of his chest. Smiled when she felt goose bumps rise on his skin. "If you must know, I was thinking about evolution."

"Evolution," he said. "Of course. That's what I always think about after sex."

"Oh, stop. Not that kind of evolution."

"No slimy amphibious creatures climbing up out of the primordial goop and exchanging gills and fins for lungs and legs? Good to know."

"Our evolution. Yours and mine. The evolution of our relationship."

"So why the weird vibes?"

"It's just—" She rolled onto her stomach and rested her chin on her folded arms. "Sometimes, I still have trouble with the transition. Sometimes, I'm not sure who I am any longer. Or who you are. There's this one guy I've loved since the beginning of time, and he's my sweet and wonderful best friend. And then there's this hot, sexy guy who turns me inside out every time he touches me. It's all so complicated, and tangled, and the threads run every which way, and I'm having trouble seeing the two of you as the same guy. Sometimes it feels as though I've traded in my best friend for that hot, sexy guy, and I'm struggling because I'm not quite sure how to deal with it."

Those green eyes softened, and he slid down in the bed until they were nose to nose. "I haven't gone anywhere," he said. "I'm still here."

"Yes, but now you're naked."

He flashed her one of those grins, the kind that always melted her, clear to the marrow. "You say that like it's a bad thing."

"Trust me. You, naked, is a spectacularly good thing."

"So this whole lust scenario isn't one-sided?"

She raised an eyebrow. "You actually have to ask that question?"

"I was just testing you." He circled a hand around her ankle and pressed a soft kiss to the calf of her leg. "Do you ever stop to think about it? What you and I accomplished? All those years of working together. All those songs we wrote. Pieces of you, pieces of me. When we put those pieces together, like a jigsaw puzzle, magic happened."

"I think about it a lot. When I held that first 45 record in my hands, everything changed for me. It all became real. It was a killer song, and we only got better as the years went on."

"*Heart of Darkness*. That little gem made us big fish in a small pond."

"It did. Sometimes I still think about the two of us, going out to hawk that record to the local radio stations. Me in my mother's pearls, a thrift shop business suit, and your sister's shoes. You came to my door looking like a rag picker, in a decrepit old Army jacket and the most hideous paisley print shirt I'd ever seen. I had to raid Danny's closet to make you semi-presentable."

"And then you turned around and covered your eyes while I changed into your husband's clothes."

"It wouldn't have been appropriate for me to watch."

"And you tied Danny's necktie for me, and you told me I should wear green more often, because—"

"—it brought out the color in those nice green eyes of yours. I meant every word of it. You were so damn cute."

"Me?" he said, taken aback. "Cute?"

"Absolutely adorable, with those gorgeous green eyes and that killer smile. Not to mention that sweet little ass."

He raised both eyebrows. "You were checking out my ass?"

"Certainly not. I was a happily married lady. I simply noticed it, in a strictly non-sexual, extremely scientific way. You wore your pants very tight back in the day. It was impossible not to…appreciate…what they were displaying."

"Hot damn, Fiore." He grinned from ear to ear. "You were totally checking out my ass."

She rolled her eyes. "Sometimes, MacKenzie, you're such a guy."

"My poor, battered ego thanks you."

"You can cut the blarney. There's not a thing wrong with your ego." She softened. "I just loved you to pieces back then, you know."

"Did you?"

"Part of it, I think, is that I was so in awe of your talent. I still am. You have whole symphonies living inside your head, and you pull them out so effortlessly to share with the world. And part of it is that you always took care of me. You kept us from starving to death when Danny was too wrapped up in his music to even notice the refrigerator was empty."

"I couldn't let you starve."

"No. You being you, that's not something you could ever do. And I have so much respect for the person you are. But that's still not all of it. I think the biggest reason I was so crazy about you was because you *got* me. You really, truly got me, in a way nobody else on this planet has ever done before or since. You got me, and you accepted me for who I was. And that, my friend, is a priceless commodity."

"That day we went out hawking *Heart of Darkness*, I thought you were so ballsy. Quiet, demure little you, bluffing your way in to see all those deejays, just so you could get them to listen to our record. Gave me a whole new perspective of who you were." He ran the tip of his finger along the inside of her thigh. "Gutsy broad."

"You were right there with me, hotshot, brilliantly playing off whatever outrageous thing I said. We had a regular good cop/bad cop routine going. And it worked, didn't it?"

"For the most part. We only got tossed out on our asses a couple of times."

"It got us the airplay we needed. That was all that mattered."

"You impressed the crap out of me. You were scared shitless that day, but you forged ahead anyway."

"I was terrified. But how did you know?"

"Geez, Fiore, I don't know. Maybe the fact that you spent half the day in various bathrooms, tossing your cookies? It was either a really bad case of the flu, or abject terror, brought on by your own audacity."

"You don't miss much, do you?"

"I'm a wizard. We know all and see all." He pressed a kiss to the crook of her elbow. "You do realize I had a wicked crush on you back then?"

She raised an eyebrow. "This I did not know. Maybe because you never told me."

"I couldn't very well tell you. You were Danny's wife, and totally off-limits. I had to settle for what I could get." He rested his head against her knee, his cheek warm against her skin. "When he wasn't around, you were mine. In a strictly non-sexual, extremely scientific way. The minute he walked into the room, you forgot I was there." He shrugged. *"C'est la vie."*

Regret clutched at her heart. She brushed her knuckles across his cheek. "Oh, Flash," she said.

He kissed her hand. "That was a long time ago. I got over it." He drew her back into his arms. "On the other hand, you might say that early passion was rekindled a while back."

She circled her arms around his neck. "Sounds intriguing. Maybe you could tell me more about it."

"I can do better than that. I can show you. The kid isn't due home for a couple more hours."

"But aren't you hungry? What about the pizza?"

"Hey, it's not often these days that I get a whole naked afternoon with my girl. The pizza will just have to wait."

"I feel flattered. You actually chose me over food."

He rolled her onto her back. "There will never come a time," he said, "when I won't choose you over food."

***

The next morning, while Rob was puttering in the studio and Paige was still asleep, Casey cut a few of the blood-red roses from the garden outside her back door, put them in a bottle of water, and drove to the cemetery.

His grave sat high on a hill, beneath a towering elm, where wildflowers bloomed in abundance between the gravestones and a breeze continually rustled the tall wild grasses that grew nearby. She knelt before a simple granite headstone that read *Daniel Fiore 1951-1987* and with her bare hands, dug into the moist soil, fashioning a trench just deep enough to hold the makeshift vase and prevent it from toppling. "I brought you roses, *caro mio*," she said. "A rich and beautiful red. You'd love them."

She rocked back on her heels and contemplated this peaceful place where he rested. "I've been thinking about you a lot lately." He didn't answer, but it didn't matter. Death had turned Danny Fiore into a good listener. She tugged at a tuft of grass. "The other day, I was out in the garden, and a couple of those big Huey choppers flew over the house. I don't know where they came from, or what they were doing way out here in the middle of nowhere. But those old protective instincts never die, do they? For an instant, my heart stopped, and I automatically looked around to see where you were."

Sixteen years ago, she'd watched him—six feet four inches and a hundred and ninety pounds of edgy, cynical man—drop to the kitchen floor of their Boston apartment and curl into a shuddering ball with his arms wrapped around his head at the sound of those whirring blades passing overhead. By the time she'd figured out what was happening and rushed to slam the window shut, it was too late; the damage was already done. There was nothing left to do but kneel beside him on the floor, wrap her arms around him, and hold him until the shuddering ended and his galloping heart slowed and his breathing stopped hitching.

Post-traumatic stress disorder. Back then, neither of them had known there was a name for it. Back then, nobody talked about it. Nobody spoke about the horrific nightmares, awash in unspeakable atrocities. Nobody admitted to waking in the middle of the night, crying and shaking. He'd called it his dirty little secret, and for more than a dozen years, she'd carried that terrible burden right along with him. Nobody knew. Not even their closest friends, not even Rob, who had spent several of those years living with them. For all that time, she'd helped Danny to keep the black, broken thing inside him hidden away from the rest of the world.

But no matter how hard she tried, no matter how hard she'd loved him, she hadn't been able to fix it. She'd been too young and too naïve back then to understand it wasn't something that could be fixed. Danny Fiore might have left Vietnam behind, but Vietnam had never left him. It had eaten away at him for two decades, corroding his insides and tainting every aspect of his life. In the end, it had killed him. It just took twenty years to get around to it.

"Sometimes," she told him now, "I can almost feel you standing behind me, feel your breath on the back of my neck. Or see you turning a corner a split second before I get to it. Almost, but not quite there. Some phantom presence. Then I realize it's not really anything new. Because sometimes I felt that way even when you were alive."

He'd been gone for nearly four years. It didn't seem possible. He'd told her once, when they were ridiculously young and madly in love and trying to glue things back together after she found out he'd cheated on her, that if anything ever happened to

him, she should get married again. Marriage, he'd said, was
something she did well. She hadn't wanted to hear it, hadn't
wanted to imagine anything might ever happen to him. They were
both going to live forever, weren't they?

In the distance, the lawn mower picked up a rock and emitted
a sharp grinding noise before resuming its staccato buzz. "You
were right, you know," she told him now. "I like being married. I
always did. I think I'm good at it. And I'm happy with him.
Sometimes I miss you so much it's an ache inside me, but I'm
happy, Danny, for the first time in years."

She raised her face to the morning sun and contemplated the
vastness of the blue sky overhead. "Something amazing happened.
Remember when you told me that if Rob would only settle down
and have kids, we could borrow his? Well, he just found out he
has a daughter. Her name is Paige, she's fifteen years old, and
she's come to live with us."

There was no confirmation on his end, but she knew he was
listening. "Of course I realize she can't be a replacement for
Katie." Nothing and nobody would ever fill the permanent Katie-
size hole inside her. "But I think it will be a healing experience,
having another little girl to love. She won't take Katie's place in
my heart, but she'll take her own place, and I hope it will help."

She plucked a buttercup and tickled herself under the chin.
Sighed, and said, "Everything just went to pieces after Katie died.
I know I blamed it all on you, but it wasn't all your fault. I should
have fought harder to save our marriage. I was just so tired of
fighting. It seemed as though I'd done nothing but fight to hold us
together right from the start. I didn't expect marriage to be easy,
but sometimes, Danny, you made it so much harder than it needed
to be. When Katie died, I was so furious. With you, with the
universe. I'd spent so many years taking care of you, and when we
lost Katie, for the first time ever I stopped caring about your pain
and started worrying about my own instead. I'm so sorry. You
were hurting so much, and instead of helping you, I let you pull
away from me.

"I don't know if you ever thought about this," she continued,
"but I think about it a lot. About how random life is. About how a
single decision, a seemingly innocuous instant in time, can alter the
course of your life. All these little decisions we make every day?

They're all connected. And once a decision is made, once a path is taken, everything else falls into place like dominoes. If only I hadn't gone to New York, if only you'd taken Katie to the hospital sooner, would she still be with us? If only we hadn't bought the house in Maine, you would never have been on that snowy Connecticut highway on that December afternoon. Would you still be alive? Or would Fate-with-a-capital-F have sent a chunk of ice falling from a 747 out of LAX to bonk you on the head, sitting on your own deck in California? I wish I had the answer to that question, because sometimes I feel so guilty. If I hadn't taken you back, you might still be alive. And how different would my life be now?"

She knew it was pointless to speculate. So why couldn't she stop doing it? *If only* were the two most useless words in the English language. She couldn't change the past; today was the only thing that was real. And she was so happy with her life today. As much as she'd loved him, she was so much happier now than she'd been with Danny. But if he'd lived, eventually she would have been forced to make a choice. And, God help her, she still wasn't sure she would have made the right one.

"He's a good man," she said, sounding defensive to her own hyper-critical ears. "What I have with him—it's nothing like what you and I had. There's no comparison. It's apples and oranges. He's the best thing that ever happened to me. The most amazing man I've ever known."

Her chest tightened, making it hard to breathe. She should stop coming here. It was bad for her mental health. Every time she left here, she felt so disoriented, her loyalties so divided, it always took her a while to regain her equilibrium. To get past the guilt she experienced on so many levels. Not only because she felt some measure of illogical responsibility for his death. Not only because she'd fallen in love with Rob while she was still married to Danny. But also because she'd survived and he hadn't.

She'd walked away from the crash. Bloodied, bruised, and in shock, but alive. He'd left in a body bag. And no matter how many times her rational side reminded her of how ridiculous she was being, her irrational side continued to feel survivor guilt. Why had she survived, when he hadn't? Had it truly been an accident, or was it all preordained? Did she have some reason for being on this planet that she hadn't yet discovered? Had he already done whatever he'd been sent here to accomplish? Or was it decided not by Fate-with-a-capital-F but by something as random and meaningless as where they'd each been sitting when the car went off the road?

It was a question she'd never be able to answer, and suddenly the unanswered questions, the memories, the guilt, were too much for her.

"I can't be here anymore," she said, possibly to Danny, more likely to herself. "I have to leave now. I'll come back another time."

And she fled, rushing down the hillside to the car she'd left parked on the grassy shoulder of the road. She climbed in and slammed the door, inserted the key and cranked the Mitsubishi's starter. The engine roared to life. For an instant, she lay her forehead against the steering wheel and closed her eyes as her stomach roiled with nausea.

"Get a grip," she muttered. She raised her head, put the car into gear, and pointed it in the direction of home.

Rob

She'd been to the goddamn cemetery again.

That grave site, high on a hill, was her own personal Mecca, and his wife went there with pious regularity to pray to her fallen god of rock & roll. Even when she didn't tell him where she'd been, he always knew. She came home reeking of it. For hours afterward, the weirdness vibes would emanate from her like strong perfume on a hot summer day, while his stomach felt like he'd swallowed razor blades. Before they got married, she'd sworn to him that she had let go of Danny, that she'd put him behind her. But it simply wasn't true. She might have made a valiant effort to exorcise her first husband, but it hadn't worked. Danny Fiore still lived inside the heart, inside the head, of the woman he loved. And Rob MacKenzie didn't know what to do with that knowledge.

For more than a dozen years, he and Casey had been something more than friends, something less than lovers. Danny had always stood there between them, larger than life. The interrelationships between the three of them, both personal and professional, had been so complex. Then Danny was gone, ripped away from them suddenly, senselessly, and without warning.

He'd had this crazy notion when they wed that because they were so solid, because of all those years of being Casey-and-Rob, the adjustments that plagued other newly-married couples wouldn't touch them. But he'd been wrong. There were times—infrequent times, fleeting times, but still very real times—when he actually wondered if they'd done the right thing. Maybe, he thought, they should have waited a little longer, dated for a while before taking the matrimonial plunge.

Then he'd look back over the years of their relationship and realize how crazy that sounded. How long was a man supposed to wait? Sixteen years should be long enough. And what would have been the point of dating? After all those years of living inside each other's pockets, inside each other's heads, they already knew everything they needed to know about each other.

No, getting married hadn't been a mistake. The mistake would have been to wait any longer. This was the woman he was meant to grow old with, to make babies with, to rock on the porch with in their doddering old age. There was respect between them, and tenderness, and a connection he'd never experienced with any other human being. The attraction between them was explosive, the sex spectacular. None of those things was the problem. The problem was Danny Fiore, the elephant in the living room, the invisible landmine they both tiptoed around for fear of stepping on it and blowing the whole thing sky-high.

He tried not to let it bother him, but sometimes the resentment bubbled up inside him until he wanted to scream. Because sometimes, he felt invisible. Sometimes, he felt as though he'd simply stepped into Danny's shoes, Danny's life, and nobody had even noticed that he wasn't Danny. After all, he was living in Danny's house. Sitting on Danny's couch, watching movies on Danny's VCR. Lathering himself in Danny's shower, and sleeping with Danny's wife.

Even though, technically, she was *his* wife now, how much had really changed? Aside from the sex, their relationship was pretty much what it had always been: They were, first and foremost, friends. They took care of each other, nurtured each other, kissed each other's boo-boos when the world hurled painful slings and arrows, and complemented each other's strengths and weaknesses. Nothing had really changed. Except that they'd stopped working together.

And it was all his fault.

The two of them had started writing songs together pretty much by accident. One afternoon, he brought Danny's wife a half-finished song he'd been writing, thinking that maybe she could add some lyrics to it. They sat down at Danny's old upright piano to work on it. Hours later, when Fiore came home from work, they were still there, sitting in the dark because neither of them had even noticed the sun had gone down and the sunny day had turned to twilight.

Casey was fond of telling anybody who would hold still long enough to listen that everything she knew about music, he had taught her. And it was partly true, except that she was deliberately forgetting the road ran both ways, that she'd taught him as much as he'd taught her. True, he'd spent months tutoring her, passing on to her every bit of music theory he'd picked up in two years sitting in a classroom at Berklee. The rest of what he'd taught her came straight from inside him, more a matter of instinct than of factual information.

They were coming at this songwriting gig from different places. Her major influences were folk/rock artists like Carole King and Carly Simon and Jackson Browne. His tastes were more eclectic: anything blues-based, anything Motown, anything written by Becker and Fagen. Her favorite album was Carole King's *Tapestry*; his was Steely Dan's *Can't Buy a Thrill*. Pretty much the only thing they agreed on was that *Stairway to Heaven* was the greatest rock song ever written. It was a little unconventional, the way they connected, but Rob MacKenzie had never been one to concern himself with rules. He just made up his own rules as he went along.

Because they were coming from such different places, they butted heads on a regular basis. Sometimes he won; sometimes she did. They might not agree on much, but they both knew instinctively that the marriage of these two vastly different sensibilities created something that was absolute dynamite. He taught her how to write a song with multiple layers of meaning; she taught him how to write one with commercial appeal. They both understood that the primary currency any song possessed was its emotional impact. Although they both wrote music, both wrote lyrics, he was better at expressing emotion through musical notation, while she was a vastly superior lyricist.

When they hit a wall, when the music or the lyrics wouldn't come, or they couldn't settle a disagreement, they would set the work aside, and they'd play the piano and sing together. Just fooling around, being silly, having fun. It was never their own music they sang—because that was work, and this was play—but other people's. Sixties pop, early Beatles, fifties doo-wop. Anything that would give them the opportunity to harmonize. They'd take turns, one singing lead while the other sang harmony. Then they'd swap parts. Neither of them had the kind of vocal talent Danny possessed, but they could both hold their own, and their voices blended into the sweetest of harmonies. Most of the time, they sounded amazing together. Once in a while, one of them would drop the ball and trip up the other one, and they'd collapse over the keyboard in fits of uncontrollable laughter.

Other times, when they needed a break from work, they'd go out and walk around the city, and they'd just talk. About the music, about the writing, about life and love and family. About hopes and dreams and disappointments. About her marriage, and about his lackluster love life. She was wise and warm and nurturing, and no matter what problem he might be experiencing, she always seemed to have the right answer.

The relationship that developed between Rob MacKenzie and his best friend's wife was impossible to classify, and after a while, he stopped trying and just accepted it for what it was. There was nothing sexual about it, nothing romantic. He'd long since gotten over his initial reaction to her, and as far as she was concerned, there was only one man on the planet, and that man's name was Danny Fiore. What they felt for each other was strictly platonic. They were simply two people with an extraordinary friendship who just happened to be male and female.

Except that there was something else, something he couldn't put his finger on, some inexplicable connection that went beyond simple friendship. Sometimes it almost felt like a marriage, only without all that messy sex stuff. Whatever this thing was between them, it was genuine, it was intense, it went gut-deep, and it wasn't going away any time soon.

In spite of the fact that she was one of the strongest women he'd ever met, he had this big-brother protective vibe going on. Sometimes Danny did stupid-ass stuff, and somebody had to make sure she was covered. Travis still hadn't fully forgiven Danny for seducing his kid sister, and Trav's idea of protection was so far over the top it was laughable. So it was up to Rob to be the one who always had her back.

He never questioned whether Danny loved her; once that gold ring went on his finger, Fiore was a changed man. But sometimes he seemed like an emotional cripple, and for whatever reason, Casey seemed to believe he needed coddling. So while she took care of Danny, Rob took care of her. It was an odd little three-way thing they had going, but for some crazy reason, it worked. For years and years.

Until one night, on a moonlit beach in the Bahamas, he screwed it all up.

For the past four years, he'd wandered alone through an arid musical desert. After four years, he should have adjusted. After four years, it shouldn't still feel as though his right arm had been amputated. But it did, and he hadn't yet figured out how to deal with it. For a dozen years they'd worked as a team. A dozen years of making beautiful music together, of living inside each other's heads. Through the lean years, when they struggled and starved. Through the fat years, when they wrote and produced hit after hit for Danny Fiore, when they won Grammy after Grammy for the magic they created. For a dozen years, they'd meshed like cogs in a wheel.

Then Katie died, and Casey's marriage to Danny went south. She hadn't spoken to her estranged husband in ten months on the night when Rob MacKenzie, mildly sloshed and without conscious intent, had kissed her on that damned beach and started something they couldn't possibly finish. The next day, he'd given her an ultimatum: fish or cut bait.

She'd chosen to fish. She'd picked Danny.

And their twelve-year musical partnership had completely unraveled.

***

She came in through the shed and saw him standing at the kitchen sink, and the look on her face said it all. While razor blades danced in his stomach, she crossed the room to him and he closed his arms around her and they clung to each other. After a time, he said bitterly, "Why do you keep doing this to yourself?" *And to me*, he thought, but didn't say it.

"Don't," she said. "Please don't. Just hold me, and don't say anything."

He opened his mouth to speak. But the words wouldn't come out. All the garbage rolling around inside him had rendered him utterly incapable of expressing what he wanted, what he needed, to say.

So he did what he always did. He shut up and just held her.

Paige

The start of the school year was always the same. The crisp
September weather, the guys with their shiny new sneakers that
would be scuffed and dirty by next week; the girls with their MTV-
inspired definitions of cutting-edge fashion. Textbooks that
needed to be covered by week's end and a locker that was located
several city blocks away from any of your classes. *The Breakfast
Club*, her all-time favorite movie, pretty much had high school
nailed: you had your jocks and your nerds, your popular kids and
your burnouts and your untouchables. You had yearbook club and
glee club and French club. Lousy cafeteria food, stunning
boredom, and a major jonesing for the lazy days and sandy beaches
of summer.

And algebra. God, how she hated algebra! While Mrs.
Silverburg wrote equations on the board in her spidery
handwriting, Paige doodled in her notebook. When the bell rang,
she was the first one out of her seat, snatching up her backpack and
heading for the cafeteria. The food might be lousy, but it was
sustenance. Juggling her backpack and her food tray, she stood
lost in the bustling crowd, searching for an empty table. When she
found one in a far corner, she squeezed between packed tables,
past snotty girls and obnoxious guys, finally dropping the
backpack and the tray on the table.

For the first two days of the semester, she'd eaten lunch with
Luke and a couple of his geeky friends. But after he dropped
Physics and picked up Lab Bio, they no longer shared the same
lunch period. Since hell would freeze rock solid before she'd sit
with those geeks without Luke there as a buffer, she sat by herself,
a lone island of solitude in the midst of chaos.

At the next table, a trio of girls who looked like they spent
too much time watching *Beverly Hills, 90210* were whispering and
giggling, undoubtedly over something trite and meaningless.
Sometimes, she really hated chicks. They were so superficial.
Guys were much more straightforward. Simpler. And their
interests didn't revolve around hair or makeup or the latest teen
idol. Paige picked up her fork and poked at the UFO—
unidentified food object—on her tray. The gray sludge may or

may not have been shepherd's pie. The jury was still out on that. She thought longingly of her stepmother's cooking, which was the second-best thing about being dragged off to this alternate universe.

She was halfway through the UFO when a red and gray L.L. Bean backpack dropped heavily to the table, and the first-best thing about being dragged off to this alternate universe sat down across from her. Those dark eyes studied her wordlessly, and a funny little flutter tickled her stomach. "Hey," she said, surprised. This was her third day at Jackson High, and the first time she and Mikey Lindstrom had crossed paths.

"Hi. How's it going?"

She set down her fork. "It's high school," she said. "How good could it be?"

"That's a valid point. You settling in okay?"

"As okay as can be expected. How come you're not eating lunch?"

"Free period. I already ate."

"Oh." She cast about for something else to say, but she'd never been good at small talk, and every time Mikey Lindstrom walked into the room, her palms began to sweat.

In an unnerving and intimate gesture, he reached out and plucked the dinner roll from her tray and tore it into two pieces. "Dad says you're in his sophomore English lit class."

"Lucky me."

"What else are you taking?" He popped a piece of bread into his mouth.

"Spanish, Intro to Western Civ, U.S. Government—" She rolled her eyes. "And the icing on the cake, my old friend, Algebra."

"Not a math person?"

"I shudder at the thought."

"If you need help, let me know. I'm a whiz at math."

"I appreciate the offer, but I don't think it would do much good. I'm a hopeless case."

"You severely underestimate my powers." He glanced at the wall clock and finished off the dinner roll. "Better eat faster, the bell rings in two minutes." He stood, picked up the backpack, and she tilted her head so she could see all six feet of him. "If I don't run into you before then," he said, "I'll see you Saturday."

"Saturday?"

"The weekly family get-together?"

"Oh. That."

He almost smiled. The corner of his mouth twitched, and for a second, she thought he was going to lose the battle. But, to her disappointment, Mister Solemn won. Shouldering the heavy backpack, he gave her a final cursory glance, and he was gone. She watched him snake his way through the crowd, greeting and being greeted by a half-dozen people, clearly some kind of demigod in this twisted microcosm of life known as high school.

The bell rang, and she gathered up her things, made her way through the crowd to deposit her tray, then shouldered her backpack and headed off in the direction of her Spanish class. A petite, dark-haired girl in jeans and a pink-and-white-striped knit shirt fell into step with her.

"Hi," the girl said. "You're new here. We have Spanish together. I'm Lissa Norton."

"Paige," she said. "Paige MacKenzie."

"So, what do you think of *Señor* Hooper?" Their Spanish teacher was a short, white-haired man who'd peppered his walls with travel posters, but Paige highly doubted he'd ever left the good old U. S. of A.

"I think it's really lame that he makes us call him *Señor*. This isn't exactly Barcelona. Or even Guadalajara."

"I know. Stupid, isn't it? So, I saw you talking to Mikey Lindstrom. How do you know him?"

She should have known Lissa had an ulterior motive. People were so predictable. And sometimes disappointing. Paige squared her jaw. "He's my step-cousin. My aunt's married to his father. What the hell difference does it make to you?"

"You can pull in the claws, New Girl. I'm on your side. I just thought I should warn you. Your little tête-à-tête did not go unnoticed. The local gossip lines are already burning up with the story."

"What story?"

"New Girl Snags Attention of Hottest Boy in School."

"There is no story. We're related. Our families break bread together."

"Whatever. I just wanted to make sure you were prepared."

She stopped dead in the middle of the hallway, causing a near-collision. Grabbed Lissa by the elbow and dragged her over to the lockers that lined the wall. "What?" she said. "Prepared for what?"

"The jealousy. The hating. Every one of the girls in the prom queen set have made a play for Mikey, but he's shown zero interest. So you can imagine the buzz it generated when he was seen sitting with the new girl. And an underclassman to boot."

"Shit." Not that she was looking to be Miss Popularity. On the other hand, she really hadn't expected to start out in a new school with all her markers in the negative column before she even spoke a word to anyone. If she was going to fail, she'd like to at least do it on her own terms. "Okay," she said. "You know these people. I don't. What do you propose is the best way to deal with it?"

They started walking toward class again. "If there's nothing going on between you and Mikey," Lissa said, "ignore them. It'll eventually die down. If there *is* something going on between you and Mikey, ignore them. It'll eventually die down. Probably."

"Great," she said. "That's just great."

Casey

When she came through the door after her morning run, the first thing she saw was the duffel bag, crammed with clothes, perched on a kitchen chair. Her Samsonite carry-on bag sat on the table, its yawning mouth open and waiting to be filled. But it was the guitar case that cinched the deal. She knew that case, knew it intimately. Could clearly remember the day, seven or eight years ago, when he'd called her and said, "I need help picking out a new guitar, Fiore. Come with me." And even though what she knew about guitars you could put in a thimble, she'd gone with him anyway, had listened intently while he explained the virtues and vices of various brands and models, then watched in mild horror as he pulled out his American Express card and paid six thousand dollars for a Fender Stratocaster. Although he kept it tuned and polished and played it regularly, he never used it for studio work. It was his performance guitar, and that one fact told her that wherever he was headed, the trip would probably involve buses or planes.

Her stomach went into free fall. It had finally arrived, the moment she'd dreaded since the day they married: He was leaving her. Not forever, of course. But once the precedent was set, more partings would inevitably follow. She should know; she'd lived the life for years with Danny. She understood how it worked. That didn't mean she had to like it.

He came into the room, carrying a fistful of toiletries. Toothbrush, toothpaste, deodorant. When he saw her standing there, he stopped dead and said, "Hey."

She glanced at him, at the assorted luggage, then back at him. "Is it something I did? Something I said?"

"'scuse me?"

"I really thought you'd give the marriage a little more time before you decided to bail."

"Hah. Very funny. You should take that comedy act of yours on the road."

"It seemed funny to me. And it looks like you're the one who's going on the road. Is there something you forgot to tell me?"

"You have no idea," he said, cramming toiletries into the bag as he spoke, "how sorry I am to be springing this on you without any warning. But you weren't here, and it was a crisis situation, and Chico needed an answer right away. So I made an executive decision without consulting the boss."

"Chico?"

"Chico Rodriguez. You remember him?"

"Of course. We drove down to Atlantic City with him back in '78."

"Woman, sometimes that steel-trap mind of yours terrifies me. How the hell do you remember what year it was?"

"It was while Danny and I were separated. The first time." After the miscarriage. And the infidelity. Both of those incidents had forever altered her life, and both were memories better left untouched.

"Well, a while back, Chico started a band called Cold House. They're on the last leg of a tour right now, and the lead guitarist just ruptured a disc in his back."

"Ouch."

"He'll be out of commission for a while, and of course, they can't function as a band without a lead guitar. They need somebody who can learn all their material in forty-eight hours, or they'll have to cancel the rest of the tour."

"And you were at the top of their short list."

"Actually, I *was* their short list."

She closed her eyes, reminded herself to exhale. "How long?"

"That's my girl. No whining, no screaming. She just cuts right to the heart of the matter."

"Damn it, MacKenzie, how long?"

"Three weeks."

She resolved to look at this philosophically. It could be worse. It could be three months. Or three years. "I know the timing couldn't be worse," he said, "with the Paige situation. I'm so sorry to leave you holding the bag. But I'll make it up to you. I promise."

His words sent an icy finger down the center of her spine. "Don't," she said. "Please don't say that."

He zipped the carry-on bag and straightened. Studied her with mild curiosity. "Why?"

"Because that's what Danny used to tell me every time he screwed up. And we both know how that story went."

He squared his jaw. "I'm not Danny."

"No," she said. "You're not."

He lay a hand over his heart and vowed, "As God is my witness, I'll never again promise to make anything up to you. From now on, what you see is what you get."

"Isn't that pretty much how it's always been with you, anyway?"

"Look, if this was my gig, I'd take you with me. You and Paige. There's no way I'd leave you behind if I had a choice. But we're talking low budget here."

"How low?"

"Tiny venues. Under 500 capacity. Roadhouses. A creaky, ancient tour bus. The occasional sleazy motel room, with hot and cold running roaches provided at no extra charge."

Dryly, she said, "Sounds quaint and lovely."

"Picture the most primitive, the most godless and soul-sucking tour we've ever been on. Then multiply the horror factor by ten, and you might have a vague picture of the next three weeks of my life."

"In other words, you're returning to your roots."

"In a manner of speaking." He moved to the refrigerator, opened the door, and stood there surveying its contents.

"I so hate to ask this question, but how much are you being paid to participate in The Tour From Hell?"

Instead of answering, he took out a bottle of Coke, closed the door, turned and leaned those lanky hips against it. Opened the bottle with a soft hiss, squared his shoulders, and just looked at her.

And she shook her head. "What am I supposed to do with you, MacKenzie? You do realize you're one of the most brilliant and sought-after guitarists in the Western Hemisphere, and you keep giving away your services for free?"

He raised the Coke to his mouth and took a long, slow swallow. "I don't need the money. If I never worked again a day in my life, I wouldn't need the money."

"That's not the point. The point is that you're devaluing yourself and your work. Tell me this. Did they ask you because you're one of the most brilliant and sought-after guitarists in the Western Hemisphere, or because you're a big enough name to give legitimacy to the rest of their little band of misfits?"

"Probably a little of both. Why does it matter? Sammy Hagar had a solo career before he joined Van Halen. I don't remember you having a problem with that."

"I wasn't married to Sammy. And you're deliberately missing the point."

"I think you're the one who's missing the point. The point is, Chico's running this thing on a shoestring. He's in a bind, and I'm in a position to help him." He crossed his bony ankles and waved the Coke bottle for emphasis. "Look, I've been there. When I had to fire Tony Izzard after he showed up for work so stoned he could barely stand. When Kitty fell off the stage during rehearsal and broke her ankle. I know what it's like to be in the middle of a tour and have to find some way to yank a miracle out of my ass. I couldn't live with myself if I turned him down. I've learned a couple of things over the years I've been in this business. One, you never forget where you came from. And two, you always remain loyal to your friends."

She let out a hard breath. "How can I argue with that philosophy? It's one of the things I admire the most about you, your immutable code of honor. You live your life by it."

"Damn right, I do. So you're not mad at me?"

"Of course I'm not mad at you. You're a grown man. You don't have to ask me for permission to do anything." She crossed the room, and he set down the Coke and wrapped his arms around her. She lay her cheek against his chest. "It's just...three weeks is a long time."

"Ish."

She stiffened, raised her head, met his eyes. "Ish?"

"Three-ish. It could be a little longer. Depending."

"On what?"

"On how well it goes. We could pick up a few more dates if it goes well."

"You're loving this, aren't you? Damn you."

"The getting back on stage and playing part? Absolutely. The leaving you behind part? Not so much."

"I should be used to this by now. After all the years with Danny."

"I hear a 'but' in there."

"But. Most of the time, I hardly noticed when he was gone. This is different."

He flashed her one of those smiles that could turn the most hard-hearted woman into a quivering pile of mush. Leaning closer, he toyed with a strand of her hair and said with an exaggerated Boston accent, "So Momma's gonna miss Poppa wicked bad, is she?"

"Don't flatter yourself, MacKenzie." She tugged her hair away from him and took a step backward. "I'll survive just fine without you. For three-ish weeks. I don't suppose you've talked to Paige."

"I wasn't about to drag her out of school to tell her. One more thing she can hold against me, skipping town without saying good-bye to her. I'm sure she's keeping tally somewhere."

"You can call her later and smooth things over."

"For what it's worth. I honestly don't think she gives a rat's ass whether I live or die."

"She'll grow out of it. She's a teenager. It comes with the territory."

"There's one more thing. Since you're not mad at me, I need a favor."

"Do I dare to ask?"

"My plane leaves for L.A. in three hours. Can you give me a ride to the airport?"

***

She wasn't able to shake the edgy, anxious feeling that took hold of her the moment he was in the air, couldn't figure out what was wrong. They'd been flying away from each other for years, but for some inexplicable reason, watching that 737 carry him into a cloudless blue sky filled her with an uncharacteristic dread. Was it leftover anxiety from the accident? She'd already lost one husband, and had no intention of losing another. Or was it simply the physical act of separation, after they'd been inseparable for so long?

She arrived home ahead of the school bus, and broke the news to Paige that her father would be out of town for an indeterminate time. The kid eyed her coolly, said, "Figures," and headed to her room. Twenty minutes later, Luke pulled into the driveway, honked the horn, and Paige blew through the door, tossing the breathy words, "Band practice," over her shoulder.

Casey killed time with housework. Whenever she was at odds, it was always her drug of choice. She vacuumed, dusted, watered all her plants. Scrubbed lavatories and toilets, the bathtub, the shower stall. She knew it was compulsive behavior, but it was comforting in some twisted way.

Paige called around five to say that she'd been invited to supper at Rose and Jesse's house, and one of the boys would drive her home. Still feeling a little lost, Casey drove to the cemetery, pulled a few weeds, and watered the rosebush she'd planted last year on Katie's grave. The habitually restless ghost of Danny Fiore was oddly still tonight, and she had nothing pressing she needed to talk over with him, so she cut the visit short and went home.

While she was out, Rob had called to leave the number where she could reach him for the next forty-eight hours. He was heading over to the studio so they could start rehearsing right away. God only knew when she'd hear from him again, but at least he was safe on the ground, and she was able to exchange a little of her anxiety for relief.

She picked a late cucumber from the garden, sliced a ripe tomato, made a salad for supper, and ate it alone at the kitchen table. When Paige came home, they watched a movie together before retiring to their rooms for the night. But sleep was elusive. For some reason, she was feeling agitated, weird, a little unglued. The room was too hot, the bed was too empty, and her insides were churning with anxiety. She rolled and flipped and thrashed, until the bedding was a totally disheveled hot mess, and then she lay for hours, watching the hands of the bedside clock move with agonizing sloth. She calculated the time difference between Maine and California, wondered whether he'd even be in his hotel room.

He could be out all night, especially if he had a mere forty-eight hours to learn Cold House's set.

At three-twenty a.m., she gave in, picked up the phone and dialed the number he'd left on her answering machine. In the darkness, she cradled the receiver to her ear, feeling a peculiar sense of déjà vu. How many late-night phone calls had they shared in that dark and murky time after Danny died? Those calls had kept her functioning, had kept her upright and breathing. They'd been an odd blend of comfort and courtship, for there had been no traditional courtship between the two of them. Only fifteen years of emotional foreplay before they became lovers. Nobody would ever accuse her of being conventional when it came to husbands. She'd married Danny three days after they met. With Rob, it had taken sixteen years.

Three thousand miles away, the phone rang. Five times, then six. Just as she was about to give up, he answered, sounding hoarse and muzzy from sleep. Something inside her went all soft, like chocolate left too long in the sun. "Hey," she said.

He paused for an instant, trying to pull himself out of sleep, then said groggily, "Hey."

"I woke you. I'm so sorry."

"S'okay." He made some kind of soft sound in the back of his throat, and her chocolaty insides went softer. "I live to be dragged out of sleep by you." He paused for another instant, then said, "Everything okay?"

"Bad night."

She heard the rustle of bedding. "What's wrong?" He sounded more awake this time.

"Nothing, really. Not anything I can put my finger on. I've been trying for hours, but I can't sleep. I've just been so antsy ever since you left. All jittery and weird."

"That's not like you, babe. If you really didn't want me to go, you should have said something. I could have called Chico back and told him I couldn't do it. You know I would've stayed with you if you asked."

"And that's why I didn't ask. You're a musician. It's what you do. It makes you happy. I would never interfere with that."

"*You* make me happy."

"Maybe it's just that this is the first time we've been apart."

"Ever since the day you tracked me down in Boston and told me we were getting married."

In the darkness, she smiled and said, "I did no such thing."

"I stand corrected. You strongly suggested we get married."

"I proposed to you. That's a little more than a strong suggestion."

"Call it what you want, I'm glad you did it. So you really miss me that much, do you?"

"Apparently so," she said, hearing the surprise in her own voice. She couldn't figure out what was wrong, why she was feeling all weak and shaky and anxious. She'd never been the clingy, needy type of woman, never been the kind to come unglued just because her man was out of town.

"Are you crying, Fiore?"

She swiped at a tear and said, "Of course not."

"You're a really lousy liar. Do you want me to come home? Because if you do—"

"I'm fine now. I just needed to hear the sound of your voice."

"Next time I go out of town, you're coming with me."

"I think that would probably be a good idea. But I'm okay now that I've talked to you. Really."

He cleared his throat and said, "So...are you in bed?"

"I am. Why?"

In a really bad Pepé le Pew accent that sounded more like the Count from Sesame Street—or possibly Zsa Zsa Gabor—he said, "So, *ma cherie*, tell me vhat you're vearing."

She let out a soft snort of laughter. "MacKenzie," she said, "you are such a letch."

"I'm just trying to be accommodating. I figured since it's the sound of my voice you needed, I could talk dirty to you. Get you all hot and bothered, then you could maybe—"

"Very tempting," she said, "but no. There will be no phone sex."

"Fiore, you are such a disappointment as a wife."

She let out another soft breath of laughter. He always had a way of making her feel better. "Babe?" he said.

"What?"

And he said softly, "Hi."

Impossible as it might seem, her sticky liquid insides went even softer. "Hi," she said.

"So Momma misses Poppa, does she?"

"Momma misses Poppa something awful. This bed feels so empty without you in it."

"So does this one. The time will fly by. I promise."

"I know it will. It's not as though I'm all alone in the house. I just didn't have any idea how much I'd miss you. I'm being silly, I know. I've slept alone before. I just need to pull on my big girl panties and buck up."

"The minute I'm done, I'll rush home to you, and we'll party. Just you and me. Alone. In the dark. Clothing optional. Maybe, if you beg, I'll put Smokey on the stereo. If you're really, really nice to me, I might even make it Marvin and Tammi."

"Are you still trying to get me all hot and bothered?"

"You can't blame a guy for trying."

"No, I can't. Especially when it's working so well."

"Yeah?" he said with interest. "So, we could still try that phone sex thing—"

"Not in this lifetime, my friend."

"That was a pretty emphatic no."

"I'm not that kind of girl, MacKenzie."

"I suppose that probably means you also don't want me to bring you home any sex toys from the big, bad city."

"You're all the sex toy I need."

"Wow. That was good, Fiore. Nice save."

And she laughed and said, "All right, my lunatic guitar man, we both need to get some sleep. Call me tomorrow?"

"What a shame. The minute I start talking about sex toys, I scare her right off. What's that all about?"

"I'm too sweet and innocent to know about things like that."

"And I'm the King of Siam. So, babydoll, since you're not interested in any phone sex tonight—"

"Or ever."

"—I'll call tomorrow. You sure you're okay, kiddo? You sounded pretty shaky there at first."

"I'm fine now. Thanks for putting up with my late-night insanity."

"I'm pretty sure it's written into the marriage contract somewhere. G'night, babe."

She hung up the phone, set it on the bedside table, and was asleep within seconds.

***

It was late afternoon the next day when the knock came on her door. She answered it to find a delivery man standing on the steps holding a florist's box. "Casey MacKenzie?" he said.

"Yes."

"These are for you."

She thanked him, gave him a five-dollar tip, and carried the box inside. Paige had come out of her room to see what was going on. "Flowers," the kid said. "Wow."

Wow was right. She must have really sounded like she was unraveling last night. Casey untied the ribbon and lifted the cover of the box, and she and Paige both gasped when they saw what was inside. A half-dozen of them. Perfect. Exquisite. Delicate. Stunning.

"I've never seen anything like them before," Paige said. "What are they?"

"Orchids," she breathed, staring at them in disbelief. "He sent me orchids."

Other men, ordinary men, sent their wives roses. Only her man sent orchids. Always, he had to be a little different. It was the way he was wired. And he always knew somehow what would please her the most. She'd never been able to figure out how he did it. She picked up the card, thumbed the envelope open, and read the message, neatly printed in the florist's handwriting: *Miss you, baby. Home ASAP. Be ready.*

Behind her, Paige was reading over her shoulder. "What does *Be ready* mean?"

Casey knew precisely what it meant. It was MacKenzie shorthand for the two of them, partying. Alone. In the dark. With Smokey on the stereo and clothing optional.

"Never mind," the kid said. "I figured it out. You just turned as red as the side of that barn out back. Too much information. Way too much information."

"I didn't give you any information."

"Oh, yeah, you did. You know, you guys are way old for that kind of thing. I just—ew."

"What kind of thing?"

"All that lovey-dovey stuff. Kissing in the kitchen. Making googly eyes at each other." Indicating the florist's card, she added, "Now this."

"Too old? I'm thirty-five. He's thirty-seven."

"Like I said. Old."

That night, she was still awake, reading by the light of her bedside lamp, when he called. It was still early, eleven-thirty her time, and when he said, "Hey, gorgeous," those three syllables turned her inside out.

"The orchids are exquisite," she said. "Thank you."

"You're welcome. I just thought you seemed to need cheering up, and since you said no to any, um—toys—I thought orchids would be the next best thing."

"You always know what I need."

"I'm a wizard. You know that."

"And I remain perpetually amazed by your wizardry. So how are the rehearsals going?"

"Very smooth. I think we just might be able to pull this thing off."

"And how's the city of angels?"

"No different than it was when I left. I can't believe I lived here as long as I did. The smartest thing you ever did was to pack your car and drive away from this place."

"I agree. But the memories aren't all bad, are they?"

"No, but the lifestyle…it's plastic and pretentious and utterly meaningless. It's not who I am. It's not who you are. Never has been, for either of us. Speaking of plastic and pretentious, guess who I ran into this morning."

"Who?"

"My ex-wife."

"Oh." No need to ask which one. "The Queen of plastic and pretentious."

"I was headed into the studio, and this big limo pulled up to the curb, and just as I walked by, she stepped out of it. And there we were, face to face on the sidewalk."

"That must have been…interesting. Did she actually speak to you?"

"She really didn't have much of a choice. People were watching. Couldn't let the world see Monique Lapierre being anything less than civil to her ex-husband. The press would tear her to shreds."

"So?"

"We exchanged pleasantries. The old European kiss on both cheeks kind of thing. *How are you? So nice to see you. Have a nice life, and don't let the door hit you in the ass on the way out.*"

"Was it weird? Strange? Did you still have, ah—"

"Feelings for her? Be serious, Fiore. That was a million years ago. I was just a kid, and it was not my finest hour. I'll admit it was a little weird. All that fake civility, just for the sake of appearances. Especially when you consider that the last time I saw her—outside of divorce court, that is—was the night I walked away from that mausoleum she called a house, and half the dishes in the kitchen cupboard came flying out the door behind me."

"You never told me that."

"There are a multitude of things about my marriage to Monique that I've never told you."

"Probably better if we keep it that way."

"Unquestionably better if we keep it that way."

"So…it was not an amicable parting."

"Definitely not. It was a very crazy time in my life. The only emotion I felt today was bafflement. Wondering what the hell I was thinking, taking up with her in the first place."

"I can answer that question for you. Danny summed it up quite nicely when he said you were thinking with what was between your legs, instead of what was between your ears."

"Danny said that?"

"He did. We were both so worried about you. The way she treated you was appalling. She was such a horrible woman. Beautiful, for sure, but her beauty was only skin deep. Underneath it all, she was very, very ugly."

"I don't know if this will make you feel any better, but the outer shell isn't looking so hot these days, either. Underneath all the layers of war paint, she hasn't aged well."

"What a tragedy."

"She hated you so much."

"Believe me, the feeling was mutual. I'd never been deliberately rude to anybody, until Monique decided she was going to keep us away from each other. What I said to her that day— let's just say it wasn't my finest hour, either, and leave it at that. But she had it coming. She was a witch. And I'm being extremely generous, because there are far worse things I could be saying about her. Far worse things, if you must know, that I actually said to her face."

"She told me what you said. The funny thing is, as furious as she made us at the time, she was right all along."

"About what?"

"About you and me. She tried to keep us apart because she thought there was something going on between us—"

"There wasn't anything going on between us! I was married, for God's sake. And pregnant!"

"Yet here we are, a decade later, together. And, quite frankly, very hot for each other. The way we feel about each other now? It was already there between us, buried so deep we didn't know it existed until another half-dozen years went by. But somehow, Monique saw it, and she had this primal recognition of you as her competition."

"I'd prefer to believe she was just psychotic and paranoid."

"Well, yeah. In addition to that. Psychotic and paranoid goes without saying."

"Speaking of hot for each other," she said, "your darling daughter loved the orchids, but she said we're too old to act the way we do."

"What way?"

"I'm thirty-five. You're thirty-seven. We're way too old to be having sex. It's disgusting. *Ew*."

"Who said anything about sex?"

"She asked me what *be ready* meant. Apparently I blushed a brilliant red, which to her delicate sensibilities was far too much information. It painted a picture she really didn't want to imagine."

At the other end of the phone, he let out a soft laugh. "I suppose that at fifteen, thirty-five does seem ancient."

"Positively geriatric."

"In that case, be forewarned, old woman: The minute I'm done with the tour, I'm blowing this Popsicle stand, and when I get home, we're having some of that tepid, geriatric sex that we're really too old for."

"You're such a perv. Be forewarned, old man: I'll be waiting."

Paige

The first postcard arrived three days after he left. On the front was a photo of the famous Hollywood sign, an unwelcome reminder that in her entire fifteen years, she'd never been farther west than Connecticut. On the back was a note written in quirky handwriting that looked like chicken tracks on the page. *I looked for the cheesiest postcard I could find, and this was it. L.A. is a zoo. Smog hovers over the city like a dirty, wet blanket. Thankfully, by the time you read this, I'll be somewhere else. ~ Dad*

Paige snorted. Right. It would be a cold day in hell before she'd think of him as her dad. But it was a novelty, getting mail. She couldn't remember ever receiving mail that was actually addressed to her. So instead of tossing it, she tucked the card inside her algebra book. That was an appropriate place to keep it, since they both—algebra, and the man who'd slept with her mother nine months before she was born—belonged in the same category, the category titled Things of Which Paige is Not Particularly Fond.

The second postcard arrived the next day. Venice Beach. A surfer on a bright yellow board. She'd heard of the place, but didn't know anything about it. Paige flipped the card over. In that same scratchy handwriting, it read: *Casey had an apartment just a couple blocks from here. We used to hang out on the boardwalk. Wish I was there now. Instead, headed for the Great Southwest. Such is the life of a traveling musician. ~ Dad*

She turned the card over, studied the guy on the yellow surfboard, then re-read the message before tucking it into the algebra book along with the first one.

After that, they arrived daily. She wasn't sure how he managed it, traveling on a bus, but for every nowhere place he stopped on the tour, he found a postcard to chronicle his journey, and wrote a personal message to her before he mailed it. At first, it seemed a little intense. A little sketchy, even. Until one day, she realized she was looking forward to getting home after school to see what he'd sent and where he'd been: *Arizona, New Mexico, Texas.* That didn't mean she accepted any part of him, but he wasn't one of those "how are you, I am fine, wish you were here" writers. His little snippets of life and wisdom were entertaining, so she allowed herself to enjoy them without ceding an inch on the issue of their non-relationship.

With school now well underway, life fell into a routine. The pain of her mom's death was still raw, but she was surviving. Sandy had often told her she was tough as nails, and it was true. Nothing could stop Paige MacKenzie. Besides, as it turned out, her father's wife was quiet and non-offensive and, strange as it seemed, with him out of the house, life almost felt…normal. Just two girls rattling around in all that space, the way it had always been with her mom. Casey wasn't one to push the relationship issue. Instead, she took each day as it came, made lemonade out of lemons, and Paige was determined to emulate her quiet strength.

It probably wasn't easy for the woman, having her husband gone like this, especially considering that they were usually joined at the hip. Paige had detected some tension in her stepmother that hadn't been there before, and she was pretty sure it was directly related to being temporarily husbandless. Casey tried to hide it, but she could see it anyway. She knew he called pretty much nightly; she heard the phone ringing at ridiculously late hours, with Casey almost always picking up by the second ring. It was possible that she was a night owl. More likely, she was waiting by the phone for his call.

Either way, the routine was easy and predictable. School every day, band practice with Luke and the boys two or three nights a week, hanging with Lissa on the weekends, and the inescapable Saturday-night family get-together. She and Casey started running together, but because the days had shortened and the sun didn't come up until a half-hour before the school bus arrived, on weekdays they ran in the afternoons, while it was still daylight. Sometimes they talked about inconsequential things. Most of the time, they ran in silence, but it was a relaxed silence.

Her father's wife was an easy person to be with, and Paige wasn't so stupid she didn't realize she'd lucked out with the hand she'd been dealt. Her stepmother could have been a monster. She'd had more than one friend, back in Boston, who'd been saddled with the Stepmother From Hell. Other friends had steered a wide berth around their stepfathers. Pretty much everyone she knew back in the old neighborhood was part of what was now referred to as a blended family. Paige could count on the fingers of one hand the number of kids she knew back home who still lived with both biological parents. Nobody stayed together. Nobody stayed married. Parents changed partners like they were playing musical chairs, and it was always the kids who paid.

Her situation was a little different; it had always been just the two of them, and it was hard to miss something you'd never had. Paige had never given much thought to her lack of a father. But she'd witnessed enough divorces among the parents of her friends to know how it ripped the heart out of a kid to see Dad packing his suitcases and leaving.

So things at home, with Casey, were low-key and calm. School, on the other hand, was a suckfest. In spite of the fact that Mikey hadn't sought her out again—or even bumped into her in the hallway—she was still the recipient of the venomous sting of rejection, as only a teenage girl could dish it out. The guys were friendly enough, but the girls—at least most of them—gave her the cold shoulder. It was more of a passive shunning than the active aggression she'd anticipated. As a kid who'd grown up on the streets of Southie and could give as good as she got in a down-and-dirty rumble, she found them laughable. Was this the best they could do? If so, then screw them. Life was too short to waste it worrying about a bunch of snotty girls who were so self-involved that their idea of punishment was to deprive her of their magnificent presence. If she wouldn't play the game by their rules, they'd just pick up their marbles and flounce off home. Well, boo-fucking-hoo.

She didn't need them anyway. She had real friends. She had Lissa, who'd quickly become her staunch ally, and Luke, who was fun and a little crazy and always up for hanging out. She even had Luke's geeky band mates, who weren't all that bad once she got to know them. Besides, once she graduated and blew this crappy town forever, she would never again have to set eyes on any of those stupid chicks, so she just put one foot in front of the other, focused on her schoolwork, and ignored them with the same elaborate grace with which they ignored her.

It was the Saturday nights that made up for all the immature high-school drama, because on Saturday nights, she always saw Mikey. Since her old man was away, it became Paige's job to carry the records while Casey did the driving. With the advent of fall weather, these little shindigs moved indoors, and because Trish and Bill's house was so tiny, the venue changed, for the foreseeable future, to the Lindstrom house.

With the stack of record albums clutched to her chest, Paige followed Casey through the front door of her Aunt Rose's house. "We're here," Casey called, juggling a bag of tortilla chips, a tub of homemade salsa, a hot container of chili and a chilled bowl of tossed salad, "and we come bearing gifts."

Through the living room doorway, Paige could see a group of men—Jesse Lindstrom, Will Bradley, Sr., Bill, Jr., and Chuck Fournier, who taught U.S. History at the high school and was Paula Fournier's husband—all circled around Mikey, who had apparently done something worthy of worshipful adulation at this afternoon's football game. She heard the words "fifty-yard line" and "touchdown," and Bill leaned over and gave his nephew an affectionate whack on the back.

"About time you got here," Trish said from the kitchen, scurrying to lighten Casey's load. "You can give the records to Aunt Rose," she told Paige. "Since your uncles have defected to football land, it looks like the women are in charge of the music tonight."

"I don't get it," Paige said. "Why are a bunch of grown men so excited about high school football?"

"Are you kidding? In a small town like this, what else do they have to obsess over? High school sports are practically a religion around here."

"Ugh. Spare me." She might not be a girly girl, but she barely knew the difference between a touchdown and a rubdown. Sports were not high on her priority list. As a matter of fact, sports were nowhere near her priority list. Maybe it was time to rethink that, since Mikey Lindstrom was captain of the football team, as well as its star quarterback.

Trish patted her arm. "Amen, sister!"

"Just set the records on the table," Rose said, closing the oven door and setting the timer. She tossed down her potholders, gathered her wayward curls into a quasi-ponytail that she secured with a rubber band, and crossed the room to take a quick look at the albums. "Hey!" she protested, picking up a Doors album and flipping it over to check the back. "This is mine! I've wondered for years where it went to. That little shit stole it from me!"

"Possession is nine-tenths of the law," Casey said, opening a drawer and rummaging through its contents until she found salad tongs. "How do you know it's yours? It's ancient. He could have picked it up at a yard sale."

"Possibly the fact that it says ROSE MACKENZIE on the back, in big black letters? Larcenous little twit."

"He's had that album for as long as I've known him, but I refuse to become an accessory after the fact. When he gets back, you can have him arrested."

"I wonder what else of mine he has?" Rose muttered as she continued working her way through the stack, absently mouthing the lyrics to *Love Me Two Times*.

Casey returned to the table, uncovered the salad, and rested the tongs against the lip of the bowl. "How are you holding out, hon?" Trish asked her.

"Me? I'm fine. It'll only be three weeks. And Paige is good company. We get along just fine, don't we, sweetie?"

"Yes," Paige said automatically, without even having to think about it. A couple of nights ago, they'd eaten dinner in the living room—grilled cheese sandwiches and tomato soup—and watched *The King and I*. Paige had never seen it before, but it was Casey's favorite movie. The plot line was hokey, its depiction of Asian people racist and demeaning, but the chemistry between the lead characters was tangible, and the music of Rodgers and Hammerstein just blew her away.

"Besides," Casey said, taking a chip from the bag and dipping it, "he calls me almost every day."

"A phone call every day," Paula Fournier drawled, "does not make up for the absence of a warm man in your bed every night."

"Truer words have not been spoken."

"Please," Rose said. "Don't turn my stomach. That's my baby brother you're talking about. I don't want to think about him warming any woman's bed." She threw an arm loosely around Paige's shoulders. "Am I right, Kemosabe, or am I right?"

Talk about racist and demeaning. Paige grinned. "You're right, Tonto."

"Hah!" Her aunt ruffled Paige's hair in enthusiastic approval. "I rest my case."

"You can't rest any case," Paula said dryly. "I'm the lawyer around here. Only I can rest cases."

Rose released her niece, picked up a tortilla chip, and flicked it at her friend. "Bite me."

The camaraderie, the joking, the ease with which these women fit together, was something new in Paige's experience. Her mom had been a loner, had never had many female friends. Aside from Meg, who'd disappeared from their lives years ago, there had been just Lorraine from downstairs and a couple of ladies who worked at the Financial District bank where Sandy processed mortgages. But those friendships had been superficial, based on proximity and convenience instead of shared interests or lifestyles. None of her mother's friends had been like these women, who were so loosey-goosey and comfortable together, throwing insults at each other without fear of repercussion, digging into each other's private lives, and talking openly about sex and husbands and kids and the joys of small-town life. Although she was too young to have any dog in this fight, she still got a charge out of listening to their conversation. Being included in their circle made her feel like an adult, one of the gang, accepted in a way the girls at school had refused to accept her.

But that acceptance was a double-edged sword. The older female cousins were all away at college. Alison, in her last trimester of pregnancy, wasn't feeling well, so she and Billy had decided to lay low and stay home tonight. Luke blew through the kitchen with his usual manic charm, greeted everyone, snagged a plate of food, and headed out for a date with some new girl. Mikey and the rest of the men wandered into the kitchen for food, then retreated back to the living room to talk football.

So she was stuck with the women. It wouldn't have been so bad, except that it meant she didn't get any time alone with Mikey. When they did cross paths, he was polite but distant. Almost as though he was deliberately avoiding her. But she couldn't imagine why he'd do that. He'd been friendly enough that day they'd run into each other in the cafeteria, had even eaten food from her tray. She'd thought they were becoming friends. Now, he seemed less like a friend than a good-looking stranger.

If her mom were still around, Paige could have gone to her for advice. Sandy had dated a number of different men over the years. She would know exactly what to say, what to do. But Sandy was gone, and Paige wasn't about to ask Casey for relationship advice. Mikey was the woman's nephew, which made asking her for advice on how to snag his interest icky on a number of levels. Besides, Casey had been married to her first husband for more than a decade before she married Rob MacKenzie. Based on what Paige had picked up here and there, it didn't seem as though there'd been anybody else in between. So what kind of meaningful dating advice could the woman give? She'd spent most of her adult life as a married woman.

It looked like she was on her own with this one.

***

She'd never even heard the term "five-and-ten" until she moved to this delightful burg. It was a sort of department store that sold a wide variety of cheap plastic crap. The building was ancient, with crooked wooden floors, the merchandise so dusty it made her sneeze. The whole place smelled like popcorn because, to her amazement, there was a working popcorn machine located near the cash register. It popped corn all day, and you could buy the stuff, hot and buttered, for ninety-nine cents a bag and eat it while you shopped.

"So," Lissa said, rummaging through a bin of eye shadow, "why the sudden interest in football?"

"No particular reason." Paige fingered a crummy plastic rain hat that looked like it belonged on someone's great-granny. These people here in East Nowhere had a stunning sense of style. "I just thought I should broaden my horizons."

"Right. I don't suppose it would have anything to do with a certain quarterback?"

"Give me a break, Lissa." She eyed her friend coolly. "Even if it did—and I'm not saying it does—what would be the point? He'd be too busy scoring touchdowns to even know I was at the game."

"Do you think this color would look good on me?" Lissa held up a packet of burgundy eye shadow and struck a pose.

"I suppose that depends. Are you deliberately trying to look like one of the Undead?"

Lissa tossed it back in the bin and kept searching. "Maybe purple would be better. So if he won't even know you're there, why are you bothering to go?"

Paige picked up a bottle of perfume, uncapped it, and took a whiff. "Look, are you with me on this or not? It's a simple sociological experiment. I want to breathe in the scent of high school athletics and see if I get carried away with hometown fervor."

"You're so weird. Has anybody ever told you that?"

Thinking of her newly-discovered family, she said, "I'm pretty sure it's a MacKenzie trait."

"So what do you think? Green or blue?"

She set the perfume back on the shelf and, studying both colors, decided that neither really went well with Lissa's dark eyes. Something in a taupe would work better. "Either one is fine," she said.

Lissa hesitated for a moment. Glanced up at the security mirror suspended from a ceiling beam. And slipped the packet of green eye shadow into her pocket.

"What the hell are you doing?" Paige said.

Lissa widened her eyes with exaggerated innocence and said, "What?"

"You know what. Are you crazy, or are you just looking to get an early start on building your criminal record?"

"Oh, stop being such a goody-goody. I do it all the time. They won't even miss it." Lissa glanced around, reached into the bin again, and pulled out a tube of eyeliner.

"It doesn't matter if they miss it, Lissa, it's against the law."

"Are you for real? You're just a big chicken." The eyeliner disappeared into the same pocket as the eye shadow. Smugly, she said, "I bet you don't even dare."

"It has nothing to do with daring. It has to do with ethics."

"Ethics? Jesus, Paige, you sound like my grandmother. Look at this lipstick. This shade of pink would be outstanding on you. Go ahead. I dare you."

Their eyes met, Paige's cold, Lissa's sparkling with excitement. "Go on," Lissa taunted. "Take the lipstick, and I'll go with you to the game."

She knew it was wrong. This whole scenario was wrong. She'd never stolen anything in her life. But Lissa had put her on the spot, and she wasn't one to back down from a dare. Nobody on this planet was going to call Paige MacKenzie a chicken and get away with it. She closed her fingers over the lipstick, sent a quick, silent message heavenward. *I'm sorry, Mom.*

And slipped it in her pocket.

Lissa winked, and Paige let out the breath she'd been holding. They turned together and coolly, casually, as though they'd just decided to break for lunch, meandered down the aisle toward the front door.

Paige got there first. Breath held, she leaned against the door. It opened, and she took a single step outside. *Almost there.* She started forward again and was about to clear the threshold when a hand clamped down on her arm.

And a voice that was definitely not Lissa's said, "Not another step, young lady."

Casey

Saturday morning. Football weather. It was one of those blue and gold fall days, so lovely it took her breath away. Paige had left on her ten-speed a couple of hours ago for Lissa Norton's house. The two girls were planning to go shopping, followed by the high school football game, and Casey was enjoying the quiet time. Paying bills wasn't her favorite activity, but it was a necessary evil if she intended to keep her utilities up and running. Carole King's *Tapestry* album playing on the stereo helped to lessen the pain.

She was comfortably ensconced at the desk in her sitting room, checkbook in hand, Leroy snoring at her feet, when the phone rang. Casey set down her pen and reached for the receiver. "Hello?"

"Casey?" The male voice at the other end seemed vaguely familiar. "It's Ted."

The name drew a complete blank, and she searched her mental file cabinets without success. He must have sensed her hesitation. "Ted Burns," he said.

It clicked. Cousin Teddy. Aunt Hilda's son, who'd spent the last nine years as one of the town's two full-time police officers. "Oh, Teddy. Hi."

He cleared his throat. "I'm calling on official business. Is your husband there?"

She could count on the fingers of one hand the number of people on the planet that Rob disliked more than her Cousin Teddy, although she'd never quite understood the reason for his animosity. Teddy was a royal pain in the ass, for sure, but Rob generally got along with everyone. He would be crushed to know he'd missed Teddy's call.

"He's out of town. What's up?"

"I'm not sure I can discuss it with you. Legalities, you know."

It was beginning to come back to her, the reason Teddy's invitations to family gatherings somehow kept getting lost in the mail. "I'm afraid I'm all you've got, since he's not reachable right now. What's this about, another parking ticket?"

She suspected that for some inexplicable reason, the animosity ran both ways. In a town with no more than two dozen parking meters, it seemed as though Rob had garnered more than his share of tickets over the past year and a half.

Teddy cleared his throat. "It's about his daughter. I should be talking to him. You not being her mother, and all."

Panic clutched her insides. "Paige? Is she all right? Has something happened to her?"

"You're not her legal guardian. I really shouldn't—"

"Oh, for the love of God, Teddy, you were at my wedding! She's Rob's daughter, and I'm his wife. She lives with us. If something's happened to her, I need to know!"

"Well—" He dragged out the word, and she wanted to reach through the phone and grab him by the throat. "I don't suppose I have a choice, seeing as how your hubby's not available."

Hubby? Good Lord. If Rob heard that, he'd probably march down to the police station, wrestle Teddy's gun away, and shoot him with it.

"We just picked her and that snotty little Norton girl up for shoplifting cosmetics from the Five-and-Ten. Eye shadow, lipstick, eye liner." His soft sound of disdain carried clearly across the phone line. "If she was my kid, I wouldn't be letting her out of the house wearing that crap smeared all over her face. But, hey, that's just me. I'm a small-town guy. I haven't lived the big-city rock & roll lifestyle like you two have."

Outside, a cloud passed across the face of the sun, erasing her good mood. "Gee, Teddy, I thought you, of all people, would realize that eyeliner is a necessary component to our Satanic rituals here at Ye Auld House of Sodom and Gomorrah." At his silence, she rolled her eyes. The sarcasm had obviously gone right over his head. "I'll be right there." And she slammed down the phone. "Cretin," she muttered.

It took her seven minutes to get to town. When she wheeled into the police station's parking lot, she noted that the local cop shop wasn't exactly doing a thriving business. One of the town's two cruisers sat out front, in need of a good scrubbing. Casey parked between a Subaru wagon and a red pickup truck with a gun rack in the rear window, snatched up her purse, and marched toward the front door.

Inside, Lynda Frechette, whose father served with her on the library committee, sat at the front desk reading *Soap Opera Digest*. In a small office at the back of the building, voices were raised in anger. Near the receptionist's desk, two teenage girls sat huddled together on a hard wooden bench she suspected was deliberately designed for discomfort. When the door closed behind her, they glanced up. She met Paige's eyes, and the kid squared her jaw, but not quickly enough to mask her fear. Casey gave her a pointed look before moving in the direction of the yelling.

"I don't give a good goddamn what you think! My daughter has never, ever done anything like this before. She's just a kid, and—" At her entrance, Biff Norton, Lissa's father, paused in his tirade. "You," he said, narrowing his eyes. "This is all your fault!"

"Good morning, gentlemen. Biff. Teddy." She nodded toward the police chief, who'd gone to school with her brother Travis. "Scotty." The only other person in the room was a woman she didn't know. Casey held out her hand. "I don't believe we've met. I'm Casey MacKenzie."

The woman took her hand in a no-nonsense grip. "Lynn Veilleux."

"Lynn's the manager over at the Five-and-Ten," Teddy said.

"Nice to meet you." She turned to Norton. "Now, Biff, what, precisely, is all my fault?"

He drew bushy black brows together. "That kid of yours is a bad influence on my Lissa. Just three weeks into tenth grade, three weeks hanging around with that little brat of yours, and now she's been arrested? This is all your fault, for bringing your riffraff to town. Maybe you should take your kid, and your long-haired freak of a husband, and go back to California, or wherever it is you've been living. Because we don't need your kind dirtying up this town."

There was a collective intake of breath, and for an instant, absolute silence reigned, while the fury rose in her so abruptly she had to clench her fists to stay their trembling.

Belatedly, Teddy appeared to remember his familial obligations. "Now, Biff..." he began.

"Thank you, Teddy," she said, drawing herself up to her full five feet, "but I can fight my own battles. Biff Norton, you stupid, ignorant redneck, have you ever even *met* my husband? I can only assume the answer is no, because if you had, you'd know he's a thousand times the man you could ever be. If he were standing here right now, he'd probably laugh off what you just said, because that's the kind of guy he is. But I'm not quite as forgiving as he is, and if I ever hear you say another bad word about him, I won't be held accountable for my actions."

Norton's eyes narrowed. "Is that a threat?"

"You'd damn well better believe it's a threat. And in front of witnesses. You can say any nasty thing you want about me, you idiot, but Rob is off limits. *Capisce?*"

Before Norton could respond, Scotty Deverell cleared his throat. "Can we just deal with the situation at hand?"

"Sorry, but I'm not finished with Biff yet. As far as dirtying this town, Norton, you and I went to high school together, and I have a long memory. I could tell a few stories about the dirtying you did back in the day. But for now, just to show I'm the bigger person, I'll hold my tongue. Unless you really annoy me again, then the gloves are off. As for Paige, that 'little brat' just lost her mother, and she's hurting. That's not an excuse. It doesn't make what she did right, but it certainly speaks to her motivation. She's been dealt a nasty blow, and she's mad at the world. I should know, because I've been there. I lost my mother at fifteen, and believe me, it almost destroyed my life. So I understand her a little better than any of the rest of you can. Underneath the anger, she's a good kid, with a good heart. Just like I imagine your daughter is. They got into trouble together, and I'm not laying sole blame on either of them. They're both to blame, and they both need to be punished. Hopefully—" She turned to Lynn Veilleux. "—by their parents, and not the judicial system."

Veilleux exchanged glances with Scotty Deverell. Scotty cleared his throat again. "It's up to you, Lynn, whether or not you want to press charges."

"We did recover the merchandise," Veilleux said. "And the total value was less than twenty dollars. And since neither of them has any record—" She paused. "But I don't believe it should be overlooked and forgotten. If the girls aren't dealt with appropriately, they'll never learn anything from this."

"I'm in total agreement," Casey said. "Maybe a little community service would be in order. Raking leaves, washing the police cruisers, picking up litter from the sidewalks."

"Sounds good to me," Veilleux replied. "How about the next four Saturdays from nine to three?"

Scotty Deverell nodded his approval. "I can supervise. Biff?"

"Fine," Norton said curtly. "Can I take my kid now?"

"Go."

He went, and a visible wave of relief rolled around the room. Casey raised a trembling hand and massaged her temple, her stomach roiling with nausea, the end result of every nasty confrontation in which she'd ever been involved. "Just so you know," Lynn Veilleux said, "I *have* met your husband, and Norton is way out of line. The guy owes you a debt of gratitude, because if you hadn't been here, I would've pressed charges against his kid, just because of his attitude. What an ass."

"Let's hope," Scotty said, "that in this case, the apple does fall far from the tree. Casey, you okay?"

"Give me a minute. I will be."

"My cousin," Teddy said, sounding like a proud parent. "She's quite the pit bull when she has to be."

"Next Saturday," she said. "Nine a.m. I'll have her here. Thanks, everyone. Lynn, it was nice to meet you. Hopefully the next time we see each other, it will be under more pleasant circumstances."

Paige waited alone on the bench in the reception area. Without speaking, Casey tilted her head in the direction of the door. Her stepdaughter sprang to her feet and followed her out the door and to the car. When they were safely inside, Casey placed her hands at ten and two on the wheel, took a deep breath, and said, "Where's your bike?"

"Lissa's house."

"It's staying there until I can find somebody with a little testosterone to go over and pick it up. Maybe Bill can do it for me. Or Jesse. I am not dealing with that man again today."

"So, am I about to get the 'Just wait until your father gets home!' lecture? Because if I am, it could be a long wait."

"No, you're not. Would you like to know why?"

Paige squirmed in the passenger seat. "Why?"

"A couple of reasons. First, because I'm quite capable of dealing with the situation myself. Probably better than your father, who has zero parenting experience. I may not have spent much time with teenagers, but in a previous life, I had plenty of hands-on experience dealing with a spoiled five-year-old. Second...I don't believe lecturing you is the answer."

Paige reached out a finger and fiddled with the dashboard air vent. "No? So what's the magic answer?"

Casey turned her head and studied the kid. Paige threw her a sly glance, then quickly looked away. "Well, now," Casey said, starting the car and putting it into gear, "If I told you, I'd be stacking the deck in your favor, wouldn't I?"

Paige

The cemetery sat at the water's edge, overlooking Boston Harbor, where gulls circled and boats scurried across vivid blue water. In the distance, she could see a line of planes waiting to land at Logan, stacked one after another, lined up like dominoes in the sky. This was the first time she'd been here since her mother's funeral, and right now, her stomach felt like she'd been drinking battery acid. Her mom's headstone, made of polished Quincy granite, bore a heart with the word *mother* at the center. That had been her idea. It seemed fitting. Especially since there was nobody left to mourn Sandy Sainsbury except her daughter.

She glanced over her shoulder. Eyes hidden behind dark glasses, her father's wife leaned against a nearby monument, her arms folded across her chest. Close enough to keep watch, but far enough away to allow Paige privacy. She couldn't figure out this woman he—her father—had married. After this morning's fiasco, she'd expected a severe tongue lashing. Possibly a grounding. Instead, Casey had returned to the house, phoned her brother to retrieve the bicycle, loaded Paige and Leroy in the car, and driven here. A three-and-a-half-hour drive to visit a dead woman. Her stepmother moved in mysterious ways, and despite her apparent kindness, Paige was still waiting for the other shoe to drop.

Casey stepped away from the monument, approached her, and crouched beside her. "After Danny died," she said, one hand braced against the ground for balance, "it was six months before I went to the cemetery. Even then, I wouldn't have gone if your father hadn't dragged me there."

Paige hazarded a glance at her stepmother, but Casey was looking at the gravestone instead of her. "I'll tell you something about my mother," Casey said, "if you'll tell me something about yours."

Their eyes met. Paige shrugged. Casey nodded. "Fine. I'll go first. When my sister Colleen and I were little girls, my mother used to dress us up in these stupid sailor dresses. Navy blue with big white collars and red bows. She'd fix our hair in tight ringlets, and then she'd drag us to church meetings and the Grange Hall and the county fair, and make us sing for people. *You Are my*

Sunshine. The Old Rugged Cross. How Much is That Doggie in the Window? Everybody thought we were adorable. Coll and I hated it." Casey shifted position. "Your turn."

"We used to go to the beach together. In the winter, when nobody else was there, and we'd just walk. It was our special place." She wasn't sure what had made her open up to this woman she barely knew. The beach had been something she shared only with her mom, something she'd never told anybody.

Casey nodded solemnly. "My mother and I used to bake cookies together. For Christmas. Thanksgiving. Halloween. Easter. All the big holidays. She'd put me in one of her aprons— which were always miles too big for me—stand me up on a chair, and let me do the mixing. Colleen was always too much of a tomboy to care. I was the one who loved to cook."

"My mom used to put music on, turn it up loud, and dance me around the living room." Paige closed her eyes to savor the memory. "I remember her holding me in her arms and dancing with me when I was too young to even understand the words. She bought every album Danny Fiore ever recorded. All the ones you and my father—" She paused, realized this was the first time she'd referred to him that way without a second thought. "—wrote and produced." She opened her eyes, looked straight into Casey's. "I'm pretty sure she was still in love with him."

"Really? Well, he is pretty special. He'd be a hard act to follow."

"I mean, she had boyfriends. But none of them lasted. Every time she'd end things with the latest boyfriend, she'd pull out a Danny Fiore album and listen to the music my father wrote. I think it was her version of crying in her beer."

"You miss her."

Paige's lower lip trembled, and she willed it to stop. "Yeah."

"I miss my mom, too. It doesn't matter that it's been twenty years. Not a day goes by that I don't think about her and remember some little thing I thought I'd forgotten. How she wore her hair. The goofy songs she used to sing to me. The wise advice I generally ignored." Casey paused. "The way she played the piano. She was an amazing pianist. That's where I got my musical talent. Dad doesn't have a musical bone in his body."

"Neither did my mom. She just loved to listen to it."

They were silent together for a time. Out on the water, a ship's horn sounded. "What was it like," Paige asked, "being married to Danny Fiore?"

Her stepmother's face grew taut with an emotion she couldn't decipher. Staring out over the harbor, Casey said, "Have you ever been in love?"

Thinking of Mikey, she said, "I've been in *like* a couple of times, but not love."

"I was so in love with him. I was only three years older than you are now when I met him. I was just eighteen, and he was...magnificent." A soft smile lit her face, changing it completely. "That probably sounds silly, but it's true. He was the most beautiful creature I'd ever seen, and there was this intensity about him that sucked me right in. He was smart, and edgy, and cynical. So talented. And absolutely certain of where he was headed. I'd never met anybody like that before. He just swept me off my feet." She grew pensive, a little wistful. "I was engaged to another man. Four weeks away from my wedding day. Danny and I eloped three days after we met. I walked away from everything, without a backward glance, to be with him. I was so in love, I would have gladly lain down on the ground and let him walk all over me." She let out a soft laugh, but there was very little humor in it. "In retrospect, I can say that's pretty much what I did." Her expression changed, grew intense, almost angry. "It was not a healthy relationship."

Surprised, Paige asked, "Why?"

"Because he always held the upper hand. Don't ever let a man do that to you, Paige. Don't ever let a man's ego crush yours."

"I don't understand."

"Danny wasn't always a good husband. I'm not saying he deliberately hurt me, or that he didn't love me—because he did—but he had his failings. His career always came first. He had tunnel vision. He could see only one thing, and that one thing wasn't me. It's not like he didn't warn me. I was simply too naïve and too dazzled to listen. Don't get me wrong. It wasn't always bad. We had some very good years, especially after Katie came along. And some very bad ones. He lied to me. He cheated on me. Sometimes he withdrew, and I couldn't get through to him.

But I just kept on loving him, no matter what. It wasn't until after Katie died, and he did something unforgivable, that I began to understand what I'd let him do to me. We separated, for almost a year. I grew so much in that year! But in the end, I took him back. I don't really understand why. Not fully. Because by that time, your father and I—" She stopped abruptly. "I had to make a choice. I'm still not sure I made the right one."

"What did he do?" Paige said. "The unforgivable thing?"

Mixed emotions flitted across Casey's face as she appeared to debate whether or not to respond. "He had a vasectomy," she finally said. "Behind my back. It was an out-and-out betrayal, because he knew how much it meant to me to be a mother."

"Jesus. That had to suck."

"Yes. It did suck." Casey hesitated, lost in thought. "It was a pain I really didn't need on top of what I already had. I'd just lost my only child, and here he was, making sure that I'd never have another. Not that I could've replaced Katie—"

"Of course not!"

"But I wanted more children. I needed to be a mother. And he took that possibility away from me. I wanted to kill him."

"Wow." She tried to imagine what it would feel like. How hard it must be to lose your kid. Even worse than losing your mother, and that was the hardest thing she'd ever known. She felt a twinge of something that felt remarkably like empathy for this woman she'd been so determined to hate.

"Maybe now you'll have a clearer understanding of the relationship I have with your father. It's genuine and open, based on love and mutual respect. We deliberately avoid doing hurtful things to each other. I know you have issues with him, but for me, life with your father is like the sunshine after the clouds."

Paige didn't say anything. She wasn't sure what to say. Her father was the villain in this piece, and she didn't want to even consider any other view of him. Her mom had died of a broken heart, and it was all his fault. If he hadn't left, she would have been strong enough to fight the cancer. But he had left, and Sandy had died. How could she ever forgive him for that?

Casey rubbed her hands against her thighs and cleared her throat. "So," she said briskly. "You ready to leave?"

Paige nodded, and they got up and began walking back toward the car. Even from this distance, she could see Leroy jumping at the window and barking. "Are we going home now?" she asked, and realized that for the first time, the word *home* meant Maine, and not South Boston.

"Not yet. We have somewhere else to go first."

***

The house was big and rambling, a little past its prime, and sat on its own postage-stamp-sized lot on a quiet street on the outskirts of Southie. The driveway was full, so Casey parked on the street in front. "Whose house is this?" Paige said.

"This," Casey said, taking the keys from the ignition, "is Mary and Patrick's place. Your grandparents. This is the house where your father grew up."

As they approached the side door, she could hear a small dog making a big racket inside. Casey knocked once, then opened the door and stepped inside the house. "Hello!" she called. "Anybody home?"

A black pug raced into the room, yapping and jumping with excitement. Casey leaned to pat him, and the look of rapture on his face was comical. "Hello, Pugsley," she said, rubbing his ears. "Where's your mother?"

The dog rolled his huge eyes, panting and dancing around Casey's feet. Beside Paige, Leroy whined. The pug approached him, and they sniffed each other warily. Mary MacKenzie came into the room, wearing a flowered apron, her reddish-gray hair a mess, her face aglow.

"Well, well! If it isn't my favorite daughter-in-law!"

The two women embraced. "Don't let her kid you," Casey said to Paige. "I'm one of four, and she says that to every one of us. We all just play along."

"Oh, you," Mary said good-naturedly. "And Paige, darling of my heart, it's so nice to see you. Come give your old Grandma a hug."

Since there was no way to graciously escape, Paige stepped forward and let the matronly woman wrap her in a bear hug. It wasn't so awful. Actually, it felt kind of nice. Her grandmother

was soft and pillowy, and she smelled like vanilla. It wasn't
Mary's fault that her son had ruined Paige's life. Mary released
her, reached out and brushed a strand of hair out of her face.
"You're a lovely girl," she said. "Just like your mother was. You
certainly didn't get it from your father. Speaking of which." She
turned back to Casey. "Where is that hard-headed husband of
yours?"

"He's away. On tour."

Mary raised her eyebrows. "He didn't tell me he had a tour
scheduled."

"He didn't. He's helping out an old friend who was in a
bind. It wasn't planned. You know how he is."

"Just getting to know his little girl, and already he's gone off
and left her?" She gave Paige another hug. "You poor thing!"

"He's a musician," Casey said. "Musicians spend a lot of
time on the road. But we're a family, and he knew Paige and I
would be fine together. Right, Paige?"

She shrugged, not knowing what to say, because to side with
either of them would seem disloyal to the other. Her grandmother
was right; her father shouldn't have gone off and left her. But
Casey had bailed her out of some pretty hot water this morning,
and she probably owed the woman something. Paige was starting
to warm up to her stepmother, something she never would have
imagined when she first arrived in Maine. On the other hand,
Casey had married Rob MacKenzie, so her judgment was clearly
flawed.

"Don't put the poor girl on the spot. Although it warms my
heart to see you defending my son. Well, never mind him. You'll
stay for dinner?"

"I don't want to impose."

Mary snorted. "As if either of you could ever be an
imposition. I have enough food to feed an army. I think we can
get by. Patrick! Michael! Get out here and say hello to Casey and
Paige!"

Her grandfather was a tall, lean man, with a quiet demeanor
and a twinkle in his eye. Michael, her father's younger brother,
kissed Casey's cheek and shook Paige's hand. The family
resemblance was strong. Michael wasn't quite as tall as her father,
or quite as slender. But he had the MacKenzie green eyes, and the

same wavy blond hair, except that his was neatly trimmed in a conventional cut.

While the men focused on eating, the two women kept the dinner conversation going. Paige remained quiet, following their conversation but not taking part. While Leroy lay on the mat by the door, Pugsley spent the entire meal sitting next to her grandfather, who kept sneaking him bites of food under the table. The meal was amazing: a perfectly-seasoned beef stew, accompanied by fresh-baked biscuits. Paige ate until she feared she would burst, and then her grandmother brought out the *pièce de résistance*: a six-inch-tall chocolate cake, smothered in chocolate frosting. Nobody turned it down, although by the time she'd finished the gargantuan piece her grandmother cut for her, she was certain she'd be rolling out the door like an overinflated beach ball.

When the meal was over, her uncle threw on a jacket, kissed his mother good-bye, said, "Paige, it was nice to meet you," and left. Her grandfather spirited Casey off to some other part of the house, intent on showing her the latest acquisitions to his stamp collection.

"Looks like it's just you and me left to clean up," her grandmother said. "That's fine, we can talk while we wash dishes."

While Mary put the leftovers in storage containers, Paige cleared the table and ran hot, soapy water in the sink. There was no dishwasher, so she rinsed the dishes, slid them into the sink, and washed them by hand. "So," Mary said, picking up a plate and drying it with a fluffy dish towel, "are you getting settled in up there?"

"I guess."

"It's very different, isn't it? I trust there's a little culture shock going on right now. How's school? Have you made any friends?"

She thought about Lissa Norton, about this morning's escapade, and felt her cheeks burn. "One or two. Mostly, I hang out with Luke."

"Well, then, that's a good thing, to have cousins nearby who are about your age. How are things at home?"

Paige picked up a dinner plate, scrubbed at a stubborn spot. "It's okay."

"You don't sound convinced. Are you getting along with Casey?"

"Casey's all right."

"And your dad?"

Paige hesitated. What could she say to this woman about her own son that wouldn't sound like whining or ingratitude?

"Ah," Mary said. "Your silence speaks volumes. You and your father have issues."

"We don't agree on much," Paige admitted. It was as close as she would come to telling this lovely woman that he'd already destroyed her life long before they ever met in person.

"Let me tell you something, sweetheart. I love all my children, and I see each of them for who they really are. The good, the bad, the ugly. Your father can be the biggest, most obstinate jackass on the planet. He's far from perfect. Sometimes, he does stupid things. He has a temper, and he still hasn't really grown up. But he has the biggest heart of anyone I know. He always did. He's the one who would bring home a bird with a broken wing and make it a soft bed and hand-feed it worms and try to heal it. Underneath the prickly man, he's still that same soft-hearted little boy. If he does things that don't make sense to you, if he gets mad and yells at you, it's only because he cares so very much. Understand?"

Head down, hands buried in dishwater, Paige nodded.

"And the other thing I have to say is this: he may have made some really bad judgment calls in his life, but the one thing he got right was marrying Casey. I've known and loved that girl since she was just a wee little eighteen-year-old child bride, in way over her head with Danny Fiore. Somehow, she managed to stay afloat in spite of it all, and over the years, I've watched her grow into a remarkable woman that I'm proud to call my daughter-in-law. The day she married my son was one of the happiest days of my life. My advice to you, Paige, is to let her into your heart. Your life will be so enriched if you do."

When the kitchen clean-up was finished, her grandmother led her into the living room, where they sat for more than an hour, looking through old family photo albums. It seemed that in the

MacKenzie household, there had always been somebody around with a camera. There were the requisite school photos, but also hundreds and hundreds of snapshots. Pictures of her father, and his siblings, at every stage of development. "Now, where was that?" Mary mused, turning pages. "Yes, here it is. Your parents, when they were dating."

And there it was. The two of them, looking young and fresh-faced and happy. A lump formed in Paige's throat. Sandy had owned a half-dozen photos of Rob, but none of them together. Nothing to document the relationship they'd had. But this—it was proof that they'd been a couple, visual evidence that testified to Paige's lineage. She studied the photo, entranced. Her mom had been so pretty. And her father'd worn the same grin she'd glimpsed a time or two, when his mood was right and he wasn't angry with her.

"Would you like to have it?" her grandmother asked.

She looked up at Mary, shocked. "Could I?"

"Of course. Let me find you an envelope to put it in, to keep it safe for the trip home."

By the time Mary returned with the envelope, Casey had made a reappearance, and was ready to leave. "Are you sure you won't stay the night?" Mary said.

"I'd love to, but your son calls me every night. I don't want him to go into a panic because he can't reach me."

"He's a good husband."

"The best. I attribute it to his amazing upbringing."

"Such flattery."

"No flattery involved. It's simply the truth."

Paige bade farewell to Pugsley, gave her grandfather a shy hug, then embraced her grandmother with enthusiasm. Mary stroked her cheek and said, "You'll remember what I told you, darling Paige?"

"I will."

"Good! Casey, I'm so glad you came." The two women embraced, Casey hugged her father-in-law, and the two of them—Grandma and Grandpa MacKenzie—watched from the door as Paige and Casey and Leroy walked to the car in the crisp evening air. "Drive safely!" Mary shouted, and Paige turned to wave before she put Leroy in the back seat and climbed into the front.

Neither of them spoke. There was no need for talk. As Casey navigated the city streets, Paige closed her eyes, reliving, examining, analyzing the events of the past few hours. It would take some time to absorb it all. But one thing was clear. No matter how angry she was with her father, no matter how determined she was to hate him, she was absolutely, utterly, one hundred percent smitten with his mother.

Casey

Half-asleep, she picked up the ringing phone and brought it to her ear. Her husband's soft, intimate voice said, "I'm sorry to call so late. I tried earlier, but I didn't get you. Where were you?"

She sat up in bed, drew the hair back from her face, rubbed her eyes. "Believe it or not, Boston."

"Boston?"

"Remember how, after Danny died, you took me to the cemetery?"

"Ah."

"I thought she needed to go. Afterward, we stopped in to visit your folks. Paige needs to know where she comes from. It's important. We stayed for dinner."

"How were things at Ye House of MacKenzie?"

"Your mom sat Paige down with the family photo albums, and while they were occupied with that, your dad had to show me the latest additions to his stamp collection. He's scored some really good stuff. Apparently."

He let out a soft laugh. "Some things never change."

"But that's good, right? Your parents are who they are, and we love them for it. Some things are so perfect you don't want to see them ever change."

"They're getting old, babe."

"Oh, sweetie, don't worry, they're as solid as ever. They'll be with us for a long time to come. Listen, Michael was there. For dinner. Without Claire."

"Oh?"

"I thought it was odd. Odder still that her name never came up. You don't suppose they're having problems?"

"I don't know. Nobody tells me anything. Hell, nobody bothered to tell me I had a kid, so why should I expect they'd share with me anything about my brother's marriage?"

"That's a good point. Your mother, by the way, is of the strong opinion that you should be here right now, bonding with your daughter, instead of on the road."

"That doesn't surprise me. My mother is a woman of strong opinions."

"I defended you. I told her we were a family and you were quite confident in my ability to handle things in your absence."

"You stood up to my mother? Gutsy broad."

"Not so gutsy. I adore your mother."

"And she adores you."

"And I always stand up for you. I always have, and I always will."

"I know. You're like a mother bear with her cub."

"No. I'm just a good wife."

"True. I'm fairly satisfied with the little woman. I think I'll keep her. Probably."

"Funny boy. Listen, I hate to have to tell you this, but Paige and Lissa Norton got picked up this morning for shoplifting a tube of eyeliner and a lipstick. Teddy called me."

"Damn it. Of course he did. I bet he was gloating the whole time. What the hell was the kid thinking?"

"She's a teenager. They don't think. If it's any consolation, she told me it was Lissa's idea."

"But she went along with it."

"Exactly."

"Ah, shit." He sighed. "What'd you do?"

"I did what I do best: I smoothed things over. There'll be no charges, but she'll be spending the next four Saturdays paying penance, picking up litter and so forth, supervised by Scotty Deverell."

"I'm sorry I left you holding the bag. Did you kick her ass from here to Kingdom Come?"

"Actually, I didn't. The whole fiasco is what prompted the trip to Boston. I did let Biff Norton have it, though."

"Who's Biff Norton?"

"Lissa's father. I went to high school with him. He was a little turd then, and he hasn't improved with age. He had something to say about you, and I took exception to it."

"Wait a minute. Have I even met this guy?"

"Not as far as I know, but he seems to know who you are. I put him in his place. Nobody talks trash about my guy and gets away with it."

"Twice in one day you defended my honor, Fiore? I'm impressed."

"Just give me a minute to blow the smoke away from the tip of my gun." In the darkness, she smiled. "Teddy called me a pit bull. I think he meant it as a compliment."

"No doubt he did. Damn, I miss you."

"I miss you, too. It just doesn't feel right. I hate sleeping alone."

"Me, too. I did it for years, and it sucked."

"Funny, I don't recall you ever sleeping alone."

"Ha-ha. You're a regular one-woman comedy act. I wasn't that bad."

"Are you kidding? I tried to keep score, but I finally had to give up because I couldn't keep track of them all. I can't imagine how you did. You must have had an abacus hanging on your headboard."

"That's really low, Fiore."

"I call it the way I see it, MacKenzie. You were quite the, ah...ladies' man. But we're okay, as long as you don't forget where you belong now."

"I could never forget. Trust me." He paused. "Remember that killer fight we had?"

She drew the covers tighter around her for warmth. "Which one?"

"The one where you threw my ugly ass out of your house."

She considered it at length. Finally said, "Which time?"

At the other end of the line, he let out a soft laugh. "I guess we've had more than our share of battles, haven't we? The time when you told me not to darken your door again until I'd cleaned up my act."

"Oh. That time. When I stopped speaking to you because you'd been running all over Southern California acting like the worst kind of slut."

"Men can't be sluts."

"*Au contraire*, my friend. And if the shoe fits..."

"Well, it all came to a screeching halt after Danny died."

"I know. Mrs. Sullivan told me."

"My landlady? You were discussing my sex life with my *landlady*?"

"It wasn't like that. She just mentioned it in passing, the last time I flew out to L.A. to visit you. She must have thought we were—ah...involved—because she told me I was the only woman you'd had in your apartment in nearly two years."

"You do realize why?"

"Fear of getting an STD?"

"I'm being serious. Try to act like it. I was waiting for you."

"Waiting?" she said. "For me?"

"I knew you'd need time, and I was determined to give you all the time you needed. But I was waiting."

Something inside her went a little melty at his words. He always had that effect on her. "But how'd you know—"

"That you'd come around? Because we loved each other. We'd loved each other since the beginning of time. There was only one direction that could go, and I knew that sooner or later, you'd figure it out. In the meantime...I just waited. It's not like it was a hardship. There wasn't anybody else I wanted. And you were worth waiting for."

Something happened inside her heart, something knife-sharp, exquisite and inexplicable. She cleared her throat. "Babe?"

"What?"

"So were you. Worth waiting for."

"I'm so glad you feel that way. Because you'll be waiting a little longer."

"Very clever, MacKenzie, the way you segued so smoothly into that little gem. How much longer?"

"Probably an extra three weeks."

"Oh, for God's sake, Rob!"

"Hey, the tour's a success. We're picking up more dates. That's a good thing, right?"

"Of course it's a success. And why do you suppose that is? It couldn't possibly have anything to do with the fact that this relatively unknown band managed to snag the illustrious Rob MacKenzie, guitarist extraordinaire, to fill in on their crappy, two-bit concert tour?"

"Is that bitterness I hear in your voice?"

"I've found that I don't much like living alone."

"What do you mean? You're not living alone."

"Are you really that dense? Do I have to spell it out for you?"

"Oh," he said.

"Yes. Oh. I'm almost desperate enough to take you up on that offer you made me a couple of weeks ago."

"Alas, and to my vast regret, due to a stunning lack of privacy, that offer will have to stay on hold for the foreseeable future."

"Let me guess. You're leaning against a dirty, graffiti-covered wall outside the men's room in some packed roadhouse, you've been up for eighteen hours, haven't eaten in twelve, haven't brushed your teeth or your hair for two days, and the minute you're done performing tonight, it'll be back on the bus for another twelve-hour drive to nowhere."

"Sometimes you scare the living shit out of me."

"I'm not psychic. I'm basing this on past experience. If you ever do come home, it'll take me weeks to rehabilitate you to a civilized state."

"A little physical therapy should work wonders."

"Lucky for you that I'm so good with my hands."

At the other end of the line, he let out a snort of laughter. Then said, "Gotta run, babe. Break's over. Hang in there. This, too, shall pass."

"If it doesn't, I'll just have to pick up some hot young stud to tide me over. Maybe I should start cruising the bowling alley."

"Hah! Fiore?"

"What?"

"You are so full of shit."

Paige

Washing and waxing a dirty police cruiser and scraping up dog turds from the sidewalk weren't exactly her idea of how to spend a quality Saturday afternoon. The work she and Lissa were performing under the supervision of that Nazi, Scotty Deverell, was tedious and exhausting. Worse, it was keeping her away from the Saturday-afternoon football games. If she wasn't afraid Deverell would handcuff her and lock her up in his jail, she'd probably shove Lissa to the ground and pound her head repeatedly against the pavement.

"Look, I'm sorry," Lissa said for the fourteenth time in the last hour. "I didn't mean to get you in trouble."

Paige pointed the high-pressure hose at the fender she'd just scrubbed. "Sorry doesn't cut it. I'm stuck doing this crap for the next month, your old man is blaming me for the whole debacle, and as if that's not enough, I'm grounded for two weeks. No football games. No hanging out after school. I can't even go to band practice! The guys have to come to my house to practice. It's humiliating. I'm reduced to sitting at home watching *General Hospital* with Leroy, and standing here scrubbing squished bug guts off the grill of a police cruiser. I have you to thank for that."

"I couldn't tell my dad the truth! If I did, I'd be stuck in the house until I turn thirty."

"My heart bleeds for you."

With her sponge, Lissa scrubbed at a particularly stubborn stain. "So, your stepmother is a hardass?"

"Not really. But she made me talk to *him*. My father."

"Did he ream you a new one?"

"He just gave me this lecture about responsibility and maturity, and made sure I understood how much I'd disappointed him. He said he'd be expecting a different kind of behavior from me in the future."

"Oh, boy. The old guilt trip. When will parents figure out that it never works?"

"I don't know, it kind of did. This whole thing makes me look like a fool. Even worse, a thieving fool."

"If you'd been a little quicker at pocketing the freaking lipstick, and if you'd looked a little less guilty, we never would have been caught."

"Excuse me?" Slowly, Paige lifted her Foster Grants and stared at Lissa from beneath them. "You're blaming this on *me*?"

Lissa had the grace to blush. "Not entirely. But, Jesus, Paige, I never got caught before. Because I know what I'm doing. I should've known better than to tag-team with you. You're such a goody-two-shoes."

Paige stood there with her mouth hanging open while Lissa went back to scrubbing. She took a deep breath, struggled briefly with her inner demons. And then caved. To hell with it. She was already in trouble. What was a little more? This time, at least it would be worth whatever punishment she was dealt. She shot a quick glance at Officer McDoofus, whose idea of supervision was to sit in a lawn chair, eating a ham sandwich and reading a paperback novel.

She adjusted the nozzle of the hose, picked its heavy weight off the ground and wound it around her arm a couple of times. "Hey, Lissa," she said.

Crouched in front of the car, Lissa looked up. "What?"

"Just this." And Paige turned a torrent of icy water, full-force, on her partner in crime.

***

"What on earth am I going to do with you?" Her stepmother, shoulders squared and knuckles white on the steering wheel, sounded really ticked off.

"She deserved it!" Paige said. "She blamed this whole mess on me! The girls at school already hate me. Now they whisper and laugh at me when I walk by. Her dad thinks I'm responsible, because his precious baby girl can do no wrong, and I'm the big, bad city kid who came here to corrupt his poor darling. Well, guess what? His poor darling has been stealing for years! When I told her it was unethical, you know what she said? That she does it all the time, and I'm just a big chicken! Now, she's saying it's my fault we got caught. That I blew it for both of us because I'm not good enough at being a thief. The little witch!"

"Have you considered the possibility that it's time you found yourself a better class of friends?"

Paige snorted. "That 20/20 hindsight thing's a real bitch."

"Biff is making a lot of noise about this. He's threatening to sue. Assault with a dangerous weapon. Pain and mental anguish. Whatever other trumped-up charges he can come up with. He knows we have money. His kind is really good at sniffing it out. If he finds himself an ambulance chaser, this could cost us a pretty penny."

"Dangerous weapon? Oh, please. Lissa's old man is a blowhard. He'll rant and rave, but in the end, he won't do anything. Bullies never do."

"Your father is not going to find this amusing."

Her own pain and mental anguish suddenly skyrocketed as a headache sprang to life directly behind her left eye. "Do we really have to tell him?"

Casey seemed to consider her question. "Why do the girls at school hate you?"

Heat suffused her face. "It's nothing."

"Paige," her stepmother said, in that parental tone of voice that meant *proceed at your own risk.*

"Fine. If you must know, I was seen talking to Mikey one day in the cafeteria. Apparently he's the sex god of Jackson High, so every feline claw in residence came unsheathed. Just in case ripping me to shreds became an option. How dare I, one of the Great Unwashed, have the audacity to actually speak to their god? Especially when he has the good sense to not even give the time of day to most of them?"

"I had no idea. It wasn't like that when I was in school. There were cliques, but for the most part, they peacefully coexisted." Casey went quiet for a moment. "Have there been any incidents I should know about?"

"It's not like that. Mostly they just pretend I'm invisible. Or they did, until this whole shoplifting thing. Now they laugh behind my back. But it's not that big a deal. I don't care about any of them. I have friends. I have Luke, and the guys in the band. And—" She laughed, but there was little humor in it. "I guess I probably don't have Lissa any more."

"After what you did to her today? Probably not. Which doesn't appear to be any great loss."

"I'm sorry. Really. I wasn't thinking about you having to deal with her old man or the cops. I just got so mad, I wanted to annihilate her."

"You have a hot temper. While I understand your motivation, that doesn't make it right, what you did."

"It's not like I hurt her. It was only water."

"High-pressure water. No, you didn't hurt her, but you could have."

"Actually, it was pretty funny. It knocked her right on her—"

"Paige! You're not making this any better!"

She'd never heard that tone coming from her stepmother, and it was shocking enough to bring her back down to earth. "Okay. So...I'll just shut up now."

"Good choice."

When they got home, the boys were already there, waiting in their eclectic collection of beat-up cars for band practice. Paige retrieved her guitar and the keys to the studio, unlocked the barn, then helped Tobey carry in the various pieces of his drum set. For a few minutes, they busied themselves setting up equipment. "Hey, Paige," Craig said, "where's the nearest electrical outlet?"

"Behind that table. You can move it out from the wall a little."

"Holy crap," Corey said, "take a look at this mixing board. Sweet!"

"Touch a thing," Paige said, "and I'll amputate your fingers. All this stuff belongs to my old man, and he dropped a small fortune on it. You break anything and I'll be homeless."

"Hey, there's Coke in this little fridge," Tobey said. "Can we have some?"

"One each," Paige said, wondering if this had been a mistake. But Casey wouldn't let her go to Tobey's house while she was grounded, and it had been decent of her stepmother to offer the studio space for their practice. Paige didn't want to blow it.

"So what's with the poster?" Tobey stood, Coke bottle in hand, studying the huge framed photo on the wall.

"It's an old publicity shot." Paige came over to stand beside him. She liked the photo, liked the way it illustrated the dynamic between her father and his two best friends. Set against a clean white background, they stood in a comfortable grouping. Danny's arms, wrapped around his wife, held her close against his chest. Paige's father, just inches away, had a forearm resting on Casey's shoulder. In his free hand, he clutched the neck of an old guitar, its butt end propped against the floor near his feet. The photographer must have stood on a ladder to take the shot, because all three of them were looking up into the camera lens. Casey's hair had been long then, hanging all the way to her waist. Danny Fiore had the bluest eyes Paige had ever seen, and a single, deep dimple in one cheek. Rob MacKenzie had been so scrawny that his legs, encased in scruffy jeans, looked miles long.

"I know your dad," Tobey said, "and your stepmother. But who's the other guy?"

She just looked at him. Raised an eyebrow. Said, "That's Danny Fiore."

He looked blank. "Who's Danny Fiore?"

This time, she couldn't help herself. She gaped at him in incredulity. "You're kidding me, right?" Tobey shrugged, unfazed by his unfathomable ignorance. She looked around the room. "Tell me he's kidding."

"I don't think he's kidding," Luke said.

She slowly shook her head in disbelief. Said to Tobey, "And you call yourself a musician? Go home and ask your mother. Meanwhile, are we here to dub around, or are we going to play some music?"

Rob

He tapped his pen impatiently against the postcard resting on his thigh. It was hard to find anything meaningful to say. He barely knew the kid, but Casey said she was reading the cards he sent, that she seemed pleased by them, so he worked daily to come up with something pithy to write. His own off-the-wall brand of humor, blended with what he hoped was paternal wisdom, was a screwed-up way to try to build a relationship, but from this distance, it was his only option. He probably shouldn't have run off and left Paige for his wife to deal with. He should have told Chico he wasn't available. The kid was, ultimately, his responsibility, and his mother was right. He should be home, getting to know his daughter. When had Mary MacKenzie ever not been right? He'd spent decades ignoring her advice, to his own detriment. He'd been well into his thirties before he finally started listening.

His mind a blank, he temporarily gave up on the postcard. The scenery that flashed by his window was flat and boring, that boredom broken only by the occasional run-down farmhouse standing solitary in the distance. There had been a time when the road had piqued his wanderlust. Now, he just wanted to go home. He'd done more than his share of wandering, and it was getting old. He was getting old. It was no longer an adventure, showering twice a week, trying to sleep slouched against the rattling side of a moving bus, eating at random intervals dictated by the location of the nearest highway rest stop. Yearning for the intimacy of lying beside his wife at night. The playing was heaven; being onstage was close to a religious experience. But the trade-off wasn't worth it. He couldn't imagine going back to this kind of lifestyle on any permanent basis.

The bus hit a bump, and his postcard fell, drifting on an air current toward the center aisle. He reached out to grab it, but Chico was faster. He caught the card in mid-air, handed it back to Rob, then plopped down beside him. "Hey."

"Hey. Thanks. Good catch."

"So what's with you, writing *War and Peace* in postcard-size bites? I've been watching you. Love letters to the little woman?" Chico waggled heavy, dark brows.

He let out a soft laugh. "Nah. They're for my kid."

Those dark brows went sky-high. "You got a kid, man? I didn't know you had a kid."

"Neither did I, until a couple of months ago. Paige. She's fifteen—"

"Oh, boy."

"—and she's a handful. Right now, she's giving Casey a real run for her money."

"Girls," Chico said, and shook his head. "You think boys are bad? They're nothing compared to girls. I wish you luck with her, my friend. So..." Chico studied him with curious brown eyes. "You and Casey."

"What? Does that seem so odd?"

"Hell, no. I had my money on you a dozen years ago. It just took you a while to catch up."

"Yeah. Well." He glanced out the window again, watched a broad expanse of brown farmland pass by in a blur. "How do you do it? At our age, how do you keep on keeping on? With a wife and kids at home, doesn't the road get to you?"

Chico leaned back on his tailbone and crossed his ankles. "Let me tell you. It's called paying the rent. It's how we make our living. My wife and kids? Three hundred days a year on the road keeps a roof over their heads and food in their bellies. We all have different journeys in life, MacKenzie, and not all of us made it big like you did. Most of us actually have to work for a living."

He opened his mouth to respond, but again, Chico was quicker. "I didn't mean that the way it sounded. You've earned everything you have. I'm just stating facts. You made it to a level in music that I can only dream about. And being on the road so much is a hardship in some ways. But I'm a musician. I may not be rich, I may not be famous, but by God, I'm making a living doing what I love. And in my book, that makes me a rich man."

"You want to hear something really dicey? You say I've earned everything I have, but the truth is, there's only one reason why I got to where I got: Danny Fiore."

"Not true. Your talent outshines all of us."

"It is true, and here's why." He shifted position, stretched out his legs as far as the cramped seating would allow. "I've never told this to anyone before, and I'd appreciate it if you didn't repeat it. Drew Lawrence—the Ariel Records executive who signed Danny—told me this a couple of years ago. It blew me away, because I had no idea. I've never said a thing about it to Casey, and I don't think she knows, either. But when Drew offered Danny that record contract—" He met Chico's dark eyes. "Danny told him it was a no-go unless we signed together. He wasn't doing it unless he could take me along."

Chico considered it. Finally said, softly, "Wow."

"That's what I call loyalty. And I feel so damn guilty. Because sometimes, I hated him for the way he treated Casey. I didn't think he deserved her. Sometimes I wanted to smash his head into a brick wall until I knocked some sense into him. And now, here I am, living off the fruits of his labor and sleeping with his wife. It really makes me proud."

"You didn't always hate him. You two, on stage together, you had this connection. You drew sparks from each other. Everybody could see it."

"In all the ways that mattered, he was my brother."

"And you have to look at it that way, man. Who's to say it was loyalty that made him do it? Maybe he was afraid he couldn't make it on his own, without you. Ever think of that?"

He shrugged. "Maybe. But sometimes, I feel invisible. And it's not a good feeling."

"Do you think I asked you to come on tour with us because you were an old friend and I thought you might say yes? I asked you because you're the best guitarist I know. And that has nothing to do with Danny Fiore. That's pure, one hundred percent Rob MacKenzie. So stop stewing over meaningless trivia. He did you a favor. *One flipping favor.* And how many did you do for him? You wrote the goddamn music. You played on the records. You produced the damn things. You toured with him in venues that packed in fifty-thousand screaming fans. I'd say your karma quotient trumps his by a mile."

"And then I ended up with his wife."

"The guy died, MacKenzie. If you've ever heard those little words 'until death do us part' you know damn well she's not his wife any more. That death thing is pretty final. You two made it legal, right? So she's your wife, and Fiore has no say about it any more. You're the one she's sleeping with these days. Be grateful. She's a good woman. Smart and kind and sexy. You deserve her just as much as you deserve anything else you have."

"I suppose you're right."

"I'm right. Now, do yourself a favor. There's a rest stop coming up in about a half-hour. Find yourself a pay phone, call your old lady, and tell her you love her." Chico stood, swaying slightly with the motion of the bus. "I guarantee you'll feel better after."

"Thanks. I didn't mean to spill all this angst in your lap."

"It's the road, man. Makes us all a little crazy after a while."

Casey

It wasn't like her to be so cranky. What Paige had done was wrong, but it was hardly time to call in the major crimes unit. In truth, what the kid had done was sort of funny, in a sick and twisted way. Even Scotty Deverell had been having trouble keeping a straight face at the sight of a bedraggled and sopping Lissa Norton. Biff Norton had, as usual, blown it all out of proportion. His threats were ludicrous, and if she told Rob about them, he'd probably laugh himself silly. So why had she lost her temper with her stepdaughter? There was no reasonable explanation. She'd simply been filled with rage, a rage that came from out of nowhere, and disappeared just as quickly.

Rob had been gone for too damn long. That was the problem. They'd been apart for more than a month, and she wasn't handling it well. That explained why she was pacing her kitchen on a lovely autumn afternoon instead of going outside and enjoying the beautiful day. This long-distance marriage thing was for the birds. And to put it bluntly, it was more than just his companionship she was missing. As Paula had so eloquently put it, a phone call every day did not make up for a warm man in her bed every night. Her hormones were obviously out of whack. If he didn't come back soon, she was going to jump in her car, track him down, and drag him home.

She paused in her pacing, wheeled around, and headed for the living room. She moved to the stack of CDs beside the stereo, shuffled through them and found the one she wanted. *The Edge of Nowhere*. If she couldn't have the real thing, she could at least have a reasonable facsimile. She popped the CD into the player and let it flow over her, the soft tones of her husband's voice, the weeping guitars, the sophisticated and bluesy arrangements that were classic MacKenzie.

The music that Rob MacKenzie created transported her to another place, some rich and vivid Shangri-La. He was an amazing composer, light years beyond her meager talents. She could always come up with a catchy melody and solid lyrics. What Rob did was turn simplicity into symphony. His arranging skills were second to none. He knew instinctively where to add strings, where to add horns, where to weave in a countermelody that brilliantly complemented the lead melody. He was the one who took their vague scribblings and turned them into hit songs. She'd never been able to figure out how he did it. He jokingly referred to his gift as auditory hallucinations, and sometimes she wondered if that was really so far from the truth.

He'd written this, his first solo album, without her, in a cabin somewhere in the wilds of Oregon, after he'd walked away from his long-time partnership with Danny. *The Edge of Nowhere*, both the song and the album, had perfectly captured his state of mind at the time, as he took faltering steps into the unknown to find out whether he had the chops to carry a solo career.

As if there'd ever been any question about that.

She'd already made her own escape. After Katie died and her marriage fell apart, she'd moved east, putting three thousand miles between herself and Danny Fiore. While Rob was searching for himself in that remote cabin on a pristine lake in Oregon, Casey had rented a tiny two-bedroom apartment in the North End of Boston, where she began her own journey of self-discovery.

He'd brought her the finished album on her thirtieth birthday, and sold her on the jazzy concept he'd been contemplating for his second solo offering. She took the bait, and they began working together on that second album. For a time, they'd worked on opposite coasts, connected by telephone and fax machine. Until one day, he packed his guitar and his cat, flew east, and moved into her guest room.

Living together had felt natural to both of them; after all, they'd lived together the entire time they were in New York. In hindsight, she realized that people probably believed they were together. A couple. But it wasn't like that. They worked together, they played together, they ran together. He was her best friend, and although she loved him—she'd always loved him—their relationship was strictly platonic.

Then he'd kissed her on that beach in Nassau, and everything had changed between them.

Kissed was, in reality, a vast understatement. Ravished would be more accurate. There hadn't been one iota of civilized behavior in the kisses he'd laid on her, standing in the frothing surf on a moonlit Bahamian beach, both of them semi-drunk on alcohol and thoroughly intoxicated on each other. It had been wonderful, and terrible, and heady, and impossible, the most exciting moment of her life. Until he remembered that in spite of a lengthy marital separation, she was still legally wed to Danny. Because somewhere beneath the raging barbarian with plundering lips and wandering hands lived a gentleman who'd been raised properly by a mother who'd managed to instill strong moral standards in nine little MacKenzies, he had backstepped and apologized for crossing the line.

The ensuing battle had been a doozy. Not their worst, not by a long shot. But a doozy nevertheless.

The next day, he'd done his best to convince her that it was the tropical setting, combined with the booze and the lengthy bout of celibacy on both their parts, that had been responsible for their lapse in judgment. And he'd told her it was time to get off the fence: Either divorce Danny and move on with her life, or give her marriage another try.

Even in her deep denial, she'd recognized the subtext of his message. As long as she was still tied to Danny, Rob MacKenzie wasn't willing to take that giant step forward with her. If she severed the tie, the next move would be up to her.

Rob, of course, was right. She couldn't continue indefinitely to live in limbo. She and Danny were still legally wed. She still wore her wedding ring, had never taken it off, even though they hadn't spoken since she'd walked out the door ten months earlier. One way or the other, the situation needed to be resolved.

For days, she'd vacillated. She'd thought about what she had with Danny, and what she might have with Rob if she was brave enough to take that leap of faith. She considered their steadfast friendship, his checkered past and his disastrous history with women. Her own disastrous history with Danny. And wasn't sure she had the courage to do what her heart was urging.

So she'd called Danny and asked him to fly to Boston. Just to talk. To find resolution to a situation they'd left hanging for nearly a year.

He'd arrived bearing flowers, stunningly handsome in a charcoal tweed jacket, neatly pressed jeans, and a shirt that precisely matched the color of his eyes. He took her breath away.

He'd always taken her breath away. He was the most beautiful man she'd ever seen.

But she had an agenda. A plan. Talking points, all laid out neatly in her head.

And then she'd looked into those blue eyes, and all her talking points vaporized, and there was nothing but Danny. Instead of talking, she'd ended up in bed with her estranged husband.

It was a colossally stupid move on her part. But she'd been making colossally stupid moves where Danny was concerned since the first time she set eyes on him. In her defense, they'd been married for thirteen years, and they'd loved each other obsessively. They'd shared, and lost, a child. In so many ways, she still loved him. Maybe not in the way she'd once loved him, but she couldn't simply erase her feelings for this man she'd fallen in love with at first sight when she was just eighteen years old.

The sex didn't resolve their differences. It didn't resolve anything, beyond the welcome physical release after a year of celibacy. But they talked afterward, and she realized that Danny had changed. That while she'd been finding herself, he'd done some growing of his own. And he was still her husband. He wanted her back. He was safe and comfortable and familiar, and those blue eyes of his were so sincere when he told her how much he loved her, how much he'd missed her.

And she was a coward.

The truth had eluded her then, but she saw it so clearly now that it took her breath away. She'd been crippled by fear, knife-sharp and devastating. Fear of the unknown, fear of losing the one solid thing in her life. If she took Danny back, and they didn't make it, at least she could say she'd given it her all. Life would go on. She'd already proven to herself that she could live without him.

It was Rob she couldn't live without.

In hindsight, her distorted logic was difficult to understand, but at the time, in her state of utter denial, it had made sense. If she started a sexual relationship with Rob MacKenzie, and that relationship crashed and burned—and Rob had a lengthy history of crash-and-burn relationships—she would lose him forever. If she was forced to choose between having half of MacKenzie and having none of him, that was really no choice at all. She'd always believed that her marriage to Danny was the most significant relationship in her life. But she'd been wrong. Her most significant, most solid and enduring relationship, the one she'd been able to depend on for her entire adult life, was her friendship with Rob. They shared a connection she'd never experienced with any other living soul. Above all else, she needed to save that friendship, that connection, even if saving it meant going back to Danny. Because to lose it would rip her heart from her chest.

Her heart had been ripped from her chest anyway, as she'd stood at the doorway to her guest room, watching MacKenzie pack what little he'd brought with him from California. A couple of suitcases stuffed with wrinkled clothes. The briefcase where he'd tucked all the sheet music for that second album on which they'd spent so many hours collaborating. His guitar and his cat. A bag of cat food, another bag of kitty litter.

She'd helped him carry his belongings down that steep, narrow staircase to the taxi that waited at the curb. He crammed it all into the back seat of the cab, and then he turned to her, standing forlorn and shattered on the sidewalk. "Are you sure?" he'd said. "Are you absolutely, one hundred percent certain that this is what you want?"

For the first time in their lives, she'd lied to him. Because she wasn't sure. Not at all. She'd believed she was making the right decision. But if it was right, why did it feel like this? Why did *she* feel like this?

"Yes," she said.

Green eyes gazed somberly into green eyes, and then he nodded.

Heart thudding, she said, "Tell me we're okay. Please tell me we're okay."

He brushed his knuckles across her cheek and stepped forward to take her in his arms. "Are you kidding? You and I, sweetheart, will always be okay."

Why was it that he smelled so wonderful? She pressed her face to his chest and clung to him. "Then you're not mad at me?"

His arms tightened around her and he buried his face in her hair. "How could I be mad at you? You did exactly what I told you to do. You stopped waffling and made a choice. What I am is proud of you."

He released her then, and without looking back, he climbed into the cab and shut the door. And as the taxi carrying Rob MacKenzie away from her slowly navigated perpetually-clogged Hanover Street, Casey Fiore stood on the sidewalk, arms crossed against a raw March afternoon, and watched until he was out of sight. Fighting the urge to run after him, call him back, tell him she'd made a mistake.

But it was too late for that. She'd made a commitment to Danny, the man whose ring she wore, the man she'd loved since she was eighteen years old, and she was determined to give her marriage one final try. She'd already told him this was the last time. If they didn't make it this time, there would be no more chances. She was a strong woman; she would simply put one foot in front of the other and march forward.

And everything would work out the way it was meant to be.

Hands trembling, stomach roiling with nausea, she had climbed the stairs to her apartment, let herself in, and closed the door. The place already felt empty without him. Lifeless. In the silence, she took a long, shuddering breath. Swiped at a damning tear. Then she, who never cried, sat down hard on the couch in that dreary March dusk and wept into her clenched hands.

When she was done, when she'd pulled herself together and had wiped her eyes and her nose, she'd marched adamantly to the phone and called her father to tell him that she and Danny would be coming to Maine on the weekend to look at houses.

Now, five years later, as she paced her solitary kitchen on a blue and gold autumn afternoon, in the house she and Danny had purchased on that long-ago weekend, with Rob a thousand miles away on a creaky tour bus, the hard, unflinching truth struck her: That kiss on the beach hadn't started anything. It had merely opened a door and released a flood of emotion that had been trapped inside her for years, buried beneath a solid wall of denial.

It was astonishing to realize, after two decades of friendship and fifteen months of marriage, that she was madly, deeply, irrevocably in love with her husband, and that she had been for years. Even more astonishing to realize that on a raw March afternoon in Boston five years earlier, letting him go had been the single worst decision of her life.

How could she have been so stupid?

Hands braced against the edge of the kitchen counter, she took a hard breath. Outside her window, that exquisite slanted light that could only be found on an autumn afternoon painted the world a burnished gold. For some inexplicable reason, everything looked different. Colors were brighter, sharper. Her own heartbeat seemed stronger, more pronounced. Her hands, pale and slender, their fingernails painted a soft pink, seemed unfamiliar, the bones prominent, veins tracing pathways she'd never noticed before. Goosebumps lay along her arms, her legs, her breasts. And inside her chest burned something she'd never felt before, something so strong, so sweet, so huge it nearly smothered her.

In the living room, the clock struck six. Somehow, she'd lost track of the afternoon, had let it slip away from her. Dusk would come soon. It was time to send the boys home, time to get ready for the weekly Saturday-night gathering.

When she shut off the stereo, the warmth he'd created disappeared, and cold silence rushed in to fill the empty space. She picked up the CD case, studied the cover photo, light filtering through a lush ceiling of green leaves and falling in dappled patterns on his face. Rattled, she dropped it, donned a jacket, and headed outside.

She heard the music before she reached the barn, instantly recognized the song, but not the voice that sang it. She knew every note of that song, knew it intimately, knew it because she and Rob had written it for Danny eight years ago, knew it because it had earned them their second Grammy and had cemented their reputation as composers, knew it because *Seasons of the Heart* had become Danny's signature song, forever connected with his name.

Casey opened the door and stepped inside the studio. The kids were so involved in what they were playing that nobody even noticed her standing just inside the door, hands tucked into the pockets of her jacket, gaping at the girl who held the microphone. She sang with eyes closed, face raised to the sky, all that tangled blond hair tossed back over her shoulders. How could this be possible? This dark, smoky, Janis Joplin voice couldn't possibly be coming from that lanky kid. It was a dark song, a song about hard living and hard loving, about loss and grief and coming out the other side still intact. It wasn't the kind of song a fifteen-year-old girl should be singing. It wasn't the kind of song a fifteen-year-old girl should even understand. Yet Paige MacKenzie not only sang it, but conquered it and made it her own.

Stunned, Casey watched and listened as her stepdaughter put her own fingerprints all over what was, without question, the greatest song she and Rob had ever written. The song snaked and twisted, built and climbed with a visceral force, moving toward a climactic moment when it would blow sky-high with a full-octave leap that few singers could achieve. Danny had done it without breaking a sweat, but he'd had a range that was unequaled, and they'd written the song to take full advantage of that range.

There was no way Paige was going to make it. She was going to fall flat on her face. Casey waited with breathless anticipation as the song climbed higher and higher, twisting and winding, until the girl reached that pivotal moment and, without any effort at all, tilted back her head and took the leap.

And nailed it.

Clean and clear, without scooping, without a single false step, she hit that sweet note and held it. A thrill shot through Casey's body, and the hairs on her arms stood up, and the last time she'd felt this way she'd been eighteen years old, standing in a smoky, overcrowded bar in Boston's Kenmore Square, and it had been Danny doing the singing.

The last note faded, and Paige finally noticed her. A mix of emotions flickered across the kid's face: shock, embarrassment, guilt. And finally, defiance. She raised her chin like a true MacKenzie, squared her shoulders, crossed her arms. In the silence, she just looked at her stepmother.

From somewhere in the midst of her astonishment, Casey managed to find her voice. With a calm that belied her true feelings, she said, "Paige, my sweet, I do believe there's something you forgot to tell us."

Paige

When Mikey came into the kitchen, all the adults greeted him, but it was his Aunt Casey he enveloped in a bear hug. Hugging him back, she reached up to ruffle his hair and said, "When did you get to be so tall?"

"I was taller than you when I was twelve."

"Who are you trying to kid? You were taller than me when you were five."

They all got a laugh out of that. Bill said, "Nice play today, kid."

"Thanks." He moved to the Crock-Pot on the kitchen counter and lifted the lid. Amazing smells poured out, permeating the kitchen. He glanced over at Paige, leaning against the counter, and said softly, "Hi."

"Hi."

"This stuff any good?"

"Casey made it. That should answer your question."

He took a paper bowl from the stack on the table and spooned chili into it. Rummaged in the drawer for a soup spoon, then leaned back against the counter, next to her, and began eating. "Oh, man," he said, "this is good stuff."

"Everything she makes is good stuff."

He took another bite. Said, "So how's the community service going?"

Her face turned twenty different shades of red. "Do we really have to talk about that?"

"You know what they say. Don't do the crime if you can't do the time."

"That's a low blow."

Those dark eyes studied her face. He scooped another spoonful of chili into his mouth. Chewed and swallowed. Said, "You're your own worst enemy, you know."

She squared her jaw. "How's that, exactly?"

"You have this huge chip on your shoulder. It's really unbecoming."

"If it's so unbecoming, then why are you standing here, talking to me?"

The smile took her by surprise. How often had she seen Mikey Lindstrom smile? He licked the spoon, dropped it in the sink, and tossed the paper bowl in the trash. "Maybe," he said, "I like to live dangerously. You want to get out of here for a while?"

"I'm grounded."

"I told you once before, you underestimate my powers. Wait here. I'll take care of it."

She watched as he threaded his way through the crowded kitchen to her stepmother. Casey glanced up at Paige, swung back around to her nephew, and said something. Mikey nodded, and she patted his arm.

He returned, somber of face, but there was something in those eyes of his that she couldn't decipher. "All clear," he said. "Be home by ten. Grab your jacket."

Outside, she hoisted herself up into the cab of his old pickup, settled into the seat, listened as the engine roared to life. He turned on the headlights, said, "Seat belt," and Paige reached to wrap it around her.

"Where are we going?"

He backed the truck around, changed direction, and pulled out of the driveway. "You'll see."

They rode in a comfortable silence, the truck rattling down the unpaved road. She had no idea where they were headed, for these back roads all looked the same to her, especially in the dark. Mikey took a series of turns, each turn gradually taking them higher until, seemingly in the middle of nowhere, he took a left onto a road that was little more than a grassy path through the woods. The climb was steep, and through the trees, she caught a glimpse of starlight. Then, suddenly, they reached the top, and came to a stop in the middle of a wide-open, grassy field. Above them, the night sky was huge, and dotted with stars. "What's this place?" she said. "What's here?"

"Magic, if we're lucky. Zip up your coat. It's chilly out there."

He grabbed a folded blanket from behind the seat and they walked side by side to the very top of the hill. While he spread the blanket on the ground, she stood, hands in her pockets, and gazed down through the darkness to the lights twinkling in the valley a half-mile below them.

They sat on the blanket together, long legs stretched out in front of them. She studied his feet in cracked leather work boots with the laces undone. "Are we here for a reason?"

"Don't worry. I'm not about to molest you."

In the darkness, she felt her face flush. "I never said that."

"You were thinking it. You warm enough?"

She was a little chilly, but she wasn't about to admit it to him. She didn't want him thinking she was some whiny, frou-frou hothouse flower. "I'm fine."

In the chill night air, his body heat drifted over to her, warm and comforting. He moved a little closer, close enough that their elbows rubbed. If he'd been any other boy, she would have thought he was about to make a move on her. But he wasn't any other boy. He was Mikey, and she knew instinctively that she could trust him, that he was a straight shooter, that he'd never do anything to hurt her.

She cleared her throat. "So," she said. "What are we waiting for?"

"It might not happen. There's no guarantee. But the time of year and the atmospheric conditions are right, and—"

Above their heads, a white light flickered in the night sky. "Look," he said, as it grew brighter, licking and darting like a flame.

"What the—"

"Just watch."

She leaned forward, hands clasped together for warmth, and watched as the light turned red, then green. Always moving, never the same, shimmering like some giant bonfire in the heavens. "It's beautiful," she breathed. "What is it?"

"Aurora borealis."

"Northern lights? But I thought you could only see them from Canada. Or the North Pole. Or the second star to the right."

"When the conditions are just so, and you get lucky, you can see them from here."

Oblivious to the cold, she sat mesmerized by the light show that Mother Nature was performing just for them. Softly, he said, "They say it may have something to do with sun flares, but I can't explain the connection. I'm no scientist."

"I don't want to know the scientific explanation. I prefer the mystery."

"Something like this," he said, "makes you realize how small you are. And how infinite the universe is."

"Wow," she said. "You're pretty deep, for a football player. Who knew?"

He nudged her shoulder playfully with his, then left it there, and they sat like that, warmth to warmth, for what seemed like hours, until Mother Nature drew the curtain and the show finally came to an end. He folded up the blanket and they climbed back in the pickup truck. Suddenly freezing, she wrapped her arms around herself, shuddering, while she waited for the truck to warm up.

The trip to her house was curiously silent. Something had changed between them. They'd forged some kind of psychic connection she couldn't explain. Mikey pulled the truck into her driveway and killed the engine. Breathless with anticipation, she waited in the dark for something, some sign that she wasn't the only one feeling it.

But all he did was open the door and walk around to her side of the truck. Ever the perfect gentleman, he held the door for her, then walked her in silence to the house.

They stood awkwardly on the steps. Maybe she'd been wrong about the connection. She would have sworn he felt it, too, but maybe that was wishful thinking. "Thanks," she said. "That was amazing."

Instead of speaking, he reached out and touched her hair in an achingly intimate gesture. While her heart beat double-time, he wrapped a single golden curl around his index finger. Paige wet her lips. Opened them and took a breath.

And he said, "I have to go. See you around, kid."

In disbelief, she watched him turn and walk back to his truck. The driver's door creaked a protest when he opened it. He stepped up onto the running board, slid into the driver's seat, and closed the door. Started the engine. And while she stood there watching, he backed the truck around, headed down the driveway, and made his escape.

As she watched him drive out of sight, a tiny crack appeared in the hard wall she'd built around her heart.

Casey

The phone dragged her out of sleep. She rolled over, snatched it up, and fumbled it to her ear. The bedside clock read 3:23 a.m. "Hey," she said groggily.

"Hey," her husband said. "Whatcha doing?"

"At 3:23 in the morning? Oh, you know, the usual. Feeding the chickens, slopping the hogs..."

"Hah. We don't have any hogs. I jus' called to say—" He paused, the open line humming between them. "—I love you."

A hard little bud of tender emotion unfurled inside her, tickling her insides as it opened like the soft petals on a rose. She said, "Channeling your inner Stevie Wonder, are you?"

"What? Oh. Hah."

"Have you been drinking, MacKenzie?"

"Maybe. Jus' a little."

"Or maybe a lot. What's with that?"

He let out a soft little belch. "Sorry. Iss a celebration. The tour's over. *Finis. Sayonara.* I'm coming home. T'morrow. Leavin' on a jet plane."

"And yet another song title. We're just brimming with lyricism tonight, aren't we?"

"I'm coming home to you, baby. Is that a song title? Wait, I got a better one. *Daddy's Home.* Almost."

"You are very drunk, my love."

"Am I? Really?"

"Without question. Totally wasted."

"Not that. Am I your love?"

"Absolutely. Even totally wasted."

"Miss you so much. Miss your snarky mouth. And that sof' skin. You have the softes' skin. Love to touch you. Makes me all shaky inside."

That tender thing blossoming inside her grew larger and more insistent. "It's a good thing you're coming home," she said, "because all those hot young guys at the bowling alley are starting to look really, really good. Those shirts. Those shoes. Those—"

"Hah. You're a one-woman comedy act." He paused, uttered another soft belch. "I'll have you know, I have been SO damn good. Girls everywhere. Hot women. Weeks an' weeks of hot women. But not for this boy. Oh, no. You are the only one. I am ud…udderly and completely blind to all of 'em. You. Are. THE. Only woman. In the world. Jus' you. My baby, with the sof' skin and the magic hands and that hot li'l bod."

Dryly, she said, "Good to know."

"And you know what? Iss always been just you. Always. Years an' years an' years. All those other girls? Di'nt count. Nope. None of 'em. But you jus' di'nt see me." He grew melancholy. "All you could see was—" He hiccupped. And said flatly, "Him."

"I see you now," she said fiercely. "I see you so clearly now."

"All those girls. All of 'em. Subst'tutes. Because you. Were not." *Hiccup.* "Available."

"I'm here now. And I'm not going anywhere."

"Promise?"

"Of course, I promise. What's gotten into you? Besides beer?"

"Bourbon. It was bourbon that got into me."

"I see. That explains a little."

"It's jus' that…I am so nuts about you. And if you lef' me, I'd die."

Her insides melted like an ice cream cone on a hot sidewalk. "Babe?" she said. "There is less than zero chance that I will ever leave you."

"You sure 'bout that?"

"Trust me, you sweet, drunken fool, I am not going anywhere. Listen, where are you?"

"Li'l Rock."

"That's not what I meant. Are you in for the night?"

"I am. In my motel room. Motel, hah! Rat hole's more like it."

"Listen, sweetheart, I think you should hang up the phone, get some sleep, and call me tomorrow when you're sober."

"You think?"

"I do."

"And when I get home, we are gonna party. Jus' you and me. We are gonna get naked and have us some of that old folks sex."

"I'm breathless with anticipation. Go to sleep now. We'll talk tomorrow. Okay?"

"Okay." And before she could say good-night, he hung up the phone and left her holding a dead receiver.

***

It was mid-afternoon the next day before he called again. "Hey, hot stuff," she said. "A little hung over, are we?"

"No hangover, but I slept three hours later than I planned." He paused. Said tentatively, "I'm sorry about last night. I was so frigging wasted. Tell me I didn't say anything embarrassing."

"I wasn't aware that you possessed the capacity for embarrassment."

"Ha-ha. Very funny. Last night's pretty much a blank. But I have this sinking feeling that I stepped over the line into purple prose."

"Let me be sure I have this straight. In the world according to MacKenzie, phone sex is a perfectly acceptable leisure time activity. But a declaration of love—to your wife, no less—is an embarrassment? Damn, Flash, sometimes you are such a guy."

"In the words of that great philosopher Popeye, I am what I am. I can't help it."

"Go ahead, blame it on that Y chromosome. That's so much easier than taking responsibility for your own actions. Well, fine. I promise not to hold it against you. Any of it."

He groaned. "Was I that bad?"

"You were actually very sweet. And very, very drunk. What the hell were you thinking? I've never seen you wasted like that. You're always so good at holding your liquor."

"It seemed like a good idea at the time. Hanging with the guys, letting go of all the tensions of the last six weeks. Kind of a grand finale after all those weeks of hell."

"I'm disappointed in you, MacKenzie. You're far too old to start bowing to peer pressure."

"Was I really sweet?"

"You seemed quite intent on assuring me of your exemplary behavior in the face of a constant onslaught of female pulchritude."

"Shit."

"And you laid on the lovey-dovey talk pretty thick."

"See what I mean? Diarrhea of the mouth."

"Are you deliberately looking for a way to take the romance right out of it? Because if you are, you're succeeding quite nicely."

"I'm not sure how you can find anything romantic in the pathetic bleatings of a drunken Irishman. But for what it's worth, I'm sorry."

"You should be. That lovey-dovey talk made quite an impression on me. Oh, and you also made sure to remind me that we have a hot date when you get home."

"That should go without saying. We've been apart for six frigging weeks. Does the term climbing the walls mean anything to you?"

"Oh, trust me, it does. Abstinence makes the heart grow fonder."

He uttered a soft, snorting laugh. "You should have that engraved on a big wooden plaque. One of those kitschy, homespun things. We could hang it over the fireplace. See what kind of response we get out of people."

"That would go over really well when your mother came to visit."

"I'm not sure that Mom understands the concept of abstinence. We're talking about a woman who gave birth to nine kids."

"If your father, in his heyday, was anything like his son, the poor woman never stood a chance."

"I haven't heard any complaints from you so far."

"And you're not likely to be hearing any in the future."

"Good to know. Listen, babe, I have to roll. The taxi's here. My flight comes into Portland at 9:15. Be there?"

"I'll be there. Have a safe flight."

***

She stood impatiently in the airport waiting area, her coat draped over one folded arm, needles of anticipation dancing in her stomach. And then she saw him, moving steadily in her direction while talking animatedly to some stranger. Her carry-on was slung over one shoulder, the duffel bag—undoubtedly full of dirty laundry—over the other, a guitar case swinging from each hand. Hadn't he left with just one guitar? He wore a faded Aerosmith tee shirt he'd owned for at least a decade, and over the tee, unbuttoned, tails hanging loose, a wrinkled, olive-green Army shirt she'd never seen before. Knowing him, he'd probably picked it up at Goodwill. Tired and rumpled and scruffy, with a two-day growth of reddish beard, he was still the most beautiful thing she'd ever seen.

He glanced up and saw her standing there, and without so much as a good-bye to his traveling companion, he came to an abrupt halt. She straightened her shoulders and watched his face as he drank her in, from the top of her head down past her bare shoulders to the strapless bodice of the frothy little summer dress, white with splotchy red and pink flowers, that draped loosely over her breasts and gathered at the waist. It ended in a full, flowing skirt that stopped several inches above her knees. His gaze continued down her bare legs to her feet, encased in a pair of shiny pumps with four-inch stiletto heels, in a screaming shade of red to match the dress.

His attention returned to her face, and his hand went to his heart in an unmistakable gesture of admiration. Then he flashed her one of those zillion-megawatt smiles, the kind that had stolen the hearts of women from Alberta to Zimbabwe. The impact was like slamming head-first into a concrete wall. Something burst wide open inside her, and she began trembling all over, and she couldn't breathe, couldn't form a coherent thought. Goose bumps popped up on her skin as he began walking toward her. Everything and everybody else faded away to pure white noise, and he was the only thing she could see, and this tidal wave of emotion made the way she'd felt about Danny seem like a grade-school crush.

How long had her feelings run this deep? How long had she been this much in love with the man who'd been her best friend for her entire adult life? Her thudding heart refused to answer, and she just stared at him in stupefaction as he moved through all that white noise toward her, bringing with him the realization that every day, every hour, every second of her thirty-five years of living had been leading up to this moment.

He reached her, set down both guitars and the carry-on bag, let the duffel slide off his shoulder to the floor. "Such a serious face," he said.

She opened her mouth to respond, but her tongue had gone too dry to form words. Instead, she reached up a hand, brushed her palm over the whisker stubble on his cheek, moved it around to the back of his neck, and watched as his eyes, fixed on her face, went from green to gray. She reached up her free hand to touch his other cheek. Her coat slid loose from the crook of her elbow, and she let it fall to the floor. He lowered his head, kissed first her wrist, then her forearm, then the corner of her mouth. Worked his way down her neck as she circled both arms around him and buried her face in that wild tangle of hair.

His mouth found her bare shoulder, and she shuddered. Against her skin, he said, "That is some dress, Fiore."

She wet her lips, found her voice, and said inanely, "I bought it on sale."

"And you wore it for me," he said, taking a gentle bite from her shoulder, "because you knew what it would do to my libido."

Of course she'd worn it for him. What other excuse could there be for wearing a strapless summer dress in October? Primly, she said, "Your libido doesn't need any extra help."

He laughed and said, "That's true enough." Nuzzled her ear. "I feel like a war hero, just back from the front lines."

"You've been on a rock tour," she said breathlessly. "In my book, that qualifies as front lines."

"Remind me to tell you my war stories. Later. After we take care of business." He ran his knuckles down her bare arm, turning her insides to molten lava. "You remind me of a cupcake. All white and fluffy and delicious, with pink icing and little red candies on top. And I want to swallow you up, one—" He pressed a kiss to her neck, just behind her ear. "—crumb—" Another kiss, this one to the underside of her jaw, and she let her head roll back limply. "—at a time." She gasped as the third kiss came dangerously close to where the little red and white dress displayed cleavage that was nothing much to write home about.

He paused there, his breath hot against the swell of her breasts. Amazing and wonderful man that he was, he didn't seem to mind that they were woefully inadequate, had always accorded them the same attention and admiration that other men would have given to a pair of 38DDs. It had been a long six weeks, and she wanted his hands on them. On her. Wanted her hands on him. Wanted to rip his clothes off and have her way with him, right here, right now.

But sanity told her that somewhere beyond the edges of that white noise, they had an audience. She pressed her cheek to his, reveling in the scrape of whiskers against her skin. Peeled free a strand of her hair that had caught in his beard. Took a step back to regain equilibrium and said, "I think we should go home."

"Before we land on the front page of the *National Enquirer*? Probably not a bad idea."

Once they were on the highway, he switched on the radio, fiddled with the dial until he found something to his liking, a seventies rock station where Mick and the boys were declaring that they were nobody's beast of burden. In classic MacKenzie style, he began singing along with Mick, a little too loud, a little off-key—deliberately, of course—adding the occasional dramatic flourish just because he could.

Tuning out his impromptu duet with Mick, she studied his face. Something had changed between them, with such devious subtlety that she'd completely missed it until now. He was the same person he'd always been. Playful, funny, a little to the left of center. Tender, caring, generous. Easygoing, laid back, until he was crossed, and then that hot Irish temper would ignite, and God help anybody who got in his way. No surprises there. With Rob MacKenzie, it had always been what-you-see-is-what-you-get.

It was she who was different.

And there it lay, the thorny issue she was having trouble dealing with. She'd lost herself so completely with Danny, had been so desperately in love that she'd allowed him to steamroll right over her until she was little more than a pale imitation of her former self. That kind of self-effacement—or maybe self-erasement would be a more accurate term—was a character trait she didn't much like, and she'd been naïvely certain that it would never resurface.

Now, her certainty was shaken. Of course she knew that Rob MacKenzie and Danny Fiore were two very different men. Of course she knew that Rob wasn't the kind of man to take advantage of a woman's most vulnerable and intimate emotions. He wasn't self-involved like Danny. He didn't have tunnel vision like Danny. He wasn't *broken* like Danny. But knowing she was capable of such self-destructive tendencies, knowing the possibility existed that she could lose herself that way with another man, was terrifying.

He stopped mid-lyric, leaving Mick to fend for himself, and said, "What?"

She looked at him blankly. "What, what?"

"Why do you keep staring at me like I'm some kind of space alien? Do I have body odor? Spinach between my teeth? Or is it my singing? It's my singing, isn't it? I'm sorry. I try so hard to color inside the lines, but it just never seems to work out for me."

Even when she was at her most fragile, he could still make her laugh. "Don't you know," she said, "that your utter inability to color inside the lines is one of the things I find the most charming about you?"

"What is it, then? I'm starting to feel like some kind of specimen under glass."

"Can't I admire my husband without getting the third degree? I'm just so glad you're home, that's all."

He turned his head and stared at her. "Why am I not believing you?"

"I just cannot imagine. I suppose you'll simply have to trust that I'd have no reason to lie to you."

"Fifteen minutes I've been on the ground, Fiore, and already you're getting all pissy with me. What's that all about?"

"You know, MacKenzie, it's a real shame that you couldn't be a little nicer to me. I had such plans for tonight. Mind-blowing plans. All of them involving you. And nakedness. Lots of nakedness." She shook her head in disappointment. "If only you could learn to keep your mouth shut."

"Permanently? Because, you know, I just want to make sure I'm clear on exactly what the ground rules are. So I can, um...participate...in those plans you made."

"It's like shooting fish in a barrel, isn't it?"

"What is?"

"Men. You're all alike. We offer you sexual favors, and you just roll over and play dead."

He grinned. "Is that what you were doing? Offering me sexual favors?"

"If you'd been a little nicer, you might've found out the answer to that question. But I guess we'll never know now, will we?"

"Hah! Keep on dreaming, babydoll."

In response, she reached across the space between them and brushed her fingertips across his cheek. He caught her wrist in his hand and kissed the underside. "Hi," he said softly.

"Hi."

"Missed you."

Stroking his face with the tips of her fingers, she said, "I wasn't sure I was going to make it. I'm still not sure. That was the longest six weeks of my life."

"You just say the word. I'll pull over to the side of the road any time you want."

"And get arrested for public indecency? I think not. As tempting as the offer is."

"No sense of adventure," he said, kissing the tender underside of her forearm. "None at all."

"I can find plenty of adventure right at home. I don't need to go looking for it on a lonely stretch of highway in the dark of night."

"No cruising the bowling alley?"

"No cruising the bowling alley. I already have all the man I need."

"You know, if this was the good old days of yore, you could just slide over here and I could wrap my arm around you, and you'd put your head on my shoulder, and we could just cruise, like a couple of teenagers. Damn bucket seats have ruined that."

"Just think what a whole generation has missed out on."

"Damn straight. Modern technology has made it really hard to grope each other while you're driving."

"It's a tragedy of epic proportions." She lay her hand against the front of his shirt and began inching it southward. "I could probably still manage a little groping, if you were so inclined."

"If you move that hand one more centimeter, woman, I really will be pulling over to the side of the road."

"I guess that means groping is out."

"I guess it does. Looks like we'll have to settle for talking."

"I guess we will. For now."

***

They came in through the shed. Casey hung up her coat and Rob kicked off his shoes and they entered the kitchen without turning on the lights. He dropped the carry-on and the duffel bag on the kitchen table and set the guitar cases on the floor. She moved past him to the sink, took a glass from the cupboard, and filled it. The water was cold and sweet, soothing her parched throat and quieting the hitch in her breathing. Behind her, he moved soundlessly, and she sensed him an instant before he touched a gentle fingertip to each bare shoulder and ran them, whisper-soft, down her arms to her wrists.

She shot from 0 to 60 in 0.2 seconds, her insides going soft and sticky and molten. Beneath her skin, there was a fine trembling, a vibration, almost a humming. Something was shifting inside her, some great tectonic plate cracking and splitting, revising history and altering beliefs she'd held for nearly two decades. This man had been her friend, then her lover, and eventually her husband. Although sometimes the edges had blurred, the progression of their relationship had been straightforward and clear. But after fifteen months of marriage, she understood that everything before tonight had been little more than dress rehearsal. Somewhere along the way, when she hadn't been paying attention, he had become her life. Somewhere along the way, when she hadn't been watching where she was going, she'd tumbled headfirst off a precipice she hadn't noticed, and she'd gone into freefall with no safety net other than the absolute trust that he would be waiting at the bottom to break her fall.

I didn't know, she thought stupidly. *How could I not know?* How was it possible for a woman to fall passionately in love with the husband she'd thought she already loved? How was it possible for a woman to reach the age of thirty-five without realizing that her one true love, the sole reason she'd been put on this planet, had been standing right by her side since she was eighteen years old?

Inside her, terror and elation battled for supremacy. She'd never experienced this kind of euphoria. Nothing in thirty-five years of living had ever felt so right as her feelings for this man. But just below the surface, it lay in wait, the crippling fear that history would repeat itself, that she would give up too much of herself for him, the way she had with Danny, and end up an empty shell. Determined to ignore that fear, she took a deep breath and resolved that tonight, elation would win. Tonight, she would allow herself to explore this maelstrom of emotions that swirled around her. Tomorrow was soon enough to face the fear.

She carefully set the glass in the sink and turned. He was leaning with both hands braced against the counter, trapping her within the circle of his arms. His body heat arced across the space between them and tangled her in its grip. In the silence, the kitchen clock ticked. Above her, his face was a pale gleam of white, blurred and indecipherable in the darkness. He smelled wonderful. Not a cosmetic scent; simply the musky scent of man. Her man. A scent so distinctive to him that, blindfolded, she could have picked him out of a crowded room. While her pulse hammered erratically and her stomach did back-flips, she lifted a hand and lay it flat against the hard muscles of his abdomen.

"Hey," he whispered, and leaned in to kiss her.

His mouth was so very familiar, yet there was something different this time. He gave her tender, sweet little kisses that made her throat tighten with emotion. Teasing nibbles. Restrained, because after a year and a half as lovers, he knew what she liked, what she craved, knew her rhythms and her desires, knew what it took to make the fire smolder slowly between them. Her hands came to rest atop his, her thumbs looped around his slender wrists, drawing in his energy, his essence, as they took their time, letting the excitement build slowly. The electric connection between them flowed from mouths to hands and back again, while their bodies, two heated, yearning bodies, maintained a controlled, torturous distance.

He was the first to break, letting out a soft groan and driving her up hard against the counter. Cool restraint forgotten, she answered him with a muted, wordless sound. Then their hands were on each other, touching, stroking, seducing. The kiss deepened, tongues darting and plunging. They broke apart with a gasp, took in air, dove back in for another helping. Her hands knotted in his hair so tightly she knew she must be hurting him. Excitement churned inside her belly, so intense it nearly made her nauseous. She wanted him so, she could barely breathe. Thrilled by his hardness pressed against her, she arched her back and opened her thighs, craving that hardness, needing it, between her legs, inside her.

Still kissing her, he swept a hand down her thigh until he reached bare skin. He touched the back of her leg, sending a shudder through her, then began inching his way back up beneath the dress. When he reached silk and lace, he hesitated for an instant before hooking a finger beneath the waistband of her bikini panties and peeling them off. She freed her mouth and whispered frantically, "What are you doing?"

The panties reached her thighs and kept going. "Shh. 's okay."

"Not here." She kissed him. "Not in the kitchen." Another breathy kiss. "Paige—"

The tiny scrap of silk and lace that she'd spent a fortune on completed its descent to the floor. "She's asleep," he whispered. "Just let me—"

"Ohhh," she breathed as he dipped two fingers inside her, wet them, and began stroking her. The man was a sexual savant, and she refused to think about the long line of women who'd warmed his bed before her, or about which of them had taught him so well. That was the past, and it didn't matter. He was hers now, and she was his, and none of those other women mattered. Their sexual histories were just that. History.

"Missed you so much," he whispered against the corner of her mouth. "Missed touching you."

"Stop," she said weakly. "Please."

"Oh, baby, your lips are saying no, but your body's saying *yes.*"

She moaned, and he crushed his mouth to hers to muffle the sound. She fisted her hands in his hair, panted into his open mouth. Closed her eyes and let her head fall back. "Stop," she whispered again.

"Why? You don't like it?"

"Of course I like it." She gasped, clutched at his arm, but her touch failed to have any effect on what he was doing to her. "You know I like it."

"Shh! Then what's the problem?"

The sensations he was causing were exquisite, and part of her wanted him to continue touching her until she imploded. It wouldn't take much; she was already halfway to paradise. She could just give in and let him have his way, and enjoy the fireworks. But this wasn't what she'd waited six weeks for, and if he kept it up, she wasn't sure how much longer she could hold onto her sanity. "I want you," she whispered fiercely. "Inside me."

"We'll get to that. But first—"

"No." She caught his wrist in an iron grip. "Bedroom."

"But you haven't—"

"Now!"

"Okay, okay. Whatever you say, Sarge."

He let the skirt fall back into place and hoisted her up into his arms. She wrapped herself around him like lichen on a tree trunk. He adjusted their fit, braced a palm against her bare butt. Kissing frantically, they made it as far as the living room doorway before she said, "Stop!"

"Shh! You'll have the kid up. What?"

"Undies. On the floor."

He backtracked, leaned to pick them up while she clung to him. He hooked them over her index finger and moved unerringly in the darkness toward the staircase that would take them upstairs. At the bottom, she said, "If you lose your balance and drop me, MacKenzie—"

"Don't worry." He hoisted her a little higher and she tightened her legs around his waist. "I have no intention of dropping you and missing this. Because, baby, by the time I'm done with you tonight, you won't even remember your own name."

"Abstinence," she reminded him, "makes the heart grow fonder."

"The abstinence," he declared, "is over."

Somehow, they made it to the top of the stairs and into the bedroom. He closed the door behind them, and in the velvety darkness, he loosened his hold on her. Still clasped in his arms, she slid lightly to the floor. He cradled her face in his hands, brushed a thumb across her cheek, and said, "You light the candle. I'll take care of the music."

Her legs had gone so weak they barely held her up. She dropped the panties on the dresser and pulled a kitchen match from the box she kept here for this very purpose. With trembling hands, she struck it and lit the fat, white candle perched on a ceramic saucer in front of the mirror.

She blew out the match, dropped it into the saucer, and turned to study him. He was so beautiful, all lines and angles, lean and lanky in tight jeans, his hair an unholy mess as he popped a cassette into the tape deck. He pushed the button and adjusted the volume. The music started—Marvin and Tammi singing *Your Precious Love*—and he turned to look at her, his expression solemn.

In the flickering candlelight, they studied each other, both of them swaying in time to that sweet, sensual rhythm, both of them aware that this night held some measure of significance, although she couldn't explain that significance to him when she could barely understand it herself. He would think she was crazy if she told him that somewhere along the line, she'd fallen head over heels in love with him in a big, bad adult way that bore no resemblance whatsoever to the feelings she'd had for Danny. He would think she was crazy if she said that despite fifteen months of marriage, tonight felt like her wedding night in a way that their real wedding night had not.

Still swaying in time with the music, he slowly crossed the room to her and said, "Mrs. MacKenzie."

Joy blossomed somewhere deep inside her. It bubbled up, spread through her extremities, and poured out of her in the form of delighted laughter. "Mr. MacKenzie," she said.

"I really like those fuck-me shoes."

She glanced down at the screaming red stilettos that raised her to a full five-foot-four. "Why, thank you, kind sir."

"If you'd like to, y'know, keep 'em on while we're engaged in, um...marital relations...I wouldn't exactly mind."

She raised an eyebrow. "Marital relations?"

"I didn't want to offend your delicate sensibilities."

Still swaying, she said, "Isn't this our song?"

"One of 'em, anyway. Would you care to dance?"

She stepped into his arms, pressed her cheek to his shoulder, and let out a deep, shuddering breath. Near her ear, he was softly singing along with Marvin and Tammi in a perfectly normal voice that bore little resemblance to the one he'd used for his earlier duet with Mick. She loved it when he sang to her. There was something so intimate about it, so sweetly romantic. So classic MacKenzie. She locked her arms around his slender waist, closed her eyes, and just let it take her. The night, the music, the magic, the man.

He stopped singing. "There's something different about you tonight. I noticed it as soon as I got off the plane."

"It's the shoes. They make me four inches taller."

"So that's it. No wonder I barely recognized you."

She tilted her head back until she could see his face. "So who did you think you were getting intimately acquainted with down there in the kitchen?"

He raised both eyebrows. "Was that you? You know what they say about all cats being black in the dark. I thought it was my other wife."

"There are no other wives, MacKenzie. There will be no other wives. There is only one wife."

"How could I forget that? What'd you say your name was?"

In response, she ran both hands down his backside, groping him unapologetically, finally leaving her hands resting there on that sweet little butt. "Does this jog your memory?"

"Oh. That wife."

"That's right, Flash." She released his butt, reached up and drew his mouth down to hers. "That wife."

This time, there was nothing remotely restrained about the kiss. The music forgotten, the verbal foreplay abandoned, they came together like heat-seeking missiles, his body pressed hard against hers, hands stroking, caressing, exploring territory both familiar and enthralling. Excitement hummed inside her and she trembled with anticipation, her tongue tangled with his in an exquisite dance as they swallowed each other's breath, each other's moans, breathed in each other's essence in a scorching need to merge and become one.

He ran his hands up and down her back, broke away, said against her shoulder, "How does this thing come off, babe? I can't get to—"

"Over my head."

He peeled the dress up and off, tossed it aside, leaving her naked except for the shoes. Never in her life had she stood in front of a man like this, naked except for a pair of red stiletto-heel fuck-me shoes. He was looking at her with a wolfish grin she'd never seen on his face before. She should have been embarrassed. Shouldn't she? Instead, she felt empowered. Was it the shoes? Did they hold some heretofore unknown secret power? She took his hands, those magical hands that could play her body with the same skill and finesse they employed to tease heated sounds from an electric guitar, and placed them on her breasts.

He was a fast learner. He cupped and lifted, squeezed and brushed and teased. "You like?" he said.

"Yes. *Oh, yes.*"

Stroking tenderly, he said, "I am *so* not leaving you again."

She let out a sound that was half laugh, half sob. "You leave me like that again, MacKenzie, I swear to God I'll stab you until you're dead."

"Bloodthirsty wench."

"Lecherous perv."

"You are so damn hot. Have I ever mentioned how hot you are?" He pressed a kiss to the swell of her breast. "These are so perfect."

"They're too small."

"Are you crazy, Fiore? They're just right. You haven't noticed how they get my engines humming?"

"Oh, I've noticed." Her own engines were humming quite nicely, too. What he was doing to her should have been a crime. Surely anything that felt this good must be illegal. "Flash?"

He was a little distracted, so it took him some time to respond. "Yeah?"

Fumbling with his belt buckle, she said breathlessly, "I want you now. Right now."

"Right now?" He circled one hard little peak with his tongue, sending her shooting off into space. "Are you sure about that?"

She pulled the belt free and dropped it on the floor. "Are you kidding? I was ready before you got off the plane."

He let out a soft snort of laughter. "Me, too. So you're ready to get this party started?"

She unbuttoned his jeans, yanked the zipper down. "I'm ready to close the sale."

"Oh, baby, it makes me so hot when you talk like that."

"Just wait until you see what else I can do." She tugged at his pants, began working them down his hips.

"Whoa, woman, slow down! Amputation by zipper doesn't sound like something I want to experience."

"No sense of adventure. None at all."

"Sadly, no." He worked himself free, shrugged the pants down, kicked his way out of them. "Not when it comes to a possible amputation of one of my favorite appendages."

She shoved the army shirt off his shoulders and dragged it down his arms. "*One of* your favorite appendages?"

"Okay, fine. My favorite appendage. Are you happy now?"

"Absolutely." She caught the hem of his tee shirt, tugged it up, peeled it off over his head, tossed it on the floor next to the army shirt. "Now I've got you naked. And it's my favorite appendage, too."

"God, I love it when you talk dirty."

She closed both hands over the aforementioned appendage. He felt thick and hot and wonderful. Tightening her grip, she stroked him gently. "Just look at you, Flash! All big and hard and ready to rock & roll."

His eyes were closed, his expression rapturous. "Oh, baby, keep doing what you're doing, and you're gonna send me right into the stratosphere."

"Poppa likes it when Momma touches him like this?"

"Poppa's spent the last six weeks dreaming about Momma touching him like this."

"Momma's planning on doing a whole lot more than touching."

His eyelids fluttered open. "Is that something I can help you with?"

"We should definitely explore that possibility." Releasing him, she placed a hand flat against his chest and gave him a not-so-gentle nudge. "Bed. Now."

Inching backward, he raised both eyebrows. "Who are you, and what have you done with my wife?"

"Keep moving."

"What the hell happened while I was out there working my fingers to the bone every night?"

The backs of his knees hit the edge of the mattress. She gave him another shove, and he sat down hard. She followed him, knelt astride him and took his face between her hands. He tilted his head and they studied each other by flickering candlelight. "Hey, there, handsome," she said tenderly.

His hands settled on her bare rump, and his beautiful green eyes went all soft and melty. "Hey, there, my gorgeous, spectacular woman."

"I missed you so much."

He gave her one of those grins, the kind that melted her all the way to the marrow. "How much?" he said.

She moved her hips closer and, eyes locked with his, aligned their bodies precisely. "This much," she said, and lowered herself onto his sleek, hot hardness.

He groaned, and she let out a raw, exultant cry. She'd needed this so bad. "Oh, Flash," she breathed.

He thrust into her, slow and deliberate. "You like this?" he whispered.

"Oh, yes."

"More?"

"Yes." The word floated out of her like a prayer.

"Tell me what you want. Anything you want, it's yours."

"Everything," she said. "I want everyth—*ohmigod.*"

Hoarsely, he said, "Babe?"

"What?"

"Wrap your legs around me."

Still on her knees, she pondered the logistics. He solved her dilemma by withdrawing. "No!" she protested. "Come back!"

"It's okay. Just hang on. Watch the shoes, they're deadly." Together, they managed the awkward rearrangement of limbs, until her feet, still in the four-inch heels, were planted on either side of his hips. He came back to her then, filled her slowly, exquisitely, deeply. Wrapped his hands around her ankles. "I could get used to this," he said.

She let out a burst of laughter. "Oh," he said. "You think it's funny?"

"Not us. The shoes."

He cocked an eyebrow. "You mean you didn't know it was the shoes that turned me on?"

"Are you saying that I might as well not be here, MacKenzie?"

"Well...I don't think I'd go that far."

She brushed a single curl away from his face. "My lunatic."

He kissed her knuckles. "Better fasten your seatbelt, woman. Because—" He pressed a sweet kiss to the corner of her mouth. "—we are going for a ride. You, me—" He kissed her bare shoulder, sending a shudder through her. "—and those shoes."

The playfulness fled as, arms locked around his neck, knees gripping his hips, she followed where he led her. Fluid and boneless, she rose and fell to his rhythm, worshiping that hot, slick, hard part of him that hammered relentlessly in and out of her. There was no world but him, nothing but his hot breath upon her face, nothing but those narrow hips driving her to a place beyond the boundaries of her mind. In some part of her, she was vaguely aware of the harsh, guttural sounds emanating from both of them, of her shock at the knowledge that those noises were coming from her own throat. Intensely aware that the sounds he was making excited her beyond belief. Shuddering, sobbing, gasping, beyond speech, beyond control, she closed her eyes, let her head fall back, and chased the rapture.

It didn't take long. They exploded together in a hot, frantic, sticky, screaming conflagration. Held each other, breathless, through the aftershocks. He fell back against the bed, gasping and barely coherent. "Holy mother of God, woman," he croaked.

"Now that I've seen the kind of welcome home I get, I might have to leave more often."

"Over my dead body."

"And what a godawful shame that would be." His hands roamed over her naked rump, found a comfortable spot, and stayed there. "We'll be keeping this body alive and kicking for a long, long time."

She wiggled around, rearranged her legs again, careful not to impale him with those four-inch stiletto heels. Finally found her sweet spot, and pressed her head against his shoulder. Brushing the hair back from her face, she said, "I'll have you know that I bought the most beautiful red lace panties I've ever seen. Do you have any idea how far outside my comfort zone that is? I've never worn red lace in my life. But I wore them for you. And you stripped them off me in the kitchen, for God's sake. In the dark! It was a complete waste of money."

His fingers tickled her backside. "Ah, baby, I'm sorry. I'm an animal."

"Yes, you are, MacKenzie. You're a barbarian. A cave man. But you're my cave man, so I suppose I'll have to keep you."

"Sixty years. That was the deal."

"I really have to put up with fifty-nine more years of this?"

"You didn't read the fine print on the contract?"

"Oh, I read it. I'm just having trouble believing I agreed to it. And the dress! I bought that for you, too, and now it's just cast aside and forgotten."

"Cast aside, but definitely not forgotten. Maybe you should rescue it. While you're at it, you can model those red lace panties for me."

"And get you all hot and bothered again?"

"Hey, we have six weeks of lost time to make up for. This was just round one."

"Um, babe? We can't make it all up in one night."

And he grinned. "Oh, ye of little faith."

She considered his words at length. Finally said, "Round one?"

"It's been six weeks. We had to get the screaming out of the way. Round two will be a lot quieter. And a lot slower."

"I have to admit that I'm intrigued. Tell me more."

"Try those panties on, and I'll show you."

She leaned forward, gave him a long, slow kiss. Carefully disengaged and slithered down his body until her feet hit the floor. While he watched with hungry eyes, she bent and picked up the dress. Shook the wrinkles out of it and lay it across a chair. When she looked back at him, he was lying on one hip, elbow propped on the mattress, chin in hand, eyes focused on her.

Grinning like a fool.

She must have been prodded by some internal devil she wasn't aware of, because what she did next was so out of character that the nice girl, the one she'd been all her life, was mildly scandalized by her actions. But there was a measure of wildness in him that called out to and connected with a corresponding wildness in her that she hadn't even known existed until he found it buried somewhere inside her and dragged it out into the light of day.

Standing before him in those ridiculous heels, legs braced apart and as naked as the day she was born, she swept back the hair from her face, wrapped both arms around her head, and began a loose, shimmying dance.

"Lift your hair," he said hoarsely. "Up over your head."

She gathered it, twisted it, held it atop her head. "Like this?"

"Keep on dancing. Oh, yeah. Now just let it fall. Oh, baby."

"Oh, baby, what?"

"Oh, baby, you are one hot, sexy bitch."

She raised her eyebrows. "Did you just call me a bitch, MacKenzie?"

"I called you a sexy bitch, Fiore. Whole different ball game."

"Good thing you clarified that, because I was really looking forward to round two."

"Me, too. What about the panties?"

She gave him a wicked grin, came back to the bed and knelt, straddling his legs. Crawled on hands and knees until she reached the place where her hair fell in a dark curtain around his face. She lowered her head until her mouth was so close to his that their breaths mingled and became a single entity.

And said, "Screw the panties."

Rob

Illuminated by soft morning light, she slept face down, this stranger in his bed, this woman who looked like his wife but was almost certainly a doppelganger. Puzzled, he buried his nose in the dark cloud of hair and took a whiff. She smelled like his wife. Sweeping aside her hair, he pressed a damp kiss to the back of her slender neck, touched her warm skin with the tip of his tongue. She tasted like his wife. He studied the way the hair grew in a soft whorl at her nape, her skin pale beneath the dark hair because it never saw the light of day. Last night had been amazing. Stupendous. Phenomenal. Except that none of those words came close. He wasn't sure the right word had yet been invented.

Who was this lush and lusty alien, and what had she done with the sweet and decorous woman he'd married? Last night, when she'd danced for him wearing nothing but a pair of red high-heel shoes and a smile, his heart had nearly stopped. The woman he'd known so well for two decades would never do that. She was far too repressed, far too shy, to ever flaunt her body that way.

After all, this was the same woman who, when they first got together, had been sleeping in a plain white cotton nightgown that looked like something his mother would wear. Because he hadn't owned a pair of pajamas since he was twelve, he'd laughed at her when she said, "But what if the house catches fire in the middle of the night?"

"If the house catches fire in the middle of the night, Fiore," he'd told her, "your local volunteer firemen seeing you in your birthday suit will be the least of your worries."

That had been the end of the cotton nightgown.

He slowly drew the bedding down to give himself a better view of the body he knew so well he could have mapped it in his sleep. It was all here, just as it should be. Every bump and dip, every line and curve, every blemish, every scar, every tiny freckle and mole, were all in their rightful places. Either the doppelganger was identical in every way, or this truly was his wife.

What the hell had happened while he'd been away?

He pressed another kiss to the center of her spine, between her shoulder blades, and she made a soft sound that might have been approval, might have been protest. He worked his way slowly southward, one knobby little vertebra at a time. When he reached the base of her spine, he paused to admire her sweet little tush before placing a kiss on one rounded cheek.

She made the sound again. This time, he was pretty sure it signaled approval. He opened his mouth and took a gentle nibble. Brushed his whiskers across her tender flesh. She rolled up on one hip, giving him access to a plethora of goodies. He rained a trail of kisses across her silky hip, up her groin to her navel, bestowing special attention on her concave little belly. Her hands, those wonderful, magical hands, tangled themselves in his hair. He worked his way northward, tasted first one breast and then the other.

In a groggy voice, she said, "You need a shave, MacKenzie."

"Good morning to you, too."

One slender hand trailed fingertips down his cheek, across his shoulder, his collarbone, down the center of his chest. The hand settled there, fingers threaded in his chest hair, and he abandoned his doppelganger theory. This was definitely his wife. In the dim light, their eyes met, and they studied each other somberly. "Hi," he said.

"Hi."

Something had changed between them, but the *when* and the *how* and the *why* escaped him. Her eyes gave nothing away, but she was sending out the weirdest vibes, and he couldn't decipher them. Couldn't figure out what was going on. But considering last night, this couldn't be bad...could it?

With a single finger, she traced the outline of his lower lip. Leaned forward and kissed him.

It felt like relief running through him, but again, he couldn't be sure. The sweet, tender kiss quickly turned heated. His heart racing, he moved his hand from her hip, slid it between her thighs, and moved it northward.

And there was a soft knock on the door.

They looked at each other, both of them startled. *Timing*, he thought. It was everything. Reluctantly, he removed his hand. Casey drew up the covers until they were both decent, and said, "Come in."

The door opened, and his daughter stuck her head into the room. "I'm sorry if I woke you," she said. "But I made breakfast. For all of us."

Jesus Christ on a Popsicle stick. Who the hell was this kid? What had Casey done to her while he was gone? He must have woke up in the Twilight Zone.

"Aw, honey, that was sweet of you," Casey said, and nudged him under the covers. "Babe? Wasn't that sweet?"

"Yeah. Absolutely. Of course."

Another surprise. He was really happy to see the kid. Her timing was abysmal, but after six weeks away, he was surprised by how glad he was to see her. "Hey," his daughter greeted him.

"Hey."

"Just give us five minutes," Casey said, "and we'll be down."

Paige eyed him speculatively, then nodded at Casey. "Okay," she said.

She shut the door, and his wife rolled away from him. Reaching out to stop her, he said, "Who was that kid? And where do you think you're going?"

But it was too late. She was already out of bed, already in her robe, already pulling her hair free and tying her belt. "I told you she just needed the right kind of attention. And where do you think I'm going? You heard her. Breakfast is ready."

"Just when things were getting interesting."

"Oh, stop sulking. Didn't you get enough 'interesting' last night?"

"I never get enough of you."

She moved to the closet, opened the door, studied her options. Took out a pair of pants and a shirt. "I'm quite certain the opportunity will arise again."

He threw back the covers and reached for his jeans, the ones he'd left on the floor last night. Yanking them on, he said, "Opportunity isn't the only thing that'll rise."

He watched with great interest as she took the red lace panties from the dresser and pulled them on beneath the robe. "You're relentless," she said, dropping her robe on the chair. "Sex and food, food and sex. No imagination at all."

"That's me. One hundred percent cave man." While he watched, she pulled on her jeans and slipped into a peach-colored silk brassiere.

"Maybe," she said, fiddling with the clasp, "I should start putting saltpeter in your food."

"Hah! That's a myth. Doesn't really work. Besides, it seems to me that—" He crossed to the bureau, opened a drawer, pulled out a clean tee shirt, and yanked it over his head. "—last night, you were the one who almost ripped my clothes off." When he looked at his wife again, she was fully dressed, standing in front of the mirror over the dresser, brushing her hair with brisk strokes. "I could help you with that."

"Not if we want to get to breakfast anytime soon."

"Well, then, little lady—" He crossed the room, drew back a hand and gave her a hard swat on the rump. "Let's get going. Breakfast awaits."

She dropped the brush, turned and gave him the Death Stare, cold enough to freeze his manhood on the spot. Her eyes ablaze and her hands curled into fists, she said, "You are in *so* much trouble, MacKenzie."

She advanced on him and he grinned, raised both hands, palms outward, and began backing away. *Mea culpa.* I plead the Fifth! I don't know what came over me."

"I'll be happy to give you a preview of what's about to come over you."

Still backing away, he said, "I couldn't resist. You're just so damn—" His back hit the wall. He was trapped, with nowhere left to go. "—adorable."

She drew back an arm, and he prepared to be annihilated. The woman had a mean right hook. Then something changed in her eyes. With a sly smile, she relaxed the fist. Moved closer. Instead of hitting him, she slipped a hand between his thighs. Turned it, slid it northward, cupped and stroked him.

And he nearly swallowed his tongue.

Her smile was evil. "Easy," she said, removing her hand and shaking her head. "Men. You're all just so damn easy."

Pole-axed, he watched her walk to the door. Who the hell *was* this woman? His glance fell on the red shoes, carelessly discarded on the floor by the bed, then returned to her retreating back. She disappeared down the hall. A moment later, he heard the bathroom door shut.

He cast another suspicious glance at the shoes. Took in a hard, shuddering breath. And said weakly, "Well. Damn."

***

The scrambled eggs weren't bad, as long as he didn't mind the occasional crunchy piece of egg shell mixed in. "Great breakfast, kiddo," he said, setting his knife and fork on his empty plate. Paige shrugged, but if he wasn't totally misinterpreting her expression, she seemed pleased.

"We've been cooking together," Casey said. "Paige is a fast learner."

"I can see that."

His daughter rolled her eyes a little, but accepted the praise. "So," he said, "I hear you made a visit to Casa MacKenzie. How'd that go?"

"I like your mother," the kid said. "She's nice."

"She is nice, my mother. As long as you don't cross her. Soft as a marshmallow on the outside. A steel rod in place of a spine on the inside. A lot like this one here." He nodded in Casey's direction. Paige glanced at her stepmother, shrugged again, but a soft smile played at the corners of her mouth. "Do me a favor," he said.

Paige glanced up, saw him looking at her. "Me?"

"You. See those two guitar cases in the corner? Go get the black one."

She glanced at him, at Casey, then shrugged. Got up from her chair, lifted the case, returned to the table. "Sit," he said. "Open it. Check it out."

Without speaking, she undid the latches, flipped open the lid, and stared at the polished black acoustic guitar inside. "Nice," she said.

"Try it out. Listen to that rich timbre."

His daughter carefully removed the guitar from its case, propped it on her lap, wrapped her fingers around the neck and played a couple of chords. Glanced at him, not even bothering to try to hide the delight on her face. "*Sweet*," she said.

"Is that or is that not the richest sound you ever heard? That's how you recognize a good guitar."

"I can't believe the difference between this and my old guitar. They're not even in the same ballpark."

"Exactly. And it's a lot easier to play, with the strings so close to the fretboard."

Paige played a couple more chords, did a little fingering. Then, with a sigh of regret, she lay the guitar back in its velvet nest. "Not so fast," he said.

She glanced up, her face awash in puzzlement. "What?"

"Do you like it?"

"Of course I like it. It's friggin' amazing."

"That's a good thing, then, because it's yours."

Her face changed, grew wary, suspicious. Not quite the response he'd hoped for. Something tightened inside his chest, temporarily constricting his breathing. *Damn it.* Kids learned what they were taught. So who had taught her not to trust?

"Mine," she said carefully. "Why?"

"Because," he said. "Because you're my kid, and I'm proud of your playing. Because I saw it in this dusty little pawn shop in Memphis, and it had your name written all over it. Because serious musicians graduate from fifty-dollar department-store guitars to the real thing. And last but not least, because I like to give presents."

"This is not a cheap guitar," she said.

"No, it's not. It's also not brand-new, but whoever owned it took damn good care of it. I'm trusting that you'll do the same. Because even though it's not new and I didn't pay full price, I still dropped a pretty penny on it."

"I don't know what to say."

"Thank you will be sufficient."

"Thank you." Her eyes met Casey's, and a silent message he couldn't decipher passed between them. "Did you—"

"I swear I did not," his wife said. "I'm as surprised as you are."

Biting her lower lip, Paige bent her head over the guitar, ran her fingers up and down the fretboard, played a few notes. "What?" he said.

"Later," Casey said, and over Paige's head, gave him a look that said *Please don't argue.*

He shot her a wink, said to the kid, "Thanks for the breakfast, kiddo. I'm off to take a shower."

And he left the two of them to whatever they were secretly plotting.

Paige

They'd been practicing for a week, she and Luke, but still she was nervous. It wasn't the profusion of relatives that bothered her, all those aunts and uncles and cousins squeezed into her father's house. She'd sung in front of people before. Hell, she'd sung solos with the school chorus before five hundred people, and been unfazed by it. Luke had a decent voice, and they sounded good together. There was nothing to be nervous about. But tonight her nerves were on edge. Because tonight, for the first time, her father would hear her sing.

Casey had written the song for her, and it wasn't some wussy, saccharine, fifteen-year-old-kid song, it was a real piece of music, complex enough to do her voice justice, simple enough to appeal to a wide audience. Her stepmother knew what she was doing when it came to writing music, and she knew how that piece of music needed to be performed. Tonight, there was no backup band, no amplification, no rocking out. Just the two of them, playing their acoustic guitars and singing.

"You ready?" Luke said.

"As ready I'll ever be." She glanced around the room, at the assembled Saturday-night regulars. Bill, with coffee mug in hand, leaning against the fireplace. Trish and Rose, side by side on the couch. Paula and Chuck Fournier, sitting in matching armchairs. Billy and Alison with their new baby, looking tired but happy. Jesse, standing in the doorway to the front hall, leaning against the door frame. And her father in the Boston rocker, long legs stretched out, ankles crossed, waiting. Casey stood behind him, her hands resting on his shoulders. Paige met her stepmother's eyes, and Casey nodded.

She beat out a soft 1-2-3-4 rhythm on the body of her guitar, the one her father had given her. And she and Luke began to play.

There were more than a dozen people in the room, but as her voice gained momentum and she lost herself in the song, only one of those people counted. Only one of those people existed. Her father sat watching, listening, with a flat expression she couldn't decipher. With Luke singing harmony, she wound her voice around the notes, wrapped herself around the lyrics. It was a song about a woman who'd given her all to a relationship and lost everything. She'd given up on love and life until this special guy came along and made her believe again. The song was raw and touching and uplifting, a perfect vehicle for her voice. Her audience seemed entranced, and she saw at least one mouth hanging open.

But still her father sat there, deadpan, sending her stomach plummeting. Was he disappointed? Did he hate the song, her singing? Had he expected something she couldn't deliver? As far as she knew, Casey had said nothing to him beyond, "Paige is going to sing for us tonight." So she had no idea what his expectations had been. Or if he'd even had expectations.

Maybe it was her own expectations that had exceeded the realm of possibility.

The song ended, and she barely heard the applause, because her father still had no reaction. While Luke, ever the ham, took bow after bow for his part in the performance, Paige set down her guitar and fled. In the kitchen, she brushed wordlessly past Mikey, who was just arriving, pulled her jacket from the coat tree in the shed, and let herself out into the crisp autumn evening.

She stood on the steps and breathed in the night air as she shoved her arms into her jacket and zipped it. Then she made her way around the house, up the seldom-used front steps, and across the porch to the swing.

Hands tucked into her pockets for warmth, she huddled in one corner of the swing, her feet curled up on the wooden slats beneath her, a confused mix of emotions tumbling around inside her. How could he have just sat there, unmoved, unspeaking? And what possible difference could it make if he did? She hated her father. Didn't she? Nothing he did or said could possibly matter. The fact that he'd wooed her with postcards and a new guitar didn't mean a damn thing. Just because he was a professional musician, the one person who should have understood, didn't mean zip. She was her own person. She didn't need him, didn't expect anything from him. She'd done this on her own for fifteen years. She sure as hell didn't need his approval to keep on doing it.

Then she saw him, a shadowy figure in the darkness, tall and lanky, coming around the corner of the house, moving unerringly toward the swing. Of course he knew exactly where she'd gone. It was the same place he always went when his own wounds needed licking. Was it too farfetched that they would have chosen the same place to do their serious thinking? After all, they shared DNA. And as much as she hated to admit it, from the prickly outer shell right through to the marshmallow center, they were so clearly father and daughter that there was no escaping the truth.

He sat down beside her, propped his ankles on the porch railing, and set the swing in motion. Paige folded her arms around her stomach and waited. After a long silence, he said, "And I thought you only liked rap."

In spite of her desire to maintain her distance, she let out a soft snort of laughter.

"So," he said amiably, "were you planning to keep this from me forever?"

"It's my thing," she said. "I'm under no obligation to share it with you."

"Don't bullshit me. You have a gift, Paige. A real gift. Don't you think you have an obligation to share that gift with the world?"

"I've never thought about it that way."

"Think about it."

"What if I said I don't want to? Share it with the world?"

He turned his head, studied her in the faint lamplight that fell through the bay window. "Then I'd say I don't believe you. I don't believe anybody can sing the way you do without wanting to share it. Without wanting to drown in the music, lose yourself in it, let it swallow you up and hold you there forever."

How was it he could see inside her soul and read what was written there? Was it because he was a musician? Or was it just another symptom of that shared DNA?

"I was blown away by what I heard tonight," he said. "Completely and utterly blown away. Do you understand that? You have the most amazing voice I've heard since Danny Fiore. I don't toss around compliments lightly. I don't bullshit. You have a talent that rendered me speechless. Have you ever seen me speechless?"

"Um…no?"

"Exactly. Casey says I came out of the womb already talking. Tonight, I couldn't believe that voice was coming from my kid."

"Mom always said I got my musical talent from you."

"Well, wherever it came from, kid, you impressed the hell out of me. I don't think I've ever been so proud."

Why did it feel like this, hearing him say those words? She hated him. Had hated him since birth. Paige searched inside herself in an attempt to resuscitate that sleeping hatred, and realized that at some point, when she wasn't paying attention, it had fled. What it had left behind in its place was a lump of raw clay, one she could mold into any shape she wanted. But the molding was up to her. She was the one who had to decide what kind of relationship she wanted with her father. Or whether she wanted one at all.

They sat for a while longer in a companionable silence. "Why don't we go back inside?" he finally said. "Your legion of fans awaits. You were the belle of the ball tonight."

She held back a smile. "I think," she said, "I'll just stay out here for a while. I have some thinking to do."

He swung his feet down off the railing and stood up. "Just don't stay out here too long," he said. "You'll turn into a Popsicle."

And he lumbered down the steps and across the lawn, disappearing into the shadows.

***

She'd been sitting for a while, arms wrapped around her folded knees, studying the night sky, when Mikey walked up the porch steps and sat down beside her. "You dad said you were out here."

"Don't be so shy. Feel free to sit down and join me."

The corner of his mouth twitched. "I hear you were quite a hit tonight," he said. "I'm sorry I missed it."

She shrugged. "It wasn't that big a deal. And it wasn't just me. Luke was there, too."

"According to Luke, he was just window dressing."

"He would say that."

"One of these days, I'll have to hear you sing."

"Band rehearsal three times a week. You're invited. Any time you want."

"Let's go for a walk."

"A walk?" she said. "Where would we walk around here?"

"Just up the road a bit. Get away from this crazy crowd. The moon's full, the stars are out. It's a great night for walking."

"It's freezing cold, Mikey Lindstrom! And you're nuts." But she slid off the swing and went with him anyway. Hands tucked in pockets, they walked, elbow to elbow, down the driveway to Meadowbrook Road. "Which way?" she said.

He looked left, then right. "North," he said.

They crossed the road and began ambling along the shoulder, facing traffic. "So," he said, "how's algebra going?"

"Better. Mrs. Silverburg's been really good. I never could get the hang of it before, but with her teaching, it suddenly makes sense."

"That's good. Do you know, my dad had her for a teacher back when he was in school? As far as he's concerned, she's a cross between Mother Teresa and Margaret Thatcher."

"Your dad's a cool guy."

"He's all right. I think he's happy with your Aunt Rose. He was alone for a lot of years after my mom left. I'm glad he found someone." He looked up at the night sky. "Life is funny sometimes. If he'd married Aunt Casey like he was supposed to, I wouldn't be here today. Or if I was, I'd be somebody different."

"What do you mean, like he was supposed to?"

"I thought you knew. It's the stuff of family legend. They were childhood sweethearts who got engaged in high school. Four weeks before the wedding, she met Danny, and married him instead."

"Wait. *Your father* is the guy she left at the altar?"

"Not quite at the altar. But, yeah. Can you imagine if they'd gotten married?"

She couldn't. Even she could see there was no spark between them. They were friends. Good friends. But boyfriend and girlfriend? She couldn't fathom such a thing.

"Wow," she said. "I had no idea. She told me she was engaged when she met Danny, but she never told me who the guy was."

"They grew up together. After she left, Dad ended up marrying her sister instead. My mom. I don't think it was a love match. She was never happy. I can remember, even as a small kid, sometimes she'd just sit and cry. Then one day, she up and left. I see her a few times a year. She hasn't neglected me. I think she's still trying to find herself."

"Getting kind of old for that, isn't she?"

He let out a soft snort that might have been laughter, but she couldn't be sure. "Look up there," he said, pointing. "See that grouping of stars? Ursa Major. And just below it, you have Ursa Minor."

"It's amazing. All I could see in Boston was electric lights."

"And over here—"" He caught her elbow and turned her. "That's Cassiopeia."

She tried to follow, but it was all too confusing. To her, all those stars looked alike. She turned to tell him so, and suddenly they were face to face, standing on the side of the road, cloaked in velvety darkness, and she couldn't breathe.

She shivered. "You're cold," he said.

"I told you it was freezing out here, but did you listen to me?"

"Here. Put your hands inside my jacket."

She hesitated, then slipped them, clasped into tight little fists, inside the unzipped football jacket. His body heat enveloped her, warmed and loosened those fists. She looked up into his face, that gorgeous face, and all the moisture left her mouth. His dark eyes, ravenous, examined her. His hair, in the moonlight, looked almost white, and she had an overwhelming urge to reach up and touch it. But her hands were trapped inside his jacket, pinned there by his arms, which had somehow managed to find their way around her. When had that happened, and how could she possibly have missed it? "I think," she said, "that this is a bad idea."

"It's a really, really bad idea."

"So...?"

"So..." He dipped his head down and kissed her.

It wasn't her first time. She'd been kissed before. Stewie Katz had kissed her after the eighth-grade graduation dance, and Sonny Malone had edged her into a dark corner at a party last summer and laid a good one on her. But those kisses had been nothing like this. They'd been child's play. This was different. This was the real thing. Her first real kiss. His mouth was soft and warm and seductive, and the kiss went on and on, until she thought she might faint right here in his arms.

They broke apart for breath. She was trembling all over, her body aching in ways she'd never imagined before. So this was what all the screaming was about. Who knew? Paige MacKenzie wrapped her arms around Mikey Lindstrom's neck and kissed him again, a kiss she could feel in every inch of her body, a kiss she wanted to go on and on forever, or until she died, whichever came first.

From out of nowhere, a car raced toward them. They broke apart, each of them taking a step backward. For a moment, they just stared at each other. "Holy shit," he said.

The car, moving too fast, raised a cloud of dust on the gravel road. Just before it reached them, she recognized it. The driver's window came down, and as he passed them, Luke leaned his head out the window and yelled, *"Whoo-heeeee!"*

And he was gone, around a corner and out of sight. She looked at Mikey, and he looked at her. "That boy," he said, "has some serious issues."

Rattled, she said, "Looks like the party's over." But she wasn't one hundred percent sure which party she was referring to.

"I'd better get you back," he said, "before they come looking for you."

"Yeah. That's probably a good idea."

He hesitated. "Look, Paige…"

Trying to slow the erratic beating of her heart, she said, "What?"

He took a deep breath. "Never mind. It's not important. Come on, let's get you home before you freeze to death."

Rob

"Alone at last," his wife said. "I thought they'd never go home." She took off her robe and hung it over the chair, then lifted the bed covers she'd already turned down and slipped between soft Egyptian cotton sheets.

"It was a little intense, wasn't it?" Sitting on the edge of the bed, he bent to peel off his socks, and she ran the fingertips of one hand up the center of his bare back.

He turned to look at her, green eyes searching green eyes, and she gave him a tender, intimate smile. "Hey there, sailor," she said. "Going my way?"

"I could probably be convinced." He stood to unfasten his jeans. Reached out to turn off the lamp, and crawled into bed and into her waiting arms. "Hi," he said.

"Hi."

"That was quite a coup you pulled off."

"She's something else, isn't she?"

"She is." He paused, unsure how to approach this for fear of trampling on toes and starting something. But he'd instantly recognized the song his daughter was singing as his wife's work. That knowledge had left a hollow feeling in the pit of his stomach. That, contrasted with his pride and elation, made him feel like he'd been run through a blender set to *puree*. "You wrote it," he said. "The song."

"With a little help from Paige. She's such a great kid."

"You haven't written anything since Danny died."

"I know. But the minute I heard her sing, I knew she had something special. And for the first time in years, I wanted to write again."

He was silent as she stroked the muscles of his back. So silent that, after a moment, she said, "Is everything okay?"

Of course everything wasn't okay. Four years he'd been working on his own. Four years he'd felt as though something inside him had died. And now, he left her alone for a few weeks, and this was what he came back to?

"I'm just surprised," he said. "That you're writing again. After all this time."

"It just bubbled up out of me," she said. "You do realize the song was about me? About us?"

"Was it?"

"I don't think I realized it was, at the time I wrote it. Not consciously. But my subconscious knew where it was taking me, even if I didn't."

She didn't have a clue. And what would be the point of enlightening her? She was almost giddy with what she'd regained. It wouldn't do any good to point out to her that he felt like something she'd just flushed down the toilet. Besides, in the end, he would cave. He always caved. She won every argument. Not because she was always right, but because he loved her too much to not let her win.

And the thought of losing her, ever, turned his insides into a tangled, bloody mess.

So he would set his feelings aside and focus instead on Paige's accomplishments. That was easier. Less likely to lead to an atomic explosion and the start of World War III.

He adjusted position, lay his head against her breast, and she tangled her fingers in his hair. "I swear to God," he said softly, "I got goose bumps the minute she opened her mouth. All I could think about was what we could do with her. How we could guide her and shape her. Help her build a career. With a voice like that, and the two of us behind her, she could be huge." He rubbed his thumb against her bare hip. "Then I came crashing back to earth and remembered that she might sing like she's been rode hard and put away wet, but she's just fifteen, and she's my little girl, and it's way too early to even think about a career. I would never subject a kid her age to that kind of life. It would eat her alive."

"Some parents do."

"Not this parent."

"I'm glad you feel that way. She acts so tough on the outside, but inside, she's just a scared kid who doesn't know which way is up."

"Why'd you end up picking a family gathering for her coming-out party?"

"It was her idea. She was too scared to sing for you alone. It was easier in a crowd. You do realize she did this for you? That was the motivation behind it. We worked on it for weeks. She may pretend she doesn't care, but I've gotten to know her pretty well, and I believe she desperately wants your approval."

"Well, she's got it."

"You need to reinforce that, every chance you get. While you were away, I got to see a few cracks in that hard shell of hers."

"I'll work on it."

They lay, limp and drowsy, her fingertips tracing formless patterns on his skin. "I love it when you do that," he said.

"This?"

"Mmn."

"And this?"

"That, too," he said. "You tired?"

"A little. You?"

"A little. You feel good in your birthday suit, Mrs. MacKenzie."

"Mmn. You, too."

"You want to, um…?"

"Can I take a rain check? Tomorrow? I'm more tired than I thought."

"Yeah, of course." He kissed her hip, pressed his cheek against her warm flesh. "Tomorrow's fine."

"Love you."

"I love you, too."

He realized, after another minute, that she'd fallen asleep. With no other options, he tucked away the hurt and the resentment, wrapped himself around her, and matched his breathing to hers.

Casey

She was vacuuming the living room when she found the cufflink.

On her knees, with the vacuum hose shoved deep under the couch to capture all the dust bunnies, she heard the metallic clink as the machine sucked up something hard, then the high-pitched whine that told her whatever it was had stalled in its journey.

Casey toed the *off* switch, waited for the machine to power down, then disconnected the hose to see what was clogging her vacuum. In the midst of a tangle of dog hair, dust, and a single Froot Loop, she found the cufflink. The square black onyx stone was embedded with a solid-gold, diamond-studded "F" fashioned in fancy script. She took it in her hand, staring at it with incomprehension, absolutely certain that she'd burned it, along with its mate and all Danny's other possessions, when she'd finally decided to exorcise him from her life.

Shaken, she closed her fist over the cufflink even as she closed her eyes against the rush of memory that assaulted her without warning.

She'd bought them for him as a tenth-anniversary gift. Ten years prior, in a city hall in a small town in Maryland, at rush hour on a weekday afternoon, they'd held hands and vowed to cherish each other until death. On this landmark tenth anniversary, they were in London, where Danny was doing a series of shows, and as usual, he'd been stuck in rehearsal for most of the day. Katie'd had the sniffles, so she had left their daughter with a hotel babysitter and, umbrella in hand, had ventured out, following vague directions from the concierge, to find an anniversary gift suitable for a man who had everything.

Ten years. A milestone. One she'd doubted, a time or two, that they would ever see. But after years of struggling, they'd achieved a hard-won success, and their life, and their marriage, had settled into an odd kind of normalcy. Danny's career had soared to heights they'd never imagined. Her career as a songwriter had brought her a great deal of money and, more importantly, the recognition of her peers. Then there was Katie, her precious Katydid, a gift from God, the angel at the top of her metaphorical

Christmas tree. Life was good. Not perfect; Danny was spending far too much time away from home, but that was a trade-off. There were always trade-offs.

Tonight, for instance, they'd be celebrating their anniversary in the privacy of their hotel room before the show, because it was so difficult for Danny to go out in public without being mobbed. But those were minor annoyances. Overall, these were the best years of their marriage.

She spent hours that afternoon wandering the streets, from gift shop to department store, searching but finding nothing suitable to commemorate the landmark occasion. She'd just about given up when she saw the antiques shop and decided to go inside. Not to find something for Danny—for what on earth would she find for Danny in an antiques shop?—but to satisfy her own desire to poke around all those wonderful, dusty antiques.

She spent a good half-hour just wandering, undisturbed, amid trash and treasure, before approaching the glass case that held antique and estate jewelry. She leaned over the case, examining hat pins and gaudy brooches. Behind the case, the proprietor, short and middle-aged and ruddy of face, gave her a wide smile and said in a lilting Irish brogue, "Might there be anything special ye'd be looking for, Miss?"

That was when she spied the cufflinks, lying on a white satin cloth inside the case. Elegant, unique, and monogrammed with an "F" for Fiore. A bit pretentious, but she knew instantly that Danny would love them. Somehow, he'd come to the conclusion that his self-worth could be measured by money and possessions, and she'd never had the heart to tell him he was wrong. "Those," she said, pointing. "The cufflinks. May I look at them?"

"Aye," he said. "An American." He slid open the case and took out the cufflinks. "These came from an estate sale in Yorkshire. They're very old. Would ye be buying them for yerself?"

She picked one up, felt its coolness, its heft. "For my husband. It's our tenth anniversary."

"Ah! Yer husband obviously likes pretty things. A man after me own heart. After all, look at the pretty girl he married. Will ye be buying them, then? Shall I wrap 'em for ye?"

"Yes. Please."

She left the shop feeling a sense of satisfaction. Danny was so hard to shop for. His tastes were very specific, and he didn't lack for anything. He made a lot of money, and he liked to spend it. As a result, it had grown increasingly difficult to find a meaningful gift that he either didn't already have or couldn't just buy for himself. But she felt confident that she'd found the one item in the entire city of London that was perfect for him.

Casey returned to the hotel, feeling almost giddy. Katie was napping in her room, attended by the babysitter who was watching daytime television with the volume turned low. Danny was still at rehearsal, so she called room service to order their dinner, then took a shower and changed into the dress she'd bought for the occasion. The Cheongsam style dress, with its keyhole neckline, was fashioned of a jade-green silk Asian print almost precisely the color of her eyes. It hugged her body, accentuating her curves, its split skirt highlighting her legs. Checking herself in the mirror, she decided she looked damn good for a woman who'd graduated from high school a decade earlier. She'd done a lot of living in those ten years, but none of it showed on the outside. The scars were all on the inside.

She checked the clock. Danny was running late. What else was new? He finally came in, gave her a quick kiss, and headed for the shower. "I'm sorry I'm late," he said. "The sound check took forever. The acoustics in that place are a nightmare."

"I ordered dinner. It should be here any minute."

"Oh, Christ." He paused, and she saw regret in those blue eyes. "I hate to do this to you, *carissima*, but I don't think I dare to eat anything before the show. Maybe later?"

And he disappeared into the bathroom.

While he was in there, room service arrived. The waiter wheeled in the cart, and she signed for the meal, giving him a generous tip. Then she went into Katie's room and dismissed the babysitter. If they weren't having the candlelight dinner she'd planned, it was pointless to pay somebody to watch over their daughter.

When Danny came back, dressed for the concert, they exchanged gifts. He loved the cufflinks, just as she'd known he would. After admiring them, he kissed her and asked, "Where did you find these?"

"In a little antiques shop here in London. I saw them and knew they'd just been sitting there, waiting for me to discover them. Waiting for you."

His gift to her was an exquisite, five-carat, princess-cut diamond necklace. She stood before the mirror, staring at her reflection, while behind her, his warm fingers fumbled with the clasp. The single stone fell, cold and hard, into the hollow between her breasts. She caught it in her hand, adjusted it until it faced frontward. "There," he said, his breath warm on her bare shoulder. "It looks beautiful on you."

She studied her mirror image with a critical eye. The necklace was all wrong for her. The stone was too big, too flashy. After ten years, he still didn't understand that big and flashy were words that didn't belong in the same sentence with the name *Casey Bradley Fiore*. But she would wear it, would cherish it, because she loved him and he'd given it to her.

After all those years, the couple reflected in the mirror still looked good together. A slender, petite, pretty—some would say beautiful—dark-haired woman. An achingly handsome blue-eyed man whose tawny hair fell in a neat line past his collar to his shoulders. He took her breath away. He had since the first moment she lay eyes on him, ten years earlier, standing in the kitchen of the house she'd grown up in, this handsome stranger, this unknown singer from Boston who had huge ambitions and was determined that she would write for him. She'd walked away from her life, her fiancé, her family, to be with him. It hadn't been all sunshine and roses. Rivers of darkness ran through her marriage. But she loved him, and she'd stood by him through it all. They had a beautiful daughter, successful careers, more money than they would ever know what to do with. A charmed life. And she had no regrets. She kept reminding herself that she had no regrets.

They each drank a single flute of champagne before Rob knocked on the door to tell Danny that the limo had arrived to take them to the venue. They'd certainly come a long way from the creaky old converted buses they'd started touring in. Immediately distracted, already someplace she couldn't follow him, Danny left her standing there with Rob and went into the bedroom to say goodnight to his daughter.

In the foyer of the hotel suite, Rob stood awkwardly, hands in his pockets, jingling loose change. He finally said, "If I may be so bold as to say so, Fiore, you are one hot ticket in that dress."

Danny hadn't said a word about the dress. She wasn't sure he'd even noticed it. Tears scalded her eyelids. She blinked them back. "Thank you," she said. "Thank you for noticing."

He studied her from beneath lowered eyelids. "Are you okay?"

"Of course I'm okay. It's my anniversary. Ten years. A milestone. You have to be okay on your anniversary. It's a law of the universe. I'm sure it must be written down somewhere."

Before he could respond, Danny blew back through, pausing to give her a quick, husbandly peck on the cheek. "Later," he said. "I promise I'll make it up to you later."

She knew he would make the effort. Danny might not always get it right, but he did try. She straightened his collar. "I know you will, darling."

And he was gone, sprinting down the corridor toward the elevator. For a long moment, she and Rob studied each other. He opened his mouth to speak.

"Don't say it," she warned him.

He clamped his mouth shut. Took a step closer, brushed a tear from her cheek. And whispered in her ear, "Smoking hot. Happy anniversary, kiddo."

Seven years later and a lifetime away from that London hotel room, kneeling on her living room floor beside her vacuum cleaner, Casey frowned at the cufflink in her hand. Why was it he could still get to her? Even now, with the way she felt about Rob, Danny could still get to her. Would it be this way for the rest of her life? He'd left her with so many scars, scars that were still raw, buried deep inside her. And certain memories could still rip her heart from her chest.

Trying to stem the flow of tears, she glanced around the room. "Are you here somewhere?" she demanded. "Did you do this deliberately, to stir things up?" She brushed furiously at a tear, shoved the cufflink into her pocket. "When are you ever going to let go of me, Danny?" Picking up the vacuum cleaner hose, she struggled for a moment to reattach it. Then she stood and took a hard breath. "For God's sake," she whispered, "leave me alone."

And she turned the vacuum back on.

Rob

"What's this?" he said.

Half-buried in the freezer in search of something to make for lunch, Casey paused, leaned back and turned to see the object he held in his hand. "It's a cufflink."

He raised an eyebrow, turned the object on its side. "I can see that. But whose?"

"It was Danny's." She snatched it away from him and pocketed it before he could get a better look.

He squared his jaw. "I thought you got rid of all Danny's stuff."

She returned to searching the freezer. From behind the door, she said, "I did."

"Then where'd it come from?"

She slowly emerged from behind the freezer door and gazed at him impassively. "I don't have a clue. I found it this morning when I was vacuuming. Why are you giving me the third degree?"

"I'm not. I'm just asking."

"Well, I don't have a crystal ball. Maybe Leroy fished it out from under the refrigerator. Are you planning to make a federal case out of it?"

A smart man knew when to shut up. He wasn't sure he qualified for that designation, but he clamped his mouth shut anyway. "No, ma'am," he said.

She gave him the Death Glare. Slowly closed the freezer door. And said, "I'm not feeling well. I think I'll go upstairs and lie down. I trust that the two of you can manage lunch on your own." And she left him standing there in the kitchen with his mouth hanging open.

Across the room, his daughter said, "Feisty one, isn't she?"

"Wipe that smirk off your face or I'll make you cook."

Paige arranged her face into a somber mask, but the amusement was still there in her eyes. "I thought you liked my cooking."

"Did I miss something crucial? Because I don't know who that woman is. Was there some memo I was supposed to get? Did the rules of the game change while I was away, only nobody bothered to tell me?"

"Maybe we should just...you know." At his probing look, she shrugged. "Get lunch?"

"Hold that thought. I'll be back."

He found his wife upstairs, flat on the bed, fists clenched tightly and a damp washcloth draped across her eyes. He sat gingerly on the edge of the mattress and said softly, "Headache?"

"I'm fine."

"You don't look fine." What she looked was pale. Ashen. Concerned, he brushed his knuckles across her cheek. "You look like crap."

"Thank you, Doctor MacKenzie, for that ego-boosting analysis."

"You know what I meant. Maybe you're coming down with something."

"I'm tired!" she snapped. "Am I not allowed to be tired?" A tear trickled from beneath the washcloth.

What the hell was going on here? Where was his sweet and stoic wife, and who was this weeping and witchy woman? "You're always tired lately," he said. "I'm worried about you. Maybe you should see your doctor. There could be something wrong with—"

"For the love of God, MacKenzie—" She tore the washcloth from her face to glower at him, and something she'd been clutching in her fist dropped to the mattress. "Will you stop hovering over me and just leave me the hell alone?"

He stared in bewilderment at the cufflink she'd just dropped. Danny's cufflink. The one she'd been clutching so tightly while she lay crying on the bed. Their bed. His and hers. The one place in this house where Daniel No-Middle-Name Fiore had no business showing his pretty-boy face.

He squared his jaw. "Fine," he said.

"Fine," she said. With a last dour glance, she picked up the cuff link, draped the cloth back over her eyes, and rolled onto her side. Away from him.

For a full ten seconds, he stared at her back, that solid wall of *leave-me-alone*, while a jumble of emotions roiled around inside him. Then he got up from the bed and did what she wanted.

He left her the hell alone.

Paige

Her father had this thing he did with his jaw that clearly signaled his mood to anybody with a functioning brain. She should know; she had the same habit. It was a little freaky, the way their body language was so similar. Clear evidence of nature trumping nurture. When Dear Old Dad came back downstairs, he was doing the clenched jaw thing, and Paige wasn't sure whether to run or offer sympathy.

She opted for somewhere in the middle. Neutral territory, like Switzerland, or Rhode Island. Clearing her throat, she said, "Casey okay?"

His brows drew together in a thunderous expression, and for an instant, she regretted saying anything. Then he relaxed, shrugged his shoulders. "She says she is, but you couldn't prove it by me. Listen, I'm not in the mood to cook. What do you say we blow this Popsicle stand and find something to eat in town?"

"In town" meant one of three options: the Jackson Diner, the pizza and sandwich shop inside the bowling alley, or Lola's, which specialized in thick and juicy steaks, a fully-stocked bar, and karaoke on Friday and Saturday nights. Slim pickings by anyone's standards. No dim sum, no plump and cheesy burritos, no handmade gelato. On the other hand, food was food, and she knew her father well enough by now to recognize that he wasn't quite as nutrition-conscious as his wife. Whatever she chose, he'd be amenable, and he wouldn't remind her that she hadn't yet eaten her daily allotment of leafy green vegetables. There were advantages to having an old man who, when he wasn't being a flaming ass, was laid back and flexible.

"Sounds good to me," she said.

They took the Porsche, which was okay with her, as there was a certain coolness factor attached to riding in a snazzy black sports car, in spite of that ridiculous and egotistical license plate. When his wife wasn't around, Rob MacKenzie didn't drive like a sedate, responsible adult. He drove that powerful car a little too fast, a little too aggressively. As if he, and he alone, owned the road. A Boston driver to the hilt. And for some crazy reason, that felt right. He did insist on seat belts, which was a little dorky, but the truth was that she felt safer wearing the thing, so she only rolled her eyes a little as she locked it around her, then forgot it was supposed to be uncool. Dead was pretty uncool, too.

He fiddled with the radio, found an oldies station, blasted something ancient at a death-defying volume. Something about a chick named Sloopy. Or maybe it was a dog named Snoopy. Either way, it was pretty lame.

He lowered the volume a few hundred decibels. "We used to play this," he said, "back in the day."

"Hunh."

"Your mom always came to our gigs wearing this cute little miniskirt thingy. Black leather. With knee-high boots. Legs up to—" He glanced at her from the corner of his eye. Cleared his throat. "Let's just say she was pretty hot."

"Really."

"And—" He reached for the radio dial, ratcheted it back up a notch. "I used to sneak her into the clubs through the back door, because she didn't have an I.D. and couldn't get in the front."

She raised her eyebrows. "My mom?" she said. "My mom snuck into bars because she wasn't old enough to drink?" She tried to picture her staid, respectable mother doing anything even remotely illegal, but she couldn't wrap her mind around it.

"Oh, she was old enough. The drinking age was eighteen then. But she didn't have a driver's license, and her folks wouldn't allow her to get a state I.D."

"But if she was of age, why did they have any say in what she did?"

"Trust me, nobody dared to cross her mother. So where do you want to eat?" He stopped for the town's lone traffic light, revved the engine impatiently, probably not even aware of what he was doing.

"Anything but bowling-alley pizza. Please God."

He turned his head, studied her. "If you could have anything you wanted, anything at all, the hell with geography, money no object...what would it be?"

"McDonald's French fries." She sighed dramatically. "I would kill for McDonald's French fries."

Still revving the engine, he nodded slowly and said, "Best fries on the planet."

She turned her head, and they studied each other for a long moment. "Good to know we agree on something."

The light turned green. He clicked his blinker and cut a hard left. "Well, then, sugar plum," he said, "we are getting us some of those McDonald's fries."

Rob

The kid had a certain charm about her, he thought as he watched her eat the last of her fries. It was an edgy, Boston-street-kid kind of charm, but charm nevertheless. "So," he said, taking a sip of Coke, "I really don't know that much about you. What makes Paige MacKenzie tick?"

She cocked her head to one side, that mop of blond curls, so like his own, falling all around her. "Why would you want to know?"

In his best, deeply resonant Darth Vader voice, he said, "Paige, I am your father." When she just looked at him blankly, he said, "Tell me you've seen the *Star Wars* movies."

"Um...no."

"A travesty. One we'll be rectifying as quickly as possible."

She shrugged. "They're guy flicks."

He clutched at his chest as if in terrible pain. "Tell me you didn't just say that. They are, collectively, the greatest movies of all time."

"Yeah? Have you talked to your wife about that? Because she seems to believe that honor should be evenly split between *Gone With the Wind* and *The King and I*."

He snorted and said, "Chick flicks. As God is my witness—" He met her eyes, saw the humor there. And they finished the line together: "I'll never be hungry again."

That pulled an actual grin from her. A brief one, but a grin nevertheless. "Look," he said, "I'm your father. Don't you think it's time we got acquainted with each other?"

"I think you're late by about fifteen years, but, hey, who's counting? So, should I start with my astrological sign? I'm a Sagittarius. Of course, you being my father and all, you ought to know that." Her smile was tight, and a little grim. "And yours?"

"Gemini."

"That figures. Don't you find this a little creepy? Like we're on a date or something?"

"Cut me a little slack, kid. I missed all the junior high school father/daughter dances. This is my way of making up for it. Talk to me. Tell me what matters to Paige MacKenzie."

Suddenly serious, she said, "Music. What else is there?"

Thinking back to when he was fifteen, he nodded his understanding. At fifteen, his music was all that had mattered to him. Hell, at thirty, it had been all he truly cared about. That and Casey. Always, Casey had been there, the center of his universe. Friend, business partner, collaborator. The one person on the planet he'd call if it was three in the morning and he needed bail money. They one person on the planet he'd take a bullet for. It had taken him years to realize he was in love with her. That knowledge had slammed into him with the force of a locomotive one night as they stood knee-deep in the frothing surf on a moonlit Bahamian beach. And without a thought, without a care, he'd hauled Danny's estranged wife into his arms, and he'd kissed her like a drowning man taking his last gulp of oxygen.

Then she'd gone back to Danny, taking all his oxygen with her.

"It's probably just PMS, you know."

He glanced up, disoriented, and it took him an instant to bring himself back. "What are you babbling about?"

"Your wife? Look, I don't have a clue where you just went, but I know exactly who you went there with."

"Ah, shit." Rubbing at his eye with the heel of his hand, he said, "Am I that transparent?"

"Like Saran Wrap. What was all that with the cufflink?"

He shook his head. "When I went upstairs," he said, "she was on the bed. Holding it in her hand. And crying."

"Ouch."

"I don't handle that kind of thing very well. Every time I think we're on an even keel, he pops up."

"The late Mister Fiore."

"And I go ballistic. He's the gift that keeps on giving."

"She talked to me about him. A little."

"Yeah?" He set his jaw. "What'd she say?"

"Nothing bad. In reference to you, I mean. Just the opposite. She told me her relationship with Danny wasn't a healthy one, but her relationship with you is built on mutual trust and respect."

"You didn't happen to hear love in there, did you?"

"If you think she doesn't love you, you're full of it."

"You don't understand. You're fifteen years old. You're too young to understand."

"I call bullshit on that. You guys have this weird connection thing going on between you. I can't explain it, but I witness it every time the two of you are in the same room. I mean, look at you. You're the crazy couple that waltzes around the kitchen while Kermit the Frog sings about rainbows. It's romantic. Sick and twisted, but romantic. Once you get past the whole frog thing."

"There's more to love than romance."

"And you've got it. Dude, you two are solid as a brick wall."

"Please," he said. "For the love of God, don't call me dude."

"I don't know what else to call you."

"Dad might be a good place to start!"

He realized his mistake the instant he saw the uncertainty on her face, she who'd made assertive, in-your-face certainty a way of life. He'd blurted it out without thinking, had simply opened his mouth, and there the words were, and it was too late to take them back. "Look," she said, "I'm not ready for that. I don't know if I ever will be."

Which one of them was the adult in this little scenario? Right now, the way his stomach felt, he wasn't sure. "I won't push you," he said. "I'm sorry if it felt that way. It wasn't intentional."

"You know—" She combed her hair away from her face with the fingers of both hands and studied him. "You're not quite the evil S.O.B. I always thought you were. It pains me to say this, but you're actually sort of okay. I mean, you drove twenty miles so I could have McDonald's fries." Her voice softened. "But we're not there yet. You know what I mean?"

"Yeah," he said. "I know."

"It'll happen, or it won't. That's the best I can give you."

"You may not understand this," he said. "But I am so damn proud of you right now. You're smart, and you're beautiful, and you're talented, and you don't take any guff from anyone. I'm not sure you realize how far we've come. We may not be there yet, but we're a hell of a lot closer than we were when we started."

"What can I say? I grow on people after a while."

"Then there's that wise-ass sense of humor. Wonder where that came from?"

They studied each other, green MacKenzie eyes gazing into green MacKenzie eyes. And then his daughter grinned. A real, live, genuine grin. "Gee," she said. "I can't imagine."

***

"Ease up on the clutch with your left foot and press on the accelerator with your right. Try to use the same amount of pressure on each pedal. If it starts to flutter, give it a little more gas. But not too much."

Her face taut with concentration, his daughter followed his instructions. The engine revved, a little too loud. Startled, she released the clutch, and the Porsche jumped so hard he almost lost his eyeteeth. "Shit," she said.

"Language," he warned.

"Um, right. Whatever you say. So what am I doing wrong?"

"You're not doing anything wrong. It's a body memory kind of thing. Do it enough times, eventually it'll feel natural. Once you've learned it, you won't ever forget. It's like riding a bike."

"With a little more horsepower."

"With a lot more horsepower. Go ahead. Try again."

This time, the car moved ahead a fraction of an inch before stalling. "Not bad," he said.

"Not good, either." She looked at him out of the corner of her eye. "You know my friend Lissa? Well, former friend."

"That would be the one you got arrested with."

"I did not get arrested. They didn't handcuff me. They didn't book me. They didn't charge me. They just took me down to the police station and—"

"Semantics," he said. "What about Lissa?"

"She wanted to know if, since you're famous and all, you could introduce her to Scott Baio."

He just looked at her, noted the slight twitch at the corner of her mouth. And said, "Scott Baio?"

"You know. *Happy Days. Joani Loves Chachi. Charles in—*"

"I know who Scott Baio is. Regrettably, we don't run in the same circles."

"No shit. And the guy's got to be like, thirty or something by now. Really old. I don't know what she's thinking."

"Language," he said again, more distractedly this time. "So what'd you tell her?"

"I asked her if she was stupid enough to think all famous people knew each other. Then I asked her if she liked me for me or because my father was a big rock and roll star. *Then* I told her to stop being a dick."

"Jesus, Paige. *Language!* Did your mother allow you to talk like that?"

"Leave my mother out of it. Can we try again?"

"You're in the driver's seat. Go for it."

She wet her lips, cranked the ignition, and hunched over the wheel. Slowly eased up on the clutch. It caught, and the car lurched forward. Started to lug. "Feather it," he said. "Feather the gas. Don't let up on the clutch yet! Give her a little more. That's it. Now bring that clutch up slowly. *Slowly.* Good girl!"

The car shuddered, then smoothed out. "I did it! Holy crap, I did it!"

"You did it. Keep giving it the gas. Steer it nice and straight. Whatever you do, don't put us in the ditch. I don't want to have to explain to Cousin Teddy why I couldn't steer the car on a straight stretch of road in broad daylight."

"Cousin Teddy is a turkey."

"I'm with you there. Get a little speed going. Okay, now put your clutch in. All the way to the floor." When she depressed the clutch, he shifted the car into second gear. She let it back up, a little jerky, but managed to keep the engine running and the car aimed straight down the road. "Good job," he said. "You know, my dad taught me to drive, back when dinosaurs walked the earth."

"In one of those Fred Flintstone cars, with your feet for brakes?"

"Something like that."

"What am I supposed to do next?"

"Third gear wouldn't be unheard of." He tried not to think about the damage she might be causing to his drive train. "Clutch down again. All the way to the floor." He shifted them into third. This time, the car didn't jerk as much when she released the clutch. "See?" he said. "You're starting to get the feel of it."

"Good thing this is a back road. Where does it go?"

"Damned if I know."

"You've lived here longer than me. You should know this stuff. What if we get lost?"

"Not that much longer. And we won't get lost. I may be a city boy, but I'm not a complete rube. Casey could tell you where it goes. She knows every back road in the county. And probably most of the snowmobile trails."

"Yee haw."

"It's not such a bad place to live. It grows on you."

"Says you. Don't tell me you actually like living here?"

"Doesn't matter. Casey likes living here. I like living wherever Casey lives."

"That is just so damn cute. Young love."

"Your day will come, little girl. One of these days, you'll open your eyes and it'll be time for your twentieth high school reunion. And you'll be looking around you, scratching your head and wondering where those two decades went."

"Um, Gramps? I think I'm ready to quit now. How do you stop this thing?"

"Clutch in. Okay, now shift her down into second."

"Me?"

"You won't always have somebody to shift gears for you, so learn to do it yourself. Remember the H pattern I taught you? Slide over, through neutral, then pull back. Good! Nice and smooth. Now brake just a little—a *little!* And ease it over to the side of the road."

They came to a shuddering halt on the shoulder. His daughter's knuckles were white on the steering wheel. "Jesus," she said. "I'm sweating like a pig."

"You think you're sweating, imagine how I feel. Do you have any idea how much I paid for this car?"

"That was pretty cool. To celebrate, I think we should go out for a couple of cold ones."

"Nice try, Sunshine. Ready to swap places, or are you still shaking in your shoes?"

"I wasn't shaking in my shoes! I was just sweating a little. This is a very expensive car. You could've taught me in the Explorer. Automatic's a lot easier."

"Automatic's boring. You just sit there and steer. Anybody worth their salt learns to drive a stick. Turn off the ignition, leave it in gear, and set the parking brake."

When she'd followed his instructions without incident, he opened the door and got out. That was when he saw the FOR SALE sign on the side of the road. The gravel driveway next to it led nowhere, but the towering maples, some of them still clinging to a brilliant orange leaf or two, told him there must have been a house here at one time. The property was mostly flat, riddled with winter-yellow untamed grass that grew waist high in places. He studied it, took it all in, listened to the wheels turning inside his head. Thought about taking down the phone number on the sign. Then shrugged, turned to walk around the car.

And saw the view.

It grabbed him by the heart and squeezed, the same way a wailing saxophone could make his chest tighten and send shivers running down his spine. High on a hill, he could see for miles and miles, just like that old song by the Who. Dark evergreen forests. Mountains as far as the eye could see. The landscape dotted with bodies of water whose names he would probably never know. God's country.

From the far side of the car, Paige circled around and stood beside him, following his gaze. "Wow," she said.

"Yeah. Wow."

His daughter crossed her arms. Still looking at the view, she said, "Can I ask you a question?"

"Ask away."

"Did you love my mother?"

The unexpected question drove a knife through his gut. He leaned against the side of the Porsche. Propping his elbows on the roof, he said, "That was all such a long time ago—"

"Stop waffling. It's not brain surgery. It's a simple yes or no answer."

Was it that simple? The wind lifted a strand of her hair and blew it into her face, that beautiful face that displayed a vulnerability she couldn't quite hide beneath the hard, brusque exterior mask she wore to face the world. He couldn't lie to the kid. She'd been lied to all her life. Right now, he and Casey were all the stability she had.

"I liked her a lot," he said. "But I think that if I'd loved her...if I'd really, truly loved her...I would've taken her with me when I left for New York."

"Yeah," she said. "That's about what I thought."

"I'm sorry. It's not the answer you were looking for."

She kicked at the gravel beneath her feet. "Hey, you were honest. You could have lied to spare my feelings. You didn't."

"Right." He wondered why that didn't make him feel any better.

"So...I guess you probably had a lot of girlfriends over the years."

Girlfriends. That was one way of putting it. There'd always been women, but especially during those hazy days following his second divorce, when he'd wandered, adrift, for far too long. A silent, solitary wraith, tall and lean and needy, beer bottle in hand, wending his way through the crowded bars of L.A., some kind of dark emptiness burning inside his gut. Beautiful faces coming at him from out of the crowd, plastic smiles, eager eyes. Hours spent cruising the winding roads of Laurel Canyon, windows open and the top down, scent of eucalyptus heavy on the night breeze as some random blonde in the passenger seat threw her head back and let the wind muss her perfect hair. Sometimes, if the night and the woman were right and the emptiness was crowding him, he'd take the Porsche out onto the freeway, open her up, and let her run. He never thought about dying. The speed, the danger, were a rush. So was the sex. Exciting, yet at the same time unfulfilling. There'd been a lot of women, so many women he'd lost track. And things he'd never told Casey. Things he would never tell her about that dark and directionless time in his life.

He hadn't understood what drove him. Not then, not until years later. It hadn't been about driving too fast, drinking too much, sleeping with too many women. It wasn't sex he'd been looking for; it was connection. He was looking to fill that emptiness inside him, searching for that slender, golden thread of connection—the connection he had with Danny's wife—in another woman.

Of course, he hadn't found it. That wasn't the kind of thing you could replicate. Back then, he hadn't understood the concept of soul mates. Hell, he wasn't sure he understood it even now, at the ripe old age of thirty-seven. But if the concept was real, if soul mates truly existed, then he'd met his when he was twenty years old. She just happened to be married to another man.

"You still in there somewhere, dude?"

He glanced over at his daughter, studied her face, the innocence that belied her streetwise attitude, and felt something tug at his heart. "Don't call me dude," he said.

"This time," she said, studying him keenly, "you went so far away I wasn't sure you were coming back."

"I'm sorry."

"It wasn't a hard question, but I bet there's a lulu of an answer."

What was it about this kid that made it impossible to lie to her? "Before Casey," he said, "yes. I had a lot of girlfriends."

"Casey doesn't strike me as the type who'd much like that."

"She doesn't. She says I was looking for love in all the wrong places. Like the song."

"Um...what song?"

"Johnny Lee?" She shook her head. "*Urban Cowboy?*" Another negative. "Travolta and a mechanical bull?" She shrugged. "Jesus, kid," he said, "we really have to work on updating your pop culture references."

Casey

She woke feeling like roadkill, irritable and exhausted, with a major headache and an upset stomach. It felt like the worst kind of hangover, which would have made sense if she'd gotten drunk last night. But she hadn't. Casey stumbled to the kitchen, still in her robe, teeth unbrushed, her hair a mess. The smell of frying bacon hit her full in the face, and her stomach lurched. Standing over the stove, Rob said, "I'm having a few people over this afternoon to jam."

When she didn't respond, he raised his head and looked at her. "You look like shit," he said.

She glared at him through bleary eyes. "Thank you so much, Dr. MacKenzie."

"Seriously." He touched her cheek, her forehead. "You don't feel feverish, but you look awful."

"I'm fine. It's just a migraine. Stop fussing over me."

"You don't get migraines."

"There has to be a first time, doesn't there?" She crossed the room, took a mug from the cupboard, and poured herself a cup of coffee.

"I wish you'd see a doctor. Something's not right. You've been sick ever since I got home, and lately all you do is sleep. Are you sure you don't have mono?"

Fighting the urge to heave the coffee mug at his head, she said through gritted teeth, "I. Am. Fine."

"Why are you so goddamn stubborn?"

"For God's sake, MacKenzie, will you stop hovering over me and just leave me the hell alone?" She slammed her mug on the counter, sloshing hot coffee over the rim. "I am going back to bed, and the first person who has the audacity to come near me will suffer the consequences!"

She slept for another four hours, awoke to bright overhead sunlight and a digital clock that read 12:36 p.m. Her headache was gone, and her stomach seemed to have righted itself. She got up, showered and dressed, and chalked it up to some 24-hour bug.

Downstairs, the house was silent, the only sound that of the ticking clock. Ravenous, she made herself a ham sandwich, washed it down with a glass of milk, then went looking for Rob. She found him in the barn, in his studio, hunched over his unplugged Stratocaster, making notations with a stubby pencil on a sheet of music paper. Walking up behind him, she lay both hands on his shoulders and said, "Hey."

He stiffened. Let out a breath. And hunched lower over his work.

"I'm sorry," she said, and kissed the top of his head. "I didn't mean to snap at you. I'm not sure why I've been so grumpy lately."

Still not speaking, he plinked a couple of notes on the guitar, erased the mark he'd just made, swiped away the eraser dust, and penciled in a correction.

"Oh, for the love of God. Is this the way you intend to play it? Well, fine. If you ever decide you want to speak to me again, I'll be at your sister's house."

And she slammed the door behind her for emphasis.

***

Rose was painting in the wonderful, sunlit studio over the garage that Jesse had set up for her when they got married. Casey sat on a wooden rocker, watching her sister-in-law slap acrylics onto an oversized canvas. "So," Rose said, "where's my little brother? The two of you are usually joined at the hip."

Casey rolled her eyes. "It's probably better if we're not in the same room right now."

Rose turned away from the canvas to look at her. "Are you two fighting?"

"Not exactly." She picked up a tube of yellow paint that had inexplicably migrated to the wrong side of the room. "He's in one of his moods. I woke up feeling terrible this morning. I hadn't slept well, I had a headache, and I was tired and dragged out. He started hovering, like a mother hen. He does that sometimes, and it makes me crazy. I snapped at him, and apparently I wounded his delicate sensibilities. I went back to bed for a couple of hours, and when I got up and tried to apologize, he got the way he gets—"

"Oh, boy."

"—and I wasn't in the mood for it, so I left and came over here, where the company is a little more agreeable."

"I'm sorry. It's that stupid jackass MacKenzie temper. He'll get over it."

"Oh, I know. He always does. But when he gets that way, it's definitely better if we're in separate places until he cools off."

"I'm just a little surprised. Every time I see the two of you, you're wrapped so tight around each other that I wonder if I should go find a fire extinguisher in case you spontaneously combust."

She sighed. And said in resignation, "My name is Casey, and I'm an addict."

Rose's brow furrowed. "Have I missed something?"

"Not that kind of addict. A MacKenzie addict. That man should come with a warning label."

"Oh," Rose said. "I see."

Casey sat up straighter. Clasped her hands and said, "I don't think you do. May I speak frankly?"

"I thought we were speaking frankly. But feel free to elaborate. As long as you're not about to go into any of the intimate details of your sex life with my brother, we should be just fine."

"It's nothing like that. It's just that something happened recently, and I really need a girlfriend to talk this over with. Somebody who might possibly understand."

"Talk away, girlfriend. I'm all ears."

"This will probably sound crazy to you, but bear with me. I've just recently realized that I'm in love with my husband. Totally, completely, utterly, madly in love."

A single beat passed before Rose said, "Come again?"

"See, I knew you'd think I was nuts."

"I don't think you're nuts, but I also don't get what you're talking about. Maybe you can translate it into some kind of English that I can understand. Because I thought you were already in love with him."

"I was. I am. But it wasn't like this. Not at first. Or…maybe it was, and I was just in denial. For a long, long time." Her sister-in-law was looking at her as though she were speaking Swahili. And maybe she was. Struggling to find the right words, she said, "I'm going to use a musical metaphor, because what else do I know anything about? When we got married, the way I felt about him…or at least the way I *thought* I felt about him, was like a sweet, tender love song, played in three or four chords on an acoustic guitar. But I've come to realize it wasn't that at all. Because underneath that tender love song, there's this symphony, with screaming electric guitars and a full orchestra, with strings and horns, and—" She glanced up at Rose, who still looked bewildered. "You're not getting it, are you?"

"Not really. I'm sorry."

"I had no idea I felt this way. I don't know when it started, or how long it's been going on. Years. Since before Danny died. Maybe even before Katie died. *Years.* I was in denial for all that time. Maybe it was like he said to me: abstinence makes the heart grow fonder. Maybe that's what made me realize the truth. I don't know. I just know that one afternoon while he was away, it suddenly hit me, and I realized that somewhere along the line, what I felt for him had turned into this."

"This," Rose said. "This what?"

She waved her arms wide. "This gargantuan *thing*. The kind of thing where your heart feels like it's going to just burst free from your chest. The kind of thing where, when he walks into the room, your throat closes up and your mouth goes dry and your palms get sweaty. And you start shaking all over, and you just sort of melt. And you can't breathe, or even formulate a coherent thought. And God forbid you should try to speak, because nothing would come out even if you tried. And you develop this peculiar kind of tunnel vision, where everything and everybody else just fades away, and he's the only thing you can see, and you just want to jump him like a starving lioness and rip his clothes off and feast on him, and—am I making myself clear?"

Dryly, Rose said, "I think I'm starting to get the picture."

"I'm thirty-five years old, Rose. I'm a grown woman who should be acting with some level of decorum. But I am so far gone that I don't care anymore. I've never felt so high in my life. It's just that…I'm also a little confused. A lot, if we're being honest. I married my best friend. My sweet, wonderful, kind and supportive best friend. And, damn it, he wasn't supposed to turn into this raging sex god!"

At a sound in the doorway, she looked up and into her brother-in-law's eyes. She flushed from the roots of her hair to the tips of her toes. Rose glanced at her husband, frowned and shook her head *no*, and without a word, Jesse turned and disappeared out the door and back down the stairs.

"Nice," Casey said.

"It's okay. I'm sure he must have heard the words *raging sex god* before. Somewhere."

"I'm really having trouble with this. I'm all afloat. I don't know who I am any more. Or who he is. Or which way is up, and I feel so vulnerable, in a way I've never felt before."

"You're afraid? Of loving my little brother?"

"Does the term abject terror mean anything to you?"

"I don't get it. Where's the down side to all of this?"

"When I married Danny," she said, "I was so in love with him. He made me feel alive, in a way I'd never felt alive before. And I just closed my eyes and jumped in, feet first, without ever looking back. It was wonderful, and it was terrible, and I was so wrapped up in him that I lost myself. It took me a dozen years to realize what I'd done to myself, and then I had to fight so hard to reclaim any sense of self. To find out who I was. To regain self-respect. And now—" She paused. "Now, I'm deathly afraid of making the same damn-fool mistake with another man. And losing myself again."

"Honey, you're not the same person you were then. You're older, and stronger, and smarter. And you've got yourself a really good guy, and I'm not saying that just because he's my brother. I mean—" Rose shrugged. "I'm not saying that Danny wasn't a good guy. But I will say—and please don't take this the wrong way—I never saw you look at Danny the way you look at my brother."

"I know. And it scares the bejesus out of me."

"I'm not following."

"The way I feel about him…it's so damn big that I don't know where to put it. If I lost myself so completely with Danny, how am I going to survive something this much bigger without disappearing like I did before?"

"Frankly, I don't understand how this could come as a surprise to you. I've been watching you and Rob for two decades.

You light up like Times Square at New Year's every time he walks into the room. You always have."

Casey clamped her mouth shut. Took a breath. "I was horrible to him this morning. No wonder he's mad at me. I've just been so angry lately. I thought it was because I wasn't dealing well with him being gone. But he's been back for two weeks now, and I'm still so irritable that I can barely live with myself."

Rose turned back to her canvas and began applying paint. "If I didn't know better, I'd think you were pregnant. Eddie used to call me Hurricane Rose because the mood swings were so bad. Without any warning, I'd go from sweet and loving to Lizzie Borden. Ax in hand, ready to chop off heads."

Casey looked at Rose's back, opened her mouth, closed it again.

Rose paused, turned to look at her, saw the expression on her face. "Hon? You don't suppose—"

Irritation. Mood swings. Exhaustion. Morning sickness. Tender breasts. She tried to remember the date of her last period, but she'd always been irregular. She would have to check her calendar. But she didn't need to check it to know she was overdue. Way overdue. Because her last period had been sometime in August, before Rob left.

More than two months ago.

"Oh, my God," she said.

***

She didn't recognize half the cars in her driveway. Mikey's old F-150 was there, flanked by a maroon Subaru wagon, a blue Ford Ranger, and a rusty brown Volkswagen Rabbit. Who were these people, and how had her husband found them? She knew that musicians had some kind of radar that made them gravitate toward each other, but he'd only lived here for eighteen months. She supposed it had something to do with the fact that he was naturally gregarious, but it still surprised her when she realized how many people Rob MacKenzie knew in this tiny backwater town after being here for such a short time.

The moment she stepped out of the car, she heard the music. Loud, crashing, classic rock. It was a good thing they didn't have close neighbors, because this would probably go on all evening and into the night. She'd learned nearly two decades ago that once a musician picked up his instrument, putting it down again was next to impossible. Back in the day, when she and Danny were newlyweds living in a third-floor walk-up apartment in a faded brownstone on the back side of Beacon Hill, the jam sessions would go on until dawn. She'd get out of work at midnight and catch a taxi home, and if it was a warm summer night and the windows were open, she could hear the music when she stepped out of the cab: Danny on the piano and Rob on the guitar, and sometimes Travis playing bass, and whoever else they'd dragged home playing whatever instrument they'd brought with them.

The only reason they hadn't been evicted was because their downstairs neighbor was a twenty-three-year-old stoner named Woofy, who, as likely as not, was right there playing along with them. She never knew his real name, or what he did for a living, although she suspected it had something to do with the jungle of greenery he grew under fluorescent lighting in a converted closet in the back bedroom of his apartment. The boys used to sneak down there sometimes and smoke with him. They thought they were getting away with something, but it was impossible to not know what they were doing; Danny would come to bed reeking of it.

Since it didn't happen often, she'd given him a free pass. But she did have a couple of ironclad house rules, and Danny had made sure that anybody he brought home understood that those rules were inviolable. Rule Number One: no drugs on the premises. What people chose to do elsewhere was their business, but anybody who walked through the door of her apartment carrying anything stronger than Tylenol would be asked to leave, and would never be invited back. Rule Number Two: guests were welcome to drink whatever they brought with them, but if they got sick, they had to clean up their own messes, and if they were driving, they had to hand over their keys when they arrived, and wouldn't get them back until they'd sobered up.

Because of Rule Number Two, they'd had a lot of overnight guests. She would get up in the morning and be climbing over them on her way to the kitchen. They ate her out of house and home, and she and Danny probably would have starved if not for

Rob, who was still living with his parents, so had money to burn. He was the one who kept her pantry stocked with luxuries like bread and milk and toilet paper. Danny had been blissfully unaware of this, and neither of them had bothered to enlighten him. It was just one of the many secrets they'd kept from Danny over the years.

Drawn by the music, she left her purse in the car and moved toward the barn. Inside, the walls and the floor were shaking to the driving rhythm of Eric Clapton's *Cocaine*. Casey stood just inside the door, taking stock, her hands in the pockets of her jeans and her body moving to that seductive, bluesy rhythm. She didn't recognize the piano player, but she was pretty sure she'd seen the guy on bass working in the produce section at the IGA. To her delight, the drummer—whose receding hairline and wire-rimmed glasses made him more closely resemble an accountant than a musician—was Buddy Theriault, who used to save her a seat on the school bus every day when they were in fifth grade.

Rob was in the middle of a guitar solo, his playing so familiar, his style so distinctive, she would have recognized it anywhere. Rock guitarists—the good ones, anyway—all had their own sound. Eric Clapton's blues-influenced playing sounded like nobody else on the planet. Eddie Van Halen, with his high-energy power chords, was immediately recognizable. And Rob MacKenzie, who had studied jazz for two years at Berklee, infused his songs with jazzy undertones like nobody else could do. His eyes were closed as he played, and the expression on his face said it all: This was what he'd been put on this planet to do.

Luke was on rhythm guitar. Rose's son was showing signs of great promise as a guitarist. It had been an adjustment for him, being moved from Boston to this godforsaken place when his mother had married Jesse Lindstrom last year. But Luke's naturally sunny disposition, accompanied by the obvious hero worship he felt for his Uncle Rob, had smoothed the transition. It hadn't hurt that Rob had taken his nephew under his wing and had nurtured Luke's love of music with private guitar lessons and jam sessions like this one. They sounded good together, and there was a connection between them, a connection so visible that, watching them play together, she felt an instant of acute physical pain because it reminded her so much of the connection Rob had shared onstage with Danny.

Rob finished the solo, opened his eyes, and saw her standing there. She went hot all over as those green eyes studied her face. He gave her a brief, quirky grin before focusing his attention back on his playing. Paige jumped into the vocals with that earthy voice of hers, and Casey glanced off to one side of the room where, perched on a table shoved up against the wall, Mikey leaned his back against the sheetrock. Long legs stretched out in front of him, he was watching Paige with such blatant adoration that Casey was momentarily taken aback.

Yikes. When had this happened? This couldn't possibly be good news, and her head swiveled around to study the girl, wondering if this crush was mutual or unrequited. But Paige was too wrapped up in her singing to give away any hint of her inner emotions. So while the music thundered around her, Casey made her way across the room and joined her favorite nephew.

"Hey there, kiddo," she said, shouting to be heard over the music.

"Hi, Aunt Casey."

She perched on the table beside him, and together they watched and listened, comfortable without speaking, she and this nephew she adored. Rob sent a glance her way. Their eyes locked, and they held a silent conversation. Satisfied that all was right with the world, he gave her a wink and focused back on his playing.

She was ravenous again. And exhausted. How was it possible she could be exhausted after sleeping past noon? She would call the doctor and make an appointment on Monday. Rose had given her the name of her OB/GYN, Deb Levasseur, and had praised her to the high heavens.

Morning sickness. That was what she'd woke up with this morning. That explained the random bouts of nausea she'd experienced for the past six weeks. She hadn't recognized it because she'd never had morning sickness with Katie. But Rose, who'd given birth to three children, had assured her that every pregnancy was different, and that her symptoms were normal.

She wasn't ready to tell Rob. Not just yet. Not until the doctor confirmed it. Not until she was certain that everything was progressing as it should. Her first pregnancy had ended in a miscarriage. Yes, that had been more than a dozen years ago, and there'd been extenuating circumstances. Still, she couldn't completely squelch the anxiety. She'd been through so much, had suffered so many losses, that the fear was never far from the surface. There'd be plenty of time for celebrating later, after she'd seen the doctor.

Eventually, driven by starvation, she gave Mikey a hug, slithered down off the table, and went in the house. She opened a can of crabmeat, mixed it with a glop of mayonnaise, debated what kind of bread to use, finally ended up wolfing it down right from the bowl. When it was empty, she let out a tiny belch, then stared at the empty bowl, shocked that she'd eaten the entire can in about five seconds. It was either pregnancy or a tapeworm, and if it was the former, at the rate she was going, she'd be big as a house within a month.

The music was still playing. From this distance, the song wasn't recognizable, but she could hear the steady boom-boom that told her they were still in full swing. Wiped out, she lay on the couch in front of the television with the sound turned down, covered herself with a light blanket, and catnapped.

When she awoke, Rob was crouched in front of her, one hand on her shoulder, those green eyes studying her with mild concern. "Hey," she said groggily.

"Hey, yourself. You okay?"

"Mmn. I'm fine. I was just napping while I waited for you."

"You were really zonked out."

She reached out a hand and touched his face. His skin was warm against her palm, and she could feel the fine rasp of whiskers. "What time is it?"

"A little after nine."

"Quitting so early?"

"We're not kids any more. Well, except for the kids, of course. The rest of us are geezers."

"You'll never be a geezer. You're thirty-seven going on twelve."

"You hungry? I have leftover pizza if you want a slice. Pepperoni and green olive. I gave Mikey some money a couple hours ago and sent him on a pizza run."

"I think I'll pass. I ate something earlier."

"How about a dish of ice cream? There's fudge ripple in the freezer."

"Little bit. Let's do one bowl and two spoons."

The kitchen on this mild autumn evening felt intimate and cozy and wonderfully peaceful. She took a spoonful of ice cream and closed her eyes while it melted on her tongue. Swallowed and said, "Where's Paige?"

"She left with Mikey."

"I'm a little concerned about those two."

"So you noticed."

"It would be hard to miss. He was looking at her like a lion watching a gazelle that was about to become its dinner." She took another spoonful of heaven, couched in the familiar flavors of chocolate and vanilla. "Should we be monitoring this situation a little more closely? She's only fifteen."

"It's awkward. I can't very well forbid them to see each other."

"Sure, you can. You just say, 'I forbid you to see each other.'"

"If only it were that easy. I'm trying to keep watch. Without looking like a Nazi."

"I think that's your job as a father. To look like a Nazi." She rested her chin on her palm and said wistfully, "The teenage years are so hard."

"Life is hard. The teenage years are just one small portion thereof."

"The world according to MacKenzie. My philosopher. So where were they headed?"

"I think the movies in Farmington. I told her to be home by eleven-thirty."

She paused, her spoon halfway to her mouth. And said, with no small amount of delight, "You gave her a curfew?"

He ate a spoonful of fudge ripple. "It seemed like the right thing to do."

With a gleeful grin, she said, "It seems like a dad thing to do."

"Don't remind me. Most people start with babies and work their way up. How'd we end up starting with a teenager?"

"Give me a break, MacKenzie. You love teenagers."

"I love hanging out with teenagers. Playing with 'em. Getting down to their level for a few hours, then sending the little monsters home to their parents. They're the ones who spawned 'em. I always figured they could deal with the results of their spawning. Of course, that was before I knew I'd spawned one myself."

"You do realize that you painted yourself into a corner? Now you have to wait up to make sure she doesn't break curfew."

"Jesus, Mary and Joseph. If I'm this tired at thirty-seven, how will I survive our babies when they get to be teenagers? Especially since we haven't even started any of them yet. Poor kids will be so embarrassed when they realize that Mom and Dad are the same age as their friends' grandparents."

"Oh, stop. We're not that old."

"Speak for yourself. Some days, I feel like Methuselah."

She stuck her spoon into the bowl of ice cream and moved it around a little. "Remember when we used to do this?"

"Sit around and talk about how old we feel?"

She rolled her eyes. "Eat fudge ripple ice cream together. In the middle of the night, when the rest of the world was sleeping."

"While ABBA sang *Dancing Queen* on that old kitchen radio you had. We'd sit up until dawn, talking about Life with a capital L. As if either of us even knew what life was about back then. We were still wet behind the ears."

"And now, of course, we're ancient."

"Sometimes I feel like it. Danny thought we were nuts."

"We weren't nuts. Running the kitchen light late at night was the only way, short of a whip and a chair, that I could keep the roaches at bay. And you could never resist the siren call of fudge ripple."

"I still can't. I'll never forget you screaming bloody murder the first time you turned on the kitchen light and those damn roaches ran for cover."

"I'd never seen anything like them before. They were arrogant little monsters. Fearless. While I, on the other hand, was quaking in my shoes."

"But after a while, you learned to peacefully coexist. You'd just swat 'em out of the way and keep on with whatever you were doing. So I'd say you were equally fearless. Those were the glory days, weren't they?"

"Bite your tongue, MacKenzie. Those were the nightmare days."

"I guess conditions were a little, ah...primitive...for a while there."

"That's a very generous depiction."

They both focused on the ice cream for a while. Eventually, she said, "For such a long time, you were the only good thing in my life."

He reached across the table and took her hand in his. They threaded fingers together and, ignoring the ice cream, studied each other while two decades of history hovered in the air between them. Eventually, he said, "That was a whole other lifetime. We're not the same people we were then."

"But it's still there. And so are those two ridiculously young people. In here." She touched her head. Then her chest, just above her heart. "And here." Studying his face, she said, "Don't you believe that everything you go through, the good and the bad, shapes the person you become?"

"Of course. But I'm not a fatalist. Our history doesn't have to become our destiny."

"Neither am I. I believe in free will. But it's all still there. Everything we've done and been and felt. The loves, the losses, the regrets. The victories, the achievements, the moments that we knew were significant just by the way they felt. The people we built connections with. It's all still inside somewhere."

"Are we feeling particularly maudlin tonight?"

"Not maudlin. Maybe just a little nostalgic, hearing you talking about old age and infirmity."

"Hey, watch it there, missy. I didn't say a thing about infirmity."

"Can I say something you'll probably think is silly and totally unnecessary?"

"What?"

"Thank you."

He lifted their joined hands to his mouth and kissed her knuckles, tangled with his. "For what?"

"For being my friend. For keeping me upright and breathing during the times when things got so awful. If I live to be a thousand years old, there's no way I'll ever be able to repay you for everything you did for me."

His eyebrows drew together in a thunderous expression. "Do I look like I'm expecting payment? That road runs both ways. What's this about?"

"I don't really know. Maybe you're right. Maybe I am feeling maudlin tonight. It's just that every so often, it hits me. Everything we went through. Sometimes it's hard to believe that was really me, living that life, when I look around me and see the amazingly normal life we live now. And I realize how much I took you for granted. You were just there, a part of my life, someone I loved so much, and I never stopped to think about it. I simply forged ahead, on fast-forward, without taking time to examine our relationship. But I realize now that if you hadn't been there, I never would have survived. You were my lifeline, for so many years that I've lost count. I want to thank you for that. And say how sorry I am that it took me so many years to realize how important you were to me."

"Would you do it all over again," he said, "knowing what you know now?"

"In a heartbeat. What does that say about me?"

"The same thing it says about me, because I'd do it over again, too, just as long as you were there. You may not realize it, but you kept me going, too. When I was nineteen, I hitched my wagon to a star. His name was Danny Fiore, and I stuck with him until he burned out. I'm not sure I would've hung around so long if you hadn't been there. You made it all worthwhile."

"We really built something big, didn't we? The three of us?"

"We did. Sometimes when I'm up on stage, playing, I automatically look to my left, expecting to see him standing in the spotlight. My front man, strutting and singing and making all the women cry. And then I realize he's not there, and he'll never be there again, and I'm the guy up front now. It's humbling, and terrifying, and sometimes it breaks my heart."

She touched his cheek tenderly. "This has nothing to do with how I feel about you. But sometimes now, my life feels a little like a table with only three legs. Lopsided and wobbly. There were three of us, for years and years and years, and now there are just two of us, and it feels so strange. He was larger than life, and it's impossible to fill the gaping hole he left behind."

He toyed with her fingers, kissed them, and said with grave solemnity, "We are two seriously fucked-up individuals."

And she laughed. "If I'd met you only yesterday, I'd love you anyway, just because you make me laugh, and it feels so good to laugh. For a long time, I didn't have much to laugh about."

"I live to make you laugh. I thought you knew that."

"I do know that. Thank you. From the bottom of my heart."

"You're welcome. From the bottom of mine." He squeezed her hand, then glanced down at the ceramic bowl that sat on the table between them. "Looks like the fudge ripple is a lost cause."

She studied the shapeless, soupy mess and said, "I could always find a couple of straws and we could drink it."

"Forget the straws. Let's find a couple of pillows instead, pop in a movie, and we can cuddle on the couch and watch it while we wait for our kid to get home."

Paige

"Your singing," Mikey said. "It's just amazing. You do realize you have to do something with it?"

Flattered, she said, "I guess."

"No," he said. "I'm serious. Singing is what you're meant to do. You have to promise me that you'll do something with it."

Something about his words made her uneasy. "Okay."

They drove for a while in silence. Until she realized they were going the wrong way. "This isn't the road to Farmington," she said.

"No."

She studied his profile, that beautiful profile, that face that could make her palms sweat and her stomach clench into a hard ball. "What's wrong?" she said.

He didn't answer. Instead, he clicked on his blinker and took a left onto a dirt road. It ended in a small gravel parking lot beside a pristine lake that shimmered in the moonlight. Mikey crammed the shifter into Park. Turned off the engine. And said, "We have to talk."

Her insides crumpled like a piece of discarded aluminum foil. "Oh, shit," she said. "You're getting ready to break my heart, aren't you?"

Mikey glanced at her, then looked quickly away, out over the lake. "I shouldn't have let this go as far as it did. I didn't intend to. It just sort of...happened."

"I don't understand."

"This can't happen," he said. "You and me. It can't happen."

"But I thought—" She broke off, puzzled, bewildered. Hurt.

"It's the timing. It's all wrong. I'm graduating in June. I did high school in three years, Paige. And I'm not going to Farmington."

She tried to breathe, but wasn't sure her lungs would allow it. "Where are you going?"

"I applied to Stanford. I've been accepted."

"Stanford," she said blankly. "Where's Stanford?"

"Northern California. Near San Francisco. Dad doesn't know yet. Remember when I said I wanted to load a suitcase in my truck and just head west? That's what I'm doing. Right after graduation. I'm spending the summer on the road before I start school in the fall."

"What does that have to do with us?"

He was silent for a long time. "I think about you," he said quietly, gripping the steering wheel. "Did you know that? I think about you all the time. And a lot of those thoughts—let's just say they're not exactly G-rated. But you're fifteen. Your father would kill me if I laid a finger on you. He'd kill me if he knew what I was thinking. And I wouldn't blame him. He's a good dad. A good man. I respect him a lot." He finally looked at her, a glimmer in his eyes that might or might not be tears. "But I don't think I can be with his daughter," he said, "I don't think I can be with you, without touching you."

"I'm not like other girls," she said.

"No kidding."

"I don't play games. I don't lie. I tell it like it is. If I want to be with a guy, I'll be with him, and I won't worry about the consequences."

"I know. You're so brave, the bravest girl I've ever known. But the consequences are still real. You can ignore them all you want, but that won't make them go away."

She tried to make sense of his words, tried to find a way to spin them that wouldn't feel like he'd just driven a knife into her gut. But no matter how she spun it, that knife was still there, buried to the hilt.

"Look," he said, "if you were older, I'd take you with me when I leave. But you're not. You'll still have two years of high school ahead of you. I wish things could be different. I really, really wish they could be different. But they can't."

"So that's it?" she said.

"If it'll help, I'll stay away from the family get-togethers from now on. I can find somewhere else to be on Saturday nights."

"It's your family," she said. "Far be it from me to tear you away from their collective bosom. You can have custody of

Saturday nights. I'll just stay home with Leroy and watch Channel 6."

"It's your family, too."

"Right. You can take me home now. You've said what you had to say."

"Don't be mad at me. Please, Paige. I'm so sorry."

She took a last long look at that face. Imprinted it on her brain so she'd never forget. Allowed herself to feel the pain of his betrayal. Took a deep, shuddering breath.

And said, "Fuck you."

***

When she came into the kitchen, her father was sitting at the table, cup of tea in hand, reading by the light of a single lamp. "Why are you still up?" she said.

He closed his book, shoved it aside. "I was waiting for you."

"How come?"

"Funny you should ask. I hear it's what parents do when their kids go out at night. Cup of tea?"

"Sure. Why not? Where's Casey?"

"She pooped out on me and I sent her up to bed." He got up and turned on the burner under the tea kettle. Took a cup from the cupboard and arranged a tea bag in it. "How was the movie?"

"We never got there."

He turned, fixed her with a steady gaze.

"Don't worry," she said, "I didn't hand over my virtue or anything."

"Good to know. So where did you go?"

"Do we really have to talk about it?"

He studied her face, apparently saw something there that deterred him from the standard parental inquisition. Said, "Not unless you want to." He poured hot water into the cup and carried it to the table.

Paige swished the tea bag around in her cup. "What would your adoring fans think if they saw you drinking tea like a little old lady?"

"Danny was the one with the adoring fans. And you can blame it on Casey. She's the one who turned me on to it. I introduced her to wine, and she introduced me to tea."

"You guys are such geeks. That sex, drugs, and rock & roll thing? You skew the stats all to hell." She pulled out the tea bag, set it beside her cup, and took a drink.

"No flying high on ecstasy and trashing hotel rooms, you mean?"

"Yeah. Something like that." She paused to stare into her cup. Sighed and said, "You two make it look so easy."

"Being geeks?"

"Love."

He took a sip of tea. "Oh."

"You're solid. A little silly, but solid."

Her father shrugged. "You don't understand the hell we went through before we finally found our way to each other. What you call silly, we call second chances." He picked up his teaspoon and squeezed his tea bag against the side of his cup. "But we're not bulletproof. You know that. Nobody is."

"Love sucks."

Her father nodded. "Sometimes it does. And sometimes it's amazing and wonderful and it takes you to a place you never knew existed. When it's right."

"So what if you think it's right, but the other party doesn't?"

He seriously considered her question. "Then I'd say it's not right. Because when it is, you both know it. You both feel it. You both want it. And just because it's not right at this point in time doesn't mean that couldn't change in the future. Look at Casey and me. Look at how long it took us to become *us*. All those years, it wasn't right, until one day it was."

She nodded slowly. "I suppose it makes sense, if you look at it that way."

"If it's meant to be, that second chance will come around when you least expect it. And if it isn't meant to be..." He reached out and chucked her under the chin. "Then it'll be right with somebody else."

She took a breath and said, "I didn't expect it to hurt this much."

He took her hand in his. Squeezed it. His hand, long-fingered and bony like hers, was warm and surprisingly comforting. A tear teased the corner of her eyelid. She said, "I don't want you to feel sorry for me."

"When I was in my early twenties," he said, "I met my first wife. Her name was Nancy. Nancy Chen. She was a Chinese-American girl from the upper east side of Manhattan, and the only woman besides Casey that I ever truly loved. Her father was a surgeon. Big money. Her parents were very traditional in their beliefs, which didn't include interracial marriage. When they tried to force her into an arranged marriage, she came to me for help. So we went down to City Hall and we got married.

"It was a huge mistake. A disaster right from the start." He grew quiet, lost in the past. "I'd committed the dual cardinal sins of being not only poor, but Caucasian. Her parents freaked. But I was in love, and in savior mode, and when they did their best to split us up, I dug in my heels. Until they took out a court order barring her from seeing her little sister. It broke her heart. I'd never heard a woman cry that way. And because I loved her, it broke my heart. So I confronted her parents. They told me that they'd welcome her back to the fold with open arms, if only she'd divorce me."

"Oh, boy."

"I thought about it for a long time. I loved her so damn much. They'd already cut off her tuition money. She was planning to be a doctor, like her father. I could've found a way to work around that. There's always a way, if you want something bad enough. But there was no way I could work around this. Her sister meant the world to her—more than me, if I wanted to be honest—and her parents wielded all the power. So I caved. I loved her enough to let her go. I sent her home to her family, and I filed for divorce. It almost killed me, but I knew it was the best thing for her. I still do. I'm sure she's a doctor now, with an appropriate Chinese husband and a houseful of kids. And I bet she doesn't even remember me."

Something clicked in some tiny corner of her heart. Softly, she said, "I doubt that."

He let out a soft snort. "Yeah. Well."

"Thank you," she said. "For not asking. For not throwing buckets of sympathy all over me. For sharing."

He squeezed her hand again, then released it. And said, "Better head off to bed, kiddo. It's getting late. Things will look better in the morning. They always do."

"Yeah," she said. "Of course. They always do."

Casey

With her hands at ten and two on the wheel and a prescription for prenatal vitamins tucked inside her purse, she sat in the parking lot outside the doctor's office, her heart nearly exploding with joy. A baby. *A baby!* Not just *a* baby, but more importantly, *their* baby. After more than a year of trying, the indefatigable team of Fiore and MacKenzie had finally succeeded at their most significant collaboration. Sitting here in her car, mentally journeying back through their years together, through everything they'd survived together, everything they'd meant to each other, she was nearly overwhelmed by the absolute rightness of this.

Pregnant. It explained so much. The exhaustion. The random nausea. The fluctuating emotions. The anxiety she'd experienced when he'd left her for those three weeks that had turned into six. The terror she'd felt when he returned and she realized how far in love she'd fallen. The tears she'd shed, she who never cried, because he hadn't been there sleeping beside her. Even the sexual aggressiveness—something so unlike her—could be blamed on pregnancy hormones.

She couldn't believe she'd missed the signs. It wasn't as though this was her first rodeo. But she'd been dealing with Rob's absence and Paige's presence, and she simply hadn't been paying attention to the calendar. Hadn't registered the significance of the rising fatigue or the mild tenderness in her breasts.

Ten weeks along. That was what the doctor had told her. Once she was able to stem the flow of joyful tears, they'd had a brief but serious discussion about how much she and Rob wanted this baby. About the sobering fact that she'd be thirty-six by the time it was born. About how her first pregnancy, at twenty-two, had ended in a miscarriage.

About the statistics indicating that scary things like miscarriages and birth defects were more likely with older mothers.

Dr. Levasseur had been calm and reassuring. "Your second pregnancy was normal," she'd said, "and there's no reason to think you won't carry this baby to term. Nowadays, thirty-six is not considered old to be giving birth. And you're in the bloom of good health. Just look at you. You have that glow!"

Now, sitting behind the wheel of her car, Casey took a deep, cleansing breath. Released it, and with that exhalation, everything simply fell into place. All the fear, all the confusion of the past few months just melted away, replaced by a certainty she'd felt this strongly only once before in her life: at the age of eighteen, when she'd walked away from Jesse to follow Danny Fiore to the moon and back. She'd been certain then, a certainty she'd felt clear to the marrow. And she was certain now. This was exactly where she was supposed to be at this point in her life.

Her time with Danny—and with Katie—had been finite. That season had been achingly bittersweet, but it was over. She'd moved on to a different season, with Rob and Paige and this new life she carried inside her womb. She couldn't wait to tell him about the baby. He would be so excited. They'd wanted this for so long. *He'd* wanted this for so long. They'd been blessed with Paige, who had stormed into their life and stolen their hearts, but this was different. This was the two of them, Casey and Rob, making a baby together. Half of that child was his genetic material, and half of it was hers, all stirred together to create someone entirely new and breathtakingly perfect.

Any way you looked at it, this was a miracle.

Both her other pregnancies had initially brought confusion, dread, torn loyalties. The first time around, at twenty-two, she'd been on the pill. The pregnancy hadn't been planned. But she'd wanted that baby so much, in spite of knowing what Danny's reaction would be. Years earlier, they'd agreed to wait until the time was right, but the timing couldn't have been more wrong. Their marriage was faltering, they were living in that godawful roach-infested apartment in the Village, and they were starving. There'd been no way she could justify bringing a child into that situation.

So she'd made the brutally painful decision to terminate the pregnancy. She hadn't even told Danny she was pregnant. It had been Rob, her dearest friend, who had grudgingly checked around, found a doctor who did abortions, scheduled an appointment for her. It had been Rob who accompanied her to that appointment. And it had been Rob, with his no-nonsense Catholic upbringing, who'd taken her in his arms and breathed a huge sigh of relief when she changed her mind because she couldn't go through with it.

And then nature, in its infinite wisdom, had taken the decision out of her hands.

She'd grieved so much for that lost baby, had grieved for years, right up until she became pregnant with Katie. With that second pregnancy, her loyalties shifted from her husband to her unborn child. She knew Danny had only agreed to having a baby because it was what she wanted. And she'd wondered, more than once during the course of that pregnancy, how she would manage to give her child a normal upbringing in the midst of the circus that was their life. She had adored Katie from the moment of conception, and had been determined that no matter what Danny did or said, their child would be raised with immense love and care.

She should have known better than to worry. His daughter had been the center of Danny Fiore's world. Life certainly had its way of playing ironic little tricks. When they lost Katie to meningitis, it was Danny—he who hadn't wanted a child in the first place—who had lost himself for a time. While Casey, in spite of battling unparalleled grief over her loss, had somehow managed to find herself in the aftermath.

She took another cleansing breath. All that was behind her now. The craziness, the drama, the tears, had all been part of another life. This time around, there was no confusion, no dread. Only joy and thrilling anticipation. This child, this new little green-eyed MacKenzie, would be wanted and adored by both its parents, as well as by a vast extended family.

She would tell him tonight, in their room, at bedtime, just the two of them. Candles, soft music. Champagne? No, sparkling cider. She had a bottle in the pantry. No more tippling for her, not until after the baby came. Her finest stemware, of course. Maybe she'd even wear the infamous dress, just so he could peel it off her. Because she had no doubt he'd peel it off. She knew her husband to the marrow. Knew the MacKenzie school of thought regarding celebrations and nakedness.

How was it possible to love a man this much? She'd adored him for decades, but that love had evolved into something so big she couldn't have imagined it just a few short years ago. It hadn't happened all at once. Loving him like this had been a process. An evolution. It had taken a year and then some of being his wife, of sleeping beside him at night and facing each new day together, of exploring her blossoming sexuality with him, to bring her to the place she stood now. It was a good place, the best place she'd ever been. MacKenzie might not be the first boy she'd kissed, but he would be the last.

If they were fortunate, they'd have the full sixty years he'd promised her on the day they wed. It wouldn't be enough. There would never be enough time. But they'd gotten such a late start on their forever that she knew better than to take it for granted. Life was too short, too unpredictable, to ever lose sight of how precious it was. Of how precious love was. Whatever time they had together, she would cherish each moment.

She inserted her key into the ignition and started the car. Just a half-hour left before dusk, and it was starting to spit snow. Rob would be looking for her soon. She hadn't told him where she was going, and he had a tendency to worry. She didn't want to leave him hanging. But there was business to be taken care of. Someplace she had to go first, before she embarked on this next stage of her life.

***

She parked atop the hill, beneath the towering elm, now shed of its leaves. Here at the top of the world, it was raw and blustery. She left the car running—she wouldn't be here long enough to shut it off—pulled on her leather driving gloves and got out. The snow that had been just a flake here and there when she left town had now become a soft blanket of white, and she picked her way cautiously over slippery ground to his grave.

While fluffy flakes of snow peppered her face and swirled around her head, she studied that gravestone. Then she reached into her pocket, pulled out the cufflink, and leaned to set it on top of the stone.

"I'm giving this back to you," she said. "I have no idea how you managed this, or what message you were trying to give me, but I can't keep it, Danny. I can't accept gifts from you. I'm not your wife any longer. It's over, you and me. I can't do this to myself anymore. Or to Rob. It's killing him, and I won't risk my marriage for anybody. Not even for you.

"I made a mistake, taking you back. A mistake I'll regret for the rest of my life, because if I'd made the right choice, you'd still be alive. It's my fault that you're dead, and the guilt has been crushing me. I loved you so much. So very much, for so many years."

Her voice softened. "We really had something special, didn't we? You were my magic man, my love, my life. And I'll never, ever regret it. Not even the bad parts. You'll always have a place here—" She touched her chest. "—in my heart. But our time ran out. I don't think it was meant to last. When I took you back that last time, although I still loved you—I'll always love you—I wasn't in love with you any more. Not the way I once was. Because by then, I'd fallen in love with Rob."

She tucked her hands into her pockets and hunched her shoulders against the bitter cold. "But we'd been married for so long, and you'd worked so hard to turn your life around, to regain my trust. I was so proud of you. I did what I thought was the right thing. And you know what? I can't explain why, but those last months we had together, even though I was in love with another man, those were good months. Some of the best of our marriage. Until it all backfired on me, in a messy, terrible, irrevocable way. I was devastated when you died. And so very sorry for my part in it. I hope you can forgive me." The wind whipped at her hair, and she swept it back from her face. "God knows, I've tried for four years to forgive myself."

It was snowing hard now, and she needed to get home. Rob would be worried. Holding her hair away from her face, she said, "I won't be coming here for our little chats any more. It feels too much like cheating on my husband. Marriage vows mean something to me, Danny. This ring I'm wearing—it means something to me. Love and trust and fidelity. He's my husband now. He's the one I owe that fidelity to. I've moved on with my life, with the man who's my soul mate, and we're starting a family together. And while I hope you're happy for us, it really doesn't matter, because I don't need your approval any more."

She stood there a moment longer, snow falling all around, big flakes now, wet and splotchy and beautiful. Said to him, "This is my last goodbye."

And turned and walked back to her car.

Rob

He was halfway home from the real estate office, his headlights on low beam because of the snow that drifted toward him in huge, hypnotic, cottony flakes. Driving past the cemetery, he was so mesmerized by those swirling flakes that he almost missed seeing the car parked beneath the giant elm at the top of the hill. A pea-green Mitsubishi. His wife's car. Beside the car stood a slender figure in a black wool coat, arms folded against the cold, a brisk wind blowing that dark, silky hair around her face.

The pain hit him low in the belly. What in bloody hell was she doing in the cemetery, at dusk, during a snowstorm? What could she possibly have to say to Danny that couldn't wait until tomorrow? He automatically hit the brakes, saw the flash of red in his rear-view mirror. Then let his foot go limp. What was the point? What was the point to any of it? What was the point in trying to build them a future when she kept running back to the past?

The anger rose in him slowly, but to be truthful, it had been building for some time. He drove home, stomped into the house in a mood so black and murky that Paige, peeling potatoes at the kitchen sink, took one look at him, instantly recognized a MacKenzie in high dander, and spun back around without speaking. He tore off his jacket, tossed it on a chair, stalked to the refrigerator and opened it. Nothing looked any different than it had two hours ago. He slammed the door shut, rattling glass jars and sending a coffee cup, inexplicably left atop the refrigerator, crashing to the floor. It broke neatly in two, and he bent and picked up the matching halves and heaved them into the trash.

Headlight beams flashed across the room as his wife swung into the driveway, climbed the hill, and parked beside his Explorer. He heard her come into the shed, pictured her kicking off her shoes and hanging her coat. Precise and fastidious person that she was, she would never leave her coat tossed on a chair the way he had. He should have seen it years ago. They weren't compatible, not in any way. Not when you analyzed their basic personalities. She was a goddess, while he was just some lax, high-functioning slob.

It was amazing that she'd stuck with him this long. Of course, with her god lying six feet deep, she could afford to go slumming.

She came into the kitchen, his goddess, exquisite in a body-hugging burgundy sweater, snowflakes still on her hair and eyelashes. There was a glow to her that he'd never seen there before. Even dead, he thought bitterly, Danny still held more sway over her than he ever would.

"Where the hell have you been?" he snarled.

Those elegant eyebrows went sky-high. "Did I just walk into the wrong house? Should I go back outside and try again?"

He squared his jaw. "Answer the question, Fiore. It's not that hard. Where the hell have you been?"

With infuriating calm, she said, "I had an appointment in town. I already told you that. What's this all about?"

"Don't lie to me. Lying doesn't look good on you."

Something in those green eyes of hers caught fire, some dark fury that set his blood pumping. Good. He'd managed to push the right button. Now they could get down to it.

"I am not lying to you, MacKenzie. I don't lie. You know that. Not to you, not to anybody. So I don't know what's gotten your ass into a pucker, but I don't intend to fight with you tonight, so you can just back off!"

"I saw you at the cemetery."

"Oh, for the love of God. I stopped there on the way home. What's your point?"

"My point? My *point* is that it's time you decided whose wife you are. His, or mine. *Because you can't be both!*"

"For God's sake, Rob, how many times are we going to play this scene? I can't believe we're playing it again."

"Yeah? Well, neither can I, cupcake. Do you have any idea what it's like for me? Every time you come back from that place, I feel like I just swallowed ground glass. But I keep my mouth shut and hold it in, even though it kills me to see you going back to him, over and over and over. The guy's been dead for four years, but you still can't break the umbilical cord."

"You are a complete and utter idiot! And you couldn't be more wrong!"

"Oh, so I'm the idiot in this little scenario? Well, I don't know. Let's examine a few facts and see what we come up with. I treat you like a queen. Hell, if you asked, I'd probably go flat on the ground and let you walk all over me wearing cleats. That's pretty much what we already do every day anyway. But that's not good enough for you. *I'm* not good enough for you. Because you'd rather live in the past, with your memories of a dead man, than build a life in the present with a man who's alive and breathing and would take a bullet for you!"

"Stop it!" she said, and glanced warily at Paige. He followed her gaze, saw his daughter standing by the sink, her face bone-white.

"Go to your room," he told her.

"But—"

"You heard me. This is between my wife and me. Go to your goddamn room!"

The kid looked stricken. She glanced at Casey, who gave her a brief nod, then back at him. Said to him, "I hate you!" And fled to her room, slamming the door behind her.

"Nice," Casey said. "You must be really proud of yourself."

"He was a shitty husband, you know. You never could see it, but it was obvious to everyone else."

"This isn't about Danny. This is about—"

"Like hell it isn't!"

"—you and your goddamn insecurities!"

"Fuck insecurities! He was a selfish bastard who was too much in love with himself to even notice you were alive!"

"Maybe you should try psychotherapy. I hear it works wonders. And that's utter bullshit. He loved me!"

"Not as much as he loved himself!"

"You are full of shit, MacKenzie!"

"You think so? Maybe I can refresh your memory. Who was it that kept you from starving when Danny had his head so far up his ass he couldn't see that the cupboards were bare? Who was it that saved you when you were drowning in your pathetic little life in that dinky apartment on Beacon Hill, and Danny was too wrapped up in his career to see how miserable you were? I threw you a lifeline and saved your ass. I gave you the music. I sat with you, day after day, month after month, and spoon-fed it to you until you could carry your own weight. Where was Danny when I arranged that abortion for you? He wasn't the one who went with you to that hideous rathole of a doctor's office, was he? And he wasn't the one who held your hand and cried with you when you couldn't go through with it!"

"I don't understand. Why are you rehashing all this now? It's ancient history!"

"You really don't understand, do you? That just proves my point. I've loved you for two fucking decades, and you still don't get it! When you lost his baby, sitting in a puddle of blood on the kitchen floor, I was the one who picked up the phone and called for help. And when they hauled you off to the hospital, and Danny went with you in the ambulance, it was me who got left behind to mop up all that blood. So damn much of it that I was terrified you wouldn't make it to the hospital in time."

"Oh, Flash."

"And when Katie was born, and Danny was six thousand miles away? I talked my way onto that private maternity ward. I was the first person, outside of hospital staff, to hold your baby. And five years later, when she was lying in that bed, fighting for her life—"

"Stop. Please."

"I was there for you. But you sent me away. Why the hell did you do that? Even after what happened in Nassau, when we both knew we could've had something amazing if only you'd opened your eyes and actually seen me, you chose him! You left me on my ass in the dust, and you went back to *him*!"

His voice broke, shaming him, but he couldn't stop now if he tried. "And when Mister Wonderful died, I cooked your meals and vacuumed your floors and reminded you to eat and sleep and bathe. I held your goddamn hand until you could walk upright by yourself again. And what did I get in return? You sent me away. Again. You always sent me away!"

His wife was on the verge of tears now. He could see them glistening in her eyes, but he wasn't ready to stop. He had to finish what he needed to say. Had to get all the poison out of his system. "You stopped writing with me. I think that's the most hurtful thing. I've been so lost, trying to work without you. My partner, my collaborator, the other half of me. I told myself it was because Danny wasn't around anymore. That you'd just given up on the music. That I was a big boy, and I could handle it on my own. But

I've been struggling, trying to reinvent the wheel, because writing without you is a whole different animal. Then I come home from tour, and I find out you've been writing with Paige. How the hell do you think that makes me feel?"

"Be serious, Rob. You know it wasn't—"

"I don't think I can do this anymore. This marriage is killing me. I feel like some emotional ping-pong ball, being bounced from one corner to the next. I've given everything I have to you, and it just doesn't seem to be enough. Well, you know what? There's this thing called self-preservation. I think it's time I took advantage of it."

"What the hell are you saying? That you're planning to leave me?"

He closed his eyes, took a deep breath, and told her the biggest whopper that had ever come out of his mouth. "Yes."

"I don't believe you!"

The fury returned. "Yeah? Well, watch me!" He strode across the room, picked up his coat, shoved his arms into it, and headed for the door.

"Stop it!" she said. "This is ridiculous! You're not going anywhere."

"You're not big enough to stop me." He crossed the shed, flung open the door and plunged out into the cold.

"It's a snowstorm, for God's sake. *Rob!*"

He squared his jaw and stalked toward the Explorer. "Leave me the hell alone."

"This won't solve anything. Damn it, we need to talk. You need to listen to me—" She caught him by the arm, stumbled along behind him as he slogged through heavy, wet snow.

Bitterly he said, "That's the problem. All I do is listen to you. But you don't listen to me." He reached the Explorer, opened the door, and turned on her. "I'm done listening!"

Behind Casey, his daughter stood in the open doorway of the house, silently watching them. "Let go of me," he said.

"No! I love you, you moron! You're a total jackass, but I love you."

She was shivering in the sweater and jeans. He could see it. Could feel it. Freeing his arm, he said, "Go back in the house,

Fiore. You'll end up with pneumonia. Jesus Christ, you're not even wearing shoes!"

"damn it, MacKenzie, you come back here!"

Ignoring her, he climbed into the Explorer, fitted the key into the ignition, and shut the door in her face. He adjusted his seat belt, cranked the engine, and rolled the window down. She stood beside the car, arms crossed, visibly shuddering, snow falling all around her while a single tear tracked down her cheek. That tear was nearly his undoing. But he couldn't back down now. He'd taken this too far. He had to carry it through to some kind of conclusion.

Suddenly drained, he said again, "Go back in the house."

"Where the hell are you going?"

He had to escape, before his own tears started falling and he humiliated himself more than he already had. "Right now? As far away from you as I can get." He rolled the window back up and crammed the car into gear. Halfway down the driveway, he glanced into the rear-view mirror.

His wife was still standing there, barefoot in the snow, watching him drive away.

Casey

What the hell had just happened?

She stood in a blinding snowstorm, barefoot and freezing, watching as his tail lights gradually disappeared from sight. Feeling a hand on her arm, she turned to see Paige standing behind her.

"Come inside," her stepdaughter said. "You'll end up with hypothermia."

Like an obedient child, she accompanied the girl into the house. "Sit," Paige said, and pushed her gently into a kitchen chair. "You stay there. I'll be right back."

Fingers stiff with the cold, she buried her face in her trembling palms. Paige returned with a blanket and tossed it over her shoulders. Teeth chattering, Casey clutched the edges of the blanket and closed it around her while her stepdaughter knelt in front of her, peeled off her sopping wet socks, and began rubbing her feet with a towel.

Casey reached out a hand to touch the girl's hair. Paige glanced up, met her eyes, then returned to her task.

He'd be back. Rob MacKenzie was generally an easygoing guy, the sweetest man she'd ever known. But every so often, he had an epic meltdown. This wasn't the first one she'd witnessed. Despite what he'd said, he would come back. No matter how mad they got at each other, he always came back.

Paige continued rubbing, while Casey desperately searched her mind for something that would explain her husband's behavior. What could have pushed him over the edge? Obviously, her visit to the cemetery. Correction: her ongoing visits to the cemetery. But were those enough to trigger a meltdown of this magnitude? There'd been the cufflink. That had really stuck in his craw. And apparently he was royally pissed because she'd been writing with Paige. She had honestly believed he would be happy to know she'd finally broken past that wall of silence.

But judging by the vitriol he'd spewed, the anger and frustration had been festering inside him for some time. He'd made some serious accusations. How much truth was there to his words? Had she been remiss in her wifely duties? Had she taken him for granted? Had she been so self-involved that she'd simply ignored his wants and needs?

"Is it my fault?" she said aloud.

"It's not your fault," Paige said, still rubbing.

"How do you know that?"

"Because." Paige rocked back on her heels. "I've seen the way you are with him. You're open, and genuine, and you clearly think he walks on water. But he has this major hang-up about Danny. He can talk all he wants about you not being able to let go, but personally, I think he's the one who's still hung up on the past."

Her stepdaughter picked up the towel and stood. "He has this sick and twisted view of things. Even I can see the truth. I've tried to tell him, but he won't listen to me. I'm just a kid."

"How do you know so much at fifteen?"

"Please. I'm almost sixteen. There's a world of difference."

"Yes, you are. And there is. Thank you. For the blanket. And the foot rub. I can almost feel my feet now."

"No big deal. Anybody would have done it."

"The Paige who came to us three months ago? I'm not sure she would have."

"You've been good to me. And I know you're not my mom, and nobody will ever replace her. But, hey. You're okay."

***

They ate a mostly silent dinner together. Every time she heard a car approaching the house, Casey jumped out of her chair and ran to the window. The plow passed, first going one way, then the other. But still no sign of Rob. She knew he'd need time to cool off. But as that time grew progressively longer without so much as a phone call, needles of fear began to dance in her stomach. Danny had died on a night like this, on a slushy Connecticut highway. It wasn't fit outside for man or beast, yet the man she loved was out there somewhere, driving around, angry and upset. She told herself he was level-headed—which was mostly true, except when he was being an idiot. Told herself the Explorer had 4-wheel drive with decent enough traction to get him over the Himalayas, let alone a back road in Maine.

Told herself he wasn't holed up in some motel somewhere, contemplating a divorce settlement.

Two hours passed, then three, then four, and she flashed back to the time, many years ago, when Danny had stayed out all night. She'd lain awake until dawn, and when she finally heard his key in the lock, she'd been furious. All those hours she'd spent awake, imagining all the terrible things that might have happened to him. At the peak of their knock-down-drag-out fight, he'd confessed to cheating on her. She'd been pregnant that time, too. She'd been so devastated by his admission that she'd lost the baby, slouched on the kitchen floor in Freddy Wong's roach-infested apartment building, the blood pouring out of her and pooling between her legs. Funny how those old memories came back to haunt you at the times when you were most vulnerable.

A little past ten, Paige went to her room and shut the door. Casey paced the floor, her anxiety growing with each tick of the clock. Where the hell was he? Off the road in some ravine, where he wouldn't be found until morning? Sitting at the Jackson Diner over a cup of lukewarm coffee with too much sugar in it? Driving aimlessly, because this was Jackson Falls on a snowy November night, and even the bowling alley was shut down? Where on earth would he go in this one-stoplight town?

Then it clicked. Six months after Danny died, she'd had a huge fight with Rob. They'd said awful things to each other, and she'd thrown him out of her house and told him not to darken her door again. Of course, being Rob, he'd come hammering at her door early the next morning, just in time for a cup of the coffee that she, being Casey, had made in anticipation of his arrival. He'd spent a mostly sleepless night on Jesse Lindstrom's couch.

The same Jesse who was now married to his sister.

Casey snatched up the phone and dialed the number. Her sister-in-law picked up on the third ring. "I'm sorry to call so late," she began, "but—"

"He's here," Rose said. "He's been here for three hours. Jesse and his friend Jim Beam are trying to peel him off the ceiling. What the hell happened?"

A solid wave of relief poured over her, and her knotted insides relaxed a little. "I don't know. I honestly don't know. I came home from town and the minute I walked through the door, he went into meltdown mode, and—oh, God." Her voice broke. "I've been so scared. I was afraid he'd gone off the road in the snow. I imagined all kinds of horrible things."

"You can stop panicking. He's right here with us, and we'll keep him until it's safe for him to drive. You might as well go on to bed. Once he calms down, I'll point him in the direction of home." Rose hesitated. "Just be forewarned: it could be a while."

"That bad? Still?"

"That bad. I honestly don't believe I've ever seen my baby brother quite this wound up."

"I'm sorry, Rose. I'm so sorry to get you involved in this mess."

"Don't worry about it. I've been dealing with his messes since birth. Get yourself some sleep, and we'll talk in the morning."

***

She awoke with her vision blurry and her head grainy. The room was still dark, and her husband was sitting on the edge of the bed with his head cradled in his arms. For an instant, her heart stuttered and scrambled around inside her chest. She rolled onto her side and reached out a trembling hand to touch the small of his back. He stiffened. "Hey," she whispered.

He raised his head. Without looking at her, he said, "Hey."

"I wasn't sure you were coming back."

He let out a soft sound, halfway between a sob and a snort. "Neither was I."

She ran her fingertips up his spine, between his rigid shoulder blades and back down, and he exhaled sharply. "When I left here," he said, "I kept asking myself what the hell I was doing, leaving you like that. But I was hurt, and scared, and pissed off. And a little crazy. I wanted to get away from you. I wanted to hurt you the way you were hurting me. I wanted to grab you by the wrists and shake some sense into you. I wanted to strip you naked and throw you down on the bed and make you forget he ever existed. I wanted to turn my back on you, say *fuck you*, and never see you again."

The hard muscles of his back refused to yield to her stroking fingers. "But it didn't take me long to figure out that no matter what I try or where I go, I can't do it. I can't get you out of my head. You've been there for too long." He finally turned and looked at her. "We're too embedded in each other to separate the strands. Almost two decades. Casey and Rob. Rob and Casey. Who the hell knows where you end and I begin?"

A flicker of pain licked and darted around her heart. "I know you love me," he said. "We've loved each other for so long, I can't begin to know where or when it all started. But, you see, the problem is, you love him, too. You're still not over him. I'm not sure you ever will be. And I just don't know where to put that any longer."

"You're so wrong," she said.

"I know it should be enough, knowing that you love me. But it's not. Because no matter what I do, no matter how much time passes, you'll never love me the way you love him. I just can't compete. I'm fighting a losing battle with a ghost. And maybe I could live with that, except for that one little inescapable truth that keeps me awake at night: If he was above ground, we wouldn't be sitting here having this conversation."

She got up from the bed so abruptly that the mattress rocked, strode naked across the room, and took her robe from a hook on the bedroom door. She pulled it on, tied the belt, and spun to face him. "You're an idiot," she said. "A complete and utter cretin, and I can't believe I have to explain any of this to you. But it doesn't look like you'll be pulling your head out of your ass anytime soon, MacKenzie, so we are going to have this out, here and now, and be done with it."

He didn't respond, just sat with his elbows resting on his knees, those green eyes unreadable.

"I am so damn furious with you! How could you do that to me? Knowing how Danny died, and what it did to me afterward— what it's still doing to me—how could you drive away from me like that, in a blinding snowstorm, mad as hell, and then not come home, and not call, and leave me spending hours wondering whether you'd gone off the road and were dead in a ditch somewhere?"

"I figured you wouldn't even notice I was gone. The way you keep wallowing in your misery—"

"That's bullshit, MacKenzie! Do you hear me? Absolute and utter rubbish! I am not wallowing, and if you'd bothered to let me get a word in edgewise, maybe you would've figured that out. In case you hadn't heard, there's this little thing called closure—"

"Something you should've gotten a long time ago, sweetheart! That train should have already left the station."

"Oh, for the love of God. How can you be this stupid and still walk upright? You are one hard-headed jackass, and I cannot imagine what I ever saw in you. That train has not left yet, not for either of us, if you want the God's honest truth. So you—" She moved closer, poked him hard in the chest with her forefinger. "— can just get down off your high horse and stop acting like a two-year-old."

"I'm not the one acting like a two-year-old! And stop poking me. If you're that mystified about what you ever saw in me, maybe it's time to rethink this whole damn marriage thing!"

"Oh, that's just priceless! We have something really good going here, and you're determined to tank it! Well, guess what?" She poked him again, hard. "I'm not letting you get away with it! Do you hear me? You may have managed to screw up your other marriages, but you're not screwing up this one. *Because I won't allow it!*"

He rose to his feet and loomed over her. "Goddamn it, stop poking me!"

"You're damn lucky that's all I'm doing, because I am so furious with you right now that I'd like to hit you!"

He squared his jaw. Braced his feet apart in a combative stance. "Go ahead. Hit me. I'm a big boy. I have broad shoulders."

"Don't tempt me, Flash. What the hell is wrong with you?"

"I'm done playing second fiddle!" he bellowed. "That's what the hell is wrong with me! I'm over it, do you hear? I did it for too long, and I. AM. DONE! I'm not standing behind any man, dead or alive, ever again. If you can't deal with that, too bad! Because that's the way it'll be from here on in. Starting right now!"

"Is there something fundamentally wrong with you, MacKenzie? Something that makes you look right through me and see what you want to see, instead of what's really there? Because I can't come up with any other explanation for how you could possibly spend more than five minutes in the same room with me and not realize that I am absolutely, utterly, batshit crazy in love with you!"

He opened his mouth to speak. Closed it as her words gradually sank in. Still furious, she said, "Of course I don't love you the way I loved him. I was a *child* when I fell in love with him! What you and I have is so much bigger, so much more than what I had with him, that they're not even in the same ballpark. All those years, I believed he was the love of my life. But I was wrong. It wasn't him. It was *you*. I've never felt this way about anybody. Are you hearing me? *Never*. How can you possibly not know how I feel about you? How can you possibly not feel it when I touch you? When we dance together in the dark? Or when we make love? *Especially* when we make love? How can you not know that you're the reason I get up every morning?"

"You haven't exactly—"

"Shut up. It was a rhetorical question, and I'm nowhere near done talking. I suppose I shouldn't blame you for not knowing, when I wasn't even fully aware of it myself. But you're so damn smart about everything else that I can't understand how you can be the village idiot when it comes to relationships. Of course he still holds a piece of my heart! He always will. That eighteen-year-old girl is still inside me somewhere, and when I'm ninety she'll still be there. She loved him at eighteen, and she'll love him at ninety. I can't help it, I can't change it, it's just the way it is. You'll have to learn to accept it if there's any hope at all of us making this marriage work."

"Good to know."

"I told you to shut up! When I'm done having my say, then you can make your editorial comments."

He scowled, but kept his mouth shut.

"The problem, you idiot, is that you have it backwards. It's not that I don't love you the same way I loved him. It's that I never loved him the way I love you."

"What the hell is that supposed to mean?"

"It means that he was a fantasy. A young girl's dream of what love was supposed to be. But you, MacKenzie—you're the real deal. And you own my heart, all but that tiny sliver that will always belong to him. You hold it in the palm of your hand, and with one wrong move, you could crush it."

"Yet you keep going back there. To the cemetery. To him. Do you have any idea what that does to me? Every frigging time?"

"I do. And that's why I went there last night. To give him the cufflink. To tell him I wouldn't be coming back again, because I'm your wife now, and every time I go there, it feels like I'm cheating on you. And I'm so tired of hurting you."

"Yeah, well, that makes two of us."

"Stop it! Do you truly have no idea what you are to me? You're my best friend, my lover, my partner. You're my foundation, my Gibraltar, and my soft place to fall. My playmate, my eye candy, and my sex toy. My teacher, my conscience, and the voice inside my head that makes me want to be a better person. My entire adult life is tangled up with yours, and like you said, we've been together for too long to untangle all those threads and figure out which of them belong to which of us. It doesn't even matter any more.

"And you know what the sad thing is? It took me almost two decades to figure this out, but it's so clear to me now that I can't believe I missed it. All those years I spent trying to fix him, trying to make him into the husband I was so sure he could be, it was you—" She paused, took a breath. "*You* who played the role of husband. All that time, while I was blind to everything but him, you were standing right beside me, doing all the husbandly things he should have done for me but couldn't ever seem to get right. *You're* the one I should have been with. And I'm doing my damnedest to make up for all that lost time now that I've finally figured it out. But you're making it really difficult, you rock-headed baboon!"

"I'm not a mind reader. I don't suppose it might've occurred to you at any point in—oh, let's say the last year and a half—to tell me any of this?"

"I'm sorry. I'm not perfect. Far from it. I've been flying by the seat of my pants with this marriage. So afraid I'd get it wrong, and I'd end up losing you. And I've learned a few things recently, things I should have realized all along, but maybe you're not the only one who's hard-headed."

He squared his jaw. "What things?"

"How about this, just for starters? When I took him back after Nassau, he wasn't the man I wanted to be with. You were. Although right now, I can't for the life of me remember why!"

"Yet you went back to him. I must be really dense, because I don't get it."

"Neither do I, damn it! I thought I was doing the right thing. Until the moment you got in that taxi and I watched you drive away, and I lost the ability to breathe. I wanted to run after you and beg you to come back. But it was too late. So I went upstairs and sat on the couch and cried instead."

"It wasn't too late! It was never too late! You knew where I was headed. You could've called me. You could have hopped in your damn car and driven to South Boston and dragged me back. I wouldn't have needed all that much convincing!"

"I couldn't."

"Why the bloody hell not?"

"I'd made my decision. I'd already made a commitment to him. How could I—"

"There's this little invention called the telephone. You could have called him and told him you'd changed your mind. Big boy that he was, he would've survived it."

"He was my husband!"

"And that says it all, doesn't it, cupcake?"

"No, damn it. It doesn't. Because I wasn't in love with him anymore. I was in love with you!"

"I—" He stopped abruptly, clamped his mouth shut, squared his jaw. "Me?" he said.

"Surprised, are you? So was I when I finally figured it out." She took a breath. "Damn it, Rob, I thought I knew what I was getting into when I married you. I thought I knew what it would be like to be your wife. I thought I knew how I felt about you. But the truth is that I had no idea. I had no idea how deep my feelings for you ran. Once I figured it out, it scared me to death."

"I don't understand. Why?"

"Because he swallowed me alive! I couldn't let that happen again!"

"Jesus H. Christ." He spun away from her, walked to the window, turned and leaned his lanky hips against the frame. Folded his arms and crossed his ankles. Furiously, he said, "Did you really think I'd ever let that happen to you?"

"I don't know. I guess I wasn't thinking clearly." She closed her eyes, sighed. Opened them again. Wearily, she said, "And of course, there's the sex."

With the fingers of one hand, he slowly rubbed his temple. "You have a problem with that, too?"

"Are you crazy? The sex is amazing. Beyond amazing. I understand that women are supposed to reach their sexual peak in their thirties, but I had no idea it would be like this. And if I'm running right on schedule, what kind of mutant does that make you? You were supposed to reach your peak two decades ago. If you're like this at thirty-seven, what were you like at nineteen? It's a good thing we didn't get together until we were in our thirties, because if you'd come at me, back when I was an innocent eighteen-year-old kid, with that out-of-control-locomotive-racing-down-a-mountainside-without-brakes thing you have going on, I would've run screaming in the opposite direction. You would have scared me to death."

He stared at her, raised both eyebrows. "So now you're scared of me?"

"Of course not. Are you even listening to me? For the love of God, MacKenzie, try to follow the little red bouncing ball. It's really not that difficult. Look, I realize I don't have the worldly experience you've gleaned from your exhaustive research. I've only been with one other man. But I was married for a long time, and I'm sorry if this makes you squeamish, but I did have a sex life. A pretty good one. Or so I thought. But sex with you—it's like a freaking trip to Disneyland, where I get to eat all the cotton candy I want, and go on every one of the rides. Some of them more than once, if you get my drift. You're like this giant candy store, and I'm standing in the window, trying to decide if I want one of these or three of those, or maybe six of that pretty one over there. This is all your fault! You've done this to me. I've never been a lustful woman. I've always been so proper, so—"

"Prudish?"

"Your word, MacKenzie, not mine! Ladylike is what I was going for. I was raised to be a nice girl. But I don't feel like a lady anymore. It's as though you've poured some kind of magic love potion over me. I don't even know who I am anymore. I don't know what happened to the me I used to be. I look in the mirror and I don't recognize myself. Instead of that nice girl I used to be, I see this bawdy, earthy, hot-blooded, carnal woman. A floozy. I don't know what that's all about. And the scariest thing is that I don't want to go back. I like the new me. I don't want to be a nice girl. I like being a floozy!"

He was looking at her bemusedly, with one eyebrow raised, but she was on a roll, and couldn't stop now. "And I swore I'd never tell you this, because it's so embarrassing, and not becoming in a woman of my age—"

"You're thirty-five years old, Fiore. Not exactly geriatric."

"Shut up. Since I've gotten this far, I might as well go for the gold. I think you are the hottest, sexiest, most gorgeous man on the planet. And every time I see you barefoot and shirtless, wearing nothing but a tight pair of jeans, I dissolve into this hot puddle of lust." She paused for breath, raked her damp hair away from her face. "And when you talk dirty to me—" She flushed hot from the tips of her toes to the roots of her hair, and buried her face in her hands. "I can't believe I'm saying this to you. But I'm just going to say it and then I'll crawl away and die of mortification. When we're alone in the dark…and you're inside me…and things are getting hot and heavy…and you talk dirty to me…I go off like a bottle rocket."

The smile hadn't reached his mouth yet, but she could see it in his eyes. "I've noticed."

"It's not funny, MacKenzie! Did you know you have the sexiest feet of any man I've ever known? How sick is that, that I'm obsessing over your feet? Did you know that all day long, while I'm paying bills and scrubbing the damn toilet and writing music and arguing with your daughter and sitting in those endless, horrible library committee meetings, what I'm really doing is counting the hours until bedtime? Because none of the rest of it is real. The only thing that's real is being in your arms, and it doesn't matter whether we're dancing in the dark, or having screaming sex, or if we're just lying in bed listening to each other's heartbeat. It's all the same, because all that matters is that I'm with you, in that magic world we've created that's just ours, and there's nowhere else I'll ever want to be again. And I've probably said way too much, but you needed to hear it."

She paused, took a hard, sharp breath. "There's one more thing I have to say, and then I'll be done. After everything we've been to each other, I am appalled that you would even entertain the notion that I'd ever want to go back to him. Yes, I loved him, and yes, it broke my heart when he died. But that doesn't mean I'd want to be married to him again. I'm not eighteen any more. I'm thirty-five, and the choices you make at thirty-five are not the same ones you made at eighteen. If you haven't heard anything else I've said today, MacKenzie, this is the part you'd damn well better listen to. If, by some miracle, he was resurrected, and he walked through that door right now, and he asked me to leave you and take him back, I'd laugh at him. I would *laugh* at him! And it wouldn't matter if he asked me a hundred times, or a thousand. My answer wouldn't change. I would never walk away from you, not in a million years. Not for him, not for anybody on this planet. Do you hear what I'm saying? I would tell him no. I would pick you. Every goddamn time. *I would always pick you!* If you were to walk out that door, right here, right now, there'd never be anybody else for me ever again. My heart would be irrevocably broken, and all the king's horses and all the king's men wouldn't be able to put it together again. Because it's just you, MacKenzie. *Just you!* So if you ever leave me—today, tomorrow, a hundred years from now—you'd best have a burial plot all prepared, because that will be the day I take my final breath!"

She turned blindly to flee. "Wait," he said, "Where the hell do you think you're going?"

"I can't be near you right now."

"Come back here!"

"No!"

She'd almost reached the bedroom door when his fingers closed around the belt to her robe and brought her to a dead halt. "Damn it, stop!" he said fiercely, and then his arms came around her from behind, and he pulled her tight against him. Breathing heavily, he whispered against her hair, "Stop."

She took a ragged breath. "Why should I?"

"Because I love you. Because I'm an idiot. Because—" He paused, his breath fluttering the hair at her temple. "—if you ever leave me—today, tomorrow, a hundred years from now—you'd best have a burial plot all prepared, because that will be the day I take my final breath."

She closed her eyes against the flood of tears, but it did no good. They fell anyway, huge, fat drops that rolled down her cheeks and plopped to the floor. She found his hands, threaded fingers with his, heard his sigh of relief.

"I'm still furious with you," she said.

"I know."

"I'll probably be furious with you again at some point in the next fifty-nine years."

He kissed the top of her head, rested his cheek against her hair. Said brokenly, "I know."

"Quite possibly more than once. Considering our track record."

"It doesn't matter. You can be furious with me as often as you need to. Just as long as you don't leave me."

"Love," she said. "It's such an odd duck. It's a continuum. I've loved you forever, and when we got married, I knew we'd moved to a different place on that continuum. I just didn't realize how far I'd moved. Until you left for those six weeks, and being without you was torture. It took me a while to figure out why. Looking back over the years, I don't know why it was such a shock to me when I realized how long I'd been in love with you. And how far I'd fallen."

"I didn't mean to doubt you. I just went a little crazy. I've always felt like sloppy seconds. I could never measure up to Danny—"

"For God's sake, MacKenzie." She turned in his arms and met his eyes. "How can you not know that you are so much more than he ever was?"

"Look at him. Then look at me, and tell me how that's possible."

"Oh, he had a beautiful face, no doubt about that. The kind of face that turned heads and made women cry. But on the inside, where it counted, he was empty. He was a good man, and I loved him desperately, but there was something missing. I don't know if it was always missing, or if Vietnam stole it from him. He was broken, in ways you don't even know about. Maybe I'll tell you someday." She reached up, touched his face with the tips of her fingers. "But you, MacKenzie, you have so much beauty on the inside, where it counts. Some people, the gods and goddesses of this world, are able to get by on their looks. The rest of us ordinary mortals have to learn to develop a beautiful interior, and that's what you have. Not that there's anything wrong with your exterior. I'm quite fond of it. And so proud to pass your DNA on to our kids."

He let out a soft, self-deprecating laugh.

"I'm serious. And yes, Danny was talented. He had a voice that could rip your heart to shreds. But without your talents, which are exponentially greater than his, do you really think he would have become the superstar he became? You put him there, my love. You may have been the man behind the curtain, but you were never second to him in any way. You are the wizard of all wizards, the great and powerful Oz. You know it, I know it, he knew it. So if I ever again hear you refer to yourself as sloppy seconds, I'll slap you silly."

"I'm sorry I went off the deep end. But I didn't know what to think, so of course, being the brooding jackass Irishman that I am, I thought the worst. You've been acting so crazy ever since I got back. Running hot and cold. Like some alien stepped in and took over your body."

"Yes, well, pregnancy will do that to a woman."

It took a full two seconds before she saw her words register in his eyes. "What?" he said.

"You heard me, Flash. This wasn't exactly how I'd planned to tell you, but your little tantrum blew my plans right out of the water."

"A baby?" he said, looking thunderstruck. "We made a baby? You and me?"

"I can assure you there were no third parties involved."

"But—when? How?"

"I trust you can figure out the answer to that second question. The answer to the first is sometime in late August or early September. Right before you left."

"So you're—"

"Ten weeks along. The baby's due the first week of June."

"You've seen a doctor? Everything's okay?"

"That's where I was coming from yesterday, when you saw me at the cemetery. And yes, everything is just fine. We did it, my love. She cupped his face in both hands and pressed a soft kiss to his lips. "We did it!"

Paige

She'd actually had the crazy idea that when he cooled off, her father would return, he and Casey would have a tearful reunion, and everything would be back to normal. Hah! She was clearly a moron. Oh, he had come back, for sure. While she pretended to be asleep behind her closed bedroom door, he had rattled around the kitchen for ten minutes before he went upstairs to face his wife. But there was no tearful reunion. The shouting started within minutes. Even though she turned up the stereo to drown it out, she could still hear it. She couldn't decipher their words, but who needed words when the voices spoke so clearly for themselves? So loud they could probably be heard down on Main Street?

It was all in the toilet. Her whole life, swirling down the drain. First her mom, then Mikey, and now her new family was imploding. She'd been so angry and bitter when she came here. But her father and his wife had worn her down with their kindness. To her amazement, she'd actually thought that she and her dad were making headway. That they'd started to build a relationship. A connection. And Casey was big sister, mother, and best friend all rolled into one. Attentive and caring and fun in a way that Paige's own mother had never been. Not that Sandy hadn't cared. It was just the opposite. She'd cared too much, had felt the weight of responsibility too heavily. She'd spent her entire life overworked, overtired, and underappreciated. Those dark circles under her eyes had sunk deeper and deeper, until one day, they just swallowed her whole.

Paige knew better than most that fairy tales weren't real. Her mom's death had taught her that. So why had she believed, for even one second, that she might find a real home here with these people? It looked like she'd been right all along about her old man, and the weight of disappointment lay heavy in her chest. How could she have trusted him? After Mikey ripped out her heart and shredded it, how could she have trusted any guy, ever again?

Upstairs, the yelling continued, and she wrapped her pillow around her head to shut out the sound. She would probably end up homeless. Or worse, once Casey ousted them from her house and her life, she would be dependent on her old man to take care of her. Not that she needed to be taken care of. But barring emancipation, she had to answer to somebody until she turned eighteen. If what she'd witnessed tonight was any indication, his parenting skills probably weren't any better than his relationship skills. And those needed some serious work. It was a shame that stupidity was going to sink his marriage, but it was pretty obvious that the ship was going down.

Angry, she tossed the pillow onto the bed. "To hell with him," she said to Leroy, who rolled his eyes and wagged his tail. "To hell with both of them. I bet if I left, they wouldn't even notice I was gone."

Leroy wagged again, and she patted him absently while she gave the idea some thought. She could leave. Take Leroy, pack a suitcase, and never come back. Hit the open road, thumb out, and make a new start in some faraway, exotic place. If Mikey could do it, why couldn't she?

Paige sighed. Who was she kidding? The open road might sound exotic and alluring, but reality would prove otherwise. What she needed was to get away from the fighting. Maybe things would look better in the daylight. She could just drive around, killing time, until they stopped fighting and it was safe to come home. For as long as this was home. And who knew? Maybe Casey wouldn't throw out the baby with the bath water. Maybe, in spite of Rob MacKenzie's idiocy, she would let his daughter stay, at least until she was eighteen.

Driving around aimlessly didn't sound all that appealing. Not that she couldn't handle the car. She'd practiced enough times with her father to know what she was doing behind the wheel. But driving around this little podunk town in the middle of the night would grow old very quickly. There had to be someplace she could go. She thought briefly of her Aunt Rose, but nixed that idea. After the debacle with Mikey, she couldn't go there. It would be too painful, too humiliating. Aunt Trish would be a better choice. She was warm and nurturing and sweet. If Paige showed up at her door in the middle of the night, Trish would take her in, no questions asked. She'd feed her and give her a warm bed and let her vent if she wanted. That was the kind of person Trish was.

Three months ago, leaving Boston had been so hard. Now, she barely missed the city. This place, this stupid, provincial, barren, dead-end spot at the far corner of the earth, had become home. She had family here, and that made all the difference. How could she have known?

"Come on, Leroy," she said. "Let's blow this joint."

The dog jumped off the bed, eager to go wherever she was going. She clipped the leash to his collar, turned the stereo down to a minimal level, grabbed her coat and tiptoed into the kitchen. Standing in front of the key rack that hung on an end cabinet, she debated briefly. But there was no real debate. Her father would probably kill her when he found out, but she was taking the Porsche. It was the only car she'd ever driven, and besides, she liked the idea of pissing him off. He'd been planning to put the car in storage for the winter, but he hadn't gotten to it yet. That was probably a good thing, because once Casey threw him out on his ass, he'd be driving it back to California anyway. Or, if not California, then wherever he ended up. Because there was no way he'd stay in Jackson Falls if he couldn't be with Casey. She might only be fifteen, but she was smart enough to know that.

It had stopped snowing, and the sky was clear. Leroy bounded enthusiastically through the soft, fluffy snow. There wasn't that much accumulation. Only three or four inches, and she knew they'd plowed the roads, because she'd heard the plow going back and forth several times earlier in the evening. Paige blipped the locks, brushed the snow away from the door with an old broom she'd found in the shed, opened the driver's door and deposited Leroy onto the passenger seat.

She spent a couple of minutes sweeping snow off the car until her windows were clear, then she leaned the broom against the side of the house and got in the car. She fastened her seatbelt, ran the passenger-side belt through Leroy's harness and clicked it. "Sorry, buddy," she said, "but we have to keep you safe." The engine roared when she started the car, and for a minute, she panicked. But their bedroom was on the opposite side of the big old house, and the way they were yelling, a 747 could crash in the yard and they wouldn't even notice.

The driveway was a slippery, slushy mess. When she reached the road, she gunned the motor a little to take her through the pile of crap left behind by the snowplow. The tires spun, and for a second, she thought she was going to get stuck. That would be just ducky, having to go back inside, climb the stairs, knock on that bedroom door, and tell her dad that his precious car was stuck in a snow bank at the end of the driveway.

But at the last minute, the wheels found traction, and she made it out onto the road. She turned right out of the driveway, because that was the most direct route to Bill and Trish's house. The windshield was fogged, and she cranked the blower and rubbed at the glass. It didn't do much good, because she and Leroy were breathing inside the car, and it was so much warmer inside than it was outside that condensation hung heavy on the glass. Paige lowered her window. Cold air rushed in, freezing her, but this time, when she wiped the windshield, it stayed clear.

Maybe this hadn't been such a hot idea after all.

There were no other cars around. Nobody else crazy enough to be out this late, on these back roads, directly after a storm. Although the road had been plowed, there was very little sand, and without snow tires, she had to fight to keep the car from spinning in circles. Sweat pooled under her arms, and she seriously considered turning around and going back home. But in this isolated rural paradise, there was no place to turn. Not even so much as a logging road between home and their nearest neighbors, Will and Millie Bradley. Their Meadowbrook Farm was two miles down the road. By the time she got there and could turn around, she'd be a half-mile from her destination, and turning would be pointless. So she forged on.

She'd forgotten about the big hill. It loomed ahead of her, a quarter-mile of downhill gradient that led directly to the river. Paige stopped at the top, feeling like Jean-Claude Killy about to race down a packed-powder slope. She'd always wanted to learn to ski, she just hadn't planned on doing it in a Porsche. Maybe she should park the damn thing by the side of the road and walk back to the house. But she was almost there, and the thought of that long trek in the cold was enough of a deterrent to keep her moving forward. She wasn't a chicken. She was the fearless Paige MacKenzie. Hard as nails, and twice as stubborn. She had brakes, for Christ's sake. No damn snow-covered hill was going to stop her.

Inching forward gingerly, she started down. The Porsche fishtailed and, heart hammering, she hit the brakes. When the car started to come around sideways, she realized her mistake and released them. She struggled with the steering wheel and the car righted itself. "Jesus," she said on a hard exhalation of breath. "Hang on, Leroy."

With a white-knuckle grip on the steering wheel, she inched forward, hopscotching down the hill that had not a grain of sand on it. Brake and skid, brake and skid, brake and skid. If she made it through this alive, she was going to write a strongly-worded letter to the Jackson Falls Department of Public Works, which she suspected consisted of one plow truck driven by a member of the volunteer fire department. Granted, this was a back road with little traffic, but considering how many times she'd heard the plow pass the house, the hill should have been sanded.

She would have made it if she hadn't lost traction two-thirds of the way down, on the steepest portion of the hill. The car skidded left, then right. Paige tried to steer, but it was useless. Tried to brake, but that only brought the Porsche around sideways. She let up on the brakes and clutched the steering wheel in terror as the car gained momentum, speeding faster and faster in its sideways journey. Through the passenger window, she could see the outline of the telephone pole hurtling towards her, but there was nothing she could do except wait for death to come and take her.

If she survived this, her dad was going to kill her.

"Oh, shit," she said, a split-second before impact.

Casey

Warm and drowsy beneath the covers, his arms tight around her as they spooned in the darkness, he said, "That was one epic declaration of love, Fiore."

"I'm so glad you liked it. Did I manage to get my point through that thick head of yours, or should I get a bigger sledgehammer? Because if the concept needs reinforcement, I could always take out a full-page ad in *Rolling Stone*. Maybe a big Valentine's heart, with the words *CASEY LOVES ROB* stenciled across the center."

"I don't think that'll be necessary. I was so damn pissed at you."

"Likewise."

"Just between you and me—" He kissed her shoulder. "— I'm pretty sure it was that hot puddle of lust thing that was the tipping point."

"Stop teasing me. Please."

"That was the sweetest thing anybody's ever said to me. The whole damn speech was sweet. I mean, I realize I'm no Jon Bon Jovi, but at least I have sexier feet than he does."

"If you don't stop, I'm going to slug you."

"Yeah, well, maybe I deserve it."

"Maybe you do, considering the way you left me standing barefoot in the snow."

"That was pretty bad, wasn't it?"

"It was. Bloody Irish drama queen."

"Hey, I only have a meltdown once or twice a year."

"Do you suppose that from now on, you could schedule them in advance, so in the future I can plan to be in Aruba during your biannual breakdown?"

"I'll try to work it into my schedule."

She floated for a time, wallowing in contentment. "You do realize I'm going to get fat and ugly? You'll probably rue the day you met me."

"You could never be fat or ugly."

"Says the man who wasn't around during my third trimester the last time I was pregnant."

"You'll always be beautiful to me. When you're nothing but a toothless hag in the nursing home, with your boobs hanging to your knees, I'll still be trying to get into your pants at least once a day."

"What a lovely picture you paint. And what happened to Paris?"

"I'm sure they have nursing homes in France."

"Funny boy." She wriggled away from him and sat up on the edge of the bed.

"Where do you think you're going, Mrs. MacKenzie?"

Tightening the belt to her robe, she said, "Bathroom. You might as well get used to it. I'll probably be spending most of the next seven months in there. Then I'm going downstairs for a drink. I'll be right back."

It was cold in the kitchen. Even though she and Danny had paid a fortune to have insulation blown into the walls, the old farmhouse was still like a barn, too hot in the summer, too cold in the winter. Without bothering to turn on the light, she got a drink of water, then walked to the window and stood with her nose pressed against the pane. The snow had stopped, and a vast blanket of stars spread across that dark winter sky.

The door to Paige's room was ajar, the stereo playing softly. She pushed open the door, tiptoed across the room and shut it down. Then hesitated. Something felt off. She listened for the sound of breathing, but all she heard were the sounds of an old house settling down on a cold November night. She moved silently to the bed, reached out, made contact with empty space. Felt around, realized the bed was cold. And empty.

She marched to the doorway and turned on the light to confirm what she already knew. Paige wasn't here. Nor was Leroy. His crate was empty and his pink leash, which normally hung on its hook beside the door, was missing.

At some point when she and Rob were too busy yelling at each other to pay attention, both kid and dog had flown the coop.

Don't panic, she told herself. *She's probably just with Luke. Or Lissa. Or*—glancing at the clock, she realized it was nearly 1:30 in the morning. And it was freezing out there.

"Rob?" she said, moving through the living room to the staircase. *"Rob!"*

A moment later, like a wraith out of the darkness, he appeared at the top of the stairs. "What's wrong?"

"Did you talk to Paige when you came in?"

"No. Her door was shut. I figured she was asleep. Why?"

"She's not here."

"What the hell do you mean, she's not here?" With his long-legged stride, he thundered down the stairs, two at a time.

"She's gone. With Leroy. His leash is missing."

He moved past her, headed toward the kitchen. "Goddamn it. When I get my hands on that kid, I swear to God I'll—"

The phone rang. He stopped dead, and they stared at each other. Her heart pounding in her chest, Casey said, "Maybe that's her."

He headed for the kitchen at a trot, caught the phone on the third ring. "Hello," he said. "Yes. Uh huh. *What?*" He glanced at the key rack on the wall, and his face went several shades paler. "Jesus Christ Almighty. Is she okay? I—yeah, of course. We'll be right there. Thank you."

He hung up the phone, rubbed his hands over his face. "Rob?" she said.

And he said, "That was Teddy. We have to go to the hospital. Paige just totaled the Porsche."

Rob

The drive to the hospital was a blur, his hands clamped on the steering wheel so tightly his knuckles lost color. Acres of darkened forests and fields whizzed past his window, while visions of death and dismemberment danced through his head. With squealing tires, he wheeled the Explorer into the County Hospital parking lot and found an empty space. They released seat belts, opened doors, and raced through the Emergency entrance. He strode up to the admitting desk and shoved aside a woman who was standing there. Her mouth fell open. Brusquely, he said to the nurse behind the desk, "My daughter's here. Paige MacKenzie. Auto accident."

"Down that hall and to your right. Hold on, I have paperwork you need to fill out! Mr. MacKen—"

He didn't wait to hear the rest of her sentence. With Casey by his side, he sprinted down the hallway, took a right at the end, and went through a set of double glass doors that read EMPLOYEES ONLY. They were in a treatment area, with a cinder block wall on one side and draped cubicles on the other. He hesitated for an instant, and then he heard her voice at the far end of the hallway. "I want my dad! Nobody's fucking touching me until my dad gets here!"

Relief weakened his knees and sharpened his tongue. He felt an instant of ridiculous, unwarranted pride. She was a MacKenzie right to the marrow. Every potty-mouthed, argumentative, prickly inch of her. He slowed his pace, moved toward the cubicle, pulled back the curtain, and opened his mouth to spill all the furious, terror-driven words that were bottlenecked inside him.

Sitting on a white-papered examining table, his daughter glanced up at him with huge green eyes. MacKenzie green. She had a nasty scrape on her chin, a bloody cut at her temple. Tiny fragments of glass in her hair and on her face. For an instant, he was hit with a feeling of déjà vu so powerful, as he remembered Casey after the accident that had killed Danny, that the room started to spin. He closed his eyes, searching for the inner strength he knew was there somewhere. He was a MacKenzie. They were all tough as nails. A little steadier, he opened his eyes again. His

daughter's clothes were bloody and torn, and she looked terrified.
But she was alive. That was the only thing that mattered.

"*Dad*," she sobbed, and began to cry.

Nothing in thirty-seven years of living had prepared him for
the impact of that single syllable. All the words he'd intended to
say simply disappeared. They would undoubtedly come back later,
after he saw what was left of his car, but for now, they were gone,
replaced by a wave of emotion so strong it nearly brought him to
his knees. *Fatherlove*. For an instant, he just stood there, amazed
by the depth of his feelings. Casey had tried to explain it to him a
long time ago, but he hadn't understood. Not intellectually, and
certainly not viscerally. Until now.

He swiped a tear from his cheek and said brokenly, "It's
okay, sweetheart. I'm here." He crossed the room, took his
daughter's hand in his, and squeezed it. "Promise me you won't
scare me like that ever again."

"I'm so sorry," she sobbed. "I wrecked your car."

"Shh. It's okay." He rubbed his thumb against the palm of
her hand. "It doesn't matter."

Struggling against a fresh burst of tears, she said, "But you
love that car so much. You paid a lot of money for it, and—"

"Jesus Christ, Paige, do you really think I give a good
goddamn about the car? All that matters is you! I've never been
so scared in my life. If anything happened to you—" He closed
his eyes, fought back nausea. Opened them again. "I can get
another goddamn car. I can't replace you!"

"But I thought—"

"You thought wrong. Have I been such a lousy father that
you actually believe I could care more about a car than I do about
you? Damn it, Paige! No matter what you do, no matter how hard
you fight me, no matter how deliberately obnoxious you act, you
can't make me stop loving you! Do you hear me? Do you
understand?"

Tears streamed down her cheeks. He dabbed at them
gracelessly, smeared a streak of blood, and realized he'd made
things worse. Leaning in close, he said softly, "Whatever the
problem is between us, we can fix it. There's nothing so bad it
can't be fixed. Right?"

She opened her mouth. Closed it. Nodded.

Some of the tension inside him began to unknot. He could breathe again, for the first time since he'd picked up that ringing phone. "Okay." He took a practice breath, just to be sure. "Now I can say it. What the *hell* were you thinking?"

Paige swiped furiously at a tear. Instead of answering, she asked, "Where's Casey?"

"I'm right here." His wife stepped through the opening in the curtain and squeezed into the rapidly-shrinking examination room.

Paige looked at her father, at Casey, then back at him. "Are you two getting a divorce?"

He gaped at her in astonishment. "A divorce? Of course not. Why would you think—"

"The fighting. It was horrible. I thought things would be okay when you came back, but they weren't. And I assumed—"

"The worst," he said in resignation. "Because you're a MacKenzie."

"Oh, honey," his wife said, squeezing past him to take his daughter's hand. "Married people fight sometimes. We get mad, we yell and scream at each other, throw a few things, slink off to separate corners to lick our wounds, and then we get over it. Because we love each other. Nothing can change that."

His daughter looked bewildered. "But he said such awful things to you."

Her words nearly tore his heart in two. This was all his fault, and only he could fix it. "I say a lot of things," he told her. "Most of them I don't really mean. Don't you worry, baby. Nobody's going anywhere. We're a solid family unit, the three of us." *The four of us*, he corrected, but now wasn't the time to divulge that little piece of information.

"You were so mad."

"And you got caught in the middle. I am so damn sorry, Paige." A tear broke loose and trickled down his cheek.

"And I'm so damn relieved. I wasn't ready to move again. Hey, do you know where Leroy is? They took him away from me. They wouldn't let him in the ambulance."

"Leroy's fine." He reached out, touched his daughter's cloud of golden curls, so like his. Felt the connection between them, that stench of MacKenzie that couldn't be removed, no matter how hard you scrubbed. "Teddy took him home to his wife. We can pick him up in the morning."

The doctor cleared his throat, and Rob got the hint. He removed his hand from Paige's hair and took a step backward. "You let the doctors patch you up," he said, "and then we'll go home. Later, we'll talk about what you did, and what Casey and I are going to do about it. But not just yet. Right now, we have more important things to worry about. *Capisce?*"

She sniffed. Nodded. "*Capisce.*" Her voice sounded stronger. More confident. More Paige-like.

He stepped away from the examining table, nodded to the doctor, and followed Casey out into the corridor. Once he was out of Paige's hearing range, he pressed his forehead to the cold cinder block wall and let out a harsh, ragged breath. Casey touched the small of his back, ran her hand up between his shoulder blades. "It's okay," she said.

"It's not okay. This is my fault. I'm the one who taught her to drive the damn car. I thought I knew what I was doing. I failed miserably."

"Kids don't come with a handbook. You learn by doing. You have to expect to make mistakes."

"She could've died."

"She didn't die. She's still the same feisty kid she was yesterday. A little humbled, maybe, but still the same warm and wonderful Paige we've come to know and love."

A soft snort of laughter rose in his chest, unexpected and uninvited. It came out of him sounding like a pig rooting for truffles.

"However," she said, "I'm thinking a little family counseling might be in order."

"Yeah." He sighed. "Okay."

"She'll be fine. We all will. And I am so proud of you right now."

He'd finally stopped shaking. Turning from the wall, he looked at her curiously. "Why?"

"You crossed a line tonight. You became somebody's dad. And you rose to the occasion with grace and dignity."

"Don't make me sound like a saint. I'm not. I'm just an ordinary guy."

"Right. You go on believing that, my darling."

Her words caught his heart and squeezed it like a fist. He took in a sharp breath. "You've never called me that before."

"An oversight I intend to rectify as often as possible in the future. A lot of firsts tonight."

"Yeah. A lot of firsts." No wonder his head was spinning. The last few hours were more than any mortal man should be expected to process.

She threaded an arm through his and nodded in the direction of the admitting area. "Come on, babe. If you don't fill out that paperwork, they'll hold Paige for ransom."

They began walking arm in arm down the corridor. "They probably wouldn't keep her for long," he said. "Didn't you ever read 'The Ransom of Red Chief'?"

His wife leaned her head against his shoulder and said, "You are so very, very bad."

"But so very, very right. And you love me anyway."

"I do. I can't for the life of me figure out why, but the disease seems to be incurable, so I guess you're stuck with me."

"Wait a minute," he said. They paused, and she gazed up at him expectantly. "I'd planned to bring this up earlier, before everything went to hell. Tomorrow morning, there's someplace I want to take you."

"All right."

"No questions?"

"You know me better than that, MacKenzie. I never question your judgment. I'll find out when we get there."

"Do you have any idea how much I love you right now?"

She smiled that amazing Mona Lisa smile, and his insides melted like butter. "Yes," she said, "I do believe I have an inkling."

Casey

She'd been down this road before. Literally. Growing up in this tiny town, she knew every back road, had ridden most of them on the school bus that traveled twice each day in a big circle from the elementary school to the town line and back. Ridge Road ran parallel to Meadowbrook Road, where she'd grown up, but at a higher elevation. She'd traveled it every school day for thirteen years. The view from up here had always impressed her, even as a young girl. Especially at this time of year when, with the trees bare of leaves, it felt like she was sitting on top of the world.

Ahead of them, on the right, she saw a bright yellow FOR SALE sign. Rob clicked on his blinker and slowed, turning into a dirt driveway that was little more than two gravel tracks winding through a field of yellowed winter grass. He stopped the car, put the shifter into Park, and looked at her.

"I suppose," she said, "you're going to tell me why we're here."

"Let's get out."

She stood with him in front of the Explorer, a cold November wind whipping her hair around her face. "There used to be a house here," she said. "It belonged to the Sirois family. I went to school with Donald Sirois. The house burned down a decade ago."

"There's twenty acres. Mostly open fields, with a few nice old hardwood shade trees. A small orchard. Lots of room for a garden. Jesse says the deer like it here, especially in the fall, when the apples ripen. Turn around." He took her by the shoulders, guided her. "Take a look at the view."

Across the road, the land fell sharply, a winter-yellow field that led to a deeply wooded hillside. In the distance, there were lakes and mountains as far as the eye could see. "The sun sets over there," he said, "right behind the mountains. At sunset, all those lakes turn sky-blue-pink. Imagine having that view out your window every day for the rest of your life."

"Why are you telling me this?" She was pretty sure she knew, but she wanted to hear it from him.

"Don't you think this would be the perfect place to build a house? *Our* house. One with no ghosts and no memories. A home where we can raise our kids." He took her hand in his, wrapped his fingers around hers to take away the chill. "I have piles of money just sitting around. Why not use some of it? We could design the place ourselves. Build it exactly the way we want it, to suit us. Roomy and beautiful, but not pretentious, because we're not pretentious people. Lots of warm wood and old-fashioned charm. A modern kitchen, with every fancy gadget you want. A master bedroom suite with a huge soaking tub. Maybe a wraparound porch, where we could put a swing, like the one we have now. Whatever you want, just name it, and it's yours. I want to build this for you. For us. To give us a fresh start."

"You want me to sell the house."

"Look, I know you love that house, babe. I like it, too. But everywhere I turn, I see Danny. If it's that way for me, it has to be a thousand times worse for you. I don't think we'll ever get past him as long as we stay there." He tugged at her hand, led her up past the cellar hole to the half-acre of flat land behind where the house had stood. "I've been doing a lot of thinking. About my life, my career, where I want to go from here. I'm a family man now. I have a wife and a daughter, and a baby on the way. I don't want to spend my life on the road, leaving you behind, missing birthdays and first steps and first smiles and all those little things that only happen once. I want to move away from performing and into the production end of the business. Writing and producing albums for other artists. With you as my partner. Like we did for Danny. We could build a studio—a real studio—right here, behind the house. Sure, we might have to spend some of our time in New York or L.A. But with a state-of-the-art facility, plus our expertise, we can make them come to us. It's like that Kevin Costner movie. If I build it, they will come."

"What about performing? You live to play guitar. You can't give that up."

"I don't intend to give up playing. But I've had enough of the road. It was fun when we were kids—"

"I'm not sure I'd go that far."

"You know what I mean. It was new and exciting. It was dreams coming true. But I've lived those dreams, and I'm ready to move on to a different dream. I'm almost forty years old. That's not how I want to live any more, spending all my time on buses and planes, living out of a suitcase, sleeping in a different town every night. I am *so* over that. I want to be here, with you and our kids, in a house we built from the ground up, a home we can leave to the kids when we're old and feeble." He raised his head, took another sweeping glance at the view. "If this doesn't tickle your fancy, we'll find another place. This isn't the only piece of land for sale in town. So what do you say?"

She thought about leaving behind the house she and Danny had worked so hard to turn into a home. A house that had never really been hers, but more a symbol of Danny's rebirth. A house that had held nothing but emptiness and sorrow after he was gone, until Rob moved in and made it a real home. A house was nothing but four walls and a roof. It was the people living there who made it a home. And no matter where they lived, as long as she and Rob were together, she would be happy.

He was waiting for her response. She gazed into those beautiful green eyes that she knew so well she could carry on entire conversations with him without either of them uttering a word. She studied the tiny laugh lines that fanned out from the corners, the pale freckles scattered across the bridge of his nose. She knew every line and angle of that face, knew how it reflected his every mood, all of that knowledge embedded deep inside her, so far inside her that she was certain it had been there for millennia, across lifetimes and continents and possibly the entire solar system, and she couldn't understand why it had taken her so many years to figure it out.

Slowly, ever so slowly, she touched him. Ran her hands up his chest, to his shoulders, and kept going. Took his face between her fingertips, drew his mouth down to hers, and kissed him. Tilted her head back and solemnly met his eyes.

Understanding warmed and softened those green eyes of his. He swallowed, his Adam's apple moving slowly up and down. And said hoarsely, "Yes?"

And she gave him a radiant smile and said, "Yes!"

THE END

Author Bio

Laurie Breton started making up stories in her head when she was a small child. At the age of eight, she picked up a pen and began writing them down. Although she now uses a computer to write, she's still addicted to a new pen and a fresh sheet of lined paper. At some point during her angsty teenage years, her incoherent scribblings morphed into love stories, and that's what she's been writing, in one form or another, ever since.

When she's not writing, she can usually be found driving the back roads of Maine, looking for inspiration. Or perhaps standing on a beach at dawn, shooting a sunrise with her Canon camera. If all else fails, a day trip to Boston, where her heart resides, will usually get the juices flowing.

The mother of two grown children, Breton has two beautiful grandkids and two precious granddogs. She and her husband live in a small Maine town with a lovebird who won't stop laying eggs and a Chihuahua/Papillon/Schipperke/Pug mix named River who pretty much runs the household.

I love to hear from readers! If you enjoyed this book, please drop me a line.

lauriebreton@gmail.com
www.lauriebreton.com
www.facebook.com/LaurieBretonBooks

12396135R00180

Printed in Great Britain
by Amazon.co.uk, Ltd.,
Marston Gate.